Where Would I Be

By

Laura T. Johnson

To Arlena Dean,

Thank you for supporting me!

Laura T. Johnson

ISBN: 978-1512229936

This is a work of fiction. Any resemblance to actual events or person(s) living or dead is strictly coincidental. All characters, incidents and dialog are the product of the author imagination and are in no way tied to real events or people.

I would like to dedicate this book to my mother. A woman who has taught me strength, dignity, and how to recognize that a person doesn't hurt what they love. You are the strongest woman I know and if I become only half of the woman, mother, and teacher you have been to me then my battle is won. I love you, mommy.

Prologue

"You'll learn, just keep on living." Those are the words echoing in Lisa's ear right now. At this moment, the words her mother would tell her over and over as she was growing up are being repeated over and over again, as if they are a favorite love song. She wishes her mother's voice will tell her what to do about the man that is standing in front of her with a gun. How could this man, who claims he loves her, be threatening to kill her? How the hell did she get herself into this? Scratch that. She knows *how* she got herself into this. The real question is how is she going to get out of it? How is she going to keep this man from killing her and her unborn child?

CHAPTER ONE

"Lisa, you have a call on line one."

"Thanks, Carol. This is Lisa Jenson...Yes, Mr. Thompson, how are you...? Good. What can I do for you...? Okay...No, I haven't received it yet. When did you messenger them over...? I should get them sometime this afternoon, then...I will call as soon as I have everything ready. Then we can set up a meeting for next week...Alright, Mr. Thompson, I'll talk to you soon...Goodbye."

A minute after hanging up, Carol buzzed in again, "Lisa, there's a Mr. James Harris here to see you."

Lisa's heart screeched to a halt. "A-Are you sure that's what he said?"

"Yes, that's what I said," a male voice came through the speaker.

"Well, Carol, please tell Mr. Harris I'm busy and to go away."

"Oh, okay."

A second later, Carol came into Lisa's office, "Lisa, he said he's not leaving without seeing you."

"Then call security."

"Security? Do you really want me –"

"Yes," Lisa said. "No, wait. No need to cause a scene. Did he say what he wanted?"

"No, but he is holding a pink rose," Carol said, smiling.

Lisa sighed and leaned back in her leather chair.

"What do you want me to do?"

"I might as well get this over with. Send him in."

"Okay."

Lisa swung her chair around, facing the view of the Mississippi River, to take a couple of breaths to kick start her heartbeat.

Then she heard, "Hello, beautiful."

She turned her chair around to face him, "Hello, James."

She could see the shock on his face for a moment, and then he said, "Lisa, you – you look –"

"Different?"

"Even more beautiful than I remember."

"What do you want, James?"

"You haven't seen me for six years and the only thing you can say is, 'what do you want'?"

"Yep."

"No 'I can't believe you're here'. Or 'long time no see'."

"I can't believe you're here and the time hasn't been long enough."

"Okay. Look, I know I shouldn't have just showed up. But, I had to see you."

"Why? No, I don't care why. I just want to know how you found out where I worked."

"It's a small town. People talk."

"Memphis isn't that small and my people don't talk to your people."

"True, but I asked around."

"Kim told you."

"Yeah," he chuckled. "I get the feeling that you guys aren't friends anymore."

"She was never a friend; it just took me longer to find that out. Now, why are you here?"

James didn't answer, he was too busy staring.

Sighing, Lisa said, "A picture will last longer."

"Sorry, I just can't get over how much you've changed."

"I haven't changed that much. What do you want, James?"

"To scc you," he said.

"You've seen me. Now, you can leave."

"Can you give me just a few minutes of your time?"

"No," she said with finality in her voice.

"Just hear me out. That's all I'm asking."

"You're asking for too much."

"One minute, that's it."

Lisa stared at him, then against her better judgment said, "You have one minute."

"Right to the point...I've missed you."

"Really," Lisa said, deadpan.

"I was hoping – I was hoping to get a chance to maybe take you out. I know that's a lot to ask, especially coming from me. But, I just want to have a chance to start over with you."

"No, thank you."

Lisa got up and walked over to her glass pitcher and poured herself a glass of water. She ignored the whispered expletive coming from James while her back was turned.

"Look, James, I don't know what possessed you to come here to see me. I'm sure you knew that I did not want to see you. Please leave."

"Lisa, it's just a bite between friends."

"Oh, so we're friends now?"

"Hoping."

Turning to face him, Lisa didn't expect him to be standing so close to her. She had to tilt her head back to look at him.

"I can't –"

"I have to tell you that you look *good*. It's taking all the restraint I have to not kiss you right now," James said, looking into her eyes.

For a minute, Lisa was lost in those light brown eyes and his words. For only a minute.

"James, you have to go."

"You always were a hard person to get too."

He handed Lisa the rose he was holding and then, playing with a curl of her hair, he whispered close to her lips, "I never give up, beautiful."

He backed up, smiled, and then he was gone. Lisa didn't realize she had stopped breathing until her chest began to hurt. Taking deep breaths, Lisa walked over to the floor-to-ceiling window overlooking the always busy Front Street. She looked out at the water and wondered how in the hell was she going to stay clear of James. Because she knew that was not the last time she would see him. She actually remembered when James first walked into her life eight years ago.

***

"Hey, how you doing?" a handsome man said to Lisa as she walked home from getting off the bus.

"Fine, you?" Lisa said, never breaking her stride.

"Can I talk to you for a minute?"

"About what?"

"If you slow down I can tell you."

Lisa slowed her pace so he could catch up.

"Damn, you walk fast!"

"Sorry."

"What's your name?"

"No," Lisa said.

"Wait, I just wanna know the name of the most beautiful woman I've ever seen," he said, giving Lisa one of the sexist smiles she'd ever seen.

"Thank you," Lisa said.

"Do you think that worked enough to get you to stop?"

So she did.

"Okay, since you won't tell me your name, how about I call you beautiful?"

The way he was smiling at her, Lisa's body temperature went up a hundred degrees. Everything about this man was sexy. He was about 5'11, creamy brown skin, with brown eyes the color of hazelnut. He looked like he was made of muscle, but not big, overdone muscles. He was just right. He was sexy as hell.

"So, beautiful, where are you headed?"

"Home."

"Do you mind if I walk with you?"

"If I won't tell you my name, how you figure I'm gonna let you find out where I live?"

"Okay, okay. How 'bout we talk here? Do you have a man?"

"No."

"Any kids?"

"No."

"Really?!" he asked, stunned.

"You sound like that's hard to believe. Not all women have children."

"All the ones I know do."

"Are you the father?"

"Oh, you got jokes."

"What, I'm serious," Lisa laughed.

"So, can I get your number?"

"What's your name?"

"James. James Harris. Your future husband," he smiled.

"Is that right? Well, James Harris, I'm Lisa Jenson."

"Nice to meet you. Can I get your number or what?"

Lisa smiled while she took out a small piece of paper and wrote her name and number down, then handed it to him.

"So, Lisa, where are you from?"

"Born right here in Memphis. Why?"

"You don't sound like it. You sound like you from up north."

"Nope, I'm from here, sorry."

"Don't be, I think you sound sexy."

"Thank you."

"Well, I'm not gonna keep you any longer than I already have, but I will definitely be callin' you."

"Alright, bye."

"See ya, beautiful."

Lisa walked up the driveway of the house they were standing in front of.

"Where is everybody?" she asked, when she walked in the house.

"In the kitchen," her mother called out.

Lisa put her books down on the living room couch and headed to the kitchen.

"Hey," she said.

"Hey. How did it go at the library?"

"Busy."

"Did you get everything you needed?" her mother asked as she took a glass dish out of the oven.

"For now."

"What do you mean, 'for now'?"

"I have to go back sometime this weekend to turn in the paper I have to write."

"Then why did you have to go today?"

"To get the information I needed in order to write the paper."

"Oh, okay."

"But I have to tell you, walking or riding the bus back and forth to the library is really not working for me."

"If you can wait a couple of weeks I can get you a computer."

"Thank you so much. That would really help me out. So, how long until dinner?"

"About another half hour."

"That would give me time to get started on a least some of my work."

Lisa turned to leave, but stopped when her mother said, "Who was that guy you were outside talking to?"

Lisa turned around and looked at her mother, "And how do you know I was outside talking to somebody?"

"Your brother said that you were outside. So I looked out to see what you were doing. So, who was he?"

"I don't know him. He was over Charles's house across the street. Why? Is your trouble radar going off?"

"I just wanted to know who he was."

"I told you I don't know. That's my first time ever seeing him."

"And just to let you know, my trouble radar only lifted a little bit. I have to meet him to determine how much trouble he is going to be."

"Well, you don't have anything to worry. I've got too much on my plate right now to worry about some man. Call me when dinner is ready."

Lisa's mother watched her go upstairs and shook her head at how naïve her daughter was.

The day passed as routine as always. They ate dinner, Anthony got on Lisa's last nerve, and she and her mother talked for a little while. Around eight the phone rang and Anthony walked into her room holding the cordless phone.

"Some man wants talk you. Who is he?" he asked.

"Boy, if you want to see your eighth birthday, you better get out of my business," Lisa said, as she pushed him out of her room and closed the door. "Hello."

"Hey, beautiful."

"Hey."

"He sounds a little young to be your father."

"He doesn't think so."

"What you up to?"

"I'm in the middle of writing a paper for class."

"For class? What do you take up?"

"I'm taking up finance."

"That's dealing with money, right?"

"Yep."

"How about taking a break and let me take you out to dinner."

"Sorry, I can't. I really have a lot of work to do."

"Aww, come on, I'll make it worth your while."

"I can't."

"Awight, then," he said. "How 'bout I call you later?"

"Alright."

"Then I'll call you later. Bye, beautiful."

"Bye," Lisa said and hung up.

Lisa already knew James was not about to call her back, he did not want to get to know her. Lisa finished out the night studying and was done by midnight. Getting into bed, she knew she wouldn't hear from him again.

CHAPTER TWO

Coming back from her trip down memory lane and concentrating on her view of downtown traffic, Lisa thought about how that night – eight years ago – wasn't the last time she heard from James. Just like today wouldn't be either.

Turning back to her computer screen, Lisa got back to work. As the work day rattled on, Lisa worked on a major account she was trying to get, and the figures Mr. Thompson had sent over arrived by one o'clock. Carol brought the packet in and said she was leaving for lunch.

"Enjoy."

When Carol left, Lisa was interrupted by a knock on the door.

"Hey, Lisa, are you busy?"

The strong and smooth voice belonged to Marc Cavell. Marc had worked at Morgan & Peterson for over eight years. He was one of the top investment bankers, Lisa was the other. They had been working together for the last three and a half years. Marc was an even six feet tall, with broad shoulders, and a chest that would make Michelangelo proud. Lisa could tell he lived in a gym. He had the sexiest dark brown eyes that looked black. His hair was coal black, thick, and wavy. Ever since she saw him, she had an urge to run her fingers through his hair. He had an olive complexion with dimples she wanted to swim in.

"Nope. Not as much as I usually am. What's going on?"

Marc walked in the office, sat on her couch, and got comfortable. She noticed he was wearing his signature cologne. She couldn't recognize it, but the scent was heady.

"Well, I wanted to know what you were doing for lunch, I wanted to discuss the Thompson account," he said.

"Oh, alright. Perfect timing, because he was my first call of the day. What time were you planning to go?"

"How about now? I'm not doing anything," he said, getting a little more comfortable on the couch.

"Well, I can't, Mr. Laid Back. I need to wait until Carol gets back from lunch."

"Okay, then I'll wait with you. And we can go ahead and get started now," he said as he got up and walked over to her desk.

As he sat in one of the chairs in front of her desk, he said, "So, how do Mr. Thompson's figures add up this quarter?"

"To be honest, they're looking pretty good."

"How good?"

"About two point three," Lisa said.

Marc looked over the paper she handed him and then stopped and looked up at her. "You're kidding?"

"Nope," Lisa said, still smiling.

"Two point three, are you sure?"

Lisa started laughing and nodding her head.

"You did it!" Marc said. "This is our biggest take since we both started working for the firm. I can't believe it, you did it!"

"Noo, we did it. Do you know how many hours we've spent working on this account? We did this."

"I guess that means we're good together," Marc said, staring at Lisa.

Lisa tried not to blush, but the way he was staring at her she couldn't help it.

"So, uhh, I guess this is a celebratory lunch," he said, smiling.

Just then Carol poked her head in, "I'm back, Lisa. Oh, good afternoon, Mr. Cavell."

"Hello, Mrs. Connors, how are you this beautiful day?" Marc asked, charmingly.

"I'm great," Carol said, smiling broadly.

Lisa couldn't believe it, Carol's face turned completely red. As Lisa tried to keep from laughing, she said, "We're about to head out for lunch, so hold down the fort."

Lisa stood up and turned to reach for her suit jacket. Carol caught Marc staring at Lisa's ass and had to laugh to herself.

"If anything important happens, call me on my cell," Lisa said, grabbing her purse.

"I always do," Carol said.

Carol was still smiling as Lisa and Marc left the office. When they got on the elevator, Lisa said, "I think someone has a crush on you."

"Carol is a sweetheart, but I don't think she'd be so nice to me if I didn't bribe her during the holidays with gifts," he joked.

When they made it downstairs, Lisa turned in the direction of the company deli.

"Wait," Marc said, grabbing her hand.

Caught off guard, they both paused for a minute. Letting her hand go slowly, he said, "Umm, why don't we go out for lunch?"

"Where do you wanna go?"

"How about the deli on Main Street? It's only a couple of blocks from here, if you don't mind hiking it?"

"I guess I'm wearing the right shoes for it," she said, as she looked down at her three inch heels.

"We'll walk slowly."

On their way to the restaurant, they continued to talk about the Thompson account. By the time they made it to the restaurant, Lisa was ready to sit down.

"Looks like we're the only ones here," Lisa said, as she walked in ahead of Marc.

"Yeah, I guess we missed the lunch rush."

"May I take your order?" the cashier asked.

"You first," Marc said.

"I'll have the Grilled Chicken Salad with Thousand Island dressing and an Iced Tea."

"Sweetened?"

"Yes."

"And you, sir?"

"I will have the Philly Cheese Steak with fries and a Sprite."

"That'll be seventeen dollars and ninety-seven cents."

"I got this one," Marc said, reaching for his wallet. "Think of it as congratulations on a job well done."

"Thank you, sir," Lisa laughed.

As they waited for their food, they took a table by the window.

"Well, Ms. Jenson, I've been working with you for over three years now and I don't know anything about you."

"That's not true."

"Let's see, I know you love your job and are damn good at it."

"What would you like to know? I am an open book."

"Okay, where did you grow up? Where did you attend college? I already know you're not married and you don't have any children, because I don't see any photos in your office."

"You don't miss a thing do you?" Lisa asked, laughing.

"Not if I can help it."

"Sir, your order is ready," the cashier said.

"Hold that thought," Marc said, as he got up from the table.

A minute later he was back with their tray.

"You were saying."

"To answer your questions, I was born and raised right here in Memphis."

"Really? You don't sound southern."

"Everyone tells me that," Lisa chuckled. "I was raised by a single mother and I have a younger brother, who is now seventeen. I graduated from U of M with a bachelor's in finance and a minor in accounting. And no, I'm not married and I do not have any children. Right now I'm concentrating on my career. I have plenty of time for a family."

"Sure you do. What are you twenty-five…twenty-six?"

"Actually I'm twenty-eight, but thanks. So enough about me, your turn."

"Alright, I was born in New York. The Bronx. Raised by both parents, only child. Attended NYU, graduated with a degree in Finance. I am not married, no children, and the rest is history. Oh, I'm thirty."

They continued to talk as they ate and learned quite a bit about each other. Lisa found out that Marc was Italian and that his parents came to America as children with their parents.

"So both sets of grandparents came here together?" Lisa asked.

"Yep, they were best friends. My parents actually have known each other all of their lives."

"Was their marriage arranged?"

"Not in the traditional sense of the word. But I'm sure my grandparents did everything in their power to get those two together," Marc laughed.

An hour later they were on their way back to the office. In the elevator, he said, "You know, we have never eaten outside the office, it was nice."

"Yeah, it was."

"We should do it again."

"Sure."

"I'll hold you to that," Marc said, winking at her.

Watching him walk away, Lisa wondered if he had been flirting with her. "Nah, I'm just reading too much into it," she said to herself as she walked into her office.

"Hey, Carol," Lisa said, as she walked passed Carol's desk.

"Yeah, right," Carol said, following Lisa into her office. "Oh, my God, that man is gorgeous! Almost every woman in this company wants him."

"I'm sure they do," Lisa said, hanging up her jacket.

"Lisa, you better open up your eyes. That man is interested in you."

"Oh, Lord. Here we go."

"Yes, here we go. Now, tell me about lunch and don't leave a thing out."

"There is nothing to tell. We went to the Main Street deli, talked, and came back. That's it."

"What did you talk about?"

"You know, normal things. Work, family, stuff like that."

Sighing, Carol said, "You are really making this hard. Did you tell him you were single?"

"He already knew that," Lisa said, as she went through her messages.

"I know he's not married. I already checked," Carol said.

Lisa just shook her head.

"Hey, I do my homework. I have to know everything about everybody. It's in my blood."

"No, it's in your nose."

"That may be so, but at least I get the real story."

"That's true."

"You two should go out on a date!" Carol blurted out.

"Carol, have you been sniffing the white again?"

"What I do on my breaks is my business. Now don't change the subject. What are you going to do about Mr. Gorgeous?"

"Absolutely nothing. Look, Carol, we work together and that is it."

"Yeah, if you say so. But, I don't think he feels that way."

That got Lisa's attention.

"What do you mean?" she asked.

"I caught him staring at your ass earlier."

"Now I know you trippin'. Don't you have some work to do?"

"Yes I do. But not until I tell you this. There are at least one hundred women on this floor alone that would like a go at him. You better snag him before someone else does."

"I'm not interested in dating anyone right now."

"Look, I have known you since your first day here. When you got promoted you made sure I did too. And for that I love you like a younger sister, and as your older and sexier sister, I'm telling you that you need to start dating."

"I'm concentrating on my career."

"Yeah, yeah, yeah. You already have it, now it's time to get your love life on track. And what's better than a man who works in the same field?"

"I don't need a man in my life right now."

"Yes, you do. And there's one right down the hall. Buzz me if you need me," she said, walking out.

Lisa shook her head and smiled as she watched Carol walk out of her office. She couldn't help but think about how she met her.

It was Lisa's first day working at Morgan & Peterson and Mr. Peterson himself was showing her around. He introduced Carol as Lisa's new assistant. After getting to know Carol that first day, Lisa knew they would be friends. She knew absolutely everything about everybody. She worked just as hard as Lisa. Which is why when Lisa got her promotion, she made sure Carol received one also. Their friendship was cemented from then on.

Bringing her back to the here and now, Carol buzzed in, "Lisa, you have a call on line one."

"Thanks...Lisa Jenson."

"Okay, since I couldn't talk you into lunch, how about dinner? And before you say no, I promise to be a perfect gentleman," James said.

"I didn't know you knew the meaning."

"There's a lot you don't know about me."

"Is that right?"

"Yeah. So, what do you say?"

"No."

"Come on. How about drinks?"

"No."

"It's just one drink, that's all. Nothing but catching up on each other's lives. I'm just asking for an hour of your time. Just to talk, that's all."

"James, I –"

"Don't say no again. I tell you what, just think about it, and tonight when you dream of me, maybe it'll be so good you'll change your mind."

Lisa just shook her head.

"And in case you forget to dream about me tonight, take these."

At that exact moment, Carol walked in holding two pink long stem roses and a card.

"James –"

"Bye, beautiful."

Lisa held the phone and listened to the dial tone humming in her ear as Carol laid two roses and a card down in front of her and walked out smiling. Hanging up the phone, Lisa picked up the envelope and took out the card. On the cover of the card was a young woman on the beach, watching a sunset. On the inside, was written:

Just like you I have changed, too. Give me a chance to introduce you to the new me. I will always love you.

James

Lisa stared at them for a minute and then threw both the card and the two roses in the garbage.

"Yeah, like that's gonna happen."

Carol walked back into the office, "Lisa."

"Yeah, Carol."

"Your three o'clock is here."

"I forgot about Mr. Keene. Give me five minutes to freshen up and then show him in."

"Will do," Carol said, and walked out pulling the door closed behind her.

Lisa got up from her desk and went into her personal bathroom to make sure her hair, breath, and makeup were perfect. As she came out of the bathroom, Carol opened the door to escort Mr. Keene in.

"Mr. Keene, please come in. How are you?" Lisa asked, as she shook his hand.

"Well, Ms. Jenson, we finally get to meet. I know I've been a hard person to conduct business with, but my company in Europe needed my personal attention."

"Everything worked out okay, I hope."

"Everything worked out just fine."

"Good. How about we get down to business?"

"Let's."

"Mr. Keene, I have been looking at your company's history, and I must say they are doing extremely well."

"Damn well, if I say so myself."

19

"But what if I told you that you could be doing better. I've put together a prospectus of what you could stand to make if you give Morgan & Peterson just one year. Your company here in the states made six point two million last year. Which is good."

"Damn right."

"What if I told you I could double that amount? If I have peeked your interest any, we can go over the prospectus."

Mr. Keene studied Lisa for a minute and then opened the booklet to the first page, "Let's see what you got."

Lisa smiled and thought to herself, *got him*. She then began their meeting.

CHAPTER THREE

Lisa walked into her house that evening feeling elated and exhausted. The meeting with Keene went perfect. By the time he left her office he was ready to sign on the dotted line. Laying her mail down after going through it, she checked her messages. According to the number blinking, she had five messages:

First message: *"Girl, I thought you would be home, it's after six o'clock. Call me."*

That message was from Lisa's best friend, Patricia, who she had known since high school.

Second message: *"This is your mother, call me."*

Third, fourth, and fifth messages were all hang ups.

Lisa headed upstairs to her bedroom; she changed out of her work clothes and put on her maroon terrycloth robe. After she hung her suit in a dry cleaning bag, she made her first call, "Hey, mama."

"Hey, you just get home?"

"Yeah. I just got your message, what's up?"

"Nothing really, just called to catch you up on your crazy aunt."

"Oh, Lord. What's she done now?"

Lisa and her mother talked every day, or maybe *gossip* was a better word for what they did. As her mother told her about her aunt's great adventure, Lisa laughed so hard she had tears in her eyes.

"Your sister is something else. When will Sharee ever learn that that man is not gonna change? She has been dealing with Larry for the last five years, and they go back and forth every few weeks or so. How many times does he have to put her out?"

"Child, I don't know. Sharee thinks the sun rises and falls on that man. So now she's moved back in the mama," Lisa's mother said.

"Well, at least Steph doesn't have to go through this."

"Yeah, is she still looking for work?"

"Yep, but I just hope her mama gets her stuff together."

21

"Now, baby, you mean get her shit together."

"Mama, watch your language!" Lisa said, laughing.

"Girl, please, you grown."

"Anyway, at Aunt Sharee's age she ain't got much time," Lisa said. "I don't understand what's wrong with her, is it that she just needs a man? I mean, does she really have to go through the getting put out all times of the night? I wouldn't be surprised if he was beatin' her."

"Look, your aunt is old enough to know right from wrong. But for some reason she just don't care. As long as that fool she is dealing with keep treating her like he do, and she keep taking it, this could go on forever and a day. Hell, nobody needs a man this damn bad. And as for getting put out at night, honey, please, he put that ass out in broad daylight."

"All I know is that she should be tired of that mess by now. I couldn't go through that. If there was a choice of being by yourself or going through that mess, I'm glad I'm single. Every time you hear about somebody's relationship, it's always bad. At this rate, the only way you gon' find a decent man is if he has one foot in a grave and the other on a banana peel with a strong wind blowing."

Lisa's mother burst into laughter and said, "Girl, you crazy!"

"No, I'm serious."

When her mother calmed down, she said, "I have told you time and time again that every man ain't the same. Just because you met one fool don't mean they are all that way. There are still some good ones out there; you just have to do a little searching. And a little praying won't hurt either."

"Mama, I've heard this speech before, I –"

"And you gon' hear it again. Every man ain't like James, baby."

"Uh, mom! I don't wanna talk about James," Lisa whined. She was not about to tell her mother that he showed up at her office today. That would be like starting World War III.

"I know he hurt you," Lisa's mother said. "But, don't let that one fool stop you from living. All you do is go to work, go home, and come over here. You barely go out. Believe me, that bastard ain't worth the time. You need to move on with your life. He just better be lucky the police got to him before I did."

"Mama, I have moved on. And what happened was a long time ago. He's not ruining my dating life."

"You don't have one."

"Whatever. All I'm saying is that I just don't feel like being worried about some man's problems. I don't want to hear about his day, his lies, or any other problems I'm sure he may have. My life is good now. I have a great job, a nice home, my family. I don't need or want a man in my life right now. When I want some drama in my life, I'll call Auntie Sharee."

"I know you have everything you need, but don't you want someone to share it with?"

"I already do."

"Who?"

"You and Anthony."

"All I know is that you shouldn't give up on love."

"Too late."

"Just watch, it will show up on your doorstep when you least expect it."

"I hope not, because I'd hate to move so it won't find me."

"Girl, you are too much, let me get off this phone. I have to call my mother before she goes to bed. I'll talk to you tomorrow."

"Okay, tell her I said hello and that I'll call her tomorrow. Oh, and tell Anthony to call me."

"Okay, bye."

"Bye."

When Lisa hung up from her mother she pressed speed dial number three.

"It's about time you called me back, heffa," Lisa's best friend, Patricia said, when she answered the phone.

"Well, hello to you, too," Lisa said.

"Yeah, yeah. Where have you been?"

"At work. Home. That's about it."

"I should have known a date wasn't included in that itinerary."

23

"Oh, God! Not you too!"

"What you mean, 'not me too'? Mama getting on you again?"

"And Carol. Don't y'all have something better to do than worry about my personal life?"

"Uh, no!" Patricia said and then laughed.

"Anyway, let's get started, who's first?"

"You," Patricia said.

"Okay."

Every week they either called or got together for their weekly talks. Lisa and Pat had been best friends since they were thirteen. From junior high to different colleges, they had maintained a constant friendship. Maybe sisters were a better word for what they were.

"I got a new account that Marc and I have been working on."

"Congratulations!"

"Thank you."

"How is Marc with his fine self?"

"Have you forgotten you're married?"   "Married, yes. Dead, no. It's a damn shame someone that gorgeous is walking around here single. If I wasn't married I –"

"But you are."

"Blocker," Patricia said.

"Anyway, can I go on, please?"

"Yeess."

"Okay, nothing else has changed in my life. Except..."

"Except, what?"

"Well, I kind of ran into James this morning."

"I hope you mean with your car. And I also hope you mean ran him over," Patricia said.

"No, he stopped by the office today."

"How did he know where you worked?"

"Guess."

"Kim."

"That's right."

"Why did she do that?"

"I don't know. But she'll tell me when I finish whuppin' her ass."

"I knew she wasn't your friend when I met her that weekend I came home from college."

"I thought Kim was cool. When I met her in class, I thought she would be a good add-in to the group."

"How you didn't see she only wanted James trifling ass, I will never know?"

"That never crossed my mind. A woman becoming friends with another woman to get her man…that mess only happens on Melrose Place."

"Uh, Lisa, Melrose Place doesn't come on anymore."

"I know that. But you get what I'm saying."

"Yeah, well I'll hold her down when you do whup her ass. Now, back to the devil. Was he shocked by your new look?"

"Yeah, but do I look that different?"

"Uh, yeah. You lost the weight; let your hair grow long."

"Well, he talked for a minute, then left."

"Talked about what, his anger management classes?" Patricia asked.

"Noo. He came by to say hello."

"Yeah, right."

"Then he called to ask me out for drinks or dinner."

"He got nerve," said Patricia.

"That he does."

"Ass."

"Pat, language!"

"Girl, please. You act like you don't cuss. I've heard words come out of your mouth that would make a sailor blush."

"Anyhoo, I said no and then hung up."

"Good. And keep saying no. If he becomes too much of a problem you tell one of us, you hear me?"

"Yes, mother."

"I'm not playing, Lisa. You don't know how dangerous he could be."

"Did it ever occur to you that I also might be dangerous?"

"Look, I know you can take care of yourself, but I just want you to know that Nic, Carol, and I are here for you. Whether you need bail money, an alibi, or a hideout, we're here."

"I know. Now, your turn."

"Let's see, Lewis is doing fine, nothing has really changed with him. My job has finally made it possible for me to be stressed out enough to pull out all my hair. Got me walking around here looking like India Arie."

Laughing, Lisa said, "Girl, you crazy."

"I'm serious. I thought after becoming partner, my workload would decrease, but it hasn't. In fact, I think it's tripled. I have so many things to deal with before I even get up in the morning. I love my job, but I am beginning to feel burned out."

"Well, Mrs. Law, why don't you and your hubby go on a vacation? Go somewhere tropical and lay in the sun. Or even better, go somewhere cold and stay in bed for a week."

"That sounds good but it might be hard for him to get away."

"Say what? Lewis owns the company, right?"

"Yeess."

"That means he's the boss. Now, go tell the boss you want to go on a vacation."

"We'll see."

"Hey, who know, you might come back pregnant."

"Ohh that would be great!"

"Oh, before I forget, have you talked to Nic?"

"Yesterday. She said she was gonna send an APB out for you."

"I'll call her."

"How's Carol?"

"Crazy as ever."

"Tell her to call me."

"I will."

"Look, honey, I have to go see what this man is burning up in this kitchen. But you remember what I said."

"I will."

"Love ya," Pat said.

"Love ya," Lisa said and hung up.

After hanging up, Lisa went to run her bath. She loved her bathroom, especially the tub. Her bathroom was huge with a separate shower and Jacuzzi tub. Actually, she loved her entire house. All four bedrooms were for guests – namely for her three best friends. Lisa's bedroom was her domain. It was filled with light. Her color scheme was mostly browns. She'd searched high and low for a dark mahogany sleigh bed. The biggest she could find. She had a sitting area in front of her big bay windows. Her chairs were cream colored, thick, and comfy. The carpet was thick and white. On the wall across from her bed was flat screen television. She loved this room. Her kitchen was huge, with stainless steel appliances and granite countertops.

Lisa poured powered milk in her tub and then turned a button on the wall to dim the overhead lighting. Then she used a remote to turn the radio on. As she slid into the tub, Luther Vandross sang to her for the next hour. After her hour soak, she dried off and put on her favorite lotion from Victoria Secret: Romance. Then Lisa got dressed in her white silk pajamas, cleaned up her bathroom, and then headed downstairs.

On the way to the kitchen, she noticed the light on her answering matching blinking.

"Now what? All I wanted to do was eat, read my book, and go to bed."

Lisa figured it was either Pat or Nic calling, but it wasn't either of them.

"Hey, Lisa, this is Marc. I got your message about Keene. I don't know how you did it, but you did. We need to have a meeting tomorrow to see where we can take this thing. I –"

The answering machine cut his message.

"Damn," Lisa said, a little disappointed that he didn't get to finish, but she didn't know why. When she made it to the kitchen, the phone rang. Lisa looked at the caller I.D. and couldn't help but smile when she saw Cavell,

Marc (901)786-2316. Lisa wanted to answer the phone, but she forced herself to let it go to the machine.

"Hey, Lisa, it's me again. Your machine cut me off. As I was saying you did a great job with Keene. And as for our meeting tomorrow, how about eleven? Let me know and I'll see you tomorrow...Umm, good night. Look, Lisa would you like –"

The answering machine cut him off again.

"Nooo," Lisa said to the answering machine. Then she pressed the play button and listened to Marc's messages again. She never noticed how sexy his voice was.

"He's a co-worker, Lisa, business and pleasure don't mix," she said to herself.

Lisa made a sandwich out of leftover chicken salad, grabbed bottled water, and headed back upstairs to her bedroom. She climbed into her bed and got comfortable. As she ate, she scanned channels until she found a movie that caught her interest.

While eating and watching television, Lisa couldn't help thinking about Marc and what he was trying to say. She was half hoping he would call back, she thought about calling him, but unfortunately neither happened. As the night passed, she chose her outfit for tomorrow, watched another movie, and was in bed by ten.

The next morning, Lisa was up by six a.m. She ate a bowl of cereal, worked out until seven-thirty, showered, dressed, and was out the door by eight-thirty. Her drive to work was only twenty minutes by the expressway especially the way Lisa drove. Everyone who rode in Lisa's car said she should drive for the Indy five hundred. The metallic red XK Jaguar with Caramel leather and wood grain interior was a blur on I-55. Lisa loved it! The car was a gift to herself when she was promoted.

Pulling into the parking garage, Lisa was already in work mode. Before heading to the elevator, she stopped to pick up a Cappuccino and a newspaper in the deli on the first floor.

"Good morning, Carol," she said, as she walked into Carol's outer office.

"Good morning," Carol said, smiling.

"What do we have today?" she asked, as she walked into her office.

Carol followed with a pen and pad, and said, "First, you have a conference with Mr. Morgan, Mr. Peterson, and Mr. Cavell in conference room A. Your file for that meeting is on your desk, it starts at ten. At eleven-thirty you have a meeting with Mr. Cavell about the Keene account. He said he called you at home, but didn't get an answer."

"He left a message."

"So, where were you?"

"At home, soaking in the tub. And yes I was alone, so don't ask."

"Okay, moving on. Then at one-thirty you have an appointment with Sheryl Hearn."

"Oh, God! What does she want?"

"She said she wants to go over this quarter's holdings. After her, then you and I have accounts to get ready for the new quarter. So get in gear girl, this is going to be a long one."

"Is there any way we can get Mrs. Hearn to reschedule?" Lisa pleaded.

"Now, you know that little white woman can work a nerve. Do you really want to postpone that meeting?"

"Yes, but a young and sexy one," she said, strutting out of the office.

"Alright now!" Lisa laughed.

Lisa looked at her watch and realized she had about forty-five minutes before the conference, which gave her enough time to check her email. When she saw that it was fifteen minutes 'til, she closed her eyes, prayed, and said, "In Jesus' name, Amen." She headed out the door to her first meeting of the day.

CHAPTER FOUR

After the conference, Lisa headed back to her office. Marc caught up to her and said, "My office or yours?"

"Yours. It's closer and has better snacks," Lisa said, smiling.

"If you get a small refrigerator, you can have snacks," Marc said, moving closer to Lisa.

To keep from blushing, which she sure she was, she took a step back.

"I'll keep that in mind," she said.

As they stood there in awkward silence, Lisa noticed two women standing in the hall to their right, staring at them.

"Okay, let's get started."

Noticing a change, he followed her line of sight and saw the two women. "Umm, yeah let's go."

Walking toward his office, Lisa made a mental note to ask Carol if she'd heard any gossip about her and Marc. As they walked into his office, Marc told his assistant to hold his calls.

"Okay, now that we are away from prying eyes. Did you get my messages last night?" he asked, once his office door was closed.

"Yeah, but you got cut off on the last one. What were you trying to say?"

"You obviously got the gist of it, so the rest doesn't matter," he said, sitting behind his desk. Lisa took a seat in one of the chairs in front of the desk. As Marc looked for a file, Lisa looked around his office. She had never really noticed Marc's office before. It was manly and well decorated, with comfortable leathers, deep browns, and wood. Lisa liked it. Then she heard Marc say, "So, what's your pleasure?"

Looking at him, she wondered if he was flirting again. "I'll start with bottled water."

"Alright," he said, as he swiveled around in his leather chair to the refrigerator.

"I also have chocolate, if you're interested. Or do you even like chocolate?"

Laughing, Lisa said, "Isn't it too early for chocolate? It's not even noon yet."

"Just like drinking, it's the afternoon somewhere. Why do you think I'm so energetic in the morning?"

"I always thought it was because you were happy with life."

"That to, but this helps," he said, waving a Hershey bar. "And you didn't answer my question."

"What?"

"Do you like chocolate?"

"Doesn't every woman?"

"I suppose, but I'm asking you."

"Of course. I love you…uh it. I meant to say it," she said quickly, hoping he didn't catch the slip up. But, when an eyebrow shot up and he smiled, she knew he'd heard her.

Marc just smiled, and said, "What's your favorite chocolate?"

"I'm a simple girl, my favorite chocolate is Godiva."

"Simple? Simple is one thing you are definitely not, Ms. Jenson."

"I'll take that as a compliment," Lisa said, staring into those deep brown eyes of his.

"I hope so."

"Okay, let's get this meeting started," she said, changing the subject.

"Right, what I wanted to know was where could we start on the Keene account and find out the ending outcome for the Thompson account?"

"As you already know, Thompson's final number is three point two. I finally got the rest of his figures and paperwork yesterday. You should have a copy of everything."

"I haven't gotten a chance to work through my stack yet," he said, speaking of the stack that was in a tray marked for this quarter. Lisa counted over thirty-five folders.

"Well, when you get a chance to look it over, let me know if you're missing anything."

"Okay. Next, the Keene account. Where can we start on this account? I was going over his past quarters and they've been pretty good. So, why does he want to change investors?"

"He didn't at first, he was just shopping around. When I got wind of it, I started calling to get a meeting with him. But for the first couple of months I just got the run around. About two weeks ago I got lucky, he had an opening in his schedule and I took it. We met yesterday afternoon, as you already know; I told him he could get a better return on his investments. He went for it." Taking a sip of water to wet her throat, she continued, "The thing is, I need your testosterone on this one."

"My what?" Marc laughed.

All Lisa could think was how sexy his smile was and how kissable his lips looked. Pushing that thought from her mind, Lisa continued, "Your man's man mentality. See, I noticed that Mr. Keene is manly, and well, that's where you come in."

"You think I'm manly?" he asked, smiling.

Laughing, Lisa said, "No, but you could pretend."

"Thanks, but he couldn't be that bad. I mean, you got him to at least try our company for a year. He has never done that with any other company."

"Yeah, but I get the feeling he feels that women have no right making the big decisions."

"Oh, one of those."

"Yep, one of those."

"What can I do? You know I don't believe in that," he said, sincerely.

"I know that, but he doesn't."

"If it will help, then alright."

"It will."

"When is the next meeting?"

"Monday. With today only being Tuesday, we have the rest of the week to prepare." Looking at her watch, she realized that it was twelve-thirty and said, "Ooo, my morning has really gotten away from me. I still have a meeting to prepare for with Mrs. Hearn. Is there anything else you need to know?"

"Nope. But I will give you my condolences. Is she still Mrs. Olivia Hearn-Sinclaire?"

"Oh, no, you are behind the times. She is now Mrs. Olivia Hearn-Winfield or should I say Mrs. Douglas Winfield III. She doesn't use her own name anymore. In her words, 'how would anyone know who I am?'" Lisa said, imitating Mrs. Hearn.

"We thought she would be better working with another woman."

"Yeah, right. You all just dumped her on me. But, you should have seen her face when she found out I wasn't married. I thought she would drop dead on the spot."

"That's our Mrs. Hearn."

"God help us all," Lisa said, walking out of the office.

When she made it to her office, she found Mrs. Hearn waiting for her in the outer office with Carol.

"Mrs. He – I mean, Mrs. Winfield, how are you?"

"I'm fine, Ms. Jenson," she said, with what one would believe was a sincere smile. But Lisa knew better. Mrs. Winfield's smile was as fake as the size Ds she'd just newly purchased. "I'm sorry for the delay. One of my meetings ran over. I didn't expect you until one-thirty, but we can get started. So, why don't you come on in?"

As Mrs. Winfield walked into her office, Lisa and Carol gave each other frustrated looks.

"Alright, Mrs. Winfield, let's get started."

For the next hour and a half, Lisa explained every current and future investment to Mrs. Winfield. She also answered every question that was thrown at her. Lisa even told her that she would have a bigger return on her profit this quarter. This bit of information made her extremely happy. Lisa figured that should keep her old ass in fur in the winter and young men in the summer.

After escorting Mrs. Winfield to the elevator, Lisa wanted to scream. When she made it back to her office, she told Carol that she should go to lunch.

As she was getting her purse, Carol said, "She's on her third husband, right?"

"Yep."

"You think she's killing them?"

"Yep. She nags them to death. When you get back, we can start on those accounts."

"Okay. Want anything?"

"No, thanks. I'm fine."

"Be back soon."

Lis went into her office and decided to get a head start on the two stacks of folders next to her desk that added up to about forty accounts.

"Hello?" a male voice called out from the outer office.

Lisa got up from her desk and walked to her doorway, where James was standing. "Now, what?" she asked, leaning against the door jam.

"I wanted to see you. That's alright, ain't it?"

"No."

"Come on, Lisa. Don't be that way. I'm trying to make amends," he said, walking closer.

Lisa had to step back into her office to make sure he didn't get to close. "What can I do for you, James?" she asked, turning to walk over to her desk.

She imagined he was staring at her ass since he hadn't answered her yet. Turning to look at him, she said, "Again, what can I do for you?"

"I wanted to see you again. To talk to you."

"About?"

"Can I take you out to lunch?"

"No."

"Why not?"

"Do you want the nice version or the truth?"

"Both."

"I can't. I have a lot of work to do," she said with a smile. Then dropping it, she said, "Now, the truth, I can't stand you long enough to eat lunch."

She saw him flinch and anger flash in his eyes, but he recovered quickly. Right then and there she saw the old James lurking around.

"Just an hour. Just to catch up, that's all."

Lisa leaned against her desk and watched him without saying a word. James sat in one of the chairs in front of her desk. Actually, he sat in the chair directly in front of her. He was too close for her comfort, but she refused to move. He wasn't gonna make her feel uncomfortable in her own office.

"Okay, I tell you what. How about tomorrow after work? We can have just one drink and talk. Come on, you know you want to," he smiled.

Right then Lisa remembered what her first attraction to him was, his smile. Again she said, "I have a lot of work to do."

"It's drinks. What, are you afraid to be alone with me?" he asked, as he stood up.

"No."

To her surprise, the word came out a lot calmer than she felt. James was inches from her. She thought he was about to kiss her, until…

"Hey, Lisa, I – Oh, sorry. I didn't know you were with a client."

"That's okay, Marc. What can I do for you?" Lisa asked, thankful for the interruption.

"How you doing?" Marc said to James. James didn't respond. Continuing to Lisa, he said, "I just needed to pick your brain about this account."

"Let me look over it and I can get some ideas. How soon do you need it?"

"No rush."

"You'll have it by tomorrow."

"Thanks. See ya later. And sorry to interrupt."

After he left, Lisa walked back to her desk and dropped the file on top of an already tall stack. Writing a note to herself, Lisa then looked at James, who was looking at her. "What?" she said.

"Are you seeing anybody?"

"None of your business."

"Ol' boy looked at me like I'm invading his space. Y'all datin'?"

"Once again, none of your business."

"It doesn't matter. I still have a chance."

"No, you don't. Look, I think it's time for you to go."

"Okay. But, I'll see you tomorrow."

Lisa just watched him as he got up to leave. Before he walked out the door, he said, "You can't keep running from me."

"Not running, just not interested."

"We'll see." He winked and then he was gone.

Lisa sat in her chair and said to herself, "Lord, give me strength."

***

By six o'clock, Lisa and Carol were finally closing up shop. Lisa packed her briefcase with the remainder of her files and headed home. Getting off the elevator, Lisa said, "I am going to try to get through as many of these as I possibly can. What are you gonna do tonight?"

"I am going to stay in bed with my husband all night."

"Lucky you."

"It could be the same for you someday if you would just let me hook you up. I know –"

"No, Carol."

"He's intelligent, good looking, never been married. He's Charles's partner."

"No, Carol. Now, go home and have fun."

"Okay. But, don't say I didn't try."

After giving each other a hug, they got in their cars and drove out of the garage in different directions. When Lisa got home, she dropped her things on her couch, looked through her mail, and checked her messages.

Taking her briefcase and purse upstairs with her, she stopped in one of her guest bedrooms that was also a home office. She left her briefcase and a stack of bills she was planning to pay tonight on the desk. She then headed to her bedroom to get out of her clothes and do her nightly ritual before getting to work.

After an hour of rejuvenating herself, she headed downstairs to see what she could make a quick dinner out of. Opening her refrigerator, she could already tell her mother had been there. There were two new Tupperware dishes in her refrigerator. Opening them, she found lasagna in one and French bread in the other. "Thank you, mommy."

Heading back upstairs to her office with a plate and a glass of white wine, she heard her phone ring. Pushing the speaker button, she said, "Hello?"

"Where the hell have you been?" her friend Nic said, without preamble.

"Working."

"Mm-hmm, I'm walking in."

"I'm upstairs in the office." Lisa then hung up, and started to eat as she booted up her computer.

Her friend walked into the room, and said, "I should shoot you."

"What did I do?"

"You haven't called or stopped by. The only way I knew you were alright was through Pat or Carol. So I had to come find you myself."

"That's what makes you a great detective."

Nic and Lisa had been friends for the past eleven years. Lisa considered all of her girlfriends to be her sisters, but Nic would always be the one she was a closet too. How could she not, Nic saved her life.

"So, what brings you out this way?" Lisa asked her.

"First things first, anymore?" Nic asked, referring to Lisa's plate.

"My mother has been here, so you know there is."

"I'll be right back," Nic said, as she left the room.

A couple of minutes later, she was back with a plate of her own and a glass of wine herself. "So, what are you doing?"

"Leftover work that me and Carol didn't finish today. You had to work tonight?"

"Just got off."

Nic was a detective for the ninth precinct. Make that a great detective, at least that's what Lisa thought.

"Anything strange or exciting happen today?"

"No, but something in the area of déjà vu happened."

"What?" Lisa asked, as she continued to eat before getting to work.

"Well, John and I got a call for domestic violence."

"Why were you –" Then Lisa figured it out. "Oh. The wife or girlfriend?"

"The wife. The husband said she just kept pushing him. He couldn't control his self."

"How did he…do it?" Lisa asked.

"He beat her to death," Nic said in a sad voice.

"How bad?"

"If it wasn't for the pictures in the house, we would have never recognized her."

"My God. What will happen to him?"

"He will be charged. For what? That depends on the DA."

"Wow."

"Yeah, I know."

For the rest of the night, Lisa and Nic talked while Lisa finished up her work. By midnight, Nic was gone and Lisa was in bed.

The next morning, Lisa made it to work by eight-thirty and was ready for work.

"Good morning," Carol sang, when she walked in at nine on the dot.

"Good morning, to you. I see your night went well."

"My night went great," Carol said with a big smile on her face.

"I would ask what you two did last night, but I'm sure I'm too young to hear those sorts of things."

"Yes, I don't want to corrupt your little mind. So, did you get any work done?"

"Yeah, I got the majority of them done. But I still have a lot to do."

"Well, give me half and I'll get started on those. And don't worry about any meetings today; you have a clear day to do some catch up."

Lisa handed her six files, then said, "Bless you. Oh, wait one of those are from Marc. I have to work that one."

"Buzz me if you need," Carol said, as she walked out of the office.

Lisa worked through the day, until Carol buzzed her to let her know she was leaving for lunch. Lisa continued to work on the accounts for the rest of the day. She actually worked through lunch. When she looked up, Carol was walking in with her coat and purse. "It's quitting time, lady."

Lisa looked up from her computer screen, and said, "I know. This day has truly gotten away from me. I didn't even get to eat lunch."

"I know. That's why I am bringing over takeout and you provide the wine."

"I don't know, Carol, I just wanted to go home and soak in my tub."

"Oh, I'm sorry, you really thought I was asking. Nooo, honey, I'll be at your house by seven-thirty."

"Alright." Lisa was actually glad Carol insisted to come over. She really didn't want to be at home alone tonight with her thoughts of James.

Lisa and Carol split up from each other to get in their cars. Due to it being summer, it was still light out. On the way home, Lisa stopped at the store to pick up two bottles of her favorite Pinot Grigio.

When she got home, she checked her messages. Her mother and Nic left messages. So, she called her mother first.

"Hey, mama."

"Hey."

"What are you up to?"

"Nothing, right now. What about you?"

"Just got home and about to jump in the tub. But, I wanted to give you a call first. Carol is coming over in a little while. She's bringing over some takeout and I have the wine. Why don't you come over and hang out with us?"

"Naw, honey. I'm going to the casino with Marilyn."

"Well, win me some money."

"You already got money, I need that money."

"For what? You need anything?"

"No, baby. I'm fine. Just going for fun."

"Okay, then."

"Ooo, Marilyn just pulled up. I'll talk to you tomorrow."

"Alright. Good luck."

"Thank you. Bye."

After hanging up from her mother, Lisa called Nic.

"Hello," Nic said.

"Hey, what you doing?" Lisa asked.

"Nothing much. What's going on with you?"

"The same. I'm just getting home from work. I'm about to change and get comfortable before Carol gets here."

"How she doing?"

"Fine."

"So, what are you two up to tonight?"

"We're having a gossip fest. Why don't you come over?"

"I don't know, y'all got room for one more?"

"Girl, please," Lisa said. "Get your butt over here."

"Well, since you put it that way. I'll be over in an hour. Is there anything I can bring?"

"Carol is providing the food. I'm providing the wine, so you can provide the dessert. Call her and tell her to bring enough for you too."

"What is she bringing?" Nic asked.

"You know I didn't ask. Oh well, whatever it is I'll eat it."

"How 'bout I bring some donuts?" Nic laughed.

"Not funny."

"Okay, okay. I'll bring a large cheesecake."

"Perfect! I'll see you in an hour."

"Bye."

"Bye."

When Lisa hung up the phone she looked at her watch and realized she had just enough time for a good soak.

Carol and Nic showed up at seven-thirty on the dot.

"Hey, ladies. Come on in," Lisa said, as she stepped aside to let them in.

"Thank you," Carol and Nic said in unison.

Lisa led them to the coffee table in the living room where the radio was playing Mary J. Blidge's new CD.

"Alright, ladies, let's get full, in both meanings of the word," Nic said, as they got comfortable in different spots around the table.

As the ladies dug into the Chinese food and poured wine, the gossip-fest began. Carol told them about her next door neighbor who was having an affair.

"Two days ago her husband came home early. She must have heard him come in, because the next thing I know, the boyfriend is on the roof buck-naked."

"What?!" Nic said, loudly.

"Yes, ma'am. But get this, now he has to quietly put on his clothes while he is still on the roof. Evidently, he wasn't, because the husband comes back outside and looks straight up at the guy. So by now other neighbors and I as well are coming outside to watch the action. All of a sudden the husband comes out of the house and yells at the man, 'You're supposed to clean the pool!' Then he gets the water hose and starts to spry the guy with water. The boyfriend loses his balance and slips and falls off the roof into the woman's flower bush."

By now all of them are in tears from laughing so hard.

"Was he hurt?" Lisa asked.

"No, but then the husband grabs the guy and beats the hell out of him. Charlotte, the wife, calls the police and have them arrest the husband for beating up the boyfriend."

"No, she didn't," Lisa said.

"The hell she didn't," Carol said.

"Is the husband still in jail?" Nic asked.

"Got out the next day, came home while Charlotte was at work and put all her shit out on the curb. I mean every knick knack and bric-a-brac. Then told people that were walking by that they could get whatever they wanted. I got a beautiful vanity set, mirror and all."

"You did not take that woman's vanity set?" Nic said, laughing.

"The hell I didn't. Shit, that's more money in my pocket," Carol said, laughing.

"You better be lucky I'm off duty, Mrs. Carol," Nic said.

"Honey, please, you don't have enough people in your department to arrest everybody in my neighborhood. Hell, those people were fighting over her stuff like it was Christmas Eve. Some of those folks I thought were dead. They probably were and just came back to get free shit."

For the duration of the dinner, all the ladies traded stories until the food was gone and the dessert and wine were on their way to being nonexistent.

Then Carol said, "So, Lisa, are you going to finally tell me who the mystery man is that keeps coming by the office?"

"What mystery man?" Nic asked, as she sliced herself another piece of cheesecake.

"That's what I been trying to find out.

"No one. Just someone I used to know. Anybody want any more wine?" Lisa asked, trying to change the subject.

"No! Now come on and tell us who he is," Carol said.

"I know who it is, it's Russell," Nic said.

"No," said Lisa.

Then Nic said, "Jason?"

"Nope."

"Damn, then who?" Carol burst out.

When Lisa didn't say anything or make eye contact with either of them, Nic said, "James?!"

Lisa couldn't even look her friend in the eyes.

"Oh, hell naw!" Nic said, loudly.

As Nic stared at Lisa, Lisa stared at the table, while Carol looked between each lady waiting for one of them to say something.

"What's going on? Don't leave a sista' out," Carol said.

Lisa and Nic looked at Carol and burst out laughing.

"What? I'm a sista' at heart. Now, tell me what's going on."

"James is Lisa's ex," Nic said, while still looking at Lisa.

"Oh," Carol said while pouring herself another glass of wine.

Then Nic asked, "What did he want?"

"He said he stopped by to say hello," Lisa said.

"How long did he stay?"

"Not long."

"What did you talk about?"

"Nothing. I told him to leave."

"How many times has he been by the office?"

"Twice. You know, this is starting to feel like an interrogation."

"I'm asking as a friend."

"It doesn't seem like it."

"Look, don't try and change the subject."

"I'm not."

"Yeah, right," Nic said under her breath. Then she said aloud, "Well?"

Lisa sighed and then said "He just came by to talk."

"About what?"

"He said he'd changed and he wanted to apologize."

"Oh, please."

"What does he have to apologize for?" Carol asked.

Neither Lisa nor Nic answered her.

So Carol said, "Hellooo, did I disappear?"

"No, Carol. Why don't you tell her, Lisa?" said Nic.

The room was completely quiet. It even seemed as if Mary J. Blidge was waiting for an answer.

"We dated about six years ago," Lisa began. "Some things happened and we broke up."

"Like what?" Carol asked.

Lisa didn't answer, so Nic did, "They dated for two years, which a year and a half of those years were spent with him beating her."

"What?!" Carol exclaimed.

Lisa still didn't say anything, so Nic continued, "When they first met, according to Lisa, everything was fine. Then about four months into the relationship. I go by her mom's house to see her and she has a black eye."

"Oh, my God," Carol gasped and looked at Lisa.

"That's not it. Then shit really gets hectic, she completely stops hanging out with me and Pat. From what her mother was telling me, she stopped hanging out with family, too."

"You don't have to talk like I'm not even here," Lisa said, while pouring herself another glass of wine.

"Anyway, he would keep track of everything she did and everywhere she went. I have to admit, she didn't let him ruin her chance of pursuing her degree. I'm so glad she didn't. But –"

"Can I tell my own story, please?" Lisa said, cutting Nic off.

"Sure, as long as it's the truth," Nic said.

Lisa stuck her tongue out at Nic, and then said, "When I met James, I hadn't been in a relationship in about four years. The last guy I dated I was really heartbroken over, and I was still sort of waiting for him to come back. Anyway, as she said, at the beginning everything was fine. We would go to the movies, clubs, and restaurants, and anything else you could think of. I was so attracted to him, so I overlooked a lot of things. Come on, even though he is evil, you saw him Carol."

Carol nodded.

"At the time, I was overweight, so someone as good looking as him showing me some interest made me feel like I was the most beautiful woman in the world. And he was older than me, so he knew how to get my young ass."

"How much older is he then you?" Carol said.

"About ten years. I was nineteen at the time, so I didn't have a lot of life experience. All I knew was going to school and what I learned from this old hooker," Lisa laughed, as she pointed at Nic.

"Whatever," Nic said, throwing a pillow at Lisa.

"So after four months, things started to change."

"Four months?" Carol asked.

"Yeah, I mean he already knew he had me. He knew all my weaknesses and even used them to get me on his side. Then he started getting meaner and wanting to spend every waking moment together. It began to be too much, it seemed like every time he would walk in he would suck all the air out of the room. It started to feel like there wasn't any room for me to breathe anymore. And I did stop hanging out with my friends and family. I just told them that I had a lot of homework. My mother tried to talk some sense into me, but of course I wouldn't listen. By then the pushing and slapping had started and I was afraid to tell my mother. Considering she never liked him, I couldn't tell her that he was hitting on me."

"Yeah, by the end, Mrs. Janice was talking about killing that fool," Nic said.

"As always, after every fight, he would be so sorry and I would believe him."

"I know this is probably a stupid question, but why would you forgive him? I mean, you don't seem to be that type of person," said Carol.

"I'm not now, but I was. It took some time for me to get here and I'm truly blessed to be."

"I've heard some people say that after they slept together, that's when the person changed. Is that what happened to you?"

"No. To be honest, it had been a minute for me, if you know what I mean. So it didn't take long for us to sleep together, to be more accurate, two weeks. He was gorgeous, I couldn't help it. He got to me through conversation. We could talk about anything. That's what attracted me. He had me believing that he was the man for me. Scratch that, I had myself believing that he was the man for me. I was addicted to him, hell part of me still is. Shut up, Nic."

"I didn't say anything," Nic said.

"So what happened to make you finally leave him?" Carol asked.

"He almost killed her," Nic said.

"What?!" Carol shrieked, looking at Lisa.

Lisa took a deep breath and said, "We were having problems, as usual, and I got tired of it. I wasn't allowed to go anywhere unless he was with me. So I told him it was over and that I couldn't go through this over and over again. At first he said he loved me and that he would straighten up. I told him I didn't believe him and that we couldn't keep going on like this. When he realized I wasn't going to change my mind, he decided to beat me until I did. He started to punch, slap, kick and everything else he wanted to do to me. Apparently, he had knocked me out, because when I woke up it was two weeks later. I was in the hospital with six broken ribs, a concussion, two black eyes and I couldn't remember what happened."

"What happened to him? Did he go to jail?" Carol asked.

"It's kind of fuzzy, but Ms. Detective here can fill you in. I have to go to the bathroom," Lisa said, getting up off the floor.

When Lisa was out of hearing range, Nic finished the story, "During her two weeks in a coma, all the pieces came together. The beating happened at his house and afterward, he left her there. When she didn't come home the night before, her mother called me and asked if I had seen her? When I told her no, she really got worried. No one knew where he stayed. I'd just got on the police department and decided to put his name in the system. We got his address and I met her mother over at his house. When we got there the door was unlocked, and when we opened the door she was laying on the floor. I tell you, Carol, when we found her, she looked dead and was close to it. The ambulance got there in time to keep her breathing, but Carol I have to tell you we didn't think she was going to make it. There was so much blood. I put out his description, but no one could find him."

"How did you find him then?"

"A couple of days had passed before he showed up at the hospital. He thought everyone had left and snuck into her room, but to his surprise I was waiting on his ass."

"You think he came to finish what he started?"

"I really do."

"Then you saved her life."

"That's my girl. If I couldn't get to her before it happened, I made damned sure it wouldn't happen again. Anyway, he pled guilty to a lesser charge and only got three years, while she's scarred for life.

Carol and Nic sat quietly until Lisa walked back into the room.

"What time is it?" Carol asked.

"Ten o'clock, ladies," Lisa said.

"It's just ten and I'm already drunk," Carol laughed.

"Me, too," Lisa and Nic said in unison, and then they all started laughing.

"Well neither of you are leaving under these conditions, so get comfortable," Lisa said.

"Girl, I already have. I packed a bag before I left home," Carol said.

"And I don't have to be at work until two tomorrow afternoon," said Nic, as she refilled her glass.

Then an idea came to Lisa. "Carol has any good gossip been going around the office lately?"

"You mean about you and Mr. Cavell?"

"Say what?" Nic said.

"Oh yes, honey. They are the talk of the office."

"What is everyone saying?" asked Lisa.

"Right now just petty stuff, nothing of any credit."

"Petty stuff, like what?"

"Actually they're saying you and Mr. Cavell have been looking quite chummy these days. And that no matter how much the women in the office try, they won't get anywhere with him. Especially, that Miss Wanna-be Melody. She has been trying to get his attention since she started working at the firm last year."

"Have they ever gone out?" Lisa asked, hoping that the tone of jealousy wasn't evident. But, both Carol and Nic noticed.

Then Carol said, "Why, you don't want him. Shit, let somebody else have his fine ass."

"I know you've had too much to drink now, because I am not interested in Marc."

"Yeah right! All I know is that you better make up your mind, because the vultures are circling, honey," Carol said.

"Lisa, you know the man likes you. Hell, that time we ran into him while shopping I could tell. He barely acknowledged me and you know that shit just does not happen," Nic said as she flipped her hair over her shoulder.

"Anyway, Miss Thing, I told you that I was concentrating on my career."

"We've heard it all before," said Nic.

That conversation went on well into the night. Looking at the clock, Lisa realized it was two o'clock in the morning. By two-thirty the living room and kitchen were clean and everyone had their sleeping assignments.

Lisa stood in the hallway of the facing rooms and asked, "Does everybody have what they need?"

"Yes, ma'am," Nic said in a little girl voice and all of them started laughing.

"Alright, ladies. Good night."

"Good night," Nic and Carol said.

The minute Lisa finished her prayers, she fell asleep. That night, she dreamed of making love to James. In her dream, they were in a room filled with candles on a large bed with silk white sheets. As Lisa straddled his lap, he kissed her deeply and passionately as she came. When they rolled over, Lisa looked into Marc's eyes as he continued to kiss her and bring her to an ecstasy that she never experienced. As Marc went deeper, he said, "I love you, Lisa." Lisa jumped up to the sound of her alarm going off. She was more tired now than when she went to sleep. She hit the button on the alarm clock and got up to start her day.

CHAPTER FIVE

"Good morning, Carol," Lisa said, when she walked into the kitchen.

"Good morning," Carol said, cheerfully.

"Is Nic awake?"

"Nope. Sleeping beauty is still sleeping."

"Well, she did say she didn't have to be at work until two."

"I've been meaning to ask you something."

"What?"

"How did someone as pretty as Nic end up becoming a cop, well, a detective."

Finishing her bagel, Lisa said, "Let's go in the gym and I'll tell you."

"You're not gonna make me workout, are you?"

"No. I know you're allergic," Lisa said, laughing.

When the ladies walked into the gym, they were surprised to see Nic already there running on the treadmill.

"Good morning, late birds."

"We thought you were still asleep," Carol said.

"Nope, I've been up about thirty minutes," Nic said.

Lisa started working out on the stationary bike, since Nic still had twenty minutes on the treadmill.

Sitting on the workbench, Carol said, "Nic, I asked Lisa, but now I can ask you."

"Shoot."

"I was just wondering why you became a detective. I mean, you're beautiful; you could have been a model. Instead you chose to be a cop, why?"

"Well, to be honest, I didn't plan on being a cop. It just kind of happened. Me and Lisa had been friends for about four years, right Lis?"

"Yeah."

"Then when she started college and I saw how much she enjoyed it, I decided to see what kind of choices were out there for me. When I decided to take up Criminal Justice, I found I really enjoyed it. At first it was difficult, but I had a lot of help. Lisa helped me in any way she could and never let me quit. Sometimes she was worse than my family."

They talked until the workout was over and it was time for Lisa and Carol to get ready for work.

Ready for work, Lisa came downstairs. When Nic saw her, she said, "I thought you were going to work."

"I am. Why do you say that?"

"The top you wearing," Nic said, as she sat at the kitchen island.

"What's wrong with my top?"

"Your back is out."

"Nobody will see it. What, it's not cute?"

"I like it, but don't you have a red scarf like that?"

"It is my scarf."

"You are lying."

"Nope. I was watching the Morning Show yesterday and this lady was showing the different ways you could wear a scarf and this was one of them. Ain't it cute?"

"Yeah, I will have to try that."

Carol walked in a second later and said, "Okay, I'm ready."

"Are you driving or riding with me?" Lisa asked Carol.

"No way, I want to get to work with my hair its natural color."

"Very funny. Hey, Nic, lockup when you leave."

"I will. I'll call y'all later," Nic said, as Lisa and Carol headed out the door.

Within twenty minutes, Lisa was pulling into the parking garage.

"Hey, Ms. Jenson. How you doing this morning?"

"Hey, Shirley. I'm fine, you?"

"Jesus woke me up this morning, so I'm great."

"Amen to that. See you later."

Lisa pulled in and parked in the first vacant spot she found. After getting her morning cappuccino and newspaper, she headed for the elevator.

Unlocking the door to her office, Lisa was already in work mode. She figured if she got right to work she might be able to get the rest of her work done that she was behind on.

Ten minutes later, Carol walked in and said, "I knew you missed that wreck on the interstate."

"Was it bad?"

"Nope, just time consuming. No one was hurt. Well, let the day begin."

"Don't I know it."

"Good morning, Mr. Cavell," Carol said on her way out of the office.

"Good morning, Carol," Marc said.

"Hey," Lisa said, as she took off her jacket and hung it up.

For a minute, Marc was speechless at the sight of her back. Right then something went through him. He heard Lisa's voice; he just didn't understand what she was saying. Shaking himself out of a trance, he heard her say, "I finished that file and put my ideas in there. If you have any questions, let me know."

"Um, o-okay," he stuttered.

"So what does your day look like?"

"Full of meetings," he said, opening the file.

"Well, let me know if you need anything."

"Will do," he said, as he turned to leave. Before making it to door, he said, "Oh, before I forget, when can we start on the presentation for Keene?"

"I'm free whenever you are."

"Okay, how about tomorrow? With it being Friday, I'm clear, if you don't mind working late?"

"Not at all. As long as you swing for dinner."

"You got a deal," Marc said and left.

Out in the hallway, Marc heard someone call his name.

"Hey, man, wait up."

"What's up, Steve?" Marc said.

"Just getting in here. Traffic was a monster."

"Not for me."

"Hell, I know it wasn't. You live right around the corner. Man, how is Lisa this morning? As fine as ever?"

"More. Man, she took off her jacket while I was in her office and her back was out. I almost passed out."

"Damn! I missed that? I would have tackled her right there," Steve said, as he took a set in front of Marc's desk when they walked into his office.

"You crazy. Lisa would have knocked you out."

"I'm telling you, she been giving me the eye. I think she wants me."

"You been saying that same shit since the first day you saw her," Marc said, laughing.

"That's because it's true."

"Has she said anything remotely sexual to you?"

"No, but it's in her body language."

"Yeah, right."

"Don't hate me because she wants me. Watch, when I hit it I'm gon' give you all the details blow by blow."

"Steve, the only blow by blow you gonna get is when she hits you with a left and right hook."

"Don't hate! You'll see, Ms. Jenson is next to being crossed off my list."

"Anyway, is there anything else, because I need to get to work?"

"Yeah, I gotta cancel tomorrow night's game. I got a date."

"Who's the victim this week?"

"This fine ass girl in processing on the second floor. Her name is Shelia, or is it Sharon? Hell, I don't know. But what I do know is that she has one of the fattest asses I have ever seen. I can't wait to hit that from the back."

"Man, you need to quit. Don't you think the women in this building talk? I mean, damn, haven't you slept with at least forty percent of them?"

"First off, wasn't any sleeping involved. And besides, it's only about eighty percent women in this company. And I have only been with half."

"Exactly."

"Hey, I'm just doing my part. You the one need to open your eyes. Between me and you, we could have our own harem."

"You crazy as hell," Marc laughed.

"Anyway, I got to go. We on for lunch?"

"Yeah, but I got to meet you there."

"Awight, later man."

"Later."

As Marc started his work day, he couldn't help wondering, what if?

Midway into his morning, Barbara buzzed him and said, "Mr. Cavell, Melody is here to see you."

Marc sighed and said, "Send her in." When Melody walked in he said, "Good morning, Melody. What do you need?"

"Well, Mr. Morgan wanted me to bring you the file you would need for the Keene account."

As she laid the file on his desk, she leaned over to show off her cleavage. Marc pretended to be too busy to notice the gesture.

"Thanks, Melody," he said.

"No problem. Is there anything else I can do for you?"

Marc wanted to say, 'yeah, get out'. But instead he said, "No that's it."

He got up from his desk and went over to his bookcase, pretending to look for something.

"Look, I was wondering if you would like to go out for drinks tonight."

"Sorry, Melody, I have plans."

"Is it with Lisa? You know the whole office is talking about you two. Everyone thinks that the two of you are sleeping together."

"Is that what everyone thinks?"

"Yeah."

"Well, to be perfectly honest, I don't care what people are saying. It's really none of their business and I need to get back to work."

"I didn't mean to make you mad or anything."

"Oh, you didn't. I just think people should mind their own business."

"I guess I better go then."

"Thanks for bringing the file."

As Melody walked out of his office, Marc could only shake his head. Although Melody was a beautiful woman, she was sort of pushy. Marc liked a chase. Melody lacked class; she was nothing like...Lisa. Marc shook that thought from his head and got back to work.

***

For the rest of the day, Lisa caught up on the work that she let slip. When she looked up, Carol was walking into her office.

"Well, that's the end of another long day. I am about to leave, is there anything else you need me to do?"

"No honey, I'm about to leave myself."

"Good, let's go. Good evening, Mr. Cavell," Carol said, on her way out.

"Hello, ladies. Are you two about to leave?"

"Yeah, it's been a long day," Lisa said, as she gathered her things.

"Good, because I could go for a drink. Would you two like to join me?"

"I can't. Charles is home from his business trip and well I missed him. But, Lisa is free," Carol said.

Marc looked at Lisa, "How 'bout it?"

"Actually, I was gonna go home and curl up with a good book tonight."

"Lisa, you can do that any night. You should go. Besides, don't you two need to get a game plan together for Mr. Keene?"

After taking a slight pause Lisa said, "Yeah, I can do with a drink."

"Great," Carol said a little too happily.

"If you're ready, we can leave now and get Carol safely to her car," Marc said.

They walked to the elevator and rode down to the parking garage in silence. When they made it to the garage, Carol said, "You guys can go ahead, I'm parked right next to Lisa."

"No, we're gonna make sure you're safely on your way," Lisa told her.

After Carol blew her horn and drove away, Marc said "Any ideas on where to go?"

"How about TGIF?"

54

"No, a few co-workers go there after work. How about the bar in the Peabody Hotel?"

"Okay, I'll follow you."

They got in their cars and Lisa trailed him to the Peabody. Parking in the parking garage a few spaces away from each other, Marc walked over to Lisa's car as she was getting out. He couldn't help but notice that she wasn't wearing her jacket and her back was out.

"Calm down, boy," he whispered to himself.

Lisa hit the button on her key chain to lock her doors. Just as they walked away from her car, they heard tires screeching and bright headlights headed right for them.

"Lisa!" Marc pulled her out of the way just in time as the car screech by them and kept going as if nothing happened. Holding Lisa close, he said, "Are you okay?"

"Yeah, I'm okay. Thank you for pulling me out of the way," she said, as she looked up at him.

"Are you sure you're okay?" he asked.

"Yeah, I just wish I had a brick."

"You wouldn't have caught him as fast as he was going."

"You don't know my throwing my arm."

Laughing, Marc said, "Let's go get you a drink."

They walked into the hotel and instantly noticed how crowded it was. They found a spot on a couch near the bar. Lisa had almost forgotten how beautiful the Peabody was. After ordering their drinks, they talked about a strategy for the Keene account.

"I think you should head the account," Lisa said, while accepting her glass from the waiter.

"Why, you're the one who got him to at least give us a try. And haven't we already had this conversation before?"

"Yes, and we are going to keep having it, until you agree," Lisa said, laughing.

"Is he really that bad?"

"I have a feeling he is, and in case I'm right, I don't want to say the wrong thing if he says something I don't like. That's where you come in, laugh at his offensive jokes, and even make some yourself. I know you know some."

"A few. You want to hear one?"

"No, thank you."

"Come on, it's funny. Steve told me this one."

"Steve. I should have known."

Lisa rolled her eyes and took a sip of her wine.

"What do you have against Steve?"

"I know he's your friend, but he's a h– I mean he's been around the office quite a bit. And for some reason he thinks I want him."

Marc, surprised, almost choked on his wine.

Laughing, Lisa said, "Oh, I see, you thought I didn't know. Women talk just like men do. And not to mention, he hasn't looked me in the eyes since I started working for the firm."

Marc just nodded and tried to keep from laughing.

"Besides, he is not my type."

"He'll be heartbroken to hear that."

"Then I'll be happy to tell him," Lisa laughed.

"Have you ever dated anyone in the office?" Marc asked, but then added quickly, "I'm sorry, ignore that question, it's the wine talking."

"That's fine, as I told you before, I'm an open book. To answer your question, no. But according to Carol everyone thinks *we* are."

"Yeah, so I'm told."

"Who told you?"

"Melody, Mr. Morgan's secretary."

"And what did you tell her?"

"I told her it wasn't anyone's business what goes on or doesn't go on between you and me."

"What if she takes her claim to Mr. Morgan?"

"Worried?" Marc teased. "Besides, that's how Mr. Morgan met his second wife."

"You're kidding, right?"

"Nope, that's who Melody replaced."

"No wonder she's all over you. My sources tell me she has staked a claim on you."

"Well, your sources are correct. But like you and Steve, Melody isn't my type. She's a little too pushy for my taste, a man likes a chase."

"Maybe she'll grow on you," Lisa said, laughing.

As Marc laughed, he said, "I don't know about that. My mother would kill me if I introduced her to someone like Melody."

"So you mother's opinion means a lot?"

"Not so much, but I would like my parent's blessing when I meet the right person. We are a close family, so it does matter what they think."

"I don't think there is anything wrong with that, actually I feel the same way."

After a moment of silence, Lisa noticed Marc was staring at her.

"Why are you looking at me like that?"

Taking a deep breath, he said, "Can I ask you something?"

"Sure."

"I can't understand why you're not married or at least dating someone."

"That's not a question."

"Okay then, why aren't you married or seeing someone?"

"Honestly, I never had any interest in getting married."

"Come on, every little girl dreams of growing up and being a bride."

"Not this one."

"You never once pretended?" Marc asked.

"Nope, it wasn't my thing. While other little girls played house, I was – I can't believe I'm telling you this," she laughed.

"What?"

"I pretended to be a lawyer."

They both laughed, and then Marc said "You pretended to be a lawyer? What were some of your cases?"

"I was a great lawyer and my cases were very serious."

"Unh huh, what were they?"

"The murder of my cabbage patch doll. That was a tough one, but I finally proved that her adopted brother killed her."

By this time, Marc was laughing even harder.

"Since you think that's funny, my next case of who burned down Barbie and Ken's house was even harder to prove."

"Who burned the house down, G.I. Joe?" he said, jokingly.

"Exactly, you must have read the article they did on the case."

"You are crazy," he said, still laughing.

"I have my moments."

By nine-thirty they had finished their third glass of wine and decided to call it a night.

"I didn't expect to keep you out this long," Marc said, as they were walking to the parking lot.

"I didn't mind at all, I had fun."

When they made it to Lisa's car, Lisa realized that this felt like the end of a date. A great date.

"Sooo, I'll see you tomorrow," Marc said, as he opened her car door after she hit the unlock button on her key chain.

"Alright."

Lisa found herself waiting to see if he was going to kiss her. He didn't. Lisa got in and rolled her window after starting her car.

"Drive safely," Marc told her.

"You, too. I'm gonna wait 'til you get in your car."

Marc leaned down and said, "Isn't it supposed to be the other way around, the man is supposed to protect the woman?"

"I guess, but it's been a while since a man had to protect me."

"And that is such a shame, Lisa Jenson."

With that said and one of his sexy smiles, he walked to his car. Starting up his car, they pulled out of the parking garage, turning in different directions. During her dinner of a chicken salad and bottled water, to her soak in the tub, she did nothing but replay the past couple of hours over and over in her mind. She found herself wondering why he didn't kiss her. Maybe she was over thinking it; maybe Marc was just being nice.

"I've been listening to Carol too much. He's just a friend, that's it," Lisa said, as she got into bed. But again, her last thoughts before she fell asleep were of Marc.

CHAPTER SIX

The next morning, Lisa made it to work by nine. And went straight to work. Carol came into her office by nine-thirty.

"So, how was it?"

"How was what?" Lisa asked, pretending not to know what she was talking about.

"Don't play with me. You know what I'm talking about."

"No, I don't."

"How did it go with you and Mr. Cavell last night?"

"We had drinks; we talked and parted in the parking lot. That's it."

"He didn't try to kiss you?"

"No. I told you we are just co-workers and friends."

"What do I have to do to get you two together?"

"Absolutely nothing. Now, can we get the work day started?"

"What am I gonna do with you?"

"I don't know."

The rest of the day went by quicker than Lisa expected. At four, she gave Marc a call.

"This is Marc," he said, when he answered.

"Hey, where are we working?"

"How about my office? I already ordered the food. How do you feel about Chili's? I remember you saying how crazy you were about their eggrolls."

"I hope you ordered enough."

"I ordered all they could make."

"I'm on my way," Lisa said, then hung up. She couldn't help but think how he could remember something she said months ago.

Carol walked in and said, "Lisa, I'm about to leave. Do you need me to do anything else?"

"Can you help me carry this stuff down to Marc's office? We're working late tonight."

"Sure."

Lisa got all of the information she had on the Keene account and her purse and briefcase. She closed down her computer and locked up her office.

"Hi, Barbara," Lisa said, walking toward Marc's office.

"Ms. Jenson," Barbara said without hiding her sneer. Lisa knew Barbara didn't like her, she just didn't know why.

"Hey, Barb. You got a hot date this weekend?" Carol asked.

"No," Barbara sneered again.

"Well, we can't all be lucky, can we?" Carol smiled.

Lisa, trying not to laugh, said, "Carol, follow me."

"Hey, you could have told me you needed some help," Marc said.

"That's okay. Carol was on her way out, so she helped me."

"So, if that's all you guys need. I'm outta here."

"Have a good weekend Carol," Marc said.

"You too, Mr. Cavell. Lisa, I'll call you tomorrow."

"Okay, bye."

After Carol walked out, Marc said, "The food should be here any minute. You want to eat first or work first?"

"Since the food hasn't made it yet, we might as well set everything up while we wait."

While they waited on their delivery, they got to work.

The next few hours were filled with working, eating, and laughing at each other's horrible jokes.

When they final finished putting their presentation together and all the food was gone, Marc said, "Lisa, can I ask you something?"

"Okay."

"Uh, the other day when I stormed into your office, I didn't cause a problem did I?"

"What do you mean?" Lisa asked, while still looking through paperwork.

"With your friend. I couldn't help but notice there was a little tension. And I could also tell he didn't appreciate my interruption."

"Everything was fine. He was just someone who didn't realize that their time was up."

"Oh. I just wanted to make sure I didn't cause any problems."

Lisa was leaning against his desk smiling, when she said, "You couldn't cause any more problems than there already are. Really, you didn't do anything wrong."

"Good," he said.

"Oh, can you hand me that binder next to you. I want to make sure everything is in order for Monday."

When he got up to hand her the binder, his office phone rang.

"Marc Cavell...Yes, Mr. Keene...Nice to finally get to talk to you, too...Matter of fact, we are preparing for that as we speak...Really...? Unh huh...Yes, sir. That will be fine...We will be there...And thank you, sir...Goodbye."

"What happened?" Lisa asked when he hung up.

"Mr. Keene had to cancel our meeting for Monday."

"Great, just what we need."

"But, there is a silver lining. He has invited us to his house for a party on the eighteenth."

"Both of us?"

"Yep. His words, 'invite that sweet thang I had the meeting with'."

"Sweet thang? I told you."

"I guess you're right."

Leaning against Marc's desk, Lisa said, "So, we did all this work for nothing?"

"No. By doing all this work we can go over it before the party and be ready for the meeting."

"I guess so," she said rubbing her neck.

Marc leaned against the desk next to her and said, "Look at it this way, I can protect you from him. I can pretend to be manly." Then he laughed.

Lisa laughed, too. Looking at him, she was about to say something, but before she could, he kissed her. Lisa had to admit she had never been kissed like that before. She found herself kissing him back.

When she finally got control of herself, she quickly pulled away.

"I – I'm sorry, Lisa," Marc stammered.

Lisa couldn't say anything; she just grabbed her purse and jacket and left his office.

"Lisa, wait."

But she didn't.

"Damn," he said, to himself. "Why did I have to do that?"

On the way down to the garage in the elevator, Lisa couldn't believe what she did. How could she have been so stupid?

"Why did I do that?" she asked herself.

Getting into her car, she berated herself the whole way home. When she got home, there were three messages on her answering machine. The first message was from her brother, the next two from Marc. He had already left three messages on her cell voicemail. Lisa just couldn't bring herself to talk to him right now. The rest of the night was spent thinking of what happened and how she felt about it. To be honest, she really liked the kiss. She liked how she felt in his arms. It felt natural.

"Oh, God, what am I going to do?" she said to her empty bedroom. "How am I going to face him?"

Lisa went to bed that night with one thing on her mind…Marc Cavell. The next morning Lisa was up by ten. Her Saturday's were mostly spent doing the things she couldn't during the week. She cleaned up the house from top to bottom, dropped off her dry cleaning, grocery shopping, and anything else she needed to do. Lisa was on her way to Barnes & Noble when her cell phone rang. Looking at the caller I.D., she saw that it was her brother's cell phone number.

"Hey, what's up?" Lisa answered.

"Why didn't you call me back last night?"

"I was tired. When I got home I went straight to bed. What did you want?"

"How do you know I want something?

Lisa didn't even answer him she just started laughing as she parked in the Barnes & Noble parking lot.

"Okay, okay, I do want something. I need five hundred dollars."

"For what?!"

"I need it for school. You know my trip to Canada starts a month after school is back in and I need to get the rest of my stuff."

"Have you paid for the trip?" Lisa asked as she walked through the door a man was holding for her.

"How you doing, gorgeous?" he said, as Lisa walked pass him.

"Hello," Lisa said and smiled.

"Who are you talking to?" Anthony asked.

"This man that was holding the door for me."

"So can you do it?"

"Once again, have you paid for the trip?"

"Yeah, mama paid for the trip when we were first told about it."

"When do you need it?"

"As soon as you can give it to me."

"Alright, I'll bring it to you after I get through shopping."

"Today?"

"Yes."

"Thanks, Lis."

"No problem."

Lisa pushed the button on her Bluetooth to hang up. She went down each aisle to see if anything jumped out at her that she already didn't have. An hour later she left the book store with two of James Patterson's new books and two books by Philippa Gregory.

After leaving Barnes & Noble, Lisa headed to Oak Court Mall. She was looking for something that would be perfect for the Keene party. After going to almost every store that sold dresses, she was about to give up until she saw a small store that had a *Grand Opening* sign over its door. Lisa thought, *why not?*

"May I help you?" the sales clerk asked, when Lisa walked in.

"I'm just looking."

"Well, we have a lot of selections, some I even made myself. What type of occasion is this for? Is it formal or casual?"

"It's a formal business dinner."

"Okay, let's see what we have."

The sales clerk looped her arm through Lisa's and led her to the back of the store.

"Where should we start? Do you have a preferred style...color?"

"I love the color maroon."

"Let's start there."

As she went through the multiple dresses, the sales clerk said her name was Elizabeth and that this was her shop. Elizabeth picked out three beautiful dresses. A maroon velvet halter dress, a light blue layered silk chiffon dress, and a slinky black floor length dress with the back out, that snapped around the neck.

"Try these on and see which one suits you best."

Each dress fit Lisa perfectly. She told Elizabeth that she would purchase all of them.

"You have truly made my day. I hope the young man who will see you in these, will be knocked off his feet."

Lisa smiled, thanked her, and left.

After leaving the mall, Lisa made a stop at the bank before it closed and then headed to her mother's house.

"Where is everybody?" Lisa called out when she walked in.

"I'm in the kitchen," her mother said.

"Hey. What are you doing?"

"Tryin' to figure out what I want to cook for dinner."

"Why you cookin' so early?"

"Marilyn is comin' to get me at five. We're going to the casino."

"Again?" Lisa said, as she poured herself a glass of orange juice.

"Yes, again. I'm cooking now, so Anthony won't burn down my house trying to cook for himself."

Laughing, Lisa said, "Where is he, anyway? I see the car is gone."

"He said he was going over that girl's house. What's her name?"

"Keisha, mama. You know you know that girl's name."

"Anyway. He said he would be back later, but by then I'll be gone."

"Well, I'll put his money on his dresser."

"How much you giving him?"

"He asked for five."

"That's not what I asked you."

"Eight."

Her mother laughed and shook her head.

"What?" Lisa asked.

"You are spoiling that boy."

"You started it."

"How?"

"You spoiled me, that's why I am like I am."

"Really? Well, just don't go overboard. I don't want him to think that everything comes to him so easy."

"I know, mama. Don't worry, Anthony's a good kid. But I promise to take it down a notch."

"Just remember what I said."

"Okay," Lisa said, on her way upstairs.

When she came back down, her mother was already frying chicken, and in the middle of making macaroni and cheese.

"Are you staying for dinner?"

"No. I am spending a quiet evening at home."

"That's all you ever do. Why don't you come to the casino with me and Marilyn?"

"You know I don't like to gamble. I'll most likely end up watching you guys play while I drink."

"You sure?"

"Yes, I'm sure."

"If you wait a few minutes, you can take a plate home with you."

"Okay."

Lisa spent the next couple of hours at her mother's. By the time she left, she didn't have to eat for the next three days. She ate two pieces of chicken, macaroni and cheese, and a slice of her mother's homemade apple pie. Well two pieces.

She waited until Marilyn came before she left. She made it home fifteen minutes later. Walking in the house with her bags and mail, Lisa checked her messages.

First message: *"Lisa, I have been trying to get in touch with you. Please call me. I just want to apologize for what happened. Call me."*

Lisa couldn't bring herself to talk to him just yet. She needed time to figure out what to do. The last four messages were hang ups, which she didn't usually get. The first thing that popped into her mind was James, but she discarded that thought as quickly as it came.

"There is no way he would have found my phone number."

The rest of the weekend was spent reading, working out, and church. Just like every weekend for the last six years. Sitting in bed on Sunday night, Lisa got to thinking about how lonely she felt sometimes. She always prided herself on how she functioned without someone in her life. She always thought she was complete without someone to come home to.

As she turned the knob on the wall near her bed, she said her prays. She also put in a little prayer for someone to share her life with. After all, her mother said, 'a little prayer won't hurt'.

CHAPTER SEVEN

Lisa made it to work Monday morning at nine on the dot. As she unlocked her office door, she remembered Carol always came in a little late on Mondays. Turning on her computer, she got herself in work mode after her morning prayer.

Starting with checking her emails and voicemails Lisa went through the files she would need to work on for the day. Through the clouds of thoughts, she heard, *"Lisa, I had to go to New York on a business trip. But, don't worry I'll be back in enough time for Saturday. I'll call later, when I think you have made it in...Bye."*

Lis didn't know if she should breathe a sigh of relief or be a little sad that he may not have thought much about the kiss.

"No, no, no, I am not going there."

"Why are you in here talking to yourself?" Carol asked, when she walked in.

"You know that's the way I think. Good morning."

"Good morning. How was your weekend?"

"It was pretty good. Got some reading done."

"No date?"

"No."

"Lisa –"

"Carol, please let's not go down this road. Not today."

"Okay, I'll give you a day off because it's Monday. But tomorrow is another day."

Laughing, Lisa said, "Thank you."

Carol left out of the office to get herself ready for the day. Fifteen minutes later, she buzzed Lisa, "Lisa, you have a call on line one."

"Already?"

"Yep. It's Mr. Cavell."

Lisa hesitated for minute, and then picked up her phone. "Marc, how's it going in New York?"

"Not too bad. A client I have thought the world would end if I didn't come straighten things out. Plus, it was a good excuse to see my parents."

"How are they?"

"They're good...Look, Lisa, I wasn't going to mention it, but I can't help it. I want to apologize for what happened Friday. I don't know what came over me. I was out of line and I promise that will never happen again."

"Marc, you have nothing to apologize for. I think that was both of us in your office. So, please don't feel bad about it. Matter of fact, don't even think about it."

"Done. So, I will be back in town on Friday. And I will be on time Saturday. I'll call if anything changes."

"Alright. Enjoy your vacation."

"I wish," he laughed.

"Bye."

"Bye."

Lisa knew she told him not to give the kiss another thought but to be honest that is all she could think of.

"Lisa," Carol said, from the doorway.

"Yeah?" Lisa said. Then she noticed how Carol looked. "Carol, what's wrong?"

"*He's* here. What do you want me to do?"

"Tell him to leave or security will escort him out."

Lisa listened as Carol relayed her message; however she did not here James's reply.

Then Carol popped back into the office, "Lisa, he said he is not going to leave until he talks to you. Should I call security?"

Lisa thought how that situation would play out and then said, "Show him in."

"Are you sure?"

"Yes."

Lisa got up from her desk and walked toward the door, where she met James just as he came in.

"Good morning."

"It was. What can I do for you, James?"

"A lot. But for now just agree to have drinks with me later."

"Look, I'm going to tell you one last time, I don't want to see you again. If you come to my office again you will be arrested. Is that clear enough for you?"

"You don't have to do all that. I just want to see you. Can't you give me a chance to show you I've changed?"

Lisa stood in the middle of her office and just looked at him. "What would your wife think of that?"

The shock on his face was priceless. "Oh, I see you thought I didn't know. See, you were right about one thing, people do talk. And you know what they told me? They told me that you were married. That you have been married for the last three years. I don't know her name and I don't want to know, but I can find out. And don't think I won't tell her what you have been doing and what you are capable of doing. I advise you to stay away from me. I don't want, nor will I ever want, to get to know the new you. Stay…away…from…me."

"I love you, not her. The marriage was a mistake."

Lisa couldn't take it anymore. She walked over to the phone.

"Lisa, you really don't want to do that."

"And what you gon' do?" Lisa said, as she dialed the extension for security. Before she knew it, James snatched the phone from her hand and slammed it down.

Lisa didn't flinch, she said, "Is that supposed to scare me? I know you can do better than that. Hell, I've seen you do better. I am not afraid of you anymore. If you don't believe me, try me," Lisa said, moving closer.

James stood there trying to control his breathing, but was doing a poor job of it.

"I'll leave, but don't think this is the end. We will be together."

"Not in this life."

Pausing at the door, James looked at Lisa and said, "If that's the way you want it."

"Don't threaten me, just leave."

With one last look, he was gone. Lisa finally took a deep breath in order to calm her heart rate and nerves.

A second later, Carol was in the office, "Are you alright?"

Lisa just looked at Carol. She couldn't hear her words even though she saw her lips moving.

"Lisa, just sit down right here, let me get you some water." Carol gave her a glass of water and went to the phone. "Yes, may I speak with detective Harvey? Nic, this is Carol. Can you come to the office? I'll explain when you get here. Lisa, Nic is on her way, okay?"

Lisa didn't answer; she just sat there in a daze. Carol sat next to her holding her hand and talking to her until Nic got there.

"What happened?" Nic said, as she rushed in.

"That James character came back. She stood up to him and was about to call security but he snatched the phone from her. I saw him when he slammed the phone down. But she stood up to him, Nic. It's when he left I heard her say, 'not in this life,' then he said, 'if that's the way you want it'. After he left, she just went into shock. Should we take her to the doctor?"

Nic pulled up a chair in front of where Lisa and Carol were sitting on the couch. "Lisa, look at me. Can you hear me? Lisa, come on, look at me."

Lisa finally looked at Nic and then said in a whisper, "Nic? What are you doing here?"

"I called her. And now we are taking you to the hospital," Carol said.

"No, no. I'm fine. No hospitals." Lisa shook her head, and then took a sip of water.

"Are you sure?"

"Yeah, I'm sure. He didn't hurt me or anything. I guess I had to reboot. I'm okay."

"Good. Now you can tell me what happened. Carol told me what she heard, but –"

"No, I told you what I saw. I was standing right there in the doorway and saw everything."

"She was standing there, I saw her," Lisa said still drinking the water.

"Do you want to get a restraining order?"

"No, there's no need for that. He can't possibly be stupid enough to try something."

"Never underestimate him, Lisa. He is stupid and crazy. He promised you a long time ago that he would never give up on you. You need to get a restraining order."

"Look, I really don't want to talk about this right now. I've got a lot of work to do."

"Oh, no you don't. You are going home and not coming back until Wednesday. You have more than enough vacation time, so you, my dear, are going home," Carol told her.

"No, I have a lot of work to do."

"You can do it at home or when you come back. But either way you are going home."

"She's right. You are going home," Nic told Lisa.

Sighing, Lisa finally said, "Okay, I'll go home."

Lisa spent the next hour packing up what she would take home and making a to-do list for Carol.

"Call me if anything happens. I can come back," Lisa said, as she walked out of her office with Nic and Carol in tow.

"Nothing will happen. Now, go home and get you some rest. I'll come over after I leave work tonight."

"Okay, I'll see you later," Lisa said, leaving with Nic.

When Lisa and Nic made it down to the parking garage, Lisa said, "You're gonna follow me home, aren't you?"

"Yes, but I'm not going to stay. I have to get back to the precinct."

"Look, go ahead and get back to work. I can make it home. I'll even promise to call when I walk in the door."

After taking a long pause, Nic said, "Okay. You just make sure you call me when you get in."

"Will do."

They each got in their cars and left the parking garage.

When Lisa got home, she dropped all her work on the desk in her office and then headed to her bedroom. She went into her bathroom and ran a bath. Then along with her book, she eased into the warm water. For the next hour and a half she read and soaked. She even turned on the Jacuzzi jets to really relax.

After her bath, she ate an apple did some more reading. She hadn't realized she'd fallen asleep until her doorbell rang. Looking at the clock on her nightstand, Lisa knew it had to be Carol. It was just after six.

Putting on her fluffy house shoes, Lis headed downstairs.

Opening the door, she said, "I was asleep."

"Sorry, but I promised to come by after work. Have you eaten?" Carol said as she walked in.

"No, I was asleep," Lisa said closing the door.

"Good. I went to the Boiling Point and went crazy. I think I bought enough seafood to last us the next couple of days."

"Ooo, let me get some plates."

Carol unpacked the bags on the dining room table, while Lisa got the plates and silverware.

"What would you like to drink? I have juice, Coke, and Sprite."

"I'll take the Sprite."

"Sprite all around," Lisa said getting the glasses out of the cabinet and the Sprite out of the refrigerator.

"Oh, before I forget, Mr. Cavell called after you left. He said he would call you after his last meeting tonight."

"Okay."

"So what happened between you two?"

Lisa almost choked on a shrimp.

"Wh – What do you mean, what happened? Nothing happened."

"Girl, please. He was so worried when I told him you didn't feel well and had to go home, I thought he would drop the phone and get on the next plane home. So again I ask, what happened between you two?"

"We kissed," Lisa mumbled.

"What?!" Carol said, loudly.

"We kissed."

"Okay, okay. I want to hear what happened and don't leave out a thing."

"It happened Friday while we were working on the Keene presentation. Then Keene called and cancelled the meeting, but invited us to the party he is having at his home. We were leaning on his desk, talking about what we could do to nail the account. He said something about protecting me from Keene, and I laughed. But, when I looked at him he was staring at me. And then he kissed me. Carol, I have to admit that I got caught up and kissed him back. I have never been kissed like that before. It felt…"

"Right?"

"Yeah."

"That's how I felt about Charles. I still remember our first kiss. I knew right then he was the man for me. So, now what happens between you two?"

"Nothing. Come on, we work together. I could never do that. What if it didn't work out? We would still have to see one another every day. Marc and I work to closely together to take that chance."

"What if it worked out and you two are meant to be?"

"Carol, please tell me you don't believe in that meant to be crap?"

"Look who you talking to. I truly believe that Charles and I are meant to be. We have been married for fifteen years. I know he is the one."

"Does he tell you that?"

"Every day."

"You guys are perfect. I hate you for that," Lisa laughed.

"Don't hate. Besides, you could have the same thing if you would just give him a chance."

"I can't do that, Carol. There's too much going on right now. You saw what happened today. I can't start something with anyone until this is over."

"What if you don't have a choice?"

"What do you mean?"

"Lisa, you are one of the smartest women I have ever met. But when it comes down to love, darling, you are clueless. Love chooses you, not the other way around. And right now it's knocking at your door."

Lisa started laughing.

"What's so funny?"

"My mother told me the same thing last week."

"Smart woman. Oh, I know that ring," Carol reached into her purse to find her ringing cell phone. "Hello, sweetheart...Yeah, we're just sitting here eating. Are you home yet...? Okay...About an hour...Sure, hold on." Handing her phone to Lisa, she said, "He wants to talk to you."

"Hey, Charles...Yeah, I'm fine...Really, I'm okay...I know...Okay...Thank you...Bye. He said he will see you when he get home. Okay, you two are perfect for one another."

"Yes, we are. Look, I know you're having a little problem now, but what's to say that something good won't come out of it."

"I hear you, but I just can't do it."

"Okay. Don't say I didn't try. Well, I am going to get out of here."

"You don't want to take some of this food home."

"No, I bought this for you."

"Well, let me replace what you spent."

"Girl, please. It was just food. I'll call you tomorrow. Remember, I don't want to see you in the morning."

"Yeah, yeah, I know. Drive safely."

"I will. Bye."

"Bye."

After watching Carol drive away, Lisa locked up the house, cleaned the kitchen, and then headed upstairs. When she walked into her room, the phone rang. Looking at the phone display, she saw a long distance number.

"Hello."

"Hey, how are you feeling?" Marc asked.

"Hey, I'm fine."

"When I called the office earlier, Carol told me you had left for the day."

"Yeah, she told me you called. How's your trip going?"

"Great so far. I'm getting to spend a lot of time with my parents since my client has finally calmed down."

"That's great."

"Yeah, so I'll be back Friday morning. I'll pick you up Saturday night at six-thirty."

"You don't have to pick me up."

"Yes, I do."

"Okay. I'll be ready."

"Alright. I'm not going to keep you any longer. Get plenty of rest and I'll call you tomorrow."

"Okay."

"Good night, Lisa."

"Good night, Marc."

When Lisa hung up, she couldn't help but smile.

"If what Carol said was right, I'm in trouble," Lisa said to herself.

She climbed into bed and turned on her radio and let the soft music lullaby her to sleep.

By Tuesday afternoon, Lisa was about to lose her mind. She got a chance to catch up on her work, finished James Patterson's new book, and had cleaned her house until there was nothing else to clean. She worked out, showered, and decided to get out of the house. Letting the top down on the car as she backed out of the driveway, Lisa headed downtown. Even though she wasn't going in, she could at least catch Carol going out for lunch.

As she pulled up in front of the building, she saw Carol walking out. Honking her horn, she pulled up next to her and said, "Shoe shopping anyone?"

"You must have been reading my mind," Carol said, getting into the car.

"I was hoping to catch you. Good thing you always go to lunch at the same time every day."

"So, where are we headed?"

"This new shoe store over on Main Street. It looks like it could be promising."

"I hope so. Because I need some shoes for this new dress I bought to wear Friday night. Do you know where we're going?"

"I have no clue. Nic didn't tell me a thing. What are you wearing?"

"A read halter dress."

"Is Charles going to let you out of the house in that?"

"He bought it. What are you wearing?"

"I found this light blue, layered silk chiffon dress. I got it at this new store in Oak Court. Now, I need to find the perfect shoes."

After parking, they walked a couple of blocks to the shoe store.

"Hello, ladies. Can I help you?"

"No, we're just looking," Carol said.

"Well, let me know if you need any help."

Carol and Lisa picked out the shoes they wanted to try on and commenced to running the staff back and forth to the back room. One associate was a little too helpful toward Lisa, but she just smiled at his advances. While laughing at Carol, Lisa thought at one point she spotted James looking through the front window at them. But when she looked again he was gone. She just brushed it off as a hallucination and continued to talk to Carol.

"So, what do you think?" Carol asked, as she modeled a pair of white stiletto sandals.

"I think they're cute. But, I thought you were looking for something to wear for Friday."

"I am, but I think I'm getting these too."

"Okay, my turn. What about these? I think I can wear these Saturday night," Lisa had tried on black sandals that snapped around the ankle. The shoes also had colorful beading that was on the strap across the toes and the strap that went around the ankle.

"Ooo, I like those."

"I have the perfect dress for these."

"Make sure to take a picture so I can see how you look."

Lisa only smiled at the sales associate and picked out a light blue pair of shoes that matched her dress perfectly.

After paying for their shoes, Lisa said, "You got time enough for lunch?"

"You're the boss. Do I have time?"

"Huey's it is."

They spent the next hour talking and eating. Lisa paid for lunch, dropped Carol back off at the office and headed home. When she got there, she put her shoes up and went through her mail. When she finished with the mail, she decided to watch some TV. After decided nothing was on, she picked out a DVD to watch. Halfway through the move, she had fallen asleep.

Surprisingly, Lisa didn't wake up until the next morning when her alarm went off. She couldn't believe she had slept a day away. Getting up and getting ready for work, Lisa was out the door by eight-fifteen.

"Good morning, Carol," she said, walking into the outer office.

"Good morning. Don't we look refreshed?"

"Yes we do. What's on the calendar for today?"

"You have two meetings set up for today. I couldn't push them back any further. Sorry."

"No problem. I am so ready to get back to work. I've been keeping up with my email, but I didn't get a chance to check it yesterday."

"Do you want me to go through it?"

"No, I can do it. But can you call Danny for me and see if he can take me Saturday morning?"

"Will do. Is there anything else I can do?"

"No that's it for right now. What time is my first meeting?"

"Ten. Oh, I haven't gotten a chance to check your voicemail yet either."

"I'll check them."

"You are in a working mood today."

"Yes I am."

When Carol went back to her desk Lisa checked her voicemail. Most of the calls had to do with business until she reached Marc's voicemail.

"Hey, Lisa. I thought you would be at your desk by now. I was sitting here thinking about you and I wanted to see if you were feeling better. I'll see you this weekend."

Lisa played the message twice. Truth be told, she had been thinking about him, too. She had found herself thinking more and more about him since she talked to Carol about the kiss. Bringing her back to the present was a voice she never wanted to hear again.

"Lisa, I know you never want to hear from me again. But, I had to call to tell you how sorry I was for what happened in your office the other day. That was not me. Not the new me. You have to for –"

"I don't have to do shit," Lisa said as she deleted the message.

After checking her voicemail, she checked her email. Within one day she had over seventy emails from clients. Pressing the intercom, she said, "Carol, can you come here for a minute?"

"Be right there." Walking in, Carol said, "What do you need?"

"My email account –"

"Already on it. Also your two o'clock meeting had to cancel. She said she didn't know when she could set up another."

"Okay. Thank you."

"No problem."

After her meeting at ten, Lisa went through the files Carol had set aside for her that pertained to each of the emails in her account. Carol came in at noon and said she was going to lunch.

"You want me to bring anything back?"

"No, I'm fine."

"I'll be back soon."

"I'll be here."

Five minutes later, her office phone rang. "This is Lisa Jenson."

"Lisa, please don't –"

Lisa hung up the phone.

Within a minute, the phone rang again. This time Lisa let it go to voicemail. After a couple of minutes she checked the voicemail, but there was no message. Now all she could do was pray that he would not come to her office. An hour later, Carol was back and they finished the work day out without another call or a visit from James.

Lisa made it home by six-thirty and quickly began cooking dinner. She had thirty minutes to cook dinner before her mother made it. Every week Lisa and her mother ate dinner together. Sometimes Anthony even came with her. But tonight when Lisa opened the door it was just her mother.

"So, how long did you have?" her mother asked when she walked in.

"Thirty minutes."

"What are we eating?"

"We are having backed fish, scallop potatoes, and English peas. What would you like to drink?"

"You know what I always drink."

"Red wine it is."

"How was your day?"

"Incredibly busy."

Lisa told her mother about her day. Everything except missing a couple of days of work and the reason why. For the rest of the night, Lisa and her mother talked about everything. By ten, they finished eating and Lisa's mother was leaving.

"Call me when you get home," Lisa told her mother, as she walked her out to the car.

"Will do. Make sure to lock up."

"I will," Lisa said, as she gave her mother a hug.

Walking back to the door as her mother drove away, Lisa saw a car parked across the street from her house. When she took a good look she could see someone sitting in it. After a minute, the car started and drove away. Lisa went in the house and locked up. She didn't know why that spooked her so much, but it did. From now on she had to make sure she watched her surroundings.

CHAPTER EIGHT

By Friday, Lisa was ready for the weekend.

"Come on, girl, we have to get home so we can get ready," Carol said.

"I'm ready. Let's go," Lisa said locking her door.

When they got down to the parking garage, they split up. When Lisa got in her car, she pushed speed dial number five.

Carol answered, "Yeess."

"I will be at you house at eight. Then we head over to Nic's."

"I will be ready."

"Alright, bye."

"Bye."

When Lisa made it home, she checked her mail and messages. Then she went straight upstairs to her bedroom. While she was standing in her closet, her phone rang.

"Hello."

"What's up?" Pat said.

"Nothing, getting my clothes together. Have you already picked something out?"

"Yeah, I'm wearing an off the shoulder black blouse with black slacks and some new Donna Karen four inch heels I ordered a week ago."

"Alright, Morticia," Lisa said.

"What are you wearing?"

"I'm wearing this light blue chiffon dress with these crystal studded three and a half inch heels I bought yesterday."

"And how are you wearing your hair?"

"I think I'm going to wear it down. What about you?"

"Up. I went to Danny today."

"I go in the morning. I have to look sharp for this business dinner thing tomorrow Marc and I have to attend."

"You got a date?!" yelled Pat.

"No! Did you not hear me say business dinner? So that means it is work related."

"I heard dinner and a man's name. I'm calling it a date."

"Whatever."

"Anyway, do you know what Carol is wearing?"

"A red dress. What about Nic?"

"I don't know. But I'm sure it will be no bigger than a napkin," Pat said, laughing.

Laughing, Lisa said, "How are you getting to Nic's house?"

"Lewis is dropping me off on his way to Carol's and Charles' house for their weekly poker game."

"Okay, well I will see him then. I'm picking her up on my way to Nic's house."

"Okay. I'll see you tonight."

"Alright, bye."

After Lisa hung up the phone, she went into her bathroom to run her bath water. After an hour and a half soak, she plugged up her curling irons. As they heated up, she put on her lotion and applied her make-up. When she figured her hair and makeup couldn't get any better, she went to get dressed. She didn't want to go too far out with the jewelry, so she decided to wear tear drop diamond earrings and a matching diamond bracelet.

By seven-thirty Lisa was ready for the night out. She had to admit, as she looked her reflection in the mirror, she looked damned good in that dress. "Here we go," she said to herself as she walked out of her bedroom.

Starting her car, she put in her new CD she bought yesterday. K Jon's voice filled her car.

In spite of how much traffic was out tonight, and the constant honking of other cars filled with men, Lisa still made it to Carol's house by eight-fifteen.

"Hello," Carol said, when she answered the phone.

"I'm pulling into the driveway."

"Come on in. Charles is opening the door."

Lisa parked her car in the driveway behind three other cars. As Lisa approached the door, it was opened by Carol's husband Charles.

"Hey, Charlie!" Lisa said, as she hugged him.

"There's my girl," Charles said in his robust voice as he hugged her back.

"Your wife said she would be ready."

"Now, of all people, you should know that beauty is a time consuming job," Charles said, as he lead Lisa toward the den.

"Not for me. I wake up looking like this."

Laughing, he said, "Come and meet the guys."

When they walked into the room it went completely silent.

"Guys, this beautiful woman is Lisa Jenson. She's Carol's boss," Charles said.

"Actually, she's my boss," Lisa joked.

"It's nice to meet you," Lewis said, as he tried to shake Lisa's hand.

"Stop playing and give me a hug," Lisa said.

"What's up, Le-Le?" Lewis said, as he hugged Lisa.

"Lisa, this Noah, Michael, and Phillip," Charles said.

Lisa shook hands with each man. When she got to Noah, she noted that he held her hand a little longer than the others. Smiling, Lisa noticed that Noah was a very handsome man. He was bald, dark skinned, and nicely built. Lisa had to admit he was quite good looking.

"Carol was right. You are beautiful."

"Well, thank you," Lisa smiled.

"Please tell me you're not married."

"I'm not married."

"Now, please tell me you will go out with me."

"That I cannot tell you," Lisa said smiling and pulling her hand away.

"You just broke my heart," Noah said, putting his hands over his heart.

"I'm sure it will mend."

"What can I say to get you to marry me?"

"Okay, Noah, give the girl some breathing room," Carol said, walking into the den.

"What's wrong with trying to get to know this beautiful creature?"

"Hey Lisa," Carol said, when she got close enough to hug her.

"Don't you look hot?" Lisa said.

"Yes, I do," Carol said, turning around so they could see her whole outfit. "Are you ready?"

"Yes, ma'am. Okay, honey, we are leaving. You boys be good."

"I'll see you ladies out," Charles said.

"It was nice meeting you all. Lewis, I'll see you later," Lisa said, as they were about to leave.

"Bye, sweetie," Lewis said.

"Lisa, I really look forward to seeing you again. I hope we can get together sometime," Noah said, gazing at her.

"Good night," Lisa said and left.

As she was walking out of the room, Lisa heard Noah say, "Man, Lewis, where do you know her from and does Patricia know you know someone who looks like that?"

"Yes, Pat does. Lisa and Pat have been best friends since they were in junior high."

"Man, I hope to meet her again…"

Lisa made it out to the car just as Carol and Charles were kissing goodbye.

"Okay, okay, that's enough. We have to go."

"Alright, you ladies have fun tonight," Charles said, as he closed Carol's door after she got in.

"We will," Lisa and Carol said as they were backing out of the yard.

"So, have you found out where we are going?" Carol asked.

"Nope, you?"

"Nope. I didn't get to talk to her earlier."

"We'll see when we get there," Lisa said.

They made it to Nic's house in no time. Even though she lived a good thirty minute drive away, Lisa made it there in fifteen.

"Girl, I am surprised you don't get a ticket every time you start your car," Carol laughed.

"They have to catch me first."

Ringing the doorbell, Lisa asked, "What do you think of my dress?"

"I think it's hot. You know if it was my color I would be borrowing it. You should wear more of this color. It brings out your skin tone. You look good, girl," Carol said.

"Hello, ladies," Pat said, when she opened the door.

"Heeyy," Lisa and Carol said as they hugged her and walked in.

"Y'all look good, come on in here so I can really look at you. Ooo, Carol, got her back out. And Ms. Lisa got out everything else," Pat laughed.

"Anyway," Lisa said, laughing.

Lisa and Carol sat on the couch as Pat poured them a glass of Hypnotiq.

"So, where is Ms. Thang?" Lisa asked Pat.

"You know it takes a minute for her to slip into her napkin."

"It did not take me that long," Nic said, as she came downstairs.

Nic was wearing a black dress that gave a new meaning to the phrase: a little black dress. The dress tied around the neck, with her back completely out, and it was so short that it barely covered her thighs. She was also wearing a pair of black stiletto sandals and her only jewelry was a pair of diamond earrings.

"Alright, beautiful ladies, it is time to show the world what real beauty looks like," Nic said.

They all climbed into Nic's white Escalade and headed out to paint the town red.

"Where are we going?" Pat asked.

"We are going to the Onyx. It's a new club that a friend of mine just opened," Nic said.

"Which friend?" Lisa asked.

"Christian."

"When did Christian open a club?"

"Actually, this will be his first night. He has been pulling out his hair trying to make everything perfect."

"Last time I saw Christian he didn't have any hair."

"You get my point. How long has it been since you've seen Christian?"

"Seven years. You two were dating then, weren't you?"

"Something like that. Now, we're cool. He was telling me about his opening and told me to make sure to be here on time."

The ride took about forty minutes from where Nic lived. Carol joked that Lisa would have made the ride in ten.

As they got out of the car, men in the parking lot were trying to get their attention. Too bad no one had the nerve to approach them.

Walking past the long line to the door, Nic asked the cashier to call Christian to the door. He was at the door in three seconds.

"Nic, it's about time you got here," he said.

"You know I have to make an entrance," Nic said as she hugged him.

"And that you did. As a matter of fact, you all did. Who are these beautiful women you came with?"

"This is Pat, Carol, and you remember Lisa."

"How you ladies doing tonight?"

He looked at Lisa, but she could tell he didn't recognize her.

"Picture me seventy pounds heavier and I was wearing my hair shorter at the time," Lisa said.

The flash of recognition shone in his eyes.

"You dated ol' boy who would – never mind, I remember you. Damn, you look good."

"Thanks."

"Real good," he said, ogling Lisa.

"Uh, Christian, are we going to stay out here all night?"

Finally getting himself together, he said, "Oh, yeah, come on in. I have the perfect table for you guys. Don't worry about anything, everything is on the house."

"You know good and well I was not going to pay," Nic laughed.

For the first couple of hours, the ladies drank Crystal that Christian sent over. They danced with just about every man in the place. Even Christian came over and asked Lisa for a dance a couple of times.

As they were all sitting around laughing and talking, Lisa noticed Carol's eyes grow ten times their normal size.

"What's wrong, Carol?" Lisa asked.

"Either I have had too much to drink or that man over there is Mr. Cavell."

"That is him," Pat said. "I'd know that good looking man anywhere."

"He's been looking over here for the last ten minutes," Carol said.

"Well, I guess they're tired of looking, because now they are on their way over here."

"Hello, ladies," Marc said.

"Hello," they all said in unison.

"At first I didn't know if it was you guys."

"Oh, it's us," Nic said.

"Ladies, these are my friends George, Jamal, and you two already know Steve," he said.

George was about six feet tall, medium built, and dark skinned. Jamal was drop dead gorgeous. He was about Marc's height and build. But he was light skinned with gray eyes. Lisa knew all the ladies were thinking the same thing: DAMN!!!

After everyone was introduced, the men joined them at the table. George sat between Nic and Pat, Jamal between Pat and Lisa, Marc between Lisa and Carol, and Steve between Carol and Nic.

"So, which ladies are married and which are single?" George asked.

"Married," Pat said.

"Single," said Nic.

"Married," said Carol.

"And Single," Lisa said.

"Not for long," Marc said, smiling at Lisa.

Lisa couldn't do anything but smile and blush.

"So, what can I do to get you to leave your husband?" Jamal asked Pat.

"Absolutely nothing."

"Do you think he would mind if we danced?"

"No."

Everyone paired off and went out on the floor, but Lisa decided to sit this one out.

"So, how was the rest of your week?" Marc asked.

"It was okay. I got a lot of work done. How was your trip?"

"Pretty good. I got to hang out with some friends."

"That's good."

"What are you ladies out celebrating tonight?"

"Nothing. We all take one day a month and we each pick out something to do. Tonight was Nic's night. How about you guys?"

"Tonight is Jamal's bachelor party."

"Oh, he's getting married. That's great."

"Yeah, we all just left this strip – uh, this other club," he laughed.

"Uh huh," Lisa laughed.

Christian came over to the table and said, "Everything alright, Lisa?"

"Everything is great. Nic and the rest are out on the floor somewhere."

"Maybe you and I can get back out there later."

"Okay."

"How about I get my dance now, then?" Marc said when Christian walked away.

"Sure."

Marc pulled Lisa's chair out for her as she got up. As they walked out on the floor, the D.J. started playing Jamie Foxx's song, 'Overdose'. Lisa had to admit that Marc could move.

"I see the surprise on your face. You thought a white boy couldn't dance. Actually, my mother taught me to dance," he said close to her ear.

"She taught you well."

They were dancing to the next song when Lisa noticed Nic, Pat, and Carol watching them out on the floor. The guys were still sitting with them, but their attention was on her and Marc.

The D.J. broke in over the song and said, "Men, grab that special woman and hold her close. This is the new one by Anthony Hamilton." The D.J. played 'The Point of it All'.

"One more?" Marc whispered close to Lisa's ear.

Lisa only nodded. He held Lisa even closer. She felt even safer and like she belonged.

"I wasn't going to bring this up, but at this moment I can't help it," Marc began. "I haven't been able to think of anything else since I kissed you. I'd somehow hoped you felt the same."

Lisa didn't say anything, she listened.

"I know I may have crossed the line, but I couldn't help myself. Please say something."

"I don't know what to say, Marc. I have to say the kiss threw me, but I've thought about it too."

For the rest of the song, they danced closely and didn't speak. When it was over, they walked back to the table hand in hand. To Lisa it wasn't a weird feeling.

For the rest of the night, they all laughed, talked, and drank. Lisa noticed earlier how Nic and George were getting along.

"Alright, ladies, it is time for us to leave," Pat said.

"Yeah, it is," Nic said.

"Let us walk you out," Marc said.

When they made it to Nic's truck, George opened Nic's car door and helped her in. The other guys helped Pat and Carol into the truck. Marc opened Lisa's door and waited for her to get in.

Instead she turned and said, "My turn."

"Wha –"

Before she could stop herself, she leaned in and kissed Marc. When they parted, Lisa said, "How's that for equal opportunity?"

"I'm all for equal opportunity. See you tomorrow?"

"Six-thirty. Good night."

Marc closed her door and watched them pull away.

"Man, I have never seen a group of fine women. There is usually at least one troll. But all of them are fine."

"Only one peaks my interest," Marc said as they walked back to the club.

"Man, I thought you were exaggerating about Lisa. She is finer than baby hair," George said.

"I told you how fine she was," Steve chimed in.

"It's something more than that," Marc said.

"I know you invading my territory. But I love a challenge," Steve said.

"Man, I have no worries," Marc laughed and patted Steve on the back.

The men celebrated Jamal's nuptials for the rest of the night.

Lisa and the girls made it back to Nic's house and they all kicked off their shoes and talked of the night's festivities.

"So, Lis, you going to tell us what that kiss was about?" Nic asked.

"I don't know. I just felt like I had too."

"That's not the first time they've kissed," Carol said.

"What?!" Nic and Pat said.

"It was last Friday. It was nice."

"That's it, *nice*?" asked Nic.

"Yes. Okay, okay, it was better than nice. It felt natural. Like something I was supposed to have always been doing, you know."

"Yeah," Carol said, looking dreamy eyed. "I get that way about Charles."

"Carol, you mean after, what, fifteen years, you and Charles are still honeymooning?"

"Yes," Lisa said and laughed. "I could tell you some stories."

"Anyhoo. The point is to keep it fresh. We all have those hellish days but when you get home it's supposed to be retreat. And Charles and I make sure that's what we have when we are together. That's what marriage is. Right, Pat."

"True. I mean, me and Lewis still have date nights. Even though we both like out alone time we make sure to spend as much time together as we can."

"Do you guys go to bed at the same time?" Nic asked.

"No," Pat said.

"Nope. Why should we?" Carol said.

"I was listening to this radio talk show the other day –"

"I already know what you talking about," Lisa said. "On the Michael Baisden Show."

"Right," Nic continued. "Some of the women felt that their men should go to bed at the same time as them."

"Girl, please. I didn't marry a child, I married a grown man. When he is ready to go to bed then he goes. Hell, sometimes you not ready to go to bed. I would act a fool if he tried to make me go to bed or do anything else I didn't want to do," Carol said, laughing.

"What about you, Pat?"

"I'm usually the last one to go to bed anyway. So, I agree with Carol."

"Lisa, what you thinking about?" Carol said.

Smiling, she said, "Marc. Tomorrow we have the Keene party to go to and I don't know what to expect."

"You mean from Keene or Marc?" Carol said.

"Marc. He was telling me while we were dancing that he could think of nothing else but our kiss. I think he wants more."

"I know he does," Nic laughed.

"Not that!" Lisa laughed as she threw a small pillow at Nic. "I think he wants more relationship-wise. The way he was talking he feels a lot deeper than I thought."

"And what do you feel?" Nic asked.

"I don't know. With everything that's been going on lately, how can I start something with him?"

"First off, I'm glad you are at least thinking about a relationship with Marc. He's a good man. But, don't let what's his name is ruin any of your happiness, whether it is with Marc or not," Carol said.

"Yeah," was all Lisa could say as she leaned her head back on the couch.

"What time is the party?" Pat asked.

"Seven o'clock."

"Don't forget about your hair appointment in the morning," Carol said.

"I never forget a hair appointment. I packed me an overnight bag, so I could leave from here. Are you leaving with me?"

"No, we're supposed to have brunch tomorrow, right Nic?"

"Yep. I'll drop her off. You just go get yourself all sexy for Marc."

"It is not like that."

"Yeah, right," Nic, Carol, and Pat said, laughing.

"Everybody has their room number, good night," Nic said, s they all headed upstairs to their rooms.

CHAPTER NINE

By ten, Danny was finishing up Lisa's hair, so she had plenty of time to make her nail and pedicure appointment.

"Thanks, Danny," she said, as she paid and him a tip.

"See you in a week," he said.

Lisa smiled and waved goodbye as she thought to herself, *It's a shame you're married.*

After running her errands, Lisa headed home. Walking in the house, she looked through her mail then checked her messages. She called her mother as she put away her groceries.

After talking to her mother, she went upstairs to her office and shredded her junk mail. By three o'clock, Lisa took an hour soak and put on something comfortable and decided to do some cleaning. As she cleaned, she listened to the new Jaheim CD she bought the other day.

By five she was done cleaning, when her phone rang.

"Hello."

"Hey, Lisa."

"Hey, Marc. What's going on?"

"Well, I want to make sure we were still on schedule. I will be at your house at six-thirty."

"I will be ready. How was the rest of your night?"

"From what I can remember, it was great. But, I can only remember the part I spent with you."

Lisa didn't know what to say that. She was actually speechless.

"Lisa, are you there?"

"Yeah, I'm here. I just don't know what to say to that."

"I understand. Like I said, I will be there by six-thirty."

"Okay, I'll see you then."

"Bye."

"Bye."

Lisa hung up the phone and walked into her closet to pick out the dress she had decided to wear earlier. She then walked into her bathroom to see if her hair needed any refreshing. It only needed a few more curls. Lisa applied her makeup slowly to make sure it was perfect. Walking into her bedroom, she put on a matching pair of maroon and black panties and bra and then her black four inch heeled sandals that snapped around the ankle. Then she slipped into her maroon velvet halter dress that zipped up on the side. Then her diamond studded earrings. By six-fifteen, she was ready to go.

She couldn't help looking at herself in the full length mirror. From the auburn curls that hung past her shoulders, to the one hundred forty-five pound frame that she worked so hard to keep after losing almost one hundred pounds. Lisa couldn't help but smile at herself. At six-twenty she heard the doorbell ring. She turned off her bedroom light and nervously walked downstairs. When she opened the door, the only thing she was thinking was *DAMN!!* Marc was standing on her doorstep looking like he just walked off the runway. He was wearing a black Armani suit and white on white shirt and tie, with diamond cuff links. He was the sexiest man she had ever seen in her life. It was going to be damn hard not to think of this as a date.

Marc took the scenic route to Lisa's house in order to get his nerves under control. He was okay until Lisa opened the door. He had always thought Lisa was beautiful ever since the first the day he saw her, but tonight seemed different. Last night was bad enough. It took all the power in the world for him to control himself.

Needless to say she was gorgeous. The only thing he was thinking was, *down boy.*

Finally, Marc said, "Hello, beautiful."

"Thank you, and hello, handsome. Come on in," Lisa said, stepping aside to let him in.

"I brought you something," Marc said, handing her a red rose and a Godiva Chocolates bag.

"Thank you," Lisa said, laughing. "Let me put this in the refrigerator and then we can go."

Marc watched Lisa go into the kitchen and couldn't help biting his bottom lip.

"Damn," he whispered.

"You say something?" Lisa asked.

"Uh, your house has really come together since the last time I was here."

"Yeah, little by little. So, do you have any ideas on how to approach Mr. Keene?" she asked, as she picked up her purse off the couch.

"What's that, a weapon?" he asked, laughing.

"Funny, real funny. It's a purse."

"Ready?"

"Let's go."

Lisa set her alarm and locked her door. Marc started telling Lisa his plan as he opened the door of his black XLR-V Supercharger Cadillac Convertible. It had gray leather seats with wood grain interior.

Waiting until he got in, Lisa realized how long it had been since a man had picked her up. So she said, "My car has wood grain interior. How long have you had this car?"

"About six months."

"It's nice."

"Thanks."

On the ride to Mr. Keene's house, they continued to talk about Marc's idea. By seven-forty-five they arrived at the Keene estate in Germantown.

As they pulled up to the valet, Lisa said, "He invited the world."

"If not more."

When the valet opened Marc's door, Marc handed him the keys and ran around to open Lisa's door. The valet gave Marc a ticket and told them to enjoy their evening. Walking up the front steps and through the double doors, they were surprised that the first person they saw was Mr. Keene.

"Ms. Jenson, I'm so glad you could make it. And let me guess, you must be Mr. Cavell?" Mr. Keene said as he shook both their hands.

"Thank you for inviting us," Marc said.

"Yes, thank you," Lisa chimed in.

"Go on in and enjoy the food, drinks, and music and we'll talk later."

Marc and Lisa walked through the foyer into the main room, where the party was being held.

"Since we have some time before our meeting, let's go get drunk," Marc said, offering Lisa his arm.

"I'm with you," Lisa said, as she looped her arm through his.

Taking two glasses from a passing waiter, Marc handed Lisa one and they started on a tour of the art. Lisa was also checking out the other women that were at the party.

"Have I told you how amazing you look tonight?"

"Yes and thank you," Lisa smiled. "I feel a little underdressed."

"You shouldn't, you are the most beautiful woman in this room."

Lisa broke eye contact and looked at a painting on the wall. Moving from different pictures and sculptures, they talked about how much each piece must have cost them. As they stood in front of one painting, trying to guess the price, Marc took a look around the room as it started to fill up.

"Damn," he whispered.

"What?" Lisa asked. Following his line of sight, Lisa's eyes landed on a woman who was staring at them. "Who's that?" she asked, as she turned back to the painting on the wall.

"Okay, quick story. She used to work for the firm, we dated until I found out she was married."

"Married? You cannot tell me you didn't know this woman was married. Hell, I can see her ring from here."

"You know, you should do stand-up. Anyway, she never wore a ring and her husband was always out of town. They had an open marriage."

96

"So? What's wrong with that?"

"I don't like open relationships."

"Point taken."

"We never went to her house, only restaurants and my place. I guess I should've gotten the picture then, but I didn't."

"How did you find out she was married?"

"John."

"John?"

"Yeah. He thought I already knew. He was having a dinner party and invited everyone and their spouses. When I showed up she was there with her husband. She even had the audacity to introduce us."

"Ouch."

"Not so much. It wasn't like I was in love or anything. It was a learning experience I know to ask the next time."

"Good. Because here she comes."

"Damn."

They watched her as she approached and Lisa saw that she was very beautiful. But she didn't hate her on sight.

"Marc! I thought that was you. How are you?"

"Hello, Judith. I've been great. What about you?"

"Wonderful. As you know I have my own firm now."

"Yeah, I heard. Congratulations."

"Thank you. I was hoping to get a chance to see you. Thought maybe I'd be able to steal you away. From Morgan & Peterson, that is."

"Thanks for the offer, but I enjoy where I work."

Lisa took a glass of champagne from a waiter as Marc and Judith talked.

"Oh, I am so sorry. Judith, this Lisa. Lisa…Judith."

"Nice to meet you," Lisa said.

"And you" Judith said, without a smile. "What do you do, Lisa?"

Before Lisa could answer, Marc said, "She also works for Morgan & Peterson."

"Well, Marc, it was nice to invite one of the secretaries. You must be new, because I don't recall you being there when I was."

"Actually, I've been with the firm for five years now. And I work *with* Marc, not *for* him."

"I didn't mean to offend you."

"You didn't," Lisa said with a smile.

"I wish my husband, Harold, could've made it. Unfortunately, he's out of the country on business."

"Sorry we missed him," said Marc, as he took Lisa's empty glass and gave her a new one."

"Maybe we should get together sometime and catch up," Judith told him, obviously flirting.

"We'd love to," Lisa said, as she grabbed Marc's hand.

Surprised at first, Marc caught on and said, "Yeah, we should."

"Right," Judith said, with her voice sounding tight.

"We will try to make that happen, but you have to excuse us, I have to dance with the most beautiful woman in the world," Marc said, looking at Lisa.

"It was nice meeting you...Judith, right?" Lisa said, as Marc led her to the dance floor.

Marc pulled Lisa close to him and whispered, "Thank you."

Breathless at being this close to him again, Lisa had to force herself to speak, "For what?"

"For saving me."

"That's what I'm here for. Is she still watching us?"

"Hmm? Oh, uh, yeah she's watching."

Marc never looked to see if Judith was really watching them. He just knew he didn't want to let Lisa go. Not now, maybe in another lifetime. It just felt so damn good to have her in his arms.

"She'll get the idea soon and give up," Lisa finally said.

Marc leaned back and looked at Lisa, "Why did you do that?"

"I didn't like how she tried to treat me. So, I decided to hit her where it would hurt the most."

"How'd you know it would work?"

"Women are just as territorial as men. If they see a man that used to date and still care about, with another woman, that means war. She already had the idea that we were dating she just wanted proof."

"Are you territorial, Lisa?"

"Extremely, but I haven't had to be in a long time."

They both laughed, but never stopped dancing. When the band finished, they went right into the next song, 'At Last' by Etta James.

Lisa turned to walk away, but Marc caught her hand, "One more?"

This time when he pulled her close, he knew something had changed between them and he knew she felt it too.

"I love this song," Lisa said.

"Me, too. I –"

"Excuse me, may I cut in?"

Bitch, Lisa thought, when Judith interrupted.

"Sorry, but this is our song," Marc said, without taking his eyes off of Lisa.

Lisa was smiling so hard you would've thought a hanger was in her mouth. Speechless, Judith stared at Marc, who was staring at Lisa, and then she stormed off.

"That was a good one, but now I'll have to watch my back when I go to the bathroom."

Marc never said a word, he just continued to staring at Lisa in a way that she thought no one had ever looked at her before…lovingly.

They continued to dance until they heard, "Excuse us, would the loving couple like us to continue playing or can we take a break?"

Marc and Lisa looked around and realized they were the only ones still on the dance floor.

Then Marc said, "Go ahead, we'll keep dancing until you come back."

Laughing, Lisa led him off the floor. She also made it her business to look for Judith, who was standing by the buffet table, throwing daggers at them with her eyes.

"I hope I didn't embarrass you out there."

"No, that was both of us out there making a scene."

Just as Marc was about to say something, someone caught his eye, "Let the games begin."

Lisa turned around and saw Mr. Keene heading their way.

"There you two are. Why don't we go to my office and do a little business?" Mr. Keene said.

Lisa and Marc followed him to a huge oversized door located on the opposite side of the room. Once inside, Mr. Keene offered Lisa and Marc a seat.

"Okay, wow me," he told them.

Marc jumped right into the pitch, "To begin we would like to tell you what we have in mind for you. We have looked over countless investments that would be perfect for you and your company."

Picking up where Marc left off, Lisa said "As you recall in the prospectus that I gave you, there are –"

"Wait, I'd like Mr. Cavell to finish what he was saying."

Lisa caught herself before she said something that would cost them the account.

"Mr. Keene, I'm not going to tell you anything different," Marc said.

"But you can. You can give me a man's point of view, after all its men who make the big decisions, right?"

At that moment, Marc could feel the heat radiate off Lisa's body.

"Listen, Ms. Jenson, why don't you go and get yourself a drink and let us men handle this?" Mr. Keene said.

Lisa was about to get up, until she felt Marc grab her hand. She looked at Marc and then at Mr. Keene, and said, "Mr. Keene, I work just as hard as Marc and if you don't see that then I withdraw our bid for your business. I've bought in big accounts for Morgan & Peterson as Marc's partner, not his assistant. Now, for whatever reason you haven't realized that women also make the big decisions, then I suggest you reread your history books."

Then Lisa walked out.

Marc and Mr. Keene sat in silence, until Mr. Keene said, "She is some kind of spitfire, ain't she? I bet she's even better in bed."

Even though Marc was fuming and wanted to go after Lisa, there was something he needed to say.

Beating him to the punch, Mr. Keene said, "Now, back to business. When do you think we can get started? I'm leaving the country in a few days and I want this settled before I leave. So, if the deal is still offered, I'm prepared to shake on it."

"As long as you understand that Lisa is my partner, we work together. And if you can't agree to that then we do not have a deal."

"Is she that good?"

"Better than great."

"Okay. But, only if…"

***

Standing at the bar drinking a glass of wine and still fuming, Lisa heard someone say, "Not turning out like you thought it would?"

Turning around, Lisa saw Judith standing behind her.

"Excuse me?" Lisa said.

"With Mr. Keene. I could have told you he only listens to women when they're a little more laid back."

"Where I come from that's considered prostitution," Lisa said, and walked away. She was headed back toward the office, but didn't go in. She continued staring at the door wondering what the hell was going on in there. Lisa got her answer when Marc came out of office looking like he had hit the lottery.

Marc walked over to Lisa and said, "No guts, no glory."

"What?" Lisa asked.

"First off, I'm glad you told that asshole off. Pardon my language."

"No problem, he deserved it. Now, what happened?"

"For starters, you were right. Second, he still wants us to take over his investments, but wants me to be the lead. Wait, let me finish, I told him no and that we were a team. Come on, you know there's no me without you," he said, softly.

"So, do we have the account?" Lisa asked, getting the conversation back on track.

"Yeah, we got it!"

Without thinking Lisa kissed Marc. Stammering, she said, "I...I am so sorry. I don't know what got –"

Before Lisa could finish the sentence, Marc leaned in and kissed her. Lisa felt as if she was thirty thousand feet in the air. She had never been kissed so passionately in all her life.

Marc pulled away and looked into her eyes and whispered, "Let's go."

Lisa didn't say a word. She just held Marc's hand and let him lead her out of the house. On their way out they passed Judith without even glancing in her direction.

CHAPTER TEN

On the way back to Lisa's house, they only talked about the rest of the meeting. Marc told Lisa that after she left, he was right behind her, but he wanted to give Mr. Keene a piece of his mind. He explained that at first Mr. Keene made a joke about her actions in bed. While Marc talked, Lisa fumed.

Then she said "So, what did you say?"

"After counting to about a million to calm down, I told Mr. Keene that we were a team and that if he didn't want you, he didn't want me. He then told me that he had already made his decision to go with us, as long as I head the account."

"And?"

"And, I told him thanks, but no thanks. He asked, did I believe in you that much? I told him more than anything. So, we got the account. If you still want it."

Lisa thought what Marc said, and she didn't want to deal with this jerk on a regular basis. Then she thought, what's wrong with letting Marc deal with him and she take the passenger seat, per se?

Marc pulled into Lisa's driveway and put the car in park. After a moment of not speaking, Lisa finally said, "Would you like to come in?"

Marc smiled and said, "Sure."

As they walked up to Lisa's door, she felt butterflies dancing in her stomach.

"Come on in," she said as she punched in her alarm code. "Would you like anything?"

"Anything you have will be fine," he said, as he followed her into the kitchen.

"Since we didn't get to eat, I know you must be hungry."

"Starving."

"Okay, what do you have a taste for? I have baked fish, or would you like something heavier?"

"That's fine."

Lisa put the glass dish in the oven and took out the bowl of mixed vegetables. As she put the bowl in the microwave and set the timer, she heard Marc's footsteps come closer."

"Lisa, are you gonna continue to act like there is nothing happening between us?"

Trying to ignore the question, she took plates out of the cabinet and silverware out of the drawer.

"Lisa?"

Lisa turned and faced Marc and said "No, I just don't know what to do about it."

"That's all?"

"Yes," Lisa said, setting the table.

When she tried to walk pass him, he grabbed her by the waist so she could face him. "I'm not ashamed to say that I feel more. Look at me, Lisa."

She looked at Marc and felt her entire body heat up.

"I know I haven't expressed my feelings publicly, but I am interested in you."

"Really?" Lisa whispered.

"Yes. I have felt this way since the first day I saw you. I thought maybe you already had someone in your life, but as the years passed, you never spoke of anyone. So when you had the house warming party, I found out that you were single. But, by then I was in a relationship. We just never seemed to be single at the same time."

"Marc, I have been single for the last six years."

"What?"

"Yes."

"What about the guy that was in your office?"

"I told you, he was someone who didn't know their time was up."

"Six years, huh?"

"Six years."

Sitting on one of the stools at the island, Marc pulled her closer to him and said, "I'm about to be brutally honest, like I said before, ever since your first day working on the twelfth floor I've learned more and more amazing things about you. Look, I'm not saying I'm in love with you, but I am attracted to you. My heart is attracted to your heart."

Lisa figured since Marc had been honest with her, she would do the same thing. So she said, "There is no denying that I am very, very attracted to you. If I wasn't, we wouldn't have…you know."

"Kissed."

"Yeah, that."

"No, kissed. You can say it, kissed."

"Kissed, we kissed. Anyway," Lisa said, laughing. "It's just that we work together and I don't want things to be weird between us."

"Things won't get weird between us. And to make sure they don't, why don't we start out as friends?"

"We are friends."

"Yes, we are. But let's try being close friends and see where it goes."

"I come with a lot of baggage. Namely, the gentleman you saw in my office."

"Who doesn't?"

"No, I –"

"Lisa, there is nothing you could possibly say to change my mind. Whatever baggage you claim to have, I would love to hear about it. When you're ready."

Lisa smiled and said, "You asked for it."

Twenty minutes later, they were eating and talking about the work they had to put into the Keene account.

"I didn't think I was that hungry," Lisa said.

"That really hit the spot."

Lisa took their plates to the sink, and Marc said, "I'll dry."

"No need, I'll just put them in the dishwasher. Let's go in the living room."

"Right behind you."

After getting settled on the couch, Marc said, "How do you take all this silence?"

"I like it, but let's get some music in here."

Lisa picked up the remote and turned on the CD player. Maxwell's voice filled the room.

"A Maxwell fan."

"Definitely, I just bought this CD over the weekend with a few others."

"I know this might be sudden and last minute, but what are you doing tomorrow?"

"I'm going to church. Would you like to join me?"

"I was going to ask you out," Marc said, laughing.

"Sorry, it's been a while."

"I tell you what, I'll go to church with you if you let me plan the rest of the day."

After thinking about it for a nanosecond, Lisa said, "Deal."

"Do you take all your first dates to church?"

"No. But my mother always told me that if you're seeing somebody and they don't take you to church, leave them."

"That's kind of strong. Why?"

"Because if they don't care about your soul, they won't care about your heart."

"Your mother sounds like a smart woman."

"She is. She's wonderful. When I was younger, I put her through so much. Nothing that involved the police, just regular teenage stuff. But I would give everything in me to go back and change some of the things I did."

"Think of it this way, the mistakes you made then, you would never make today."

"You got that right."

They were quiet for a moment as Maxwell's 'Pretty Wings' started to play.

"Lisa, may I have this dance?"

Smiling, Lisa aid, "Yes."

When they stood up, he said, "You're a lot shorter without your heels."

"Stop it," she chuckled.

After a few seconds into the dance, Lisa said, "This is nice."

"Yeah, it is."

They danced to the next two songs without saying a word. Neither one of them wanting to spoil the moment. Then Lisa felt him lean away from her, and when she opened her eyes he was staring at her.

For a moment she was lost in his eyes. Then he leaned in and kissed her gently. Soon their kiss became more passionate with every passing minute. Lisa didn't remember how they ended up on the couch, but she didn't object. It had been so long since she'd been held that she never wanted this to end. But it did, because Lisa could feel Marc pulling away. When she opened her eyes, those dark brown eyes were starting right back at her as if they could see into her soul.

"What? What's wrong?"

"You don't know how much I want to carry you upstairs."

"You don't know how much I want you to carry me upstairs."

"So, I think we better stop."

"Yeah, you're right."

But neither of them moved, they just stared at each other.

"I want to make love you, Lisa. That's why we have to stop. Because if we went upstairs tonight it would only be about lust. And I want more than that with you."

"There's nothing wrong with lust."

They both laughed.

Pushing her hair out of her eyes, he said, "I want more than that with you, okay?"

"Okay."

Marc leaned down and kissed her again. Getting themselves under control, Marc got ready to leave.

"I'll see you for church tomorrow?" Lisa asked.

"Just tell me what time."

"Be here at ten-thirty."

They walked to the door and Lisa opened it, Marc turned at the door and kissed her. When they parted, he said, "Make it ten. I'm going to need all the prayer I can get."

Laughing, Lisa said good night and watched him get in his car. After he pulled away, Lisa locked up and went up to her room. A half hour later she was climbing into bed, and she already knew what she would be dreaming about that night.

***

Lisa's alarm went off Sunday morning at eight-thirty. After washing her face, she went downstairs to have a bowl of cereal. While pouring the milk, the telephone rang. She expected to see her mother's number on the display, but to her surprise she saw Marc's number.

"Hello."

"Good morning, beautiful," Marc said.

"Good morning."

"Did I wake you?"

"No, I just sat down to have a bowl of cereal."

"I called to see if we are still on for today?"

Lisa was shocked that he still wanted to go to church. Most men would have made up some excuse to back out.

"Of course," she said.

"Next on the agenda, do I still have you for the rest of the day?"

"You sure you want to spend the entire day with me?"

"More than anything."

"I don't know."

"Don't think, just say yes."

Lisa was quiet for a moment and then said, "Okay, you have me for a day."

Laughing, he said, "Forgive me, Lord, for thinking what I'm thinking. I'll see you in an hour, beautiful."

"Okay, bye."

She couldn't help but smile as she hung up the phone. On her way upstairs to her bedroom her phone rang again. Thinking it was Marc, Lisa said, sweetly, "Helloo."

"Good morning. And what's got you so happy?" her mother said.

"Hey, mama," Lisa said changing the tone of her voice. "And nothing has me happy this morning, but going to church."

"Do you have company?"

"No!"

"Uh huh, are you coming to church?"

"Of course. And I'm also bringing a friend."

"Who, Carol?"

"No."

"Then, who?"

"Someone from work."

"Carol is someone from work. Now, who are you bringing?"

Lisa didn't answer.

"Girl, you hear me talking to you."

"Marc. Marc Cavell."

"Date number two?"

"It's not like that, mama."

"You must've forgotten who you talking too. I know you like this man. Look how you answered the phone, 'helloo'," Lisa's mother said, imitating her. "He must have called before me for you to answer the phone like that."

How did she know that? Lisa thought to herself.

"The last man you brought to church was James."

"Yeah, I know. But Marc and I are just friends."

"If you say so. I'll see you guys after a while."

"Okay, bye."

By the time the doorbell rang, Lisa was ready to go.

"A man on time," she said heading downstairs.

"Hello, Mona Lisa," Marc said, when Lisa opened the door.

"Hello, Mr. Cavell."

"Are you ready?"

"Yes," Lisa said, as she locked up."

"You look beautiful this morning."

"Thank you. You look quite handsome yourself."

Backing out of the driveway, Marc said, "So where is your church?"

"Don't worry, I'll show you. But so you won't worry about my directional skills, it's on Ford Road."

"Okay, I trust you."

As Lisa gave him directions to the church, she also told him how happy her mother was to hear that he would be joining them for church.

"That makes two of us," he said.

Pulling into the parking lot of Great Temple Baptist Church, Lisa realized how big this was going to be. The church wasn't large and the congregation was close knit. Everybody knew each other and their business. So Lisa knew everyone would want to know who Marc was. Marc parked, got out, and came around to open Lisa's door. He even took her hand and helped her out. Lisa felt like royalty.

"Thank you," she said.

Waving at her family, Lisa and Marc walked up the front steps to join them.

"Hello, hello, hello," she said hugging everyone.

"Hey, baby," her grandmother said.

Lisa turned to Marc and said, "Everyone, this is Marc Cavell. Marc, this my mother, Janice Jenson, my grandmother, Beverly Dodson, and my brother, Anthony."

"Jenson," Anthony laughed.

"Anyway," Lisa said, laughing.

"It's nice to see you all again," Marc said.

Janice smiled and said, "I'm glad you could join us this morning, Mr. Cavell."

"Marc, please. And thank you for having me."

"Alright, Marc."

"Grandma, are you singing this morning?" Lisa asked.

"No, I'ma sit with y'all today. Now, let's go in, before service starts."

Everyone went into the church and found an empty pew. Service started with a selection from the choir and then a sermon was given by Reverend Williamson. Love and marriage was the subject.

As Reverend Williamson preached, Lisa looked at Marc and noticed that was completely engrossed in it. When Reverend Williamson finished his sermon, he turned the service over to Deacon Robinson.

Deacon Robinson called for visitors and Marc stood up. When Lisa saw movement in her peripheral vision, she turned to see James stand up. At first she thought she was hallucinating, but he stood there as clear as day.

Marc was the first to speak, "Good morning, I'm visiting this morning from Saints Cathedral in New York. A good friend brought me here today and I'm glad she did. Thank you for having me."

"Who brought you here today?" Deacon Robinson asked.

"Lisa Jenson."

"Little Lisa? Girl, stand up." Lisa stood up. "Well, she ain't little no more, but she will always be little Lisa to us. Thank you for bringing another soul to hear the word."

As Lisa and Marc sat down, Deacon Robinson said, "And you, brother."

"Good morning, Saints. I'm actually not a visitor. I used to attend Great Temple about five years ago and I'm glad to be back."

"Well, we welcome you back and we welcome our first time visitor. Our sermon today touches on friendship, love, and marriage. A lot of people don't understand how to be friends first and get to know one another. There is so much divorce that nobody believes in love anymore. Everybody wants a wedding not a marriage. My wife and I have been together for ten years and she is my life. We put God first in our lives and in our marriage and for that I know our marriage is blessed. Just as God took a rib from Adam to make Eve, I know my wife was made for me. I want to say, I love you, Barbara, and I always will."

The congregation clapped as the deacon walked over and hugged his wife. Marc took hold of Lisa's hand and winked at her. As they stared at one another, it seemed as if everyone in the church disappeared and they were the only two left.

After service was over, Lisa introduced Marc to the pastor and a few other members of the church. On their way out to meet up with Lisa's family, Lisa saw that James was headed toward them.

"Oh, no," Lisa said.

"What's wrong?" Marc said. Then he saw what was wrong.

"You remember your little problem with your ex?"

"Yeah."

"Well, here comes mine."

Marc watched as the same man he saw in Lisa's office headed their way and Marc grabbed Lisa's hand.

"Hey, Lisa," James said.

"Hello."

"How you doing?"

"Fine, you?"

"I'm great."

Looking at Marc and noticing he was hold Lisa's hand, James said, "How you doing, I'm James."

"I'm Marc," he said, shaking his hand.

"I remember seeing you in Lisa's office last week," James said, looking at Lisa.

"Yeah, I remember you."

"Lisa, can I talk to you for a minute?"

"No."

"Only to talk, that's it."

"No."

"I –"

"Look, I don't mean to get in the middle of this, but I believe she told you no. Now, if you will excuse us," Marc said.

"And who are you supposed to be? From what Lisa told me, you two are just co-workers," said James.

"I didn't know she had to answer to you. But in case you missed the bulletin, she is not available. So, do yourself a favor and stay away from her," Marc told him.

"Look, I don't need to talk to –"

"Is there a problem here, Lis?" Anthony asked, as he stood behind James.

When James turned around he was shocked to see how much Anthony had grown.

"Hey, Anthony! Man, look at you! What are you sixteen...seventeen?" James said.

"Lisa, you alright?"

"I'm fine, Anthony. Marc and I were just on our way out."

"Ma and grandma are waiting."

"You don't remember me, Anthony?" James asked.

Anthony walked closer to James and said, "Oh, I remember you. And if we weren't in church I would show you just how much I remember."

Lisa stepped between them and told Anthony, "You know better. We're in church."

Realizing that Anthony wasn't going to back down, Marc said, "Anthony, why don't we go see if we can talk your mother and grandmother into going out to lunch. I think I might need to do a little kissing up. You can tell me what they like."

Marc put his arm around Anthony's shoulder and walked him toward the door. They went off talking like they were old friends.

"Take care, James."

"Lisa, wait."

"No," Lisa said and walked out of the church to catch up with her family.

"Just co-workers. I'll bet," James said, as he watched Lisa walk away.

CHAPTER ELEVEN

"Wait for me! Y'all tryin' to leave me?" Lisa said, catching up to her family. "Do you guys wanna go to lunch with us?"

"That's what we were just talking about," Marc said.

"I know you're not gon' act like that didn't happen," Janice said, angrily.

"Mom, not now."

"Then, when? Be –"

"Um, I'll just wait by the car," Marc said.

"No, I'm sorry, Marc. But, we will talk about this," Janice said.

"Where we gon' eat?" asked Anthony.

"How 'bout O'Charley's, they have good food?" Lisa said.

Everyone agreed and headed to their cars.

Walking to the car, Lisa felt Marc's hand on the small of her back. She felt as if it was the most natural thing.

As they pulled away from the church, Lisa caught a glimpse of James standing on the church steps watching them drive away.

After a few minutes of silence, Lisa wanted to find out what Marc was thinking.

"So, did you enjoy the service?"

"I really did, thank you for inviting me."

"Good."

"I hope it's an open invitation."

"Completely open. I also want to thank you for running interference. I don't know what would've happened if you didn't."

"No problem. Besides, I didn't want your brother to hit the guy."

"I know you might be wondering what's going on, but considering we're almost at the restaurant, I don't want to get into it right now."

"Understood. But can I ask you something? You don't have to answer."

"Shoot."

"Did he hurt you? I mean, did he hit you?"

"What made you ask that?"

"It wasn't hard to figure out after seeing how Anthony and then your mother reacted to seeing him. And the fact that you were breaking every bone in my hand."

Laughing, Lisa said, "Sorry about that."

"I won't break. If you need to lay – I mean lean on me, I'm strong enough." Then turning serious, he said, "I understand. I really do."

Lisa sat silently wondering what Marc thought of her now.

"If you feel like talking, I'm here," he said, taking hold of her hand.

Pulling into the restaurant parking lot and parking, everyone walked in and was seated immediately. Then the grilling began.

Lisa's grandmother, Beverly said, "I'm little older than anyone at this table, so I need my memory refreshed. How did you and our Lisa meet, Mr. Cavell?"

"We work together, ma'am."

"Do you often date your co-workers?"

"Grandma, it's not a date. We are just friends."

"Hush, child," Beverly said.

"It's okay. I have dated another person that I worked with, but that was years ago."

"Do you have any children?" Lisa's mother asked.

"No, ma'am."

"Ever been married?" from Beverly.

"No, ma'am."

Then Janice, "Have you ever been in jail, on drugs, or on the down low?"

"Oh, God," Lisa said.

"No, no, and definitely not."

"Anything else you wanna ask him mama?" Janice said.

"Yes, and excuse me for this question, Mr. Cavell. What is your…ethnic background?"

"I'm Italian."

"And how do your parents feel about Lisa, son?"

"They haven't met her…yet."

Lisa caught the yet word, but didn't say anything.

"Why not?" Beverly said.

"Because we're friends," Lisa told her grandmother.

Ignoring Lisa, Beverly went on, "I grew up in another time, and in my time, men and women didn't date outside their race. Now, I know this is a different time from when I was a young girl, about five years ago." Everyone laughed, as she continued, "Now-a-days things like this happen all the time, so it's not that taboo. So I'm not going to make a big deal about it, but let me make this clear. You protect my granddaughter, you make sure that beautiful smile she has stays permanently glued to her face. She is a strong woman. That's the way we raised her. And she needs an equally strong man. You hear me? If you can't protect her and treat her like the beautiful woman she is, move on and don't waste her time. Or you'll have to deal with me."

"And then you'll have to deal with me and I'm much worse," Janice said with a smile.

"Um, if I didn't know what kind of family you were at first, I sure do now," Marc said, laughing nervously. "To be honest, I have been in…awe of Lisa since the first day I saw her. And then I met her and knew she was extraordinary. She's smart, funny, and passionate about her work. And yes, strong, and that's another reason to be even crazier about her. Lisa knows how I feel about her, but she wants to go slow, and I respect that. But, if given the chance, I truly believe I can make Lisa very happy," he said looking into Lisa's eyes.

"Well, alright then. Now that that's cleared up, let's eat," Beverly said.

"And Lisa, don't think you off the hook either. You treat this gorgeous man with the same love and respect he is obviously going to treat you with. You hear me?" Janice said.

"Yes, ma'am," Lisa said and smiled at Marc.

After the questions, everyone ate, laughed, and talked. Lisa noticed how well Anthony and Marc were getting along. He asked Marc so many questions; Marc could barely keep his answers straight.

"Do you make as much money as Lisa?"

"Anthony, you know better than to ask him that!" Janice said.

Marc laughed and said, "It's okay. Anthony, I do pretty well. After college I came to Memphis to work for Morgan & Peterson."

"Why did you want to come to Memphis?" Anthony asked.

"During college I interned with the company and I like the city, so I moved her about eight years ago."

The rest of the lunch consisted of the family getting to know Marc, whose name was actually Marcello Cavell. Lisa thought his name was sexy.

After an hour lunch, everyone was leaving the restaurant and hugs and handshakes went around.

"Don't forget to call me tonight," Janice told Lisa. Then her mother looked at Marc and said, "On second thought, call me tomorrow."

"Good-bye, mother."

"Bye, kids."

"Hey, Anthony don't forget next Saturday," Marc said.

"Fo' sho'. You just make sure you bring yo' game," Anthony said.

Getting into Marc's car, they sat quietly as if waiting for the other person to say something.

Marc was the first to speak, "Would you like me to take you home to change?"

"No, I'm fine. We don't have to go through all of that. What have you planned for the rest of the day?"

"First, do you trust me?"

Without hesitation, Lisa said, "Yes."

Smiling, Marc said, "Good, because I couldn't think of a thing. So, I'm offering you a day of movies and a great dinner cooked by me. What do ya' say?"

"Okay."

Getting off on the next exit, they made it to Marc's house which was located downtown on Riverside Drive. When they walked in, Lisa's eyes were drawn immediately to the view of the Mississippi River.

"Let's take the tour," Marc said.

First, he started with the living room, which was decorated with a black leather sofa and love seat, with a large oak coffee table. There was a large plasma television that hung on the opposite wall in front of the sofa and above a wood burning fireplace. In front of the patio doors that led to the balcony, was a beautifully set table. Next, the kitchen. This was a chef's dream. It had marble countertops, dark wood cabinets, stainless steel appliances, and a subzero refrigerator with a clear door. The kitchen also had a breakfast nook in front of a large window.

"The back door leads down to the garage. It also leads down to the back sidewalk. Some mornings I can get an actual run in down by the water."

Lisa followed him back in the house when he said, "Would you like to see more?"

"Of course."

Heading upstairs, Marc opened the first door on the right to his home office. The office was a mirrored reflection of his office at work. The view was of a busy downtown traffic jam.

"I know you're thinking it's not that different from my office at work, but when I find something I like, I stick with it," he said, as he looked her straight in the eyes.

"I'll keep that in mind," Lisa said as she smiled and walked out of the room.

Next, they went across the hall to a room that was being used as a home gym.

"There's really nothing to see in here."

The next room was a guest room that was furnished with a huge canopy bed, sitting area by a window that also looked over downtown traffic.

Walking back out of the room, he said, "That door is the other bathroom, and this is my bedroom."

The bedroom was furnished with a huge comfy bed covered with a chocolate colored duvet` and matching pillows. Across from the bed was another large plasma television on the wall. Underneath it was a two-sided fireplace. Lisa could see through to the bathroom. There was also a sitting area with chairs that matched the bedding. They faced the doors that lead to the balcony. It was beautiful. Lisa thought it was a room that a woman could not resist.

On their way back downstairs, Lisa said, "You have a beautiful home."

"Thanks, I'll tell my mother you said so. Have a seat."

"That explains a lot."

Marc turned on the television, "What type of movies do you like to watch?"

"I'm pretty open."

"Can you narrow it down just a little?"

"Okay. Old movies. You know Humphrey Bogart, Joan Crawford, and Betty Davis."

"Barbara Stynwick. My mother has a weakness for those movies. She brings a suitcase full every time she visits. So I ordered her copies of each movie she has so she wouldn't have to lug them wherever she goes." Marc pulled out a draw under his coffee table and said, "Pick one."

Lisa pulled out *The Two Mrs. Carrols.*

"Humphrey Bogart it is," Marc said, as he put it in the DVD player. "Would you like something to drink before the movie?"

"Um, do you have any bottled water?"

"No, but I can run to the store."

Lisa smiled at him and said, "No, you don't have to do that. How about you tell me what you do have."

"I have sodas, juices, and wine."

"I'll take the juice."

"Okay, I have orange, apple, and a combination strawberry-banana."

"I'll take the strawberry-banana."

"Two strawberry-bananas coming up."

After the juices were served, Marc sat down and started the movie. During the next two movies, which were *The Two Mrs. Carrols* and *In This Our Lives,* neither Lisa nor Marc moved from their spots on the couch. Lisa with her feet pulled under her and Marc with his feet up on the table.

Around eight, Marc said, "Are you hungry?"

"Yeah, I could do with a little something."

"Let's see what I can whip up."

"I'll help," Lisa said, slipping her feet into her shoes.

"Leave them off, I don't mind."

"Okay."

Lisa got up to follow Marc in the kitchen, but she stopped in her tracks and said, "Well, look at that."

"What?" Marc asked from the kitchen.

"The sunset. I haven't watched one of these in years. I remember when I was nineteen, I used to come downtown just to watch the sunset."

"You and your boyfriend?" Marc said, coming out of the kitchen to stand next to her.

"Not all the time. Sometimes it was nice to just come alone. I used to wonder about the people who lived up here in these houses. I know you get to watch this every day."

"Not often as I'd like. Have you forgotten who we work for?"

Lisa laughed along with Marc.

As the sun finally dipped into the water, Lisa notice he was staring at her.

"What are you looking at?" she asked.

"At the most beautiful woman I have ever seen."

"You should really stop that."

"Why? You are." Marc took another step toward Lisa. "You know, I meant everything I said to your mother and grandmother. If you let me, I know I can make you happy. All you have to do is let me."

"Are you always this straightforward? I mean, outside of business."

"Yes."

"Marc, I haven't been in a relationship in a long time. It's been hard for me to put my trust in someone ever since…never mind."

"No, tell me," he said, taking her by the hand and leading her to the kitchen.

"My mother says the best way to get to a woman's heart is to listen to her secrets and keep them as if they were your own."

Lisa watched him as he moved around the kitchen and said, "Your mother sounds like a smart woman."

"She is. And I'm still waiting, Mona Lisa," he said, while gathering everything he needed to cook.

"Marc, that is too much to explain in one day."

"Then you better get started."

After a moment, Lisa started talking, "You met the cause of the problem after church. I met James in college. Let me rephrase that, I met him while I attended college. At the beginning everything was good, we just clicked.

We could talk about anything, we got each other's stupid jokes, we – uh anyway you get what I'm saying."

"Yeah," Marc said, chuckling.

"About four months into the relationship, the real James introduced himself. Can I help with something?"

"You are helping, keep talking."

"The first time was a slap, for what, I don't even remember. I was in such shock, that I didn't even hit him back. I guess he saw that as fear."

"We're you afraid of him?"

"That's the thing at first I wasn't. But as the first year passed I did become afraid of him. The second time he hit me was over my friend Nicole. He couldn't stand her and she felt the same way. We went out one night and he thought I came back too late. When I got home, my mother said that he had been calling all night. So the next day I went to his house after classes and the moment I walked in he knocked me to the floor. I remember fighting back that time, but that just made it worse. From then on, anything would set him off; it was like he enjoyed it. He would always say, 'I been waiting for this'. But I never knew why he wanted to hurt me. You know... I never knew a man could rape his girlfriend or wife."

Turning to look at her, Marc said, "How many times did that happen?"

"Twice. So, when I realized that he'd take it no matter what I said, I stopped saying no. He did things to me I thought I would never let a person do to me. It got to a point where I didn't have any fight left in me anymore. I stopped caring what happened to me. All I did was go to school, his house, and then home."

"Wait a minute. You were in school while all of this was going on?"

"Yeah."

"And you didn't stay with him?"

"Nope."

"Did your mother ever see any of the bruises?"

"They were never where anyone could see them. I mean, she knew something was up, but she didn't know to what extent. She tried to keep me away from him, and he wasn't allowed at the house. But nothing she did worked."

"So what finally did?"

"Toward the end of the relationship, I couldn't take it anymore, it was like he just took over everything. I started to realize he would never change, so I decided to break it off. At first everything was fine, he was just trying to talk me out of it. He told me he would change, get counseling; do anything if I stayed. When he realized that I didn't believe him, he punched me. That's where everything gets a little fuzzy. The rest Nic had to fill in for me. You might remember her; you met her at my house warming."

"Yeah, the detective, right?"

"That's her. Anyway, from what she tells me, they found me unconscious on his living room floor."

"Wait, from what they tell you? You don't remember?"

Lisa took a deep breath, and then said, "No. Nic told me my mom had called her looking for me when I didn't come home from school. Nic, being the best friend and cop ever, found out where James lived. She told me when she found his apartment, the front door was unlocked and when they opened it, I was laying on the floor. She thought I was dead. Apparently, there was so much blood…" Lisa took another deep breath and then continued. "When I arrived at the hospital, my family was told that I had six broken ribs, both of my eyes were swollen shut, a concussion, and a lot of other problems. During my two week coma, Nic said that they looked for him everywhere and couldn't find him. But every night Nic would sit and talk to me. Then one night, when he figured everyone was gone, he came to visit me. Nic and her partner arrested him then. A month after I was home, he was sent to jail for three years."

"For attempted murder?"

"Not attempted murder, for assault. Needless to say my, mother was livid. She told him in court that the best place for him was jail, because if he was free she'd kill him."

"I'm sure she meant it," Marc said.

"And so here I am. I went to counseling, finished school and applied to Morgan & Peterson. And I've been living a very blessed and happy life since then."

"Good for you," Marc smiled. "Are you ready to eat?"

"Definitely, but let me freshen up first."

When Lisa came out of the bathroom, Marc had dimmed the lights, lit candles, and John Legend was singing softly.

Walking toward her and taking her hand, he said, "Dinner is served, Mona Lisa."

Pulling her chair out and then taking the seat across from her, he said, "We have blackened fish over ricotta and a great bottle of white wine."

"This looks almost too good to eat."

As Marc poured the wine, Lisa looked out at the twinkling lights on the Mississippi Bridge. Smiling, she said, "This view is amazing."

"It sure is," he said, looking at Lisa. Then he said, "I'm glad you came over today, I hope you'll be back."

"I'd like that."

"Dig in."

As they ate dinner, Lisa asked Marc about his life.

"Well, if you have to be all in my business," he said, laughing. "I already told you my parents still live in New York and I try to get up there to see them as often as I can. My father was a mailman, my mother a nurse. I'm an only child and I hated it, there was never anyone around to blame when I did something wrong."

Laughing, Lisa said, "I'm glad I had Anthony."

"Tell me more about your life. What does your mother and father do? Did you have a good childhood?" Marc asked.

"I had a great childhood. My mother is a homemaker and my dad was never around. I saw him and even got to spend a little time with him when I was younger. But as I got older I saw less and less of him."

"What does he do?"

"He's a CFO at Johnson & Johnson."

"Oh, so that's where your love of numbers comes from."

"I guess so."

"Do you speak to him often?"

"Not really. We're just not that close."

"May I ask why?"

"He hasn't been around. We speak a couple of times a month and he thinks he's done his fatherly job."

"And you're okay with that?"

"At first, no. Then the older I got, I realized that I couldn't make him be there. I made up in my mind that as long as I had my mother, I would be alright."

"You know your eyes light up when you talk about her."

"Really? Well they should. She's a great woman. I don't think I know another woman who is as strong and as smart as my mother."

"I can see that you guys are close."

"Yes, we are. But back to you, have you enjoyed living here?"

"Yes, everything is so much calmer and slower. I love the fireworks on the fourth of July, the concerts during Memphis in May."

By ten, dinner was over, the dishes in the dishwater and Marc and Lisa were sitting on the couch with a glass of wine each.

"Did you enjoy the rest of the day?" Marc asked.

"I really did. In fact, I've enjoyed the past two days."

"It doesn't have to end."

"Eventually, we'll have to go back to the real world."

"Let's save that for tomorrow," he said, as he leaned in and kissed her.

After a minute, Lisa pulled away.

"Stay the night, Lisa," Marc said, as he set his glass on the table along with Lisa's.

"I don't think that's a good idea."

Lisa got up and walked over to the balcony door and stared at the water.

Marc walked over and put his arms around Lisa, "Why not? We don't have to do anything. I just want to be with you tonight."

The room became quiet as the CD change and then Nat King Cole began to sing Mona Lisa.

"I don't want the night to end yet," he whispered.

Lisa was quiet for a minute, then said, "Me neither. But if I stay what will happen to us just being friends?"

"Hopefully, turn us into something more. Now let me ask you something, what happens at work?"

Lisa thought about that and then said, "I like to keep my personal life personal, but I promise not to act weird about what's going on between us."

"Can I kiss you at work?"

"Depends on my mood," Lisa said jokingly and then turned to face him.

"I'll make sure to keep you in a good mood. Now, I'm going to ask you again, will you stay the night?"

After thinking for a minute, she said, "Yes."

This time they both leaned in to kiss. Then Lisa felt him pull away. He bent to pick her up and carried her upstairs. She felt like she weighed two pounds.

On their way upstairs, he whispered, "Tell me when to stop."

When they made it to the bedroom, there was no need to turn on the light. The entire room was lit by the full moon. Marc laid Lisa on the bed and then lay next to her. He stared into her eyes as if he could read every secret she ever had. Then he started to laugh.

Lisa looked at him like he lost his mind. "What are you laughing at?"

"I know this is the wrong time to say this, but my mother would always tell me that if you look into a woman's eyes and see forever, then you know you have found the one. I finally understand what she meant." Marc leaned in and kissed her.

Lisa felt like she just had an orgasm and he hadn't even touched her. Lying on his bed, they did something she hadn't planned; they held each other and looked out at the moon and water.

After a few minutes, Lisa said, "Marc, be patient with me."

"Always."

Turning toward him, Lisa kissed him deeply. They started exploring each other's body to almost the point of no return. She unbuttoned his shirt and pushed it off his shoulders. Marc following suit, unbuckled Lisa's belt and dropped it to the floor. He then unbuttoned her shirt and slipped it off of her. Then Lisa turned on her side so he could unzip her skirt.

Feeling her tremble, he asked, "Are you cold?"

"No," she whispered.

"It's okay, we'll take things slow."

Lying in Marc's bed, in her lace black bra and panties and Marc in his boxers, they kissed for what seemed like a lifetime. Realizing that they needed to stop before they went too far, they spent the rest of the night holding each other. They eventually fell asleep listening to Nat King Cole sing about Mona Lisa.

Chapter Twelve

Hurrying through her front door after being dropped off by Marc, Lisa ran upstairs to get dressed for work. As she took a quick shower, she couldn't help but think about how she woke up this morning. Around six, Lisa was awakened by the sound of the shower and the sun shining through the balcony door. Looking around the room and realizing where she was, Lisa smiled. Getting out of bed, she walked over to the balcony door and looked at the view. She heard the shower turn off and a minute later the door opened.

Marc walked up and put his arms around Lisa's waist and said, "Good morning, Mona Lisa. Did you sleep well?"

"Good morning, Marcello. And I have never slept so well."

"You know, you and my mother are the only two people who can call me that. But I like it more coming from you."

"I'll remember that," Lisa said, turning around to face him and putting her arms around him. Seeing that he was just in a towel and still wet, about a million raunchy ideas ran through her head. She looked at his wet hair and said, "I have a confession."

"What?"

"Every day I would see you, all I wanted to do was run my fingers through your hair."

"Well, you got your wish and I got mine."

"And what was yours?"

"To hold you at night and wake up to see you lying next to me."

"That's two wishes."

"What can I say, I got lucky."

Lisa laughed and was about to walk away, but he didn't loosen his grip. Instead he said, "Let's play hooky."

"And do what?"

"Anything you want."

Lisa gave him a wicked smile and then said, "Anything?"

Marc nodded yes. Before Lisa could answer, Marc's phone rang. Not moving to answer his phone, he waited until she gave him an answer.

"Yes."

"Great!" he said, smiling. Finally, he walked over to answer the phone, "Hello…Good morning, Paul."

Lisa and Marc stared at each other as he listened to their boss.

"Yes, everything went great. Just as I'd hoped it would," he said, and then winked at Lisa. "I was actually planning to take a –…Yes, sir…Alright…No, I haven't talked to Lisa yet…I'll see you at the office." Marc hung up and said, "Our plans have been changed, Paul wants to meet with us at ten to discuss how Saturday went."

"Oh, this should be fun," Lisa said, while zipping her skirt.

"Rain check?" Marc asked.

"Definitely."

On the way to her house, Marc offered to wait for her. She told him that wasn't necessary and that she'd see him at the meeting.

By eight-forty-five Lisa was dressed and out the door. She made it to work by ten minutes after nine, practically skipping to her office. When she made it to Carol's outer office, Carol was nowhere in sight. Lisa went into her office to get ready for the meeting. She hung her suit jacket and purse on her coat rack, and nearly jumped out of the window when Carol walked out of her bathroom.

"Oh, Carol, you scared me half to death!"

"Scared you, you scared me," Carol said, while she put down the vase of the most beautiful red roses.

"Those are beautiful, Carol. You must have been real good over the weekend."

"Oh, I was. But these are not for me. There for you."

"Me?"

"You. Now, who is he?"

"Who is who?"

"Don't play with me Lisa. Just read the card before I do."

Lisa took the card from her and read it. By the time she finished reading the card she was smiling so hard she looked like the joker. She dropped it immediately when she saw Carol looking at her.

Lisa said, "What?"

"Well?"

When Lisa didn't answer, Carol snatched the card and read herself. "'For my Mona Lisa.' What does that mean?"

"It means none of your business."

"Oh no, no, no. You don't get off that easy. Over the weekend you have met a man that actually got you to look at him twice, tell him where you work, and that could turn you into the Joker. Did you meet at the Keene party?"

"Yes."

"Wha –"

"I wish I had time, but I have a meeting to get ready for."

"I know tha –." Carol paused and then stared at Lisa and said, "How did you know that?"

"Know what?" Lisa knew where she slipped up.

"How did you know you had a meeting?"

"Um, Paul called me."

"But he told me he could only get in touch with Mr. – Oh my God!"

"What?"

"You and Mr. Cavell. I knew he was interested in you, I knew it. Did you sleep together?"

"First off, I don't know what you're talking about. Second, we haven't done anything."

"Well, how did you know about the meeting?"

"Paul left a message."

"Unh-huh. I still want the story about this weekend over lunch later."

"There's nothing to tell."

"Those flowers say there is, Ms. Mona Lisa," Carol said, walking out.

Twenty minutes later Lisa walked into the conference room where Marc and Mr. Morgan were waiting.

"Good morning, Paul…Marc. Am I late?"

"Morning, Lisa," Paul said.

"Good morning, Mo – uh, Lisa," Marc said.

Lisa smiled, and then Paul said, "You're not late. We're just waiting for John. So kids, how was the party?"

Looking at one another, Marc spoke first, "It was good, considering it was work."

"I know Keene comes off as an asshole, pardon me," Paul said. Lisa only nodded.

In the next minute, John walked into the conference room, "Good morning, everyone."

Everyone said good morning in return and then they all got to work.

During the two hour meeting, they discussed the Keene account. They discussed paths to take, stocks to look into, and other areas to produce a great outcome for Mr. Keene's account.

After the meeting, Marc said, "Lisa can I see you in my office when you get a chance today?"

"I have some time now, if you do?"

"Okay."

They all filed out of the conference room talking, then parting and going in opposite directions.

While Marc and Lisa walked towards his office, they discussed other areas to look into for the account.

"Barbara, will you hold my calls? I don't want any interruptions for the next hour," Marc told his assistant.

Looking at Lisa first and then Marc, Barbara said, "Yes, sir."

The minute Lisa walked into Marc's office, he closed his door and grabbed Lisa around the waist and asked, "Did you like your roses?"

"They're beautiful, Marcello. Thank you so much." Without even thinking, she kissed him, but abruptly pulled away.

"No, don't pull away. You don't ever have to pull away from me. If you ever feel the need to hug, kiss, or anything else, please do."

"Okay." Lisa put her arms around Marc's neck and kissed him. After a moment the two separated and sat on Marc's couch.

"So, what did Carol say?" Marc asked.

"First, when did you order them?"

"On my way here."

"Well, Carol guessed they were from you, but I veered her off the path."

"Why?"

"I wasn't ready to tell anyone yet."

"Why not tell her? She would be happy."

"And how do you know that?"

"Because she's always setting us up and smiling when she sees us together."

"That's true."

"So, can I see you tonight?"

"Already? You're not tired of me yet?"

"That will never happen. It took me too long to get here and I am not letting you go." Marc was about to kiss Lisa, but was halted by the buzzer. Surprising Lisa, he kissed her anyway.

A second later, Barbara buzzed in again.

"Ignore it," Marc whispered, as he tried to pull Lisa beneath him.

Between kisses, Lisa was able to say, "She's letting you know our hour is up."

Looking down at Lisa, Marc sighed, "I asked for a whole hour." He got up off the couch, and pushed the button on his phone. "Yes, Barbara?"

"Melody is bringing down some files from Mr. Morgan."

"Tell her to leave them with you."

"I am about to go to the copy room, sir. So, I won't be here."

"Wait for her." Marc turned back to Lisa and smiled. "Now, where were we?"

"Right here," Lisa said walking toward him and putting her arms around him.

As soon as it was getting good, there was a knock at the door and it opened. Lisa and Marc separated quickly enough in hopes of not being seen by the intruding Melody.

"Hello, Melody," Lisa said, walking toward the door.

"Hello," Melody said, with a sneer.

"Hello, Melody. Thanks for knocking," Marc said.

"I needed to give you these," she said, walking toward Marc.

Smirking, Lisa was heading out the door, until Marc said, "Hey, don't forget."

"I won't."

When Lisa walked out, Marc said, "Now, what can I do for you Melody?"

"First, Mr. Morgan wants you to look over this file for the Mike Webster account."

"Thanks."

"Second, maybe we can go out after work."

"Um, Melody that wouldn't be a good idea."

"Come on, Marc," Melody said, walking closer. "All work and no play can make for a very boring life."

"I happen to like my life," he said, as he stood up and walked behind his desk.

"What about a late dinner? I know I can be lot more fun than work."

"Like I said before, that would not be a good idea."

"It's not like you're seeing someone."

Marc didn't respond.

"So, the rumors are true."

"What rumors?"

"That you and Lisa are sleeping together."

If she saw the shock on his face, she didn't mention it. He was hoping she didn't see him and Lisa in an embrace when she barged in.

"That's really none of your business, now is it?"

"I think it is. I have to know who my competition is."

"Melody, there is no competition. Now, if you will excuse me, I have a lot of work to do."

"I'll come back when you're less busy," Melody said, smiling seductively as she turned and walked out of the office.

After she left, Marc sat back in his chair and shook his head in amazement at how pushy some women can be. He has always appreciated a good chase. Even though Melody was great to look at, Marc felt there was something missing. Melody had all the outside traits a man could possibly want. She was beautiful, great breast that she loved to show off, legs that went on for days, but she was still missing something. She wasn't like…Lisa.

Lisa had everything he wanted. She was beautiful, smart, after a couple dates she wouldn't turn stalker. She was okay with doing her own thing. She was never pushy, not when it counted anyway. He finally got what he always wanted, someone he could fall in love with. Making that revelation brought an idea to mind. He made a phone call.

"How'd it go?" Barbara asked when Melody walked out.

"It didn't," Melody said, while buttoning up the two buttons she had undone before going into Marc's office. "But, he did tell me that he would never go for someone like Lisa. So, those rumors everyone has been spreading around are lies. He wants me. He's just taking his time about it. You'll see," Melody said, and walked away.

***

"Hey, I was wondering when you would get back?" Carol said when Lisa walked in.

"Can I talk to you for a minute?" Lisa asked.

"Only if you tell me who sent you those flowers," Carol said following Lisa into her office.

"Girl, get over there and sit down."

"Okay, okay."

When Lisa sat down behind her desk, she took a deep breath and said, "Alright, where should I start?"

"How about from the beginning?"

"Well, I did sort of meet somebody."

"What does that mean? Either you did or you didn't."

"I did. But, I didn't meet him at the Keene party."

"Okay, where?"

Lisa proceeded to tell Carol everything. From her and Marc's first kiss in his office through to how she found out about the meeting that morning. Needless to say, Carol was speechless.

Lisa said, "And we have our first date tonight."

Finally Carol said, "The roses are from him?"

"Yes."

"I knew it! I knew you two had the hots for one another. Did you sleep together?"

"No!"

"You will. How long has it been for you? What…a year?"

"Try six," Lisa mumbled.

"Say what?"

132

"It's been six years."

"Girl, I'm surprised you haven't been attacking men on sight," Carol laughed.

"Shut up!" Lisa said, laughing.

They talked for another twenty minutes, and by one-thirty Carol was off to lunch and Lisa was trying to get some work done.

"Excuse me."

Hearing the deep male voice, Lisa almost jumped out of her chair, "Oh."

"Sorry, didn't mean to frighten you. There wasn't anyone at the desk. I'm looking for a Lisa Jenson."

"You've found her. What can I do for you, Mr. –?"

"These are for you." He walked out and came back in with the most beautiful maroon calla lilies. "I also have a message for you."

"Alright," Lisa said, still looking at the flowers.

All of a sudden the man began to sing. When Lisa heard what he was singing, she looked up and saw Marc standing in the doorway smiling.

"May I have this dance?"

Smiling from ear to ear, Lisa walked over to Marc and they danced while the man sang 'Mona Lisa.'

When Carol came back to have lunch with Lisa she heard the singing. She peeked into Lisa's office and saw a man singing and Lisa and Marc dancing. Closing the door softly, she smiled and thought how much they reminded her of her and Charles. Picking up the phone, Carol dialed his office number.

Ten minutes later, Carol hung up just as the singing florist was coming out of Lisa's office.

"Miss."

"Good bye," said Carol.

A couple of minutes later, Marc walked out. "Good afternoon, Carol."

"Afternoon, Mr. Cavell." Carol was doing everything she could not to jump up and hug him. "How are you today?"

"You know, Carol, I couldn't possibly be any better. How 'bout yourself?"

"Fine, I'm fine."

"Great."

After he left, Carol went into Lisa's office. When she walked in, Lisa was looking out her window. Carol also saw the new flowers. "Oh, Lisa, that was the most romantic thing I have ever seen."

Lisa continued to stare out the window without saying a word.

Coming to stand next to her, Carol said, "Lisa, are you alright? Oh, Lisa. What's wrong?" she asked, as she handed her a Kleenex when she noticed Lisa was crying.

"What if –?"

"Oh, no you don't. You are not going to "what if" yourself right out of this relationship before it even gets started. Mr. Cavell is a good guy. Don't make him pay for something some asshole did. Let me ask you something, do you believe in your heart that Mr. Cavell will treat you right?"

Without hesitation, Lisa said, "Yes."

"Will you allow him to treat any other way?"

"Hell, no."

"Then that's all you need."

"Thanks, Carol."

"No problem. That's what I'm here for."

Looking at her watch, Lisa said, "My day has flown by, it's almost three."

"But what a way to spend it."

"Why don't you go home spend some time with that husband of yours?"

"You don't have to tell me twice. How much longer are you gonna be here?"

"Probably another hour."

"Then I will see you tomorrow."

"Bye."

The next hour and a half passed by quickly and Lisa couldn't wait to get home and get ready for her date with Marc. As Lisa put on her suit jacket, her phone rang.

"This is Lisa."

"Hey, you," Marc said.

"Hey, yourself."

"What time are you leaving?"

"Actually, you caught me as I was getting ready to leave."

"Don't let me stop you. I'll see you at seven."

"I'll be ready."

After hanging up, Lisa couldn't get out of her office quick enough. But she couldn't shake the feeling that something would come along and try to ruin her happiness.

Chapter Thirteen

As usual Marc was on time. He was dressed in a dark blue suit looking good enough to eat. Lisa was dressed in a black spaghetti strapped dress with her hair in big curls hanging to the middle of her back. Tonight she decided to show a little more skin.

"Good evening, Mr. Cavell," Lisa said, when she opened the door.

"Good evening," he said, eyeing her from head to toe. "Ready?"

"Yes. Where are we going?"

"To a restaurant near my house. The Pier."

Taking a nice ride through town gave them each some time to get to know each other outside of work. To be honest, he knew Lisa a lot better than she thought he did.

Walking into the restaurant, the host greeted Marc as if they were old friends. They were shown to a booth by the window that overlooked the river. While they waited for their drinks, Lisa said, "Thanks to you I didn't get any work done today."

"I hope I didn't go overboard."

"Honestly, this was the most romantic day I have ever had. Thank you."

"You don't ever have to thank me for showing you how I feel." With that being said, Marc leaned over and kissed her.

"Excuse me," the waiter said, as he served their drinks. "Would you like to start with an appetizer or with the main course?"

"What would you like?" Marc asked Lisa.

Looking at the menu, Lisa finally said, "I'd like the Cajun shrimp in crab sauce."

"And I'll take the seared salmon and asparagus spears with hollandaise sauce."

They continued talking when the waiter left their table.

"Lisa?"

Lisa turned and saw Pat and her husband Lewis.

Pat walked over to the table and smiled at them and said, "I thought I was hallucinating at first. How are you?"

Hugging Pat and then Lewis, Lisa said, "I'm good. What are you guys doing here? I thought it would take divine intervention to get you out of the house, Pat."

"It did," Lewis joked.

"Hi, Marc. How are you?" Pat said.

"I'm great. How about you?" Marc said, gently shaking her hand.

"I'm good. Marc...This is my husband, Lewis. Lewis...Marc," Pat said. Marc and Lewis shook hands.

"So, is this a work thing?" Pat asked, as took a sit in the booth next to Lisa.

"Celebration, actually. Lisa has finally worn me down and got me to go on a date with her. I just couldn't allow her to keep begging me," Marc said.

"Yeah, right!" Lisa said and punched him in the arm.

"How do you think I got married?" Lewis joked.

"Uh, don't get yourself in trouble," Pat told her husband.

"I can already see you're a bad influence," Lisa told Marc.

"We're here to celebrate that this beautiful woman has agreed to marry me," Marc said, looking at Lisa.

It seemed as if the entire restaurant was on pause.

Lewis was the first to speak, "I see that this was also a surprise for Lisa. Marc, it was nice meeting you. Hope we can all get together soon. Honey, let's let these two continue their dinner, and later in the week you two can run up the phone bill talking about this."

Pulling Pat from the table, Lewis led her to their table.

Finally finding her voice, Lisa said, "You are insane. Do you know how long that conversation is going to be?"

Marc started laughing, and said, "But you should have seen your faces."

Lisa couldn't help but to laugh herself. "It's not funny, Marc. You have started something that crazy woman is not going to let go."

"Well, let's see," he said, looking past her.

When Lisa turned, she saw that Pat was headed back to their table and Lewis was sitting at another table shaking his head.

"Oh, God," Lisa mumbled.

"Lisa, come to the ladies room with me." Pat pulled Lisa from the booth without waiting for Lisa's answer.

Lisa looked back at Marc and mouthed, "I'm gon' get you."

The minute they made it to the restroom, Pat said, "First, he is even more gorgeous in the light. I didn't get to see him that well Friday night. Second, that marriage thing had better been a joke. And third, you are wearing the hell out of that dress."

"Pat, it's just a date."

"No, it isn't. You haven't been on a date in years. So, I know this is something more. Carol called me and told me everything."

"I knew she would. I was going to tell you and Nic this week."

"Girl, please! You know there is no way anyone of us can keep anything from each other."

"I know," Lisa laughed.

"How is it?" Pat said, getting serious.

"Scary. But, it's also natural. Like it's something that has always been happening or should have been happening."

"Like it was meant to be?"

"Look, don't start that fate stuff again."

"That's what it is."

"We're just taking things slow. So, yes, that marriage thing was a joke."

"Good."

"Now, can I get back to my dinner?"

"You may, but we will talk about this."

"I know."

When Lisa came back to the table, the waiter was serving their dinner.

Marc stood up as Lisa sat down, and said, "Did I get you in a lot of trouble?"

"Not as much trouble as you are. You can't joke like that with my family. They will start making plans and reserving a church."

"Lisa, when did you hear me say I was joking?"

Fork in mid-air, Lisa stared at him. "What?"

"Look, don't get nervous, I'm not proposing now. But, I hope when the time is right…"

"And how do you know that the time will ever be right?"

"I'm psychic."

"More like psycho."

For the rest of the dinner, they learned a little more about each other and surprisingly there were no more interruptions from Pat.

By nine, they finished eating and Marc paid the check, "So, Mona Lisa, what would you like to do next?"

"Surprise me."

On their way out, they stopped by Pat and Lewis' table to say goodnight.

Finally making it outside, Marc said, "Why don't we walk off some of this food on Beale Street?"

"I'm willing."

Marc drove to a parking garage close to Beale. As they walked, Marc took Lisa's hand in his as if it was the most natural thing in the world.

"I've been wondering something," Lisa said.

"What?"

"Why are you just now showing me how you feel? Why didn't you say something sooner?"

"Because you wouldn't have believed that I was serious. You would have thought that I was just after one thing."

"True. But, why now?"

Stopping in the middle of Beale, Marc looked at her, and said, "I didn't want my chance to pass me by."

Then, with people walking by, he kissed her.

Ending their kiss, Lisa said, "I'm glad you didn't."

"Now, what?"

"Pool?"

"Huh?"

"Do you play pool?"

"Yes, but that is not what I had in mind."

"I know. Come on."

Going into the pool hall, Marc paid for a table and they started a game. Lisa won the first one.

"Oh, it's like that?" Marc laughed.

"Hey, what can I say," Lisa gloated.

"I see who I'm dealing with. Rack 'em."

As the next game got under way, four men walked in talking and laughing loudly. When they spotted Lisa bending over the table, they started making crude statements about her body. She ignored them and kept playing even though they were getting louder.

When she noticed Marc wasn't paying much attention to the game, she said, "Ignore them. They're drunk."

Lisa walked around the other side of the table to take her shot, when she heard, "Hey man, ain't that yo' ol' girl?"

When Lisa looked up, she saw James with some of his friends by the bar. "Oh, great," Lisa said to herself.

Marc, having already recognized James, said, "Do you want to leave?"

"Yeah, I think that's a good idea."

Before they could head to the door, James was already standing in their way.

"What's up, Lisa?"

"Move James," she said.

"I need to talk to you...alone," James said, eyeing Marc.

"That's not gonna happen," Marc said.

"Was I talking to you?"

"Look, James you need to get out of our way. It's obvious you've been drinking. Go home and sleep it off." Lisa said, and walked pass James.

Grabbing her arm, James said, "I said I need to talk to you."

Marc suddenly grabbed James's hand and bent his arm behind his back, "Don't touch her."

He moved so quick that Lisa was shocked that he didn't break James's arm.

"Yo, man, let him go," one of James's friends said. Then the rest of them were heading toward Lisa and Marc. Standing beside a table, Lisa picked up a beer bottle. Marc reluctantly let James go.

"And what you gon' do, white boy? You can't handle me. Hell you probably can't handle Lisa."

"Don't let this suit fool you," Marc said, moving closer to James.

"Wait. No, don't." Lisa said, getting between Marc and James. "James, like I said before you need to move. Nobody here is afraid of you, as you can obviously see. And in case you don't remember, I have always loved a good bar fight. Now, gentlemen, if you don't want to see your boy get his ass whipped, I suggest you take him home...to his wife," Lisa said.

"This ain't over," James said.

"Anytime," Marc told him, as he and Lisa walked out of the bar. Outside, he said, "Are you okay?"

"Yeah," Lisa said, taking deep breaths to calm herself.

"Good, because I could never want you more than I do now."

Laughing, she said, "Than show me."

Nothing else was said, until they were back in the car.

Marc spoke first, "Are you sure you want to do this?"

Nervously, Lisa said, "Yes."

"I don't believe you."

"I'm just nervous."

As they drove, Lisa realized he was taking her home. Fifteen minutes later they were in Lisa's driveway.

"Your house was closer."

"I want you to be comfortable."

Walking into the house Lisa said, "Would you like to something to drink?"

"No, I'm fine."

"Then, how about some chocolate?" Lisa asked, as she went into the kitchen.

"You haven't opened them yet?" Marc asked when he saw Lisa take the box of chocolate covered strawberries out of the refrigerator.

"Nope. Follow me."

They went upstairs to Lisa's bedroom, with her showing him around on the way. When they made it to her bedroom, Lisa hesitated at the door, but she got her nerve up to walk in anyway. Getting out of her shoes, she stood in front of Marc.

"What kind of music do you have?" he asked.

"It's in the cabinet under the stereo."

Marc walked over and kneeled down to look in the cabinet, and then he said, "Perfect."

In the next minute, she heard Gerald Levert's voice come through the speakers.

"Stroke of Genius. Good choice," said Lisa.

"Thank you," Marc said, as he dimmed the lights and climbed into bed next to Lisa and wrapped his arms around her. They laid there listening to Gerald and feeding each other strawberries.

Chapter Fourteen

"Are you ready?" Marc asked.

At that moment, Lisa tensed up.

"No, that's not what I meant, Mona Lisa. I meant are ready to tell me everything?"

"Why do you call me that?"

"What, Mona Lisa? Well, I noticed every time I called you beautiful, you flinched. So, I had to come up with something else. And what's better than one of the most beautiful paintings in the world?"

"Is there anything that you don't miss?"

"Not about you. When it comes to you I notice everything. That's how I know that you never told me the whole story about you and James."

Lisa began talking without preamble, "I loved him more than anything in the world and I thought he felt the same. Hell, he was the one to say I love you first. When I met him I was overweight and didn't think to highly of myself."

"You were overweight?"

"By one hundred pounds. And for me to have a handsome man like him to find me attractive, I was on top of the world. Like I said before, at the beginning everything was fine," she said, and then biting another strawberry Marc held to her mouth.

After swallowing she went on, "In my opinion, everything went wrong when we slept together. Then it seemed like he changed. I noticed that when he would walk into the room, I would tense up. It was like he was always there. But I never said anything. Whatever he did or said I went along with. It was like he knew my weaknesses and used them against me."

"Bite," Marc said. "Now, go on."

"He even started to turn me against my mother and what's worst, I believed it. He would tell me she was saying mean things about me. And I believed that, like a fool."

Marc heard the croak in her voice and held her tighter.

"Go on," he told her.

Picking up another strawberry and feeding it to him, she said, "Then the hitting started. And, you know, during every fight we had he would always tell me, 'I been waiting to do this'. And it never dawned on me that this man hated me."

"That's a strong word."

"Well, it's true. But the sad thing about it is I didn't know why. After every argument or fight, he would apologize and I would forgive him. Everything I did was for him, everything."

Lisa didn't even know she was crying until Marc wiped a tear away. Lisa buried her face between his neck and shoulder.

"Let it out," he whispered.

"No, I'm not going to cry over him anymore; I did that for a year."

"Can you tell me something?"

"What?"

"Did you ever consider going back to him?"

"Yes. But, that was a short lived feeling."

"Are you completely over him?"

Lisa looked up at him and said, "It has been six years since I have seen or heard from him. It only took me two of those years to get myself together. I am completely over James Harris."

"Good."

After a long minute, Lisa said, "I can't have children."

"What?"

"That's what the last argument was about. I told him I was leaving him because I didn't want to raise a baby with him. I was pregnant. He said that that was exactly what he needed to change, but I didn't believe him. I remember I was about to leave when he grabbed me by my hair and told me since I didn't want to have a baby with him, I wasn't going to have one at all."

Feeling her tremble, Marc held her tighter and whispered, "It's okay, I'm here."

Looking into his eyes, she knew he would be, so she told him the truth.

"I lied about not remembering what happened. I just couldn't bring myself to tell you. I didn't know what you would think of me."

"There is nothing you could say that could make me change my mind about how I feel about you. Tell me."

"He dragged me by my hair to the floor and started to kick me in the stomach. I remember being kicked and punched everywhere. After a while he stopped. I recall looking at this clock and realizing that almost an hour had passed. Can you believe that someone had that much hate in them to be able to go that long? It's funny how you never forget the smallest detail. After a while, I heard him say, 'if you can hear me, you bleeding. I guess you ain't pregnant no mo'. And he laughed. I couldn't believe I had loved a man that could be so cruel. Figuring that he had finished, I got up and was headed toward the bathroom when all of a sudden he grabbed me again and this time I didn't think he would stop. It seemed worse this time. I actually remember praying that he would go ahead and kill me."

"Oh, baby," Marc whispered, then kissed her on the lips.

"Two weeks later, I woke up in the hospital, childless and with a lot of other injuries."

As Lisa cried, Marc felt protective of her. All the pain this beautiful woman had been through and she still made it. She didn't need his protection, but he would for damn sure make sure she would never have to go through something like that again.

"I've never told anybody that. I don't know why I told you. I guess that was a great story to tell on a first date, huh?"

"I'm glad you told me, this way you can move on…with me." Starring into her eyes, Marc kissed her.

Feeling her relax against him, he kissed her more passionately. Lisa started to unbutton his shirt.

Looking at her, he said, "You know we don't have to do anything."

"We're not."

"I know this is a personal question, but how long has it been for you. You don't have to answer."

Without hesitation, Lisa said, "Six years."

The shock showed on his face. "Six years? How –"

"How was I able to hold out that long? I haven't been out with a man in six years. I couldn't trust my judgment about men, so I just turned that part of my life off and concentrated on my career."

"So, why are you here with me?"

"You were a surprise. I didn't expect to…to feel the way that I do about you."

"I'm glad you do," he whispered and then kissed her.

As they kissed, the CD changer clicked and Anita Baker began to serenade them. Eventually, they feel asleep in each other's arms.

***

The next morning, Lisa's alarm clock went off as usual, but on this morning she didn't wake up alone. Turning over to look at Marc, she smiled at him.

"So, it's your turn to stare at me?" Marc said, with his eyes still closed.

"Do you ever sleep?"

"It was hard, but I finally fell asleep. I woke up few minutes before your alarm went off." Marc smiled as he opened his eyes.

Lisa threw her brown and cream duvet off her and was about to get up until Marc grabbed her around the waist. "Where are you going?"

Laughing, Lisa said, "Well, every morning before work I workout."

"You don't have to leave the bed to workout. My workout plan is far better for the body. It covers the back, shoulders, stomach, thighs, and uh other places with muscles," he said, kissing each part named.

Dazed for a moment by his kisses, Lisa finally said, "Okay, we better stop. If we start now we might not ever stop."

"I hope so," he said, pulling Lisa beneath him.

"I guess I can work out any morning," Lisa said, rolling Marc over so she could be on top. Kissing him, Lisa felt like she would not be able to contain herself for much longer. Looking down at him, she said, "You know, you are bad for my celibacy streak."

Smiling up at her, Marc said, "And you are good for me." Pulling her down toward him, he kissed her deeply. Eventually, they were interrupted again by Lisa's alarm clock.

"Ignore it," Marc whispered between kisses.

"We have to go to work," Lisa said, kissing his neck and then his chest.

"I think this work is more important."

Sliding off him, Lisa got out of bed. "Come on."

Watching Lisa's naked body as she walked over to the closet, Marc didn't hear a word she said.

Gathering his jumbled thoughts, he said, "I have to get my bag out of the car."

Five minutes later they were in her home gym. During the workout they talked about work, their expectations from a relationship, and could they handle the fact of having people at work know about them.

"Today is as good as any, Mona Lisa," he said, lifting the heaviest weights Lisa had.

Watching him, Lisa lost her train of thought.

"Mona Lisa, Mona Lisa," he sang to get her attention.

"Huh? Oh, sorry."

"What do you think?" he asked.

"Are you sure you want everyone to know about us so soon? It's new. What if –"

"No. No, what ifs," he said, putting down the weights and walking over to her while she was on the treadmill. "I know I want to be with you. I know I'm supposed to be with you. I also know you feel the same way, but not ready to admit it yet."

"Psychic thing, right?"

"Right. But I'll wait for you."

Smiling, Lisa said, "You won't have to wait that long."

Marc leaned over the treadmill and kissed her. "Today is the day we go into work together."

Lisa smiled and nodded.

They finished working out and then headed downstairs to eat breakfast.

When they made it to the kitchen, Lisa said, "What would you like to have?"

"Besides you, how about an omelet?"

"Alright, two omelets it is."

By seven-thirty, Lisa and Marc had finished eating breakfast and were heading back upstairs to get dressed for work.

"There is a bathroom in either of the bedrooms," Lisa said.

"Wouldn't it be quicker to shower together?" Marc asked, as he hugged her from behind.

"No, I think we would actually waste time. Now go and get ready," she said, laughing.

"Oh, alright."

An hour later, Lisa met Marc downstairs.

"You look beautiful, Mona Lisa."

"Thank you. You look as handsome as always."

"Ready?"

Taking a deep breath, Lisa said, "I'm ready for anything."

Kissing her hand they walked out of the house. In the car they talked about what was next for the Keene account and how much work they would have to invest in it. Twenty-five minutes later, Marc pulled into the parking garage.

"Good morning, Ms. Jenson...Mr. Cavell," the security guard said.

"Good morning, Shirley," Lisa said.

"Morning, Shirley," Marc said.

"You have car trouble this morning Ms. Jenson?"

"No."

"Oh, well have a good day."

As Marc drove into the garage to park, he said, "Nervous?"

Seeing how calm he was, made her relax. "No."

Getting out of the car and walking up to the door, he said, "To be on the safe side, I'll talk to Paul this morning. I don't want anyone to give him a bad idea about us."

"Okay."

"Did I tell you how good you look this morning?"

Smiling, Lisa said, "Just good?"

As they stood in front the elevator, he said, "To be honest, you look good enough for me to eat. You know, we could press the stop button when we get on the elevator."

"Mmm, I might take you up on that offer."

Seeing movement behind Marc, Lisa focused in and saw Melody heading their way.

"Good morning, Mr. Cavell...Ms. Jenson," Melody said, looking only at Marc.

"Morning," Marc said.

Lisa didn't say anything, after all, Melody wasn't interested in her.

"Mr. Cavell, I was wondering if you've gotten a chance to think about what I said."

Looking straight ahead, Lisa was hoping and praying the elevator would hurry up, because she was about two seconds away from snatching Melody's ass.

Then Marc said, "Melody, I believe we've already discussed that and I said no."

On the inside, Lisa was laughing her ass off.

Ding

Finally, Lisa thought to herself as she walked into the elevator first.

"Maybe if you mulled over the offer some more you might change your mind."

Nervously, Marc cut his eyes toward Lisa, and then said, "I doubt it."

Making it to the top floor, Melody walked off the elevator, swaying her hips in an exaggeration toward Mr. Morgan's office.

"She is something else," Lisa said, shaking her head.

"Would you like me to walk to your office?" Marc asked.

"You don't have to do that, Marc. Go and get some work done."

Lisa leaned in and kissed him and walked into the outer office area of her office. Leaving Marc to watch her walk away smiling to himself.

"Good morning, Carol."

"Morning, Lisa," Carol said, cheerfully.

"What do we have today?" Lisa asked, as she walked in her office.

The scent in her office was glorious when she walked in. Carol came in with her legal pad, while Lisa sat at her desk and booted up her computer.

"Alright, first you and Mr. Cavell have to get started on the Keene account and go over the Thompson account."

Lisa couldn't help but smile at the sound of Marc's name.

"And what are you smiling about?"

"Nothing," Lisa said, but she couldn't stop smiling.

"We'll talk about that in a minute. Next you have a ten o'clock with a Sara Blakely. She's a new client with a small company looking to expand. Basically, your day is pretty much tied up with the Keene and Thompson account. Now, how is it?"

"How is what?"

"Don't play dumb with me. You and Mr. Cavell. What have you decided?"

"To let whatever is happening between us happen."

"Have you slept with him?"

"No, and I'm about to bust. I have never met a man that evokes so much sexual attraction. I've almost caught a rape charge at least fifty times. Especially when we woke up this morning."

"You what?!"

"Calm down. Last night at dinner we ran into Pat and Lewis."

"I know she couldn't believe what she was seeing," Carol laughed.

"You got that right. She dragged me into the ladies room. Then after dinner, we went to play pool and ran into James and some of his friends. There was almost a bar fight."

"Who started the bar fight?"

"I said almost a bar fight."

"There must have been a bottle somewhere close," Carol mumbled.

"You know it. But we got out of there without a fight."

"What did Marc say?"

"He told James, 'don't let this suit fool you'. I thought I would die from laughing at the expression on James's face. After that we went to my house."

"How do you feel about him?"

"I feel like we've always been together. I really care about him. He is amazing, kind, romantic, and sexy as hell."

"Are you falling in love with this man, Lisa?"

"I think I am."

"Wedding bells," Carol sang.

"Hold up, slow down. You know you talking to a woman who gets hives when we get to talking about marriage."

"No, what I see is a woman who has found the man that she was made for and who was made for her. And I think he feels the same way about you, Mona Lisa."

"Funny."

"Alright. Let the work day begin."

"We're not going to hide our relationship," Lisa blurted out. "I mean we're not going to flaunt it, but we're not going to hide it."

Turning back to Lisa, Carol said, "That had to have been his idea. How do you feel about that?"

"I'm actually okay with it."

"Well, you know I am you guys biggest promoter and I will slap anybody who says something I don't like."

"Well, get your powder out. But let me do the honors of slapping Ms. Melody."

Laughing, Carol said, "Deal. You have five minutes before Mrs. Blakely arrives."

"Okay."

As Carol walked out, Lisa's phone rang.

"Lisa, here."

"Hey, has Carol told you about your work day?" Marc said.

"Yep. When is a good time for you?"

"How about one o'clock? I have a couple of meetings this morning."

"Perfect."

"See you later."

After hanging up, Carol buzzed in, "Ms. Jenson, Mrs. Blakely has arrived."

"Send here in."

Carol showed her in and Lisa said, "Hello Mrs. Blakely, come in and have a seat."

"Thank you, Ms. Jenson. And thank you again for seeing me on such short notice."

"Not a problem at all. Would you like some coffee?"

"Uh, no thank you."

"So, what can I do for you?"

"I just started my own business, which is a security company that deals with businesses and homes. And I'm looking to find different areas of investments that might work for the company."

"Okay, we'll start from the beginning by getting you financial information and I'll go over the information and we can see where to go from there. When can you have all your information?"

"I can have it by the end of the day and send them over."

"That will be fine. Let's see, how about we set up an appointment for next Wednesday at ten. Is that good for you?"

Looking into a day planner, Mrs. Blakely said, "That will be fine."

"So, tell me a little more about your company."

For the next thirty minutes, Mrs. Blakely told Lisa about her company. Then she said, "I really do thank you for seeing me so soon."

"You're welcome. See you next week," Lisa said, as she walked Mrs. Blakely to the outer office.

Going back to her desk, Lisa got back to work. She decided to look up some information on Blakely Security Systems.

"Working hard?"

Lisa looked up at the sound of Marc's voice.

"Not as much as I usually am. What are you doing here? I'm supposed to come to your office."

"I needed to talk to you."

"Is this good news or bad news?"

Marc walked over behind Lisa's desk and kneeled down in front of her.

"Marc, what are you doing?"

"What does it look like?"

"It looks like you've lost your mind. Now get up before Carol comes in and get her hopes up."

Marc started to laugh, "You should see the look on your face. Calm down, I just wanted you to know that I talked to Paul."

"And, what happened?"

"He said as long as we're not quitting, what we did was our business."

Smiling, Lisa leaned in and kissed Marc.

After parting, Marc said, "Now, do you feel comfortable with me?"

"I was never uncomfortable."

"Unh-huh."

"What did you tell him?"

"I told him that I had something to talk to him about," he said, as he stood up and leaned against Lisa's desk. "I said that it concerned me and you, and that I wanted to be the first tell him before he heard rumors. I told him that you and I are dating. He said as long as it doesn't interfere with work, what we do is our business. So, to celebrate, I'm cooking you dinner Friday night at my place."

"In that case, I'll bring dessert."

"Mmmm, what are you going to make?" he asked, as he leaned over her.

"I'm sure I'll think something," Lisa said, seductively.

"Then I know I'll like," he said, leaning in and kissing Lisa neck.

"Don't start something you can't finish."

"I'm a finish it."

Kissing, they were soon interrupted.

"What are you two doing?" Carol asked. "And with the door open, might I add. Anyone could walk in."

"Anyone did," Lisa laughed.

"How are you today, Mr. Cavell?"

"I'm doing great, Carol. Especially, since things have obviously changed for the better. Why don't you call me Marc?"

Being charmed, Carol smiled and said, "Okay, Marc. I'll give you two some privacy."

"No, Carol, I'm leaving. I have a meeting to get to. See you in an hour?"

"Of course."

After he left, Carol said, "What happened?"

"He talked to Paul so we wouldn't get crushed by the rumor mill."

"What did Mr. Morgan say?"

"Marc said that he was fine with it, as long as it doesn't interfere with work."

"That sounds fair. Lisa you look so happy, and it's only been what…four days? I'm so happy for you and Mr. – uh, Marc."

"I am happy, Carol. I just hope nothing – "

"What did I tell you? Don't think about the bad; just let this relationship take its course."

"I know, I know. I'm being negative and that is not what my life is about now."

"Enjoy yourself, Lisa. You deserve it."

"Thank you, Carol. Thank you for being my friend."

"Always, honey. Now, I have to get back to work. Need anything?"

"Yeah, some advice."

"I'm all ears."

"Well, from what I have already told you, you know how difficult it is for me to contain myself any longer."

"Yeah."

"Well, he is cooking dinner this weekend and I think I am going to finally end my six year draught."

"Hell, you grown! Who says you have to wait months before you sleep with somebody. Hell, I slept with Charles on our first date."

"You didn't!"

"Oh, girl, please. I knew he was the one. Let me ask you something. When you all went on lunch or business trips did you ever just talk business?"

"No."

"Y'all got to know each other on both levels. So, don't worry about time. You need to worry about if he can handle all that pent up sexual need."

"It's not that bad. I have barely thought about sex for the last six years."

"Trust me when you get down to it, a whole other person takes over. You need to buy some lingerie."

"You think?"

"Hell yeah!"

"Maybe."

"Definitely. Now, go freshen up for your meeting."

"Excuse me, am I disturbing you?"

The two ladies looked toward the door and found James standing just inside the door.

"You must have detected my happiness and decided to come and fuck it up," Lisa said with a fake smile and anger in her voice.

"Lisa, I came to apologize. I shouldn't have done that last night."

"You damn right! Look, James, I think you better leave before I show my true colors."

"Lisa should I call –" Carol started.

"Look, you don't have to call nobody," James snapped. "I just wanted to say that I'm truly sorry to you and your...friend."

"You are sorry and he is more than my friend."

Anger flashed in his eyes and then disappeared.

"Now will you leave or do I need to call security?"

After a moment, he walked out.

"Are you okay?" Carol asked, standing next to her.

Breathing hard, Lisa said, "I'm fine, just give me a few minutes."

"Okay."

Lisa stared out her window while she steadied her breathing. When she felt herself was calm, she headed to her meeting.

Chapter Fifteen

Making it home by six-thirty, Lisa checked her messages and her mail on the way to the kitchen. Half listening to Pat's ranting, Lisa stopped dead in her tracks. In her hand she was holding a letter from James. The letter didn't have a return address, but she remembered what his hand writing looked like.

"How the hell did he find out where I lived?"

Right then she remembered the car that was sitting across from her house the night her mother came over for dinner.

Hearing her mother's voice but not the words, Lisa opened the letter.

Lisa,

I hope you haven't torn this up before reading it. Considering you won't talk to me, I hope you could at least read this letter. Lisa, I know you're still hurt by what happened and you have every right to be. But you have to believe that I've changed. I know this might not mean much, but I've suffered too. I lost the one woman that I loved and will always love. You were the woman I was to supposed to marry. My heart forever belongs to you. Please, Lisa, give me a chance to really show you that I've changed. Call me at 316-2282 if you're willing to listen. You know he's not the one for you, I am.

James

"Yeah, like that's gonna happen," Lisa said, balling up the paper and putting it in the trash.

On her way upstairs to her bedroom, Lisa's phone rang, "Hello."

"I knew I would eventually catch you at home," Pat said.

"Yeah, I just walked in," Lisa said, as pulled off her shoes.

"You ready?"

"Yeah."

"Okay, you first. And start with Marc."

"We went out for drinks last week and we talked about everything but work. Our childhoods, parents, and friends. You get the idea. Anyway, we had to work late on Friday night for an upcoming meeting and he asked about James."

"What did he ask?"

"He saw him in my office that first time and wanted to know who he was, so I told him that he was just a pass mistake. Long story short, he kissed me. And I have to tell you Pat, that kiss was like nothing I have ever experienced."

"What did you do?"

"Ran out."

"What?!"

"I know, but I didn't know what else to do."

"That's why you two were acting so cozy at the club. We knew it was something between you two. Go on."

"That Saturday we had a business party to go to and we ran into one of his exes. Needless to say she treated me like I wasn't there and then had the nerve to think I was some secretary he was banging."

"No she didn't?"

"Yes, she did. But Marc straightened her out. Then, when she asked him about having lunch I jumped in and pretended that we were an item. She could have practically attacked me on the spot. While out on the dance floor, to make her even more jealous, we kissed again. Thank God the client didn't see that. Anyway, we spent Sunday together and I spent the night at his house. And no we didn't sleep together. But Lord knows I wanted to when I saw him walk out of that shower Monday morning. I guess you can say that we are seeing each other."

"From what he said, you two getting married."

"He was joking, Pat."

"How do you feel about him?"

"I really like him, Pat."

"Are you falling in love with this man?"

"I think I am."

"And you two haven't slept together?"

"No."

"Well, honey, I am truly happy for you. You deserve it."

"Carol said the same thing. Have you talked to Nic?"

"Nope, but I am calling her as soon as we get off this phone."

157

"Tell her to call me when she gets some free time. Now, it's your turn."

"Nothing is different, except me and Lewis are going to Montego Bay for our anniversary next month."

"That'll be so romantic. Can I go?"

"Have your husband take you."

"Ha ha."

"Work is good; it's just piling up on me. My assistant is leaving next week for good and I don't know what I'm going to do about a replacement."

"How about Stephanie?"

"Isn't she in school?"

"Yeah, at night though. She's looking for work to help pay for college and I know you pay well. You want me to call her?"

"Hell, yes! Call her, now!"

"Hold on."

Lisa clicked over to call her younger cousin.

"Hello."

"Hey, Stephanie."

"Hey, Le Le, what's up?"

"Hold on."

Lisa clicked back over. "Pat?"

"I'm here."

"Okay. Stephanie, you remember my best friend Patricia?"

"Yeah. Hey, how you doing?"

"Fine, sweetie. How are you?"

"Good."

"Well, Steph, Pat and I have called to offer you a job."

"Really? Who hiring?" Stephanie asked, excitedly.

"I am. Can you type?" asked Pat.

"Yes, ma'am. I type fifty-five wpm. I'm catching up to you Le Le."

"Yeah right," Lisa laughed.

Then Pat said, "Can you file, know Microsoft, and be on time?"

"Yes ma'am."

"A fast learner?"

"Definitely."

"Okay, I want you to be at my office at ten-thirty tomorrow morning. The address is 6005 Poplar Ave., fifteenth floor, Ste. 1503. You got it?"

"Yes, ma'am. Can I ask you something?"

"It pays fifteen dollars an hour."

"You're kidding?"

"Nope. You interested?"

"I'll be there at ten."

"Alright, but don't forget to dress for the office."

"Oh, you don't have to worry about that. Thank you so much! And thank you, Le Le."

"You're welcome, honey."

"See you tomorrow morning, Mrs. Cole."

"Alright, bye."

"Bye."

After Stephanie hung up, Pat said, "Thank you, girl that was a godsend."

"No problem. Now, finish your side."

"Actually, that's it."

"Then I can take my soak early."

"You're not seeing your man tonight?"

"No. We've been together since Saturday night, actually Friday night. So, we decided to take a night off."

"In that case, enjoy your soak."

"Love ya."

"Love ya."

Hanging up, Lisa went to run her bath water and was about to slide in when the phone rang. Answering the portable she had laying on the floor by the tub, she said, "Hello."

"You finally made it home?" her mother said.

"I've been here about an hour and a half. How you feeling today?"

"I'm fine, honey. Just sitting here watching TV."

"Where's Anthony?"

"At a friend's house."

"What you cook today?"

"Nothing, I just ate a sandwich today. How was work?"

"Tiring as usual."

"How's Marc?"

Smiling at the sound of his name, Lisa said, "He's fine."

"Look at you smiling. How was the rest of the weekend?"

"It was really nice. We talked a lot and got to know each other."

"Since you have been working together for the last three years, I know that was a short conversation."

"Not really. I told him about James."

"And what did he say?"

"That he was glad that I told him. Asked if I was over him, I told him yes. Right now, we are just taking things slow."

"Well, I'm glad you finally taking a chance somebody."

"Yeah, me too."

"I'm not gonna keep you, go ahead and get some rest."

"Okay. Oh, mama before I forget, Pat hired Stephanie to be her assistant."

"Really? That'll be so good for her."

"Yeah, she goes in tomorrow."

"I'm so happy for her. Well, I am gon' let you go. Call me tomorrow."

"Okay, bye."

"Bye."

Lisa soaked in the tub for the next hour and then went through her ritual of putting on lotion and brushing her teeth and hair. She went downstairs to fix dinner and decided to order Chinese food.

After hanging up, her phone rang. Looking at the caller ID, she smiled. "Hello."

"Hello, Mona Lisa. What are you doing?"

"Waiting for my takeout."

"What did you order?"

"Sweet and sour chicken and shrimp fried rice."

"Mmmm, sounds good."

"Have you eaten?"

"Yeah, I had an early dinner with a client."

"How'd it go?"

"Pretty well. It was just one of those 'you're still my number one client' dinners.

"Gotcha. So, what are you doing?"

"Sitting in the living room looking out at the view, thinking of you."

"What about me?"

"How I would love to pour some that sweet and sour sauce all over your
_"

Right then the doorbell rang."

"Saved by the bell," Lisa laughed. Lisa paid for her dinner and then locked the door.

"Back to what I was saying," Marc said. "I would love to pour that sweet and sour sauce all over you."

"I like the sound of that."

"You know it's hard for me to contain myself when I'm around you. Especially, when Robert delivered the flowers."

"And serenaded us, don't forget that."

"I haven't. To be perfectly honest, I wanted to make love to you right there."

"Why didn't you?"

"Trust me. I want let that moment pass again."

"I hope not."

"What are you wearing?" he asked.

"Nothing."

"Seriously?!"

"I just got out of the tub."

"Didn't you just open your door?"

"I have on a robe."

"Maybe I should make a delivery."

"Maybe you should."

"You gon' make me walk over there."

Laughing seductively, she said, "It'll be worth the hike."

They talked for the next couple hours. By ten, they were both hot and bothered, and they finally ended their conversation with promises of lunch tomorrow.

"I'll see you in the morning," Marc said.

"Alright, bye."

"Bye, Mona Lisa."

Going to bed that night Lisa didn't think she could wait another two days.

***

The next morning, Lisa did her usual routine and arrived at work at nine. She was dressed in a cream colored suit with a skirt that hugged her just right and was about mid-thigh in length.

Walking to the elevator, Lisa ran into Melody.

"Good morning, Ms. Jenson," Melody said, with her usual fake smile and enthusiasm.

"Good morning," Lisa said, cheerfully.

Melody didn't expect this reply. Usually, Lisa is never this nice to her. So, she said, "And why are we so happy today?"

"Oh, nothing. I guess I just love Wednesdays."

Just as Melody was about to say something, she spotted Marc heading their way from the coffee shop. Standing up straighter, Melody was ready for war. She was not about to let him turn her down this time. Definitely, not in front Lisa. She knew Lisa wanted Marc. All that acting like she doesn't need a man was bullshit. She also didn't believe the rumors that Mr. Cavell was interested in Lisa. Melody had seen the good looking man that has been coming to see Lisa lately. She and the other secretaries figured he must have been her boyfriend or even her husband. Maybe they were trying to work things out. That would leave Mr. Cavell in the clear. In the clear for Melody, that is.

"Good morning, Mr. Cavell," Melody said.

"Morning, Melody. Good –"

Melody chimed in again, "You're looking quite handsome this morning."

Melody figured she had to keep the conversation between him and her going so Lisa wouldn't jump in.

"So, Mr. Cavell, my friend is throwing a dinner party this Friday, would you like to go?"

Without hesitation, Marc said, "Melody, I'm dating someone and I don't think she would appreciate me going out with other women."

"I won't tell her if you won't."

"I tell you what, I'll ask her." Turning to Lisa, he said, "Lisa, would you – wait, first off, good morning, gorgeous." He then leaned over and kissed her. Continuing, he said, "Now, would you mind if I went to dinner with Melody?"

Loving the stunned look on Melody's face, Lisa said, "I'm sorry, but we have plans this weekend. And to be perfectly honest, I...don't...share."

Lisa made sure that last statement hit home by saying it directly to Melody.

The elevator arrived and Marc said, "Ladies first."

Both ladies walked into the elevator. Lisa was standing against the back wall with Marc and Melody was standing in the front of the elevator. Melody could hear Marc whispering and Lisa laughing softly. She was so mad she could have spit fire. The elevator couldn't have made it to the twelfth floor fast enough. Storming out of the elevator as soon as the doors opened, Melody almost knocked a co-worker down.

Walking off the elevator, Marc said, "I guess we put an end to that."

"Don't bet on it. If I'm right, and I usually am, this is just the beginning," Lisa said, watching Melody walk away.

"I don't believe we will have a problem out of her."

"There is no *we*. I won't have a problem. I already have another idea if this didn't get through to her."

"I don't even want to know," he chuckled.

Laughing, Lisa said, "Yes, we must protect the innocent."

When they made it to Lisa's office, they were both surprised by who was waiting for them.

"Mr. Keene, good morning. Did we have a meeting this morning?" Lisa asked.

"Good morning, Ms. Jenson and no. I actually came to talk to Mr. Cavell."

"Is there a problem, sir?" Marc asked.

"I figured we could go over some business," Mr. Keene said.

"Since we're all here, we can just go in," Marc said.

"I was hoping we could go to your office, Mr. Cavell," said Keene.

"Mr. Keene, we have already discussed this, Ms. Jenson and I are a team."

"Marc, its fine. I have quite a bit of work to do, so you handle this without me," Lisa said.

Staring at Lisa, Marc said, "Okay. Um, Mr. Keene, why don't we go to my office?"

Looking back at Lisa, Marc winked and led Mr. Keene away.

Walking into her own office, Lisa was mad as hell. Pacing in her office, she was so worked up she didn't hear Mr. Morgan come in.

"Paul, I didn't see you there."

"I can see that. Are you alright?"

"Yeah, trying to get some ideas for the Keene account."

"Can I interrupt you for a moment?" he asked, walking all the way into the office.

"Sure, what's on your mind?" Lisa asked, even though she already knew what it was.

"I'm sure you know Marc came to see me and told me about you two."

"Yes, he told me."

"Now, I'm here to talk to you. I'm not gonna repeat what he told me, but I wanna know where you stand."

Caught off guard for the second time this morning, Lisa didn't know what to say at first. And then decided to be honest about what was going on.

"Paul, as you already know we are seeing each other. This will not interfere with our working relationship. I firmly believe that my personal business remains outside of the office. There will not be a problem for the company or our clients."

"Glad to hear it, but that's not what I was talking about. Lisa, I have watched you from the time you started working for us up 'til now. I just wanted to let you know that I'm happy for you two."

Surprised, Lisa said, "Thank you, Paul."

"Now, back to business. What are you doing here and not in Marc's office with him and Mr. Keene?"

"Paul, that man is safer with Marc."

Laughing, Paul said, "He's getting under your skin, huh?"

"More, he has my blood boiling."

"Good, now get in there and show him why you earn the big bucks. You and Marc are the best for this account. Don't let Keene being an ass change that. Alright?"

"You're right."

Walking out the door, Paul said, "Keep me posted."

Smiling, Lisa walked out of her office and headed to Marc's office.

"Hey, Barbara. Is Marc still in his meeting?"

"Yes he is."

"Good. Tell him I'm here, please."

Hesitating for a minute, Barbara pushed the buzzer.

"Yes, Barbara."

"Sorry to interrupt, Mr. Cavell, but Ms. Jenson is here."

"I'm coming out."

A second later, Marc walked out of his office, closing the door behind him. Taking Lisa by the hand, he said, "Are you sure? Because this guy is much worse than we thought."

"Yeah, I'm sure."

"Then let's go."

Walking into the office, Marc said, "Sorry about that, but Lisa was able to join us after all."

Sitting in the empty seat in front of Marc's desk, Lisa nodded a hello to Mr. Keene.

"To bring you up to speed, we have been discussing some options that might work for Mr. Keene," Marc said to Lisa as he rounded his desk.

"I have a few ideas, if you don't mind me cutting in."

"We're all ears," Marc smiled.

For the next twenty minutes, Lisa laid out perfect plan after perfect plan.

At the end of her spiel, Mr. Keene said, "I think those were pretty good. How soon can you get started on them?"

"As soon as possible," Lisa said.

"How do plan to go about this?" Keene asked Lisa.

Lisa knew he was an ass from the word go, but she kept her temper in check and explained how they could bring each of her ideas to life.

After thirty minutes, the meeting finally wrapped up with handshakes and goodbyes.

"So, how did I do?" Lisa said when they were finally alone.

Walking toward her, Marc said, "I thought you were brilliant, you really showed him. I think he's finally seeing we work well together."

"Just work?"

"Among other things," he said and kissed her.

Breaking their kiss, Lisa said, "Paul came to see me, before I came here."

"And?"

"He wanted to know how I felt about you. So I told him."

Holding her, he said, "What did you tell him?"

"I told him it was purely sexual and that he has nothing to worry about."

Laughing, he said, "We need to get started then."

Taking the hint, Lisa kissed him.

"Excuse me, Mr. Cavell," Barbara said, over the intercom.

"God, every time. Yes, Barbara," he said, pressing the button.

"Your ten-thirty is here."

"Thank you." Turning to Lisa, he said, "I forgot about the meeting. Can we meet back here for lunch about one o'clock?"

"I'll be here."

Kissing each other, Lisa left his office, and headed back to hers.

"Good morning, come lately," Lisa said to Carol.

"Good morning. And sorry about that. I kind of got caught up," Carol blushed.

"Being bad early in the morning. Have you had coffee yet?"

"Nope."

"Come on."

On the way down in the elevator, Lisa told Carol about the morning activities as Carol laughed.

As they were walking into the coffee shop, they passed Melody and another woman that Lisa didn't recognize.

"Good morning, Melody…Stacey," Carol said.

"Good morning, Carol," the ladies said, then continued on their way.

"I'm glad looks can't kill," Carol said to Lisa.

"Please, she is not even on my worry list."

"What is on your worry list?"

"You know, the usual things."

"Is James also one of the usual things?"

"No."

"Liar."

"Okay, a little."

"Has he tried to contact you? Never mind, he wouldn't know how to."

Lisa didn't say anything as they stood in line in the coffee shop.

Then Carol said, "Something you not telling me?"

"You got to promise not to tell Pat or Nic. Not yet anyway. I don't know what to do about it yet."

"About what? And I don't promise anything until I hear it. So tell me."

"Good morning. What can I get for you?" the cashier asked.

"The usual," Lisa said.

"I'll also have a cappuccino, but instead of her usual, make mine mocha."

"Okay, two cappuccinos, one French vanilla and one mocha. That comes to $4.34."

"I got this one. Consider this payment for your silence," Lisa laughed.

"Only a trip into your closet will pay for that."

When they got their coffees, they headed back to the elevators.

"Okay, give it up. What's going on?"

"I got a letter in the mail from James yesterday."

"How does he know where you live?"

"I don't know. The only thing that comes to mind is that he followed me from work. The reason I say that is because the envelope didn't have a stamp on it. Now, unless the rules of mailing letters have changed, he put the envelope in my mailbox."

"What are you gonna do?" Carol said, lowering her voice, as they got on the elevator with three others.

"I have no idea," Lisa said, trying to sound stronger than she felt.

"You have to tell Nic."

"I can't do that. If she knew she would have twelve cop cars surrounding my house twenty-four/seven."

"That's what you need."

"I don't know yet. I have to think about it. I can't close down my life for this idiot."

"You are not closing down your life, you're just taking precautions."

"Yeah, I know. I have to think about it," Lisa said, walking into her office.

Sitting at her desk to finally get started on her work day, Lisa still couldn't shake this feeling of fear she had in the pit of her stomach.

***

At twelve-thirty, Carol stuck her head in Lisa's office, "I'm going to lunch. Can I bring you anything?"

"No thanks. Enjoy."

"Okay."

Getting back to work, Carol's phone rung and Lisa answered it from her own extension.

"Lisa Jenson."

"Hello, Mrs. Jenson," James said.

Lisa hung up.

"Knock, knock."

Looking up, Lisa plastered a smile on her face when she saw it was Marc.

"Hey, you," she said.

"Hey, yourself," he said, walking into her office.

"Is it one already?"

"A little after. You are late. Are you ready to eat?"

"Yeah, but Carol isn't back from her lunch yet."

"Yes, I am," Carol said, walking in. "It was too crowded to eat at the deli. Hello, Mr. Cavell."

"A –"

"Sorry, Marc."

"Better."

"Carol I'll be back in an hour. You know where to find me, if you need me."

"Alright."

Marc and Lisa headed to his office.

Reaching his office, Marc told Barbara that he didn't want to be interrupted, unless it was important. When Lisa walked in to his office, she was surprised to see that he'd already ordered lunch.

168

"I hope you don't mind me ordering for you. I ordered the lunch special from TGIF, is that alright?"

"Of course."

"Good, come on and sit down."

As they sat down on his couch and got comfortable, Marc handed her bottled water.

"We have a lot to choose from," he said. "We have deli sandwiches, quesadillas, and two choices of dessert. One is strawberry cheesecake or chocolate cake."

"Now, who is going to eat all of this?"

"I guess I did kind of go overboard, huh? But I didn't know what you would like."

"I'll take the quesadillas."

As they ate, they discussed different accounts, some they worked on together and some they didn't.

"So, you really think Mr. Keene liked my ideas or is he just patting me on the head?"

"I think he really likes them. All the ideas are great, as usual. He can't deny something that will make him money."

"What were the ideas you were pitching? I mean, before I came in stepped on your toes."

"Honestly?"

"Yeah."

"I didn't have any. He caught me off guard. So, in actuality, you saved me today."

"Glad I could help," Lisa said, while picking at her food.

"Hey, don't let him get to you. You have knocked bigger jerks than this guy down."

Smiling, Lisa said, "Great motivation speech."

"The best," he said, giving her a kiss. "Now, eat."

"How was your meeting?"

"Too long. But it went well. He is extremely meticulous, which just means he's an ass."

Laughing, Lisa said, "Sounds like you have a male version of Mrs. Hearn. Oh, sorry, I mean, Mrs. Winfield."

"Of my very own," he said, laughing. "Are we still on for Friday?"

"Yes."

"Dinner is at eight, so I'll pick you –"

"You don't have to that. I can drive over, after all you are cooking."

"No deal."

"Well, at least let me bring something. What can I bring?"

"Nothing but your sexy self. And maybe a bag for the weekend."

"I don't know about that."

"Well, you could spend the rest of the weekend naked. I wouldn't mind that at all."

"I bet you wouldn't. I'll pack a bag."

"You just won't let me have any fun."

"Oh, we'll have some fun."

"I like the sound of that."

Just as they were about to kiss, there was knock at the door.

"Damn, is there a camera in here?" Marc said, sounding frustrated.

Laughing, Lisa said, "Tell them to come in."

"Do I have to? We still have forty minutes left on our lunch."

"Yes, you do. Now, answer the door."

"Come in," he said.

"Hey, man. What's up? Oh, my bad, I didn't know you were having a meeting. I didn't see Barbara at her desk so I knocked," Steve said.

"That's cool, man. What can I do for you?"

"I need a little help with this Kimball account. I am stumped."

"Okay, but can you give me 'til two? This might run over a little while."

"Okay. How are you today, Lisa?"

"I'm fine, how about yourself?"

"I'm better now that I see you."

"That's nice," Lisa said.

"Maybe tomorrow you and I could have lunch, Lisa."

"I don't think that would be a good idea, Steve."

"Marc can handle things without you for an hour...or two," Steve said, with a sly grin.

"Say what? I –"

Before Lisa good her words out, Marc said, "Look um, give me half an hour."

"Okay," Steve said, leaving. But before closing the door, he winked at Lisa.

When he closed the door, Lisa said, "You need to talk to your friend before I do."

"I will, don't worry. Now, let's get back to where we were."

"You mean...?"

During their kiss, Lisa only had one thing on her mind. How was she gonna be able to control herself until Friday?

Before it got too heated, Lisa backed away.

"No, no don't do that. You are driving me crazy. Do you have any idea how much I want you right now?"

"Trust me I do. That is why I am leaving. I have a job to think about, I can't be in jail on rape charges."

Laughing, Marc said, "I won't tell, I promise."

Getting up to leave, Lisa straightened out her skirt.

"I guess you're right. I mean I'd hate for Barbara to walk in and catch us up against the window," he said, as walked toward Lisa.

With each step he took, she could have sworn her body temperature went up. She was not gonna make it 'til Friday.

Continuing, he said, "Or on my desk, on my couch, or –"

"In your desk chair," Lisa whispered, before they kissed. This time she didn't pull away.

"Lisa?" he whispered, against her lips.

"Yes, Marc."

"Wanna leave?"

Looking up at him, she wanted to say yes with every fiber in her being.

"What about Steve?"

"Who?"

Smiling, Lisa said, "Steve. You're supposed to help him with something."

"Right now I need you to help me something."

"Look, we're not teenagers. We can contain ourselves for a couple of days."

"I don't know about that," he said, as he pinned Lisa against his desk.

"Okay, I know I better go. I just got a flash of you and me on your desk. Whew, I got to go."

"I'll just jump out the window."

"Over dramatizing. I'll see you later." Lisa kissed him and headed out the door.

When she made it to Carol's outer office, Carol was coming out of Lisa's office.

"How was lunch?" Carol said, with a smirk.

"Yummy."

"Good because we have work to do."

"What?"

"Well, the Thompson account has had some changes. It seems he wants us to handle his new company's account. Mr. Peterson called about fifteen minutes ago with the news, and needless to say, he was happier than I have ever heard him."

"It must be big if he sounded happy. How many boxes?" Lisa asked, as she walked into her office.

There were three big boxes on the floor in front of her desk.

Carol walked in behind her and said, "Working late?"

"Yep," Lisa said, sounding miserable.

"I'll call Charles."

"Thank you, Carol."

"No problem."

Shaking her head, Lisa walked over to the first box, took the lid off and took a stack of manila folders out and put them on her desk.

She was about to take out another stack when she heard Carol say, "Sir, sir you can't go in there!"

Walking back to the doorway, Lisa was met by James. She automatically noticed how angry he looked. That was a look you don't forget. Ever.

"Lisa, should I call someone?" Carol asked.

"No, Carol. I'll take care of this."

Besides, Lisa knew who that someone was. And she didn't want him involved. She could handle this.

Looking back at James, Carol said, "Alright, but I will be right out here."

"You didn't have to hang up on me," James finally said, when they were alone.

"Are you crazy?" Lisa asked.

"What?"

Walking closer, Lisa enunciated each word, "Are...you...crazy? Because when someone keeps telling you to stay away, a sane person would do just that. Now, since you didn't understand the first couple of times, let me put it this way, I will have your ass locked up so fast they won't have time to put up the welcome home banner. Is that a little clearer to you?"

"I need to talk to you."

"You want talk to me, but you don't seem to understand that I don't want to talk to you. Now, get the hell out of my office."

"I'm not leaving," James said, standing his ground. "I love you and I know you still love me. In spite of everything we've been through I know you still love me."

Right then Lisa knew he wasn't quite the same anymore. He hadn't heard a word she said. Even though she was a little frightened, she knew she couldn't show it.

"I'm not giving up on you. We can make this work."

"I don't think the lady feels the same way," Marc said, as he stood in the doorway.

Seeing him standing there, Lisa wasn't surprised, but relieved. James was just shocked.

"Marc, everything is okay," Lisa said.

"I don't think it is Lisa. Mr. Harris, I think it's time for you to leave," Marc said, as he walked into the office.

To surprise Lisa even more, Steve followed Marc into the office.

"What, you bring your back up because you can't handle me man to man?" James said.

"He's here to make sure I don't kill you," Marc said, standing face to face with James. "I know all about you. Lisa told me everything. Now, I'm going to tell you something...Stay away from her, because if you don't the only way they'll find you is by boat." Smiling and dropping his voice down to a whisper, he said, "I'm Italian, I can make it happen."

As Marc walked past James toward Lisa, James, not meaning to step out of Marc's way, stepped aside.

Watching Marc talk to Lisa quietly, James walked out.

No one talked for about a minute, then Lisa said, "How did –"

"Carol called my office. Barbara told her where I was. Are you alright?"

"I'm fine and thanks. You didn't have to do that."

"Yes, I did. That's what I'm here for," he said, as he took her into his arms.

"And thank you, too, Steve," Lisa said.

"No problem," Steve said, smiling.

Marc then kissed her on the forehead and held her a little tighter. She tensed up a little when she thought about Steve standing there watching them.

"He told me," Steve said.

"He's okay with it," Marc said.

"I'm gonna leave you two alone. Oh, and Lisa if he messes up once, I'll be here."

"That'll never happen," Marc said, laughing.

After leaving the office, Steve remembered he had to tell Marc something. When he got back to Lisa's office, he saw them still standing in the same spot, holding each other. He decided to leave them alone and to also take Lisa off his list.

Chapter Sixteen

"Well, it looks like we made some kind of dent in this mess," Carol said, surveying the piles of folders and paperwork.

"Yeah, so let's close shop and start back tomorrow," Lisa said, stretching.

"I'm already out the door. Since it's only seven, I can spend the rest of the night with my husband."

"Tell Charles I'm sorry for keeping you late at work."

"He'll forgive you, if you bring Marc over to meet the extended family."

"Sure, what day? And is Charles cooking?"

"Of course, that's why I'm making it next week. It's his week to cook. How about Thursday? Ask Marc if he can make it and let us know."

"Ask Marc what?" he said, as he walked into the office.

"Carol invited us over for dinner next week," Lisa said.

"Can you do it?" Carol asked.

"As long as this beautiful lady and good food are involved, I'm there."

"Good, I'll tell Charles, and then let you know the details. I will see you two in the morning," Carol said, as she put on her shoes.

"Wait, we're all walking out together," Lisa said, gathering the rest of her things and locking up the office.

They all walked to the elevator talking about the work week. When they made it to the garage, Lisa and Marc walked Carol to her car. Watching her drive away, they walked hand-in-hand to their cars that were parked next to each other.

"I came out and moved my car earlier," Marc said.

"I figured as much. But you know you didn't have to go through all of this trouble," she said, as she leaned against the trunk of her car.

"We discussed this earlier, case closed. And I am also following you home."

"You –"

"Case closed," he said, cutting her off.

"I was going to say, only if you promise to stay."

"For how long?" he said, moving in closer and kissing her.

175

They were so engrossed in their kiss, that they never saw the car pull up.

"Hey!"

Marc turned around quickly, blocking Lisa. Only to see Shirley the security guard.

"Do I need to turn the hose on you two? I felt like I was watching the first scenes of a porno," Shirley said, leaning out the window of the security car.

Laughing, Marc said, "Sorry about that, we tend to get carried away."

"Yeah, I saw. But you making us lonely people real jealous," Shirley said, laughing and pulling away.

"Okay, back to you. How about we stop at the nearest burger place and go all out?" Marc asked Lisa.

"I like the sound of that. I can deal with little pig out."

"What's your favorite burger joint?"

"Dixie Queen. They have these huge juicy burgers and the best shakes I have ever had."

Marc started laughing and said, "Sorry, it's just that –"

Laughing too, Lisa said, "You nasty, you know that?"

"I hope to get to show you soon...real soon."

"I like the sound of that, too. Now, let's go before we give Shirley scene two."

"We stop for food first, and then your house."

"And milkshakes. Don't forget the milkshakes."

"Of course."

Forty minutes later Lisa and Marc walked through her front door.

"Where do I set up?" he asked.

"Depends. Do you want music or television?" Lisa said, as she went through her mail.

"Television," he said.

"Then follow me."

Walking into her bedroom, she said, "Is there anything you specifically like to watch?"

"Besides you?"

"Yes," she said with a smile.

"What do you have?"

"Let's see," Lisa said opening her cabinet. "Do you want comedy, suspense, or action?"

"Action."

"How about *Law Abiding Citizen*?"

"I haven't seen that yet."

"Then *Law Abiding Citizen* it is," Lisa said, as she put the movie in the DVD player.

Getting comfortable on the bed, they started the movie.

For the next couple of hours, they ate and yelled at the people on the TV screen. By the end of the movie they had eaten everything in sight.

"That was good," Marc said, leaning against the headboard.

"Yeah, I haven't eaten like that in a long time. Do you wanna watch another movie?"

"No, I actually want to talk to you about something."

"Uh oh, what?"

"It's not like that. I just wanna know where I stand with you. The reason I'm bringing it up because James seems adamant about you two getting back together."

Turning to look at him, Lisa said, "First, what James thinks is none of my concern. He and I getting back together will never happen. Second, I have enjoyed every moment we've spent together. Even the ones when we were just friends. It's you and no one else. Just you."

"Really?" Marc smiled.

"Really," Lisa said and kissed him.

She could feel him run his fingers through her hair and against her cheek. His tongue caressing hers in a kiss that Lisa hoped would last forever. As he kissed her neck, he whispered that he would stop when she told him to. The only response he got was the low moans of pleasure.

He started unbuttoning her blouse and she followed suit with his shirt and tie.

Marc looked into her eyes, "Are you sure?" he asked.

"Yes," she whispered.

"Positive?"

Lisa kissed him and took off his shirt and tie.

Marc undid her bra and took her left breast into his mouth. Lisa arched her back in greeting to this wonderful feeling. He then moved to her right breast. Lisa couldn't remember ever feeling this good. He then moved down to kiss her stomach as he unzipped her skirt and slipped it off her hips.

Finally catching her breath, Lisa said, "Do you have protection?"

"Yeah," he said, reaching for his wallet. When he looked through it he realized he didn't have one. "Damn!"

"What's wrong?" Lisa grumbled.

"I guess I was wrong. But, I can run to the store. I wouldn't even need my car."

Laughing, Lisa said, "No, I don't want you to leave."

Staring at her, he said, "I'll be right back."

Pretending to pout, Lisa stuck out her bottom lip.

"Okay, okay. We'll wait. I can continue to take cold showers. I'm saving a bundle on hot water."

"I know what you mean."

"I can do this. It's no big deal. I can do this," he kept repeating.

"Can you really?"

"Can you?"

Looking at each other they both said, "No."

Then the doorbell rang.

"Who is that?" Lisa said, looking at the clock.

"I'll go see," Marc said, grabbing his shirt and heading downstairs.

Lisa went to her closet and put on her bathrobe. As she headed downstairs she could have sworn she heard Nic's voice.

"Nic, what are you doing here?"

"I was looking for you, of course. But something better answered the door," Nic said, looking at Marc with his shirt half opened. "Anyway, I wanted to tell you about my day."

"I'll leave you two alone," Marc said, walking toward the stairs.

"You won't get out of it that easy. This concerns you too," Nic told him.

Stopping in his tracks and looking at her, he was about to ask Nic what she was talking about but Lisa beat him to it.

"Mr. Cavell did you threaten to kill a James Harris this afternoon?" Nic asked, shocking both Lisa and Marc.

"What?!" they both said.

"I'll take that as a yes. Now, Mr. Cavell, a James Harris came into my precinct today to press charges against you."

"Are you kidding me?" Marc asked, getting angrier by the second.

"Afraid not," Nic said, opening the bottled water she had got out of Lisa's refrigerator. "He walked into the station and stopped me on my way out. Do you know the fool didn't even recognize me? I just stood there and looked at him. Anyway, he started telling me that his life was being threatened by a Mr. Marc Campbell, and the man works at Morgan & Peterson. When he said the name of the company I realized who he was talking about and that he had been back up to your office. Lisa, how long has he been coming to your job?"

Sighing, Lisa said, "Almost a month."

Nic didn't say a word. She stared at Lisa.

"So, what happens now?" Lisa asked, looking a little worried.

Realizing how upset she was, Marc walked over to the couch where she was sitting and sat beside her and held her hand. Nic made a mental note.

"I had him fill out a form for these charges and gave him my card."

"Wha –"

"Wait," Nic said, holding up her hand to fend off their questions.

"Somehow the form was put in the shredder and the card has my old number on it."

Smiling, Lisa got up and hugged her friend, "You are something else you know that?"

"I am a stinker, ain't it?"

"What if he wants to check on the case?" Marc asked.

"He won't. And besides the mere thought of the cops talking to you gave him great happiness. Don't worry. If he does, I'll handle it. But, I have to know something."

"What?" Marc asked.

"Did you tell him you were in the Mafia?"

"Not in so many words," Marc smiled.

"If you can make his ass disappear, I'll give you an award myself," Nic said. "Now, on to other things. Mr. Cavell, how do you feel about my girl?"

While asking the question, Nic had stood up and put her hand on her gun. The gesture did not go unnoticed and Marc smiled.

"I care deeply for Lisa. I know you may not believe me, but I will prove it to you."

"Don't prove it to me, prove it to her."

"Oh, I will," he said, looking at Lisa.

By the look on Lisa's face, Nic could tell he was succeeding.

"I just want you to remember something, Mr. Cavell. If you hurt her, I'll shoot you. Be sure of that."

"Understood."

"And now you can call me Nic."

"And I am Marc."

"Alright. Now, I'm going to leave, since I have obviously interrupted your evening," Nic said, eyeing their attire.

"Pat called you?" Lisa asked, as she followed Nic to the door.

"You know she did. We'll talk some more tomorrow. Good night, kids," Nic said, as she walked to her truck.

Watching Nic drive away, Marc said, "Your friends are something."

"Yeah, they're great. And you know what, so are you."

"I am?"

"Yes. Will –"

"Shh, you don't even have to ask. I'll stay."

The rest of the night was filled with soft caresses and kisses until they couldn't contain themselves anymore and had to stop before things went too far. As she fell asleep, Lisa couldn't shake that constant feeling that something was going to come along and ruin this.

Chapter Seventeen

Waking up and hitting the buzzer to her alarm clock, Lisa turned over to wake Marc, but he wasn't there. Getting up to put on her robe, Lisa went to the bathroom to wash her face and brush her teeth. Leaving the bathroom, she went into her home gym expecting to see Marc working out, but he wasn't there.

Heading downstairs, she was hit by wonderful smells that came from the kitchen.

Walking in, she said, "Good morning."

"Good morning, Mona Lisa. Ready for breakfast?" Marc said, turning from the stove.

"It's five-thirty in the morning, how long have you been up?"

"About half an hour. I wanted to cook for you."

Lisa was surprised by all the food on the island. There were blueberry waffles, sausage links, croissants, and the best smelling coffee she had ever smelled.

"You sure you only been awake for half an hour?"

"Yes, now go sit down and I'll set you up."

"Yes, sir. Everything looks so good."

"Including the guest of honor," he said, as he kissed her.

Five minutes later, they were eating and talking about the day ahead.

"Do you have a busy day?" Marc asked.

"Yeah, Carol and I are getting the Thompson account together. What about you?"

"Absolutely, the Aaron Burks account has turned to sh –, you know what I mean."

"It'll work out. You're Superman when it comes to this stuff. That's actually the first thing that I noticed about you."

"The first thing?"

"Well, the second thing."

"You're no slacker yourself. You are one of the smartest women I have ever met. Most of the women I've dated were either selfish or had no plans for the future. Before you, I dated women that were spoiled and into themselves. You were different. When I first met you I could tell you had plenty of drive."

"Sounds like you really know me."

"I think I do."

"As for the women you dated, maybe those were the kind of women you were looking for."

Marc's left eyebrow shot up.

"Wait, let me finish. One thing I know about men is that every woman they have dated or will ever date, they chose for a reason. All those women you chose, you chose for a reason. As you got older you wanted more, but you never changed your type of women. That's all."

"Well, thank you, Dr. Phil."

"Ha ha. Are you working out with me?"

"Of course."

They cleaned up the kitchen and went upstairs to get dressed for their workout. For the next hour they worked out, and by eight-forty-five they were dressed for work.

Lisa was dressed in black wide leg slacks and a white blouse that showed off just enough cleavage.

"Hello, angel. Your chariot awaits."

"Well, thank you, kind sir. You really know how to make a girl feel special."

"You are. To me," he said, and then kissed her.

Heading out the door, Lisa set the alarm and locked the door.

"Are we making good time?" Lisa asked.

"Yep," he said.

Listening to the morning radio show hosted by Steve Harvey, they laughed and commented on the topics.

By five minutes after nine, they were parking in the company garage. Walking to the elevator, Marc asked, "Are we having lunch today?"

"I think I will be working through lunch today with that Thompson account."

"Well, I can probably catch something with Steve. I'm sure he's feeling a little neglected."

"I'm sure he is."

After getting off on the top floor, they split up after wishing each other a good day.

"Good morning, Carol."

"Good morning, Lisa. How was the rest of your night?"

"Not how I planned, that's for sure. But all in all, it was nice."

"I'm right behind you. Tell me what happened."

"You won't believe this…" Lisa proceeded to tell Carol all about last night.

After getting over the initial shock, Carol said, "I can't believe he did that. What are you going to do?"

"I don't know." Turning on her computer, Lisa then said, "My first instinct was to tell Nic to get me a restraining order and have it sent to his house, but I don't know where he lives."

"Nic found him the first time, she can find him again."

Laughing, Lisa said, "I know that's right."

"Lisa, you can't let him take over your life again. You're stronger than that."

Smiling at her friend, Lisa said, "Yeah, I know."

"Ready to get started?"

"Yep. We got a long day ahead of us."

"I already have my beginning pile on my desk. Call me if you need me," Carol said, as she walked out to her desk.

Instead of dwelling on James, or better yet wasting her time on thinking about him, she began her work day. She realized that as the day passed, she was thinking more and more about getting a protection order.

✳✳✳

"So man, how did it happen?" Steve asked Marc, as he looked over the menu at *Sauces* restaurant.

"How did what happen?" Marc said.

"Come on, man! You and Lisa. No, forget how, when?"

Sighing, Marc said, "In my office one Friday we were working late."

"You hit that in your office?!"

"No. I couldn't take it anymore, man. I have wanted this woman from the first day I saw her in the garage at work. We were talking and the moment just hit me. I couldn't help it. So, I kissed her."

"What happened?"

"She grabbed her things and walked out."

Steve looked at Marc and then burst out laughing. Marc shook his head.

"Anyway, at the Keene party, we ran into Judith."

"For real?"

"For real. So when I spotted her heading in our direction, I told Lisa who she was. So, Lisa decides to help me save face and play my loving girlfriend. After making Judith mad as hell, we went out on the dance floor to jam the knife a little deeper and put on a show. To end this long story, I kissed her again."

"Did she run again?" Steve asked laughing.

"No, she kissed me back," Marc said, smiling to himself.

"And that's all it took?"

"No. After getting the account, I took her home and she invited me in. We talked for a while and danced, and then we ended up –"

"You slept together?" Steve asked, excitedly.

"No, I left before things went too far. Sunday morning I went to church with her and her family."

"Well, when did you two finally sleep together?"

"We haven't," Marc said.

"What?!"

"Look, I really like this woman. She's not like any woman I've ever met."

"Man, you and every other man at the firm. You mention Lisa's name and all you'll get is smile and a nod."

"I know. But it's more than that. She's smart, funny, and sexy as hell, and man, don't laugh, I cooked breakfast this morning."

Steve started laughing even harder this time. After a couple of minutes, he was finally able to talk.

"You cooked breakfast for her, and you ain't even hit it yet?"

"Nope."

"Man you whipped."

"I have seen every inch of this woman. She can whip me anytime she wants," Marc said, looking off into space and shaking his head.

"You sure you're not sleeping together?"

"I wouldn't tell you if we were, but no."

"Excuse me gentlemen, what can I get you?" the waitress said.

"Yeah, I'll have the honey sauce wings and a Coke," Steve said.

"Okay," the waitress said.

"And I'll have the butterfly shrimp, a large platter, and a Sprite."

"Is that all?" she asked, flirtatiously.

"Yep, that's it," Marc smiled.

"I'll be back with your order."

"See, what I mean?" Steve said when the waitress walked away.

"What?"

"You have got to be kidding me. You didn't see how that waitress was hitting on you?"

"No."

"Oh, you're sprung."

"And proud of it."

Twenty minutes later, the waitress showed up with their orders.

"Alright gentlemen, here are your orders. Enjoy," she said, smiling again at Marc.

In fact, half the wait staff was ogling him.

Steve, finally said, "Man, you must be crazy to give all these women up for one. I know I wouldn't be able to do it."

"I can. Lisa is more than enough for me. Like I said, she's special."

"Is it because she's black?"

"What? No, that's not it."

"Don't get your panties in bunch. I just asked. I've seen you date women of all races, but never a black woman. Is she the first black woman you have ever dated?"

"No. I've dated black women before. Color doesn't matter, the person does. It's just that it's something more about Lisa. She has it all."

"Yea, she is fine as hell," Steve said, smiling.

"Yes, she is. And watch it."

"Awight, man. I'm just saying. But hey, I'm happy for you, man."

"Thanks, man. I thought you might have a problem with this."

"We tighter than that. She's just another incredibly fine, smart and funny woman. I can find another one…in a hundred years," Steve said, then started laughing. "Now, let's go before these women attack yo' ass."

"Not just me. The other half is jockin' you," Marc laughed.

"Oh, that I got time for."

"Come on, man."

"But the women –"

Laughing, they paid the bill and left tip.

Walking out, Marc said, "When you're in love, there are no other women."

"Oh yeah, you got it bad," Steve said, laughing.

Chapter Eighteen

Realizing what time it was, Lisa got up from her desk stretching and trying to clear her mind of figures. Her and Carol had finally finished the Thompson account and as a reward Lisa told her to go home early.

"You ready, Mona Lisa?"

Smiling at the sound of Marc's voice, Lisa said, "I was past ready an hour ago."

"I know what you mean. I am worn out," he said.

"Let's go."

Talking on their way down to the garage, Lisa told Marc she couldn't wait to soak in her tub and read her book.

"What are you reading?" he asked.

"James Patterson's *Don't Blink*."

"Is it good?"

"Better than that. I have every book he has written so far. I think I'm about a step from stalking him."

"Should I be worried?" Marc laughed.

Laughing, Lisa said, "Not yet."

Pulling into Lisa's driveway twenty minutes later, they were still talking about James Patterson books.

Walking to the door, Lisa said, "Thank you for chauffeuring me today."

"No problem. Proud to be at you service my lady. Should I pick you up in the morning?"

"No, I can drive in the morning. Besides, you're picking me up tomorrow night."

"That's right. Alright then, you sure you're gonna be alright?"

"Yes."

Marc leaned in and kissed Lisa and said, "Good night, Mona Lisa."

"Good night," she whispered.

Closing and locking her door, Lisa leaned against her door smiling.

Then, "Marc!" Lisa yelled when she opened her door.

But to her surprise, he hadn't moved.

"What took you so long?" he asked.

Kissing her and backing her into the house, he closed the door with his foot while Lisa undid his tie. She only got as far as his top button on his shirt when the doorbell rang.

"Ignore it," he said.

"Done," she said, as kissed him and continued to unbutton his shirt.

Ding Dong Ding Dong. "I know someone is here, there's a car in the driveway."

Marc looked at Lisa.

"My mother," Lisa said, as she tucked her blouse back in.

Marc straightened his shirt and tie as Lisa headed toward the door.

"Hey, mama. What are you doing here?"

"You forgot? I – Oh, I see why you forgot. Hello, Marc."

"Hello, Mrs. Jenson," he said, as he stood up to shake her hand.

"I didn't mean to interrupt," Lisa's mother said.

"You didn't," Lisa and Marc said at the same time.

"Uh huh. Anyway, have you checked your messages?"

"No, I just got home. What was – oh, no. I did forget."

"Yes, you did. But since you were in the middle of something, we can have dinner another night."

"No, Mrs. Jenson. Don't let me ruin your plans, I was just about to leave," Marc said.

"Don't run off, stay and have dinner with us."

"Thank you. But, I got a lot of work to do tonight. Can I get a rain check?"

"Of course you can. It was nice seeing you again."

"You too, Mrs. Jenson."

"Five minutes, mama."

"Okay. Bye Marc," Lisa mother said, as she went into the kitchen.

Turning toward Marc, Lisa said, "Sorry about that."

"Another couple of minutes and we would really have some explaining to do."

"Don't I know it?"

"And no apology needed. I will have you for an entire weekend with no interruptions," he said, taking Lisa into his arms.

"Yes, you will."

"See you in the morning?"

"Yes."

"Good night," he said, and then he kissed her.

"Good night."

Lisa watched him get in his car and drive away. After getting her hormones together she walked into the kitchen.

"So mom, how was your day."

"Pretty routine. How about you?"

"Tiring as usual. I'll tell you about it over dinner. Where do you wanna go?"

"How about Bahama Breeze? I have a taste for some Coconut Shrimp."

"Sounds good to me. You drive," Lisa said, as she ran her fingers through her hair and checked her makeup.

During the drive, Janice said, "So, what did I interrupt?"

"I knew it was coming. You didn't interrupt anything, we were just talking."

"Mmm-hmm. Didn't look that way to me."

"There was nothing going on mother. Now change of subject, what have you been up to?"

"Making sure your brother has everything for this trip. I didn't know he needed this much stuff just to go to Canada."

"Well, they'll be gone for like two weeks, right?"

"Yeah."

"You wanna stay with me while he's gone?"

"Nope, I'm gonna enjoy my privacy."

"Hot date?"

"Yeah, right," Janice said, laughing.

Finally making it to the restaurant, they continued to talk during their fifteen minute wait for a table.

As soon as they were seated, Janice said, "You look happy, Lisa."

"Don't I always," Lisa said, looking at her menu.

"Yeah, but now you have a glow about you."

"Carol said the same thing."

"So, how do you feel about him?"

"He's a good man. We're taking things day by day. It's nice."

"Good. Have you heard from James?"

Lisa's head snapped up at the mention of his name. Lisa knew her mother. She knew her mother only asked questions when she already knew the answer.

"Matter of fact, I have."

"Why didn't you tell me?"

"Who told you?"

"Lois said that he was going around asking about you."

"Then he found someone, because Kim told him where I worked."

"He's been up to your job?"

"Yes he has."

"When was the last time he came to see you?"

"Yesterday."

"Besides the obvious, what did he want?"

"The obvious."

"Girl, do I really have to keep asking you these questions to get the information?"

"No, ma'am. He really didn't get to talk long because Carol went and got Marc and he put James out. Then get this…James went to the police and filed a report that Marc threatened his life."

"What?! How do you know that?"

"James went to the same station that Nic works in and talked to her. She said that he didn't even recognize her."

"Damn fool. Well, good for Marc. Maybe now that James knows a man is around he will go back to hell where came from."

"I guess so."

"Why do you say that?"

"I didn't want my past to interfere with this. I thought all this was over. It's been six years. And just when I meet someone I actually care about, James pops up. There is no way Marc is going to want to deal with this mess."

"Did –"

"Good even, ladies. I'm Todd and I'll be your waiter this evening.

"Hello," Lisa and her mother said.

"What can I get for you two ladies to drink?"

"I'll have a *Bahama Mama*," Lisa said.

"And I'll have a *Pina Colada*," Janice said.

"Would you like an appetizer?"

"We'll have the Coconut Shrimp."

"Alright. I'll be back with your drink orders," he said.

"Todd is cute," Janice said when the waiter was out of earshot.

"Yeah, he is," Lisa agreed, but not really paying any attention to the waiter.

"Back to what I was saying," Janice said. "I want you to be careful, you hear me? You remember what we talked about when you got out of the hospital?"

"Yes, ma'am."

"Good."

For the next couple of hours they talked about new clients Lisa had, the family, and Janice's plans for her cruise. By nine-thirty, they had finished dinner and Lisa feeling a little tipsy from her three *Bahama Mamas*. They continued to talk on the forty-five minute drive back to Lisa house.

"Do you wanna stay the night?" Lisa asked when they pulled into her driveway.

"Naw, honey, Anthony should be at home by now."

"Okay. Call me when you get home."

"I will. And don't get in that tub, you been drinking."

"I won't. Good night, mama."

"Good night and lock up."

"I will."

Lisa watched her mother back out of the driveway and pull away, as she set her alarm and locked up for the night. Twenty minutes later, she was in her pajamas and climbing into bed. She was literally asleep in seconds.

***

The next day, Lisa couldn't help feeling nervous about her weekend plans. She'd made it to work by eight-thirty.

Making it to her office with coffee and newspaper in hand, Lisa said, "Good morning, Carol."

"Good morning," Carol said getting up from her desk and following Lisa into her office.

"What's on the book for today?"

"Absolutely nothing. With us finishing the Thompson account early, you have no appointments or meetings today. So you have time to catch up on other accounts and get your mind together for this weekend."

"It's too early, lady."

"That's okay, I'll wait until you've finished your coffee," Carol said, then walked out of the office.

Laughing, Lisa turned on her computer. She decided to go over the Thompson account. Lisa was something of a meticulous nut. She had to make sure everything was right and in place before she could move on to something. Lisa considered this to be the lower level of OCD.

"Good morning," Marc said, as he walked in.

Looking up from her computer, Lisa smiled when she saw him.

"And a good morning to you, too."

After a quick kiss, he said, "Soo, how was dinner with your mother?"

"Difficult, but good. I kind of had other things on mind."

"I know what you mean. I spent two hours in a cold shower."

"Sorry about that. I'd forgotten that we were supposed to have dinner."

"I'm sure you'll find some way to make it up to me."

"A few things have crossed my mind," she said, then kissed him. This time a little deeper than before.

After a couple of minutes, Lisa pulled away abruptly.

"Are you okay?"

"Yeah, I'm sorry. My nerves are on edge today."

"What's wrong? Tell me all about it," he said, as he took her hand and led her over to the couch and pulled her down in his lap.

"Nothing, just drunk to many *Bahama Mamas* last night, I guess."

"You sure that's all?"

"Yeah."

"You know there is nothing for you to be nervous about. This is just a weekend for us to spend some time together without any interruptions. Nothing more. No pressure. Just you and I enjoying each other's company. Again, no pressure. Okay?"

Lisa looked into those deep dark eyes of his and felt this pull at her heart. "Okay."

This time he just held her close.

That sat like that for what seemed like forever until Carol walked in.

"You know you should really try closing this thing," she joked.

Laughing, Lisa said, "I'll have to remember that."

"Good morning, Marc."

"Morning, Carol. How's it going?"

"Not as good as it's going for Lisa. I'll give you guys some privacy." She went out of the office and pulled the door shut behind her.

"So, what's your day looking like?"

"Rather slow, just fact checking and research. What about you?"

"A couple of meetings and some power planning for a major account I'm working on."

"Need any help?"

"Nope, I've been studying this account for some time now and I think I know what the client likes and want."

"Good."

"See you later?"

"Of course," Lisa said, as she got off his lap.

"See you later, gorgeous," he said with a quick kiss before leaving.

Sitting behind her desk and looking out her picture window, Lisa thought about what her and her mother talked about last night.

"Hey lady, what are you thinking about?"

"This weekend, that's all."

"Stop worrying. Everything will go just as it's supposed too. Is there anything I can do for you?"

"No, Carol. On second thought, you can. You can go home."

"It's only ten."

"I know. And I've been keeping you here past our usual time. Go and play catch up with your husband."

"You sure?"

"Yes. Go."

"And you're going to be okay?"

"Yes."

"Okay, I'll see you Monday and enjoy your weekend."

"I'll call you."

"Girl, if I get a call from you before Monday I will kill you. Enjoy...your...weekend," Carol enunciated.

"Bye, girl."

"Bye," Carol said, walking out.

After Carol left, Lisa got back to the little work she had left and did a little online shopping.

"Knock, knock."

Looking up and seeing Nic in the doorway, Lisa said, "Did Carol call you?"

"No and hello to you, too."

"Hello. Did Carol call you?"

"I told you no. I was expecting to see her. I wanted to see if y'all want to do a little shopping today and some lunch."

"You a couple of hours late. I sent Carol home early."

"She isn't sick is she?"

"No. We had been working hard on an account and I sent her home early for a job well done."

"I wish you were my boss."

"So, are you buying today?"

"Depends on the damage we do while shopping."

"Let's go," Lisa said locking up her office.

On the way down in the elevator, Nic said, "I got a date tonight and I need a new outfit."

"Oh, okay."

"Where's Marc?"

"I don't know, probably still at his meeting."

"Any plans this weekend?"

"Yeah, he's planned something. I just don't know what they are. I do know the expression on your face the other night was priceless," Lisa laughed.

"What? Look, I knew he was handsome from meeting him at your house warming and that night at the club. But when he answered your door...girl, all I could think was DAMN!! I don't see how you took so long to get at him."

"We were friends."

"Damn that! He fine as hell!" Nic said.

"Yes he is!" Lisa said, shaking her head.

"Lisa."

Turning to see who called her, Lisa saw her boss John heading toward her and Nic.

"I'll go get my truck," Nic said.

"Okay. Hey, John, what can I do for you?"

"I'm glad I caught you. I wanted to talk to you about the Thompson account."

"I'm on way to lunch, but I –"

"No, don't rush. Everyone is taking advantage of the half day, including me. I was thinking we could meet Monday morning around ten."

"That'll be fine."

"Alright, have a great weekend."

"You too, John."

As Lisa got into Nic's Escalade, Nic asked, "What was that about?"

"A meeting."

"What time do you need to be back?"

"Oh, no, it's not until Monday. I am officially off the clock for the rest of the day."

"Cool. Let's go put some sales clerk's children through college."

"Where are we headed?"

"I was thinking about Wolfchase."

"Okay."

"Maybe we can find something at Victoria Secret for your weekend."

"I wouldn't even know what to buy it's been so long."

"We'll find something."

"You never said who your date is with."

After a moment of silence, Nic finally said, "Michael."

Lisa was updating her calendar on her iPhone for the meeting on Monday and stopped in mid key punch and looked at Nic.

"What?" Nic said.

"Michael? You mean Michael the –"

"Yes, that Michael."

"When did this happen?"

"He asked me Wednesday and I said yes."

"That's nice."

"And what does that mean?"

"Nothing."

"Yeah, right. I know you don't approve, but I like him."

"I didn't say anything."

"Yeah, I know. But your silence speaks volumes."

"Just be careful, Nic. Okay?"

"I will."

Lisa was about to say something else until her cell phone rang. "Lisa Jenson...Hey you...Yeah, me and Nic are out shopping...No, I left my car in the garage...Where are you...Oh, really...Yes, I'll be ready and yes I remembered...Okay, see you then...Bye."

When Lisa hung up, she saw Nic smiling. "What?"

"I want that."

"Want what?"

"That smile that's plastered on your face."

"You can, Just –"

"Don't say it, Lis."

"Okay, okay. Just be careful."

"I will."

Parking the truck, Nic added, "Is there a limit?"

"No."

"My girl."

They started on the first floor. Going from store to store, seeing some nice items but nothing that caught their eye. With no luck on the first floor, they moved to the second. Their first stop was Victoria Secret.

"Are you looking for anything special?" Nic asked, holding up what Lisa thought was a shoe string.

"If I wear that, I might as well be naked," Lisa laughed.

"That's the idea."

"How about this?" Lisa asked, holding up a white bustier with matching thong panties

"That's cute, buy it. Are you gonna buy something for every night?"

"I guess I should, huh?"

"Yeah. Variety, honey."

Putting the thong set back, Lisa spotted something else, "Oh, what about this one?"

This was a sheer white nightgown with matching underwear.

"Cute, but no. How about this?" Nic held up a sheer black baby doll top with matching boy-cut panties.

"Oooo, I like that! Do they have in white?"

"What the hell is with you and white all of sudden?"

"I like white."

"Girl, please. You haven't been a virgin in twenty years. Pick a color."

"Give me the black."

"Good, now find a couple more. I'll be in the back where the good stuff is."

"I wanna see."

"No, baby, this is strictly for the professionals. You're a beginner."

After twenty minutes, they paid for their items and left.

They only walked a couple of steps before Lisa said, "Bingo! Shoe store!"

"Girl, what is your infatuation with shoes?"

"Look, you knew what my addiction was when we met. Come on."

"Does Marc know about your addiction? Better yet has he seen your closet?"

Laughing, Lisa said, "No. I'm saving that until I've known him a bit longer."

Following her insane friend into the store, Nic said, "Girl, we gon have to find you a twelve-step program."

"I'm not that bad."

"Yeah, right."

"Hello, ladies. Welcome to *Soles for the Soul*. How can I help you?"

"Actually, we're just looking around," Nic told her.

Then, "Excuse me, do you have this in a seven in a half?" Lisa yelled across the store.

With a slight smirk on her face, the sales clerk went to help her.

All Nic could think was thank God they were the only ones in the store. Doing some looking around herself in the back of the store, Nic suddenly heard Lisa say, "What the hell are you doing, following me?"

Looking for who she was talking to, she spotted James standing close enough to Lisa to see her tonsils.

"I was just walking by and saw you trying on shoes. Is it a crime to want to say hello?"

"Depends on who you ask. Is there a problem her, Mr. Harris?" Nic said.

Looking at Nic like she was crazy, James said, "No and how the hell do you know my name?"

"A couple of days ago you came into my precinct to file charges against a Mr. Campbell. Remember now?"

"Uh, yeah," James said, looking at Lisa.

"Let's see if we can jog your memory a little more. My name is Nic and I am Lisa's best friend. Do you remember now? I'm gonna let that bit of information sink in. And here is something else to think about, Ms. Lisa Jenson has filed a restraining order against you. If you come within two hundred feet of her you will be arrested. Since you are apparently breaking the law, you can either leave or be taken away."

"This ain't over Lisa."

"Is that a threat Mr. Harris?"

With one last look, he walked away.

Watching him walk away, Lisa couldn't help think about how much worse this could get.

"He's following me now."

"I have no doubt about that. Here's your copy of the order."

"How did you get a restraining order?"

"I have friends in high places."

Taking a seat, Lisa said, "Thanks, Nic. But, there's something I need to tell you."

"What?"

"He knows where I live. He sent me a letter, but it didn't have a stamp on it. That means he had to have put in my mailbox."

"Do you feel safe at home?"

"Yeah."

"Okay. I'll keep a look out and you do the same."

"How did I get here? How did dating him turn into this?"

"I don't know Lisa. I don't know. But we are not going to let him ruin our day of shopping. We have two gorgeous men who can't wait to spend the weekend with us. Pep up, it's time for pedicures."

Lisa bought a pair of sandals she thought would go perfect with her dress.

By four o'clock, they had done more shopping than they intended to and got pedicures. Pulling into the garage where Lisa worked, they were still talking about their plans for the weekend. Lisa took her bags from the back of Nic's truck and put them in her trunk.

Nic noticed a note on Lisa's windshield and pulled it from under the windshield wiper and read it.

"Lisa, you have a message," she sang.

Closing the trunk, Lisa walked to the front of the car and took the note from Nic.

While Lisa read it, Nic recited it, "Didn't want to bother you on your girl's day out. See you at seven, Mona Lisa."

Lisa couldn't hide the smile that this two sentence note put on her face.

"Look at you, all giddy," Nic teased.

"Shut up," Lisa said, blushing.

"He is fine."

"Nic, that's not all. He's smart, he's romantic and passionate, and he even made it through questioning with my mother and grandmother."

"I can tell he's crazy about you. And that background check I did only brought up a ticket he got in college."

"Good."

"I can't believe you asked me to do that."

"After dealing with James, I learned that a woman needs to know what she's dealing with."

"From what you told me and from what I found out he's an honest guy. So go for it."

"I am."

"Let's go get ready for our men."

"Why don't you get ready at my house?"

"You know you don't like Michael."

"I promise to be nice. Have him pick you up at my place."

"Alright, I'll call him on the way. And don't make me pull you over on the expressway."

"You have to catch me first."

Because of traffic, they got to Lisa's house in thirty minutes instead of the usual fifteen. Walking into the house and dropping her bags on the couch, Lisa checked her messages and looked through her mail.

While listening to her message, Lisa was already dialing her mother's number.

"Hey mama. What are you doing?"

"Nothing. About to cook dinner."

"Hey, mama," Nic yelled.

"Hey, Nic, baby. How you been?"

"Fine. What about you?"

"I'm good. What you two up to tonight?"

"Your daughter broke me in the mall," Nic said.

"No, I didn't mama. She started it."

"Y'all a mess. What did you get?"

"I got shoes, some accessories and perfume. Nic bought everything in sight."

"I did not." Nic said, from the kitchen.

"Where's Anthony?" Lisa asked her mother.

"Gone. You know on Friday nights he is out with his friends."

"Where'd they go?"

"His friend Cedric is having a party."

"Oh, okay. You okay being there by yourself?"

"I won't be here by myself for long. You aunt called and said that her and a new friend are coming over. And Marilyn is on her way over, too."

"Nic and I need to come over there with y'all."

"Naw baby, this grown folks."

"Mama, me and Nic are almost thirty."

"Hey speak for yourself," Nic said.

"Well, this is for forty and over. What you two got up for tonight?"

"We both have dates."

"Are you going out with Marc?"

"Yes, I am."

"And, Nic, who are you going out with?"

"His name is Michael and we work together."

"Good. So, you ladies go ahead and get beautiful for your dates. Call me tomorrow."

"I will. Bye."

"Bye, mama," Nic said.

"Bye, y'all."

Looking at her watch, Lisa said, "Girl, it's already five-thirty and I still don't know what to do with my hair."

"Girl, please, you only where it two ways: up or down."

"Okay, let's get ready."

Nic went into one of the guest room while Lisa went in hers to get ready.

"Damn, I forgot to get earrings," Nic said.

"Come and pick a pair out of my box."

Nic walked into the room and headed towards Lisa's jewelry box. Noticing the packed bag, she said, "Did you pack your new stuff?"

"Ooo, I'm glad you said something." Lisa emptied out her Victoria Secret bag and packed them in her weekend bag.

Picking out a pair of earrings and holding them up to her ears, Nic said, "How about these?"

Looking at her, Lisa said, "I like them. They match the dress you bought."

"They're not too dangly?"

"No."

"These are it, then."

"Well, let the makeovers begin," Lisa said.

***

By six-forty-five they were ready for their dates. Lisa met Nic downstairs when she finished dressing.

"Look at you. I like that color on you," Lisa told Nic.

Nic was dressed in an emerald green silk dress. The dress was knee length, backless, with silk straps that tied around her neck. Her hair was an upsweep of ring curls with tendrils hanging down.

"Thank you. You don't look so bad yourself."

"I know," Lisa said, twirling around. Lisa was wearing a red spaghetti strapped dress. The pencil skirt was a little above her knee. Lisa had done an extra hour of workout every day this week just to fit in it. "You don't think it's too tight do you?" Lisa asked.

"Yes, but you got the body for it. Hell, ass was made to be seen."

Lisa walked over to a mirror she had hanging on her living room wall to see how far her butt was sticking out.

"Ain't no need in being self-conscious now. You knew you had a big ass a long time go."

"Go to hell, Nic," Lisa said, laughing while she looked at herself in the mirror.

At seven on the dot, the doorbell rang.

Thinking it was Marc, Lisa answered the door. To her surprise it was Michael at the door instead.

"Hey, Michael. Come on in."

"How you doing, Lisa," Michael said.

Lisa had to admit Michael was a good looking man. He had the smoothest dark skin Lisa had ever seen. It reminded her of dark chocolate.

"Hello, beautiful," he said to Nic. "These are for you." He handed Nic a bouquet of wild flowers.

"They're beautiful, Michael. Thank you," Nic said, smiling.

Lisa was closing the door, when Michael said, "Another car is pulling up."

"Oh, okay. So, what are you two doing tonight?"

"Dinner and hopefully dessert," Michael said, eyeing Nic.

"Depends on how good dinner is," Nic said.

"Mmm, I am a lucky man," Marc said, walking in the door.

Lisa smiled and walked into his outstretched arms.

"Hello," Lisa said.

"I have something for you," he whispered in her ear.

"What?"

"Oh, sorry. How you doing?" Marc said, looking at Nic and Michael.

"Marc, this is Michael. Michael, this is Marc."

They shook hands.

"Now what's my gift?" Lisa asked.

"Your first of many for this weekend," Marc said.

Marc walked back out the door and Lisa looked at Nic. Marc came back in holding a rose and handed it to Lisa.

"Thank you," Lisa smiled.

"That's not all."

All of a sudden, delivery men started bringing in bouquets of red roses. Lisa stopped counting after the fifth deliveryman walked in.

"Marc, what is all of this?"

"All this is for you," he said, kissing Lisa.

"By the way, you look sexy as hell."

When the last deliveryman walked out, Lisa looked around her living room and counted at least a dozen vases of red roses.

Turning back to look at him, she said, "This is too much."

"Not from where I'm standing," Marc said.

"Man, you making me look bad," Michael joked.

"Sorry about that. Nic, you're looking beautiful."

"Thank you," Nic said, blushing a little.

Lisa laughed at her friend.

"Nic, we better go babe."

"Okay. But first I have to take a picture of you two. No, I don't wanna hear it. You two stand over there in front the forest," Nic joked. "Alright smile."

Lisa and Marc stood in front of the roses with their arms around each other smiling. Nic snapped the picture.

"Oh, that's a good one. Okay, you two have a good weekend."

"Okay. You guys have a good night," Lisa said.

After they left, Marc said, "Are you packed?"

"Yes. Packed and ready to go."

"Let's go."

Lisa set the alarm, but before closing the door she took one last look at all the vases of red roses. It was the most beautiful sight she had ever seen.

Locking up, her and Marc head for his car.

Chapter Nineteen

In the car, Lisa said, "So, Mr. Cavell, what do you have planned for this weekend?"

"It's a weekend of surprises."

"A whole weekend of surprises? Well, I could get use to this."

"I hope so. Did I tell you how sexy you look tonight?"

"Yes and thank you. You don't think it's too tight do you?"

Marc looked at her like she was crazy.

"I will never have that problem with anything you wear."

Pulling into his driveway and parking, Marc got out and went around to help Lisa out of the car.

Opening the front door, Marc said, "After you."

Smiling, Lisa said, "Thank you."

Walking through the door, Lisa gasped, "Oh, my God."

"You like surprise number two?"

"I love it."

Lisa walked farther into the house and saw that she was walking on rose petals. In fact, roses and rose petals were everywhere. They were all over the floor, out on the balcony, and going up the stairs.

"Lisa?"

"I'm sorry," she said, wiping away a tear. "I'm being silly. This is the most romantic thing anyone has ever done for me. It's been so long since – this was my first reaction. I'm okay," she smiled.

"So I did good?"

"You did wonderful," she said, turning to him and kissing him.

"I'm glad you like it. I'm gonna take you bag upstairs and I'll be right back."

When Lisa turned toward the balcony, Marc couldn't help but to look at her ass. *Lord, she's blessed,* he thought to himself as he went upstairs.

A minute later, he was back at Lisa's side. "You don't know how good you look in this dress."

"Thank you. I wore it for you."

"Then, thank you. Are you ready to eat?"

"Yes, I am."

"Well, follow me."

Marc took Lisa's hand and led her out onto the balcony. Pulling her chair out for her, he said, "I have cooked what I hope will be the best meal you have ever had. I cooked Lobster Tails with Shrimp Scampi. And for dessert, well that's upstairs."

Smiling, Lisa thought to herself, *you have no idea.*

Sitting at the table looking at the view, Lisa couldn't help but think back to when she would sit on a bench and think about the future. At that time, a man like Marc was not imaginable.

She was brought back by hearing Marc say, "Here we are."

He placed their plates on the table and sat down himself.

"This looks delicious," Lisa said.

"Thanks. Would you like some wine?"

"Please."

"Now, before you taste it, it's not the wine you usually drink. A client of mine gave me three bottles when I first started at the firm. He told me to only open them on special occasions. This is my first bottle. I figured this was the best time to open one up."

Tasting it, Lisa said, "This is incredible. What's it called?"

"Honestly, I don't know, it's in French. At least I think it's French," Marc laughed.

"Well whatever it is, it's good."

"Eat up before it gets cold."

During dinner they talked about everything they could think of. There were no uncomfortable minutes of silence.

"Are you enjoying yourself, so far?" Marc asked.

"I'm having a great time."

"Good. I'll clear the table, you relax."

"I can help," Lisa said, picking up her plate.

"Oh, no you don't. This weekend is all about you. Relax."

While Marc cleared the table and cleaned the kitchen, Lisa leaned on the rail and watched the traffic go by on Riverside and the couples walking hand in hand in the park.

"It's a beautiful night, isn't?" Lisa asked when Marc put his arms around her.

"Not as beautiful as you."

"I could stand her like this all night."

"Good, because we have all night."

Lisa turned and put her arms around his neck and they moved slowly to the soft jazz that was flowing from the living room out to the balcony and making all the sounds of the city disappear.

"Tonight has been wonderful, Marc. Thank you."

"You don't have to thank me. Besides the night isn't over yet. You ready for your next surprise?"

"I think my heart can stand another one."

"Good." He then reached into his pocket and pulled out a black velvet box. "Open it," he said.

"What have you done?"

"Open it and see."

Lisa opened the box and was completely stunned.

Inside the box were the most beautiful sapphire earrings she had ever seen.

"I didn't know what you would like, so…"

"These are gorgeous, but I can't –"

"Shhhh. Yes, you can. Let me do this for you."

Lisa couldn't say one word. She stared at this man, who seemed to enjoy making her happy. What could she have done in her life that would have reaped this kind of reward?

"Thank you," she whispered.

Then she kissed him. She kissed him with every bit of passion and…love? Is this what this is? Was she falling in love with this man?

"Now, that's the kind of thank you that makes it all worthwhile," he said, against her lips. "There's also something I want to tell you."

"Oh, God. Please don't tell me you're married."

"No, nothing like that," Marc laughed. "I've fallen in love with you Lisa. I may be moving a little fast for you, but I can't help how I feel about you. So, if by chance I'm moving too fast tell me now and I promise to pull back."

Lisa was quiet for a moment. She didn't exactly know what to say, so she said what was in her heart.

"Marc, I haven't been in a relationship or dated someone in a long time. I don't know what is fast or slow these days. I stopped trusting my judgment about men and it's not like they were beating my door down either."

"That's hard to believe."

"I used to be a big girl."

"Doesn't matter if you were big or small, your heart is still the same."

"Thank you for saying that, but a lot of men don't see pass weight. Marc, I never thought I could feel the way I do about you. But I do. I think I'm falling in love with you, too. I don't think you're moving too fast at all."

"Thank you for trusting me," he said, then leaned in and kissed her.

The rumble of thunder made them look up.

"I'm glad we already ate," Marc said.

"I don't know, I kind of like the rain."

"I'll remember that. Now, follow me."

Walking inside, Marc locked the balcony door and led Lisa up the stairs. When they walked into his bedroom, Lisa was surprised to see that the rose petals led to the bed and were on the bed. He had candles lit everywhere and bowls of strawberries and whipped cream on one of the nightstands.

"Surprised," he whispered.

"It's beautiful."

Marc walked Lisa over by the bed and started to kiss her neck and shoulders.

"Wait, I have a surprise for you."

"I already have what I want," he said, and kissed her.

Breaking the kiss, Lisa said, "You'll like it. I'll be right back."

Lisa picked up her bag and went into the bathroom. As she changed, she was taking deep breaths to slow down her heartbeat. Changing into her black lace babydoll and boy-cut underwear, she also put on the earrings he gave her. Ten minutes later, she walked out of the bathroom to see Marc standing in front of the balcony door watching the rain fall. When he turned and saw her, he was speechless.

"How do you like your surprise?" Lisa asked.

"I would say wow, but that wouldn't be close to describing how exquisite you look."

Picking Lisa up in his arms and carrying her to the bed, he laid her down on the bed and lay next to her. He then placed the two bowls between them.

Listening to the rain and thunder they feed each other. Marc picked out a strawberry, dipped it in the whipped cream, then spread it across her chest and licked it off. He dipped the strawberry again and did the same thing.

He then bit the strawberry and kissed Lisa. With every passing moment, their kiss became more fervent, more need than just want. Then Marc slipped her top off of her. Caressing her right nipple while he smeared whipped cream on the left one and licked it off. Lisa moaned softly. He switched to the right one and did the same thing.

He slowly made a path down her stomach to her thighs. He could smell a mixture of her perfume and her sex. It was intoxicating. As he kissed the inside of her thighs, Lisa moaned softly and ran her fingers through his hair.

Moving back up to kiss her, he whispered, "I don't think I've ever felt skin as soft as yours."

Not being able to contain herself, Lisa rolled him over so she could be on top.

"Oh, so you're in charge now?" Marc asked.

Lisa smiled, nodded yes and kissed him deeply. She became another person.

She started from his neck, to his chest, to his stomach. Running her hands underneath the waistband of his pajama bottoms that he changed into made his breath quicken. She slowly pulled them off of him and dropped them to the floor. At the sight of him, she couldn't help but smile.

"And what are you smiling at?" he asked, looking down at her.

"My next gift."

Reaching over to the bowl of strawberries, she took one and dipped into the whipped cream and rubbed it from the bottom to the tip of his penis. She then took him into her mouth. She could feel him tense up, than relax. Hearing him moan only excited her more.

"Ohhh," he moaned.

With every moan, she took more of him her mouth. She became so engrossed in it she couldn't have stopped if she wanted to. Which she didn't. Feeling the vein harden, Lisa released him and started to stroke him. He came with such vigor, his entire body shook.

Lying next to him, Lisa waited until he caught his breath.

After a flash of lightening went across the sky, Lisa said, "Are you alright?"

Turning to look at her, Marc said, "I'm better than alright, I'm in love. I wasn't expecting that."

"Well, I wanted to give you a gift."

"That you did. I'll be right back."

While Marc went to the bathroom, Lisa watched the rain fall in sheets. Climbing back in the bed, Marc pulled Lisa close to him and kissed her. He then whispered against her lips, "You know you've started something don't you?"

"I hope so."

"Now it's your turn. Remember the muscles to use for a great workout. The shoulders, stomach, thighs, and of course the most important muscle," he said, kissing her in each place. Then he kissed Lisa through her underwear.

Lisa nearly lost her mind.

He pulled her lace underwear off, and kissed her again. As she shuddered, she felt something cold and automatically tensed up.

"Relax, it's just a strawberry," Marc said, as he rubbed the strawberry over her clit, than sucked the juices off. He continued to suck on her clit until he felt her hands in his hair and pulling him closer.

"Yes, Marc. Yes!" she moaned.

At one point she couldn't tell if the low rumble was outside or the beginning of a massive orgasm. His movements became faster and faster and before she knew it she was cumming and calling his name. Loudly.

When she collapsed back against the pillows, she heard Marc say, "Stay with me. I'm not through with you yet. I'll be right back."

Lisa couldn't speak, so she nodded.

After a few minutes of deep breaths, she finally got her heart rate down. She got out of bed and walked over to the balcony door to watch the rain.

Behind her, she heard Marc say, "I brought you a glass of wine. I figured your throat would be dry."

"You were right."

Kissing her shoulder, he said, "It's really coming down out there."

"Yep."

Setting his glass down and wrapping his arms around her waist, he said, "Have I told you how beautiful you look?"

"Yes," she smiled.

"Well, now let me show you." He then moved Lisa hair to one side and kissed her neck.

"Mmmm," she said.

"Mmmm, indeed."

Turning her toward him, he kissed her and picked her up and carried her back to the bed. Laying her down on the bed, he kissed her. They kissed each other passionately, while Lisa pushed Marc's robe off his shoulders. Breaking their kiss, Marc reached over in his nightstand draw and pulled out a condom.

Lisa continued kissing his neck and chest as he put the condom on.

"Come here," Lisa said, pulling him on top of her.

Kissing each other deeply, Marc gently pushed into her.

"Ahhh," Lisa moaned.

Not moving, Marc said, "Are you okay?"

"Yes, I'm okay."

He began to move inside of her tight walls, as he kissed her again. As they moved in sync with one another, he said, "You are so beautiful. I love you, Lisa."

"I love you, Marc," she said, staring into eyes.

Marc knew at that instant that he would love her forever. They seemed to curve to one another, to perfectly mold into each other. Marc made love to Lisa as if it was her first time. He was gentle, yet strong, he catered to her body as if he was the creator of all her sweet spots. Even though she didn't drink enough to be drunk, it appeared as if the room was spinning. The voice she heard calling out to Marc and the heavens above didn't sound like her voice.

With each stroke there was a rumble of thunder, at least that's the way it seemed to Lisa. Just as their bodies intertwined, so did their voices, their love, their futures, and their pasts. As Marc's thrusts speeded up, Lisa realized it wasn't just thunder she heard; she was also hearing the rumbling of her orgasm.

Moaning louder and calling each other's names even louder, they came blissfully together in waves after waves orgasms. Looking at her as they both came, Marc felt Lisa shake uncontrollably beneath him. Collapsing on top of her, they both were breathing heavily. When he moved away, Lisa realized right then that making love to Marc was as if she found her other half. She also realized she didn't want him to move, she wanted him to stay inside her just as a puzzle pieces fit together to form a beautiful picture. They didn't say anything after that, they just held one another and kissed and listened to the storm outside.

Chapter Twenty

Lisa hadn't realized she fell asleep until she felt Marc kissing her on the neck and saying, "Baby, wake up."

"I'm awake."

"No, you're not."

Laughing softly, Lisa said, "Well, I'm awake now. What time is it?"

"It's one-thirty."

"I guess I did fall asleep. The last time I looked at the clock it was a little after midnight. Did you sleep any?"

"Yea, but I'm wide awake now."

"Mmmm, really?"

"Yep. Come on."

"Where are we going?"

"I told you I wasn't through with you yet."

"Let me through something on."

"You don't need to put anything on. Just follow me."

Doing as she was told, Lisa followed him into the bathroom. The lights were dimmed, there were more rose petals on the floor leading to the Jacuzzi, and they were also inside. In fact, there were so many petals in the Jacuzzi; you couldn't even see the water. The circular shaped tub was big enough to seat four.

"Come on," he said, helping her. "One more thing."

Lisa heard soft music feel the room, when he pressed a button on the wall. Marc, then climbed into the tub.

"You want the jets on?" he asked.

"No, this is perfect. This whole night has been perfect."

"Glad to hear it."

They sat quietly, Lisa leaning back against him and listening to the music. She didn't think the night could get any better than this.

"You want me to heat the water?" Marc asked, after a while.

Turning toward him and straddling him, Lisa said, "Why don't you let me do that?"

"Have I created a monster?"

"No, but you sure as hell woke one up," Lisa smiled.

As they kissed, Lisa felt Marc become hard against her inner thigh.

"Mmm, you are wide awake," she said, kissing his neck and nibbling his ear.

"Told you," he said. "I guess we won't be in here long."

Laughing, Lisa said, "Probably not. But, I wouldn't mind trying some things in here."

"I like the sound of that."

"Speaking of sounds," she said, leaning back to look at him. "What were you whispering in my ear earlier? I didn't understand a word you were saying."

At first Marc looked confused, then it dawned on him, "Ohh, yeah. Sorry about that."

"No, don't be sorry, it sounded soo sexy," Lisa said, kissing his neck. "What were you saying?"

"Italian."

"I had you speaking another language. Hmm, I kind of like that thought," she smiled.

"I have never done that before."

"What were you saying?"

"That you're everything I ever wanted in woman. And multitude of dirty words."

"Well, let's see how many times we can get you to switch up," Lisa said, gently biting his ear.

After a couple more minutes of that, Marc said, "You are driving me crazy."

"I hope so," she moaned.

"You better stop before we get started in this tub. And might add I'm not wearing protection."

"Mmm-hmm." But, she didn't stop what she was doing.

All of a sudden Marc changed positions, this time it was her turn to be driven a little crazy. Marc began kissing her deeply, and then moving down to her neck and throat, continuing down to her breast, where he spent the majority of his time, moving from one breast to the other.

"Hot yet?" he asked.

"In flames."

"That's what I like to hear."

"I didn't think it would be like this," Lisa said, as she pulled him closer.

"I'm glad to surpass your expectations."

"Oh, you did more than that, you created a whole new level."

"I aim to please."

"That you do."

Marc moved and sat next to Lisa and pulled her close to him, "You're amazing," he said.

"So are you."

"I know this may be out of the blue and weird, but I need to know something."

"What's that?"

"How do you feel about dating me?"

"What do you mean?"

"Am I the first white man you've ever dated?"

"Yes. But not the first one to have tried," she smiled.

"I'm sure of that. A couple of my clients have even asked about you."

Turning to look at him, Lisa said, "Who?"

"It doesn't matter now, I have you. Now, back to the subject. How do you feel about that?"

"Has someone said something to you?"

"No, of course not. I just wanted to know."

"Well, I've never thought about it. All I know is that you are a caring, strong, smart, loving, and gorgeous man. And most importantly, I feel safe with you. I feel like nothing could hurt me. I trust you. No other man has done or been all those things to me. And all these things make me love you." She said the last part more to herself than to him.

"Let's get out of this tub. I want make love to you."

Not saying a word, Lisa got out of the tub dried off and went into the bedroom, while Marc cleaned the bathroom.

With the towel wrapped around her, Lisa took a bottle of lotion out of her bag and sat on the bed.

"Need help with your back?" Marc asked, climbing into bed.

"Yeah, thanks."

As Marc massaged lotion into her back, he noticed a scar on the lower part of her back.

"What's that?" he asked as he touched the scar.

"A reminder," she said, sighing.

"How'd you get it?"

"Let's just say I moved in time."

Getting up and putting the lotion back in her bag, she saw that her lingerie was still on the floor. Picking it up, she felt Marc's hand on her arm.

"James?" he asked.

"Yes."

"Come here." Pulling her back over to the bed and down beside him, he said, "You're safe with me. I will never let you have another sad day for the rest of your life. I love you, Mona Lisa."

"Can you really do that?"

Looking her in the eyes, he said with assurance, "Yes, I can. I'm Superman, remember?"

For the rest of the night they made love slowly, sensually. There was no need to rush. Lisa had never felt so satisfied in her life. The last thing she remembered was falling asleep in his strong arms.

***

Waking up around nine, Marc slipped out of bed without waking Lisa and went downstairs. He had some calls to make.

"Good morning, is this Nicole?"

"Yes. Who is this and at nine in the damn morning?"

"I'm sorry to be calling so early, but this is Marc."

"Oh, my God. Is Lisa okay?"

"Yes, yes, she's fine. She's wonderful and it's for that reason I want to propose to her."

"What?!" Nic was wide awake now.

Laughing, Marc said, "I hope she'll be this excited."

"Where is she?"

"She's asleep, and that's why I'm calling you."

"I'm listening."

Marc told her his plans for that day in hopes of her helping him with everything.

"Marc, do you love her?"

"With everything I have in me."

"Do you promise to protect her?"

"Yes, I do."

"Are you ready to take Pat's, mine, and Carol's place as her best friend?"

"That, I could never do, but I hope to be added to the list."

"Oh, you're good. Here's the number." Nic called out the number and then said, "I'll call you when I've done my part."

"Thank you, Nicole."

"You're about to be in the family, call me Nic."

"Thanks, Nic."

"Okay, bye."

"Bye."

After hanging up, Marc took a deep breath and made another call.

After the second ring, "Hello?"

"Hello, Mrs. Jenson, this is Marc. How are you this morning?"

"I'm fine, you?"

"I'm good. Hopefully, I'll be better by the end of this conversation."

"Yes, I'm listening."

"I actually wanted to talk to you face to face. If I could?"

"Well, I have somewhere to be by eleven. Can you come now?"

"Yes, ma'am."

Lisa's mother gave him the address. After getting dress as quickly and quietly as he could, he wrote Lisa a note and left the house.

Using his GPS system in his car, he made it to Lisa's mother's house in about ten minutes.

"Hey, Marc, come on in," Janice said, when she opened the door.

"Good morning, Mrs. Jenson."

"You want some coffee, I just made some?"

"No ma'am. I don't think I need it this morning."

"Let's sit down so you can get whatever it is off your chest."

Taking a seat in the chair facing Janice, Marc took a deep breath.

"Okay, son, I'm listening."

"To start off, I love your daughter with all my heart. She is an amazing woman, and...I want your permission to propose to her."

After a long pause, one of the longest pauses Marc had to ever sit through, Janice said, "Marc, I'm pretty sure Lisa has told you everything that happened to her a few years ago."

"Yes ma'am, she did."

"You should know that she doesn't trust people like she used to. It's hard for her to let her guard down and I don't want her rushed if she isn't ready."

"Yes, ma'am."

"Do you think she loves you?"

"Yes, I do."

"What makes you so sure?"

"Because I love her. I love her enough to wait if she isn't ready. I love her enough to marry her tomorrow if she will let me. I have enough love for this woman to cover whatever she is not ready to provide."

"You're good. Well, let me be the first to welcome you to the family. We are crazy bunch," Janice laughed.

"Thank you, Mrs. Jenson."

"Call me Janice. Now, when will I get to congratulate you both?"

"That's the other reason why I wanted to see you..." Marc told her the same plan he told Nic. After making arrangements with Janice, Marc headed to his favorite jewelry store. He had a ring to pick out. On his way to the jewelry store, he made one last important call.

"Hey, ma..."

By the time he made it to the jewelry store he had finished his call with his parents. After their initial shock they were happy and excited to meet the woman that finally got their son to settle down. Even though they couldn't make it until next week, he promised to call them right after Lisa accepted his proposal. At least he hoped she would accept his proposal.

"Mr. Cavell, welcome! Were the earrings a big success?" The tall, white haired man asked.

"Actually, they did. In fact they worked so well, Mr. Waller, that I am here for an engagement ring," Marc said.

"An engagement ring?! Congratulations, Mr. Cavell. Let me show you the best rings we have," Mr. Waller said opening the glass door.

After about a half an hour of looking, Marc decided on a four carat princess cut diamond ring. The jeweler agreed that the ring was perfect.

Thirty minutes later, he was walking into his house. Walking through the front door he was greeted by the sound of Jill Scott playing on the stereo and Lisa singing along as she cleaned the kitchen.

Leaning against the kitchen door jam, he said, "Hello, Mona Lisa."

Turning around Lisa smiled, ran, and jumped into his arms.

"Hey, you. Where have you been?"

After a kiss and putting her on the countertop, he said, "Didn't you read my note?"

"Yes, but you could have woke me."

"You looked so beautiful sleeping that I didn't want to disturb you. So, what have you been doing?"

"Cleaning," Lisa said, looking guilty.

"I see. But you know you didn't have to do that."

"Don't worry. After I worked out, alone, I cleaned the bedroom, the bathroom, and the kitchen."

"You shouldn't have done that. This is supposed to be a weekend of relaxation," Marc said, and then kissed her. "What do you want to do today?"

"My mother called me and said that she's having a barbecue today and wanted me to bring you. You up for it?"

"Of course. What time?"

"Two o'clock."

"It's noon."

"Yep," Lisa said, pulling him closer to her and kissing his neck.

"We do have some time to waste," Marc said, picking Lisa up off the counter as she wrapped her legs around his waist.

As we walked up the stairs, Lisa grabbed the railing.

"Here?" he asked.

"Here," she whispered in his ear.

"I don't have –"

Lisa pulled a condom out of her cleavage.

"You are so bad," he said, laughing.

He gently laid her down on the steps and began to undress her, while she did the same to him. When Marc pushed into her, Lisa felt just as she had last night, complete. Her moans turned him on even more and before he knew they both climaxed. Breathing hard, neither of them moved.

Lisa was the first speak, "Shower?"

"Together?"

"Of course."

Gathering their clothes, they went upstairs. Walking into the shower, Marc turned on the faucet, water came out of spouts in every direction.

"I gotta get my shower to do this," Lisa said.

Soaping up a towel, Marc said, "If you move in you could have this option every day."

Taking it as a joke, Lisa said, "Then where would you live?"

"Funny."

In the shower, they did more fondling than showering. After a thorough cleaning, they got out and helped each other dry off.

Lisa then unpacked her hair dryer, curling iron, and her bag of toiletries. Drying her hair as she waited for her curlers to heat up, Marc shaved, brushed his teeth and went to get dressed. After drying and curling her hair, Lisa brushed her teeth, and then applied her make-up.

Coming out of the bathroom still in her towel, she repacked her things and said, "The curlers on your sink are still warm, so be careful."

"Will do."

Combing his hair, Marc watched Lisa take off her towel and slip on a pair of black lace panties.

For a minute, he stared at her, and then said, "You keep walking around like that and we'll be late for the barbecue.

Laughing, Lisa said, "I'm getting dressed. Besides, you're not really helping either walking around shirtless.

Walking over to her and pulling her close, he kissed her.

After a minute, Lisa pulled away and said, "Alright Mr., that's enough. We have to get dressed."

"We still have a little time."

"No we don't," Lisa laughed.

Lisa put on a pair of wide leg blue slacks with a matching halter top. She also had on a pair of matching three inch heeled sandals. Her only jewelry for today was the earrings that Marc had given her the night before. In Marc's eyes she was the most beautiful woman he had ever seen. He thought the diamond engagement ring would be great add-on.

"Are you ready to meet my whole family?"

"I can't wait," Marc said, setting the alarm as they walked out.

Chapter Twenty-One

Walking through the front door, Lisa yelled, "Hello."

"In the kitchen," her mother said.

"Hey," Lisa said, giving her mother a hug.

"Hey, baby. Don't you look pretty?" Janice said.

"Thank you."

"Hey, Marc, how you doing?"

"Fine, Mrs. Jenson. How are you?" Marc asked, as he kissed Janice on the check.

"I'm doing fine. Lisa, go and introduce Marc to everyone."

"You want me to come back and help?"

"Nope, I think I got everything covered."

"Alright."

Leading Marc through the patio door, Lisa was surprised to see Nic and Pat.

"What are y'all doing here?"

"Girl, you know we don't miss mama cooking," Nic said.

Lisa gave them both hugs and then asked, "Pat, where's Lewis?"

"Over there with the rest of the men," Pat said.

"Hey, Marc," Nic said, shaking his hand.

Then Pat followed suit.

"I'll be right back. I'm going to introduce Marc around."

Lisa proceeded to introduce Marc to aunts, uncles, cousins, friends of the family, and neighbors.

Leaving him with the rest of the men, Lisa headed back to Nic and Pat.

"Mama invited the entire family," Lisa said, sitting in an empty chair at the table.

"As long as I get plate, I don't care," Pat said.

"So, how did you guys find out about the barbecue before me?"

"I ran into mama at the store this morning and she told me about it," Nic said. "Then I called Pat and Carol."

"When is she supposed to get here?" Lisa asked.

"There she is," Pat said, nodding past Lisa.

"Hey, ladies," Carol said, as she hugged all of them.

"A table full of beautiful women. There is a God," Carol's husband, Charles said.

Each lady said hello and gave Charles a hug.

"Well, I guess I will head over where the men are. I'll see you gals later."

Watching him head toward the men, Carol said, "He is just too much."

"That's your husband, girl," Pat laughed.

"Don't I know it?"

"So, now that we are all together, how is the weekend going so far?" Nic asked.

"Better than I expected," Lisa smiled.

"I think somebody's six year drought is over," Carol joked.

"All I have to say, is that man made miracles happen," Lisa said.

All four of them burst out laughing at the same time.

"But for real. I have never felt like this before. I told him last night that I love him."

All three ladies looked at her without saying a word.

Nic said, "Do you?"

"Yeah, I do. I have known him for over three years, as a co-worker, then as a friend. And now as the man I love. And it feels natural. I feel happy and safe with him. It's not at all what I expected to feel about him, especially so quickly. But, I do. I…" Lisa trailed off as she looked at Marc, who was laughing and talking with the other men at a table. He must have felt Lisa looking at him, because he looked at her, smiled and winked.

"I love him," she said.

"Did he say it back?" Carol asked.

"Actually, he said it first. But even if he didn't I would have."

"We are so happy for you," Pat said.

"Hey, Lele."

"Hey, Curtis," Lisa said, standing up to hug one of her cousins.

"What's up Nic…Pat…Carol."

They all said hello, but was preoccupied with girl that was with him. To say that the girl was damn near naked was understatement. Looked like all she had on were shoes.

"Introduce us to your friend, Curt," Pat said.

"Aw, this is Paradise," he said.

"Is that your real name or your stage name, baby?" Lisa asked.

Pat choked on her drink and Nic and Carol had to pat her on her back.

The girl looked at Lisa and said with attitude, "It's my real name."

"Well, it's nice to meet you, Paradise," Nic said.

"I'll catch y'all later," Curtis said.

Lisa, Pat, Nic, and Carol watched Paradise as she headed toward the men.

"Two things I can't believe. First, I can't believe she wore that shit out in public. Second, I can't believe you said that," Carol laughed.

"What? Y'all know I say what's on my mind. Besides, my grandmother told me that when I turn eighteen, I don't have to hold my tongue for nobody."

"Lord knows you live by that rule," Pat said.

Lisa's mother walked out of the house, "Chil' did y'all see what Curtis brought up in here?"

"Yea, we saw," all four ladies said.

"Uh-oh, Nic. She's talking to Michael," Pat said.

"Girl, please. Michael knows I got good aim."

"Honey, she is making her rounds. Now, she's all in Marc and Lewis's faces," Carol said.

Lisa watched the scene from where she was sitting and was about to get up, when Marc looked at her and winked. She smiled. Marc excused himself and walked over to where Lisa and the other ladies were sitting.

"What was Miss Thang talkin' about?" Nic asked Marc.

"Something about not really being that guys girlfriend. She said she was a single agent," Marc explained as he sat down in a chair between Lisa and Carol.

"Anthony, play something so these people can work up an appetite," Janice said.

The next sound everyone heard was Maze. That got everyone up to dance.

"You wanna dance?" Marc asked.

"Sure," she told Marc. Then she said to the girls, "Y'all get those husbands and come on."

For the next couple of songs everyone was up dancing. After the second song ended, people started heading for the table with food and drinks.

"Are you hungry?" Lisa asked Marc.

"No, not yet."

"Well, I'm going to get me something."

"Can that wait a few minutes?"

Looking at him, Lisa smiled and said, "What's the matter?"

Marc didn't say anything; he just pulled her close and started to dance slowly.

"Uh, Marc there's no music."

"I hear music."

The next thing Lisa knew, she heard Anthony Hamilton's *The Point of It All*. Looking over at Anthony, Lisa didn't understand why he was smiling at her. In fact, when she looked around everyone was watching them.

"Oh, God. Sorry about this. I guess it's been a while since I brought someone home and they're in shock," Lisa laughed.

"Lisa."

"Hmm?" she said, looking up at him.

"You remember when I told you that this would be a weekend of surprises?"

"Yes."

"I have another one for you."

"Mmm, you wanna leave so you can give it to me," Lisa smiled.

Smiling himself, Marc said, "I'd actually wanted to give it to you right here."

"What are you talking about?"

Suddenly the entire yard was quiet.

"Lisa, this came as a surprise to me too, but when it came to me I knew I was supposed to do this."

"Do what?" Lisa asked nervously.

Marc reached into his pocket and then kneeled down on one knee.

"Get up," Lisa said.

Marc smiled.

"They are gonna think you're serious."

"I am. Lisa, I have loved you since the first day I saw you in the parking garage at work. I think I've loved you even before I knew you existed. God made you just for me and I am happy to receive this beautiful gift."

Lisa was near tears now.

"Lisa, will you do me the honor of being my wife?" he asked as he opened the small velvet box.

Lisa eyes never left his. She didn't even glance at the ring.

"Yes, I'll marry you" she said in a shaky voice.

Marc happily slipped the ring on Lisa's finger and kissed her hand. Standing up he hugged her tight and kissed her all over her face.

"Thank you," he whispered in her ear.

As Lisa family surrounded them to congratulate them and look at the ring, all Lisa could think was, *I love this man with everything I have in me. Please God, don't let anything ruin this.*

Hugging her mother, Lisa whispered in her, "You approve?"

"Baby, I approve of everything you do. I am so happy for you."

"Thank you, mommy."

Janice then went to Marc and hugged him, "Welcome to the family."

"Thank you for helping me."

"Thank you for making her happy."

Marc hugged Lisa and then said, "Oh, I forgot something." Then he pulled out his cell phone.

"Who are you calling?"

"My parents, they're waiting on our call."

"You already talked to your parents? You have a lot of explaining to do later."

Laughing, Marc said, "Yeah, I know. But if I go down I'm taking a lot people with me. Nic, Pat, Carol, and your mother helped me."

Lisa looked over at her friends, "I'm going to get every last one you."

"Girl, please," Pat said.

"And besides, you're getting married!" Carol screamed, as all four of them hugged.

"Lisa, my mother wants to speak to you," he said handing her the phone.

"Hello…Yes, how are you?...No, ma'am I don't have any children…My mother, and I also have a younger brother…I love your son very much…Okay, I'll see you soon…Hold on." Lisa hand Marc the phone back.

"I'm here…Yes, she is…I now understand what you told me once, pop. I really do," he said, looking at Lisa smiling. "Okay, I'll see you guys next week…Love you, too. Apparently, you make a good first impression over the phone."

"Why?"

"Because they can't wait to meet you. They will be here next week."

"Good, that will give me enough time to get used to this," Lisa said, looking up at him.

For the rest of the day and into the early evening they danced, ate, and drank. By eight-thirty the crowd was thinning down and Lisa, Anthony, and Marc were helping with the cleanup.

When the house and the yard were spic and span, Marc and Lisa walked out in the front yard. Lisa leaned her head back against his chest as he stood behind her and wrapped his arms around her waist.

"What are you thinking about?" he asked.

"This house. Everything important that has happened to me, happened in this house. I had my college graduation party here; I found out that I was hired by Morgan & Peterson here. After working there for one week, I told my mother, 'I saw the most beautiful man in the parking garage today.' Now, I've gotten engaged in this house."

"When I first saw you in the parking garage I thought you were the most beautiful woman I had ever seen. I knew you were taken. And then when Steve saw you, he made it his life's work to get you. I'm so glad you waited for me."

"I've been waiting for you all my life," Lisa said turning toward him.

"I want you to know that I will do my damnedest to make you the happiest woman in the world."

"I promise the same thing."

"You already have. You said yes. You know you still haven't looked at the ring."

"I don't have to."

Marc took her hand into his and held it up. The ring sparkled in the moon light. Lisa smiled at the ring and looked up at Marc and said, "It's beautiful. But you could have gotten it out of a cracker jacks box and I would have still said yes."

"I wish you had of told me that this morning."

Laughing, Lisa said, "You need to stop. But, seriously, it's beautiful. Thank you."

"For what?"

"For rescuing me."

"Ditto." Marc then leaned in and kissed her.

"Ahem, excuse me. Can I talk to you two for a minute?" Janice asked from the front porch.

Looking at each other first, Lisa and Marc said, "Okay."

Following Janice into the house and then into the living room, they all sat down. Marc and Lisa sat on one of the sofas, while Janice sat in a chair facing them.

"First off, congratulations. I hope you two will be happy together. Second, Lisa are you sure? Have you thought this thing through, I mean really thought this through? The both of you," said Janice.

"I am sure, mom. I love him," Lisa said looking at Marc.

"Well, Marc, you have done something no man has been able to do."

"What's that, Mrs. Jenson?"

"You've actually gotten Lisa to tell me she loves someone. She's never done that before."

"I'm a lucky man."

"Yes, you are," Janice said. "And I can tell, so is she. Well, that's all I wanted to talk to you two about. I am tired and I am going to bed. Welcome to the family, Marc."

"Thank you, Mrs. Jenson."

"I think Janice is more appropriate. Good night," Janice said, heading for the stairs.

"Good night," Lisa and Marc said.

"What's up y'all?" Anthony said coming into the living room.

"Hey, what are you doing tonight?" Lisa asked.

"Me and some friends going downtown on Beale."

"Looking for girls?"

"Women, Lisa, women."

"What time are you leaving?"

"In about an hour."

"Well, we're leaving now and mama went up to bed. So, lock up when you leave."

"Will do. And Marc, man, welcome to the family. I am so happy there's another man in the family. All these women were wearing me down."

Lisa laughed and shook her head.

"I got you, man, "Marc said.

"And congratulations, sis."

"Thank you, Ant," Lisa said, as she hugged him.

"See y'all later."

Walking to the car, Lisa got in when Marc opened her door. As she waited for him to get in, she stared at her ring in disbelief. When he got in the car, she said, "This is beautiful, Marc. I think now would be as good of a time as any for you to tell me what you've been up to today."

"Okay," he said, as he backed out of the driveway. "Waking up to you this morning was the happiest moment in my life. And right then I knew that I wanted to wake up to you for the rest of my life. So, I called Nic and she gave me your mother's phone number. I asked if I could come over. We talked for about an hour. And after I got her blessing, I went to the jewelry store."

"Basically, everyone knew but me?"

"Yes."

"You have been busy."

Laughing, Marc kissed the back of Lisa's hand. "So, I vote that we stop off and get some champagne and then I take you home and make love to my fiancée."

"It's amazing how much we think alike."

On the way home, Marc stopped and bought two bottles of champagne.

"Two bottles?" Lisa asked.

"We can drink one and find other ways to get rid of the other."

"Mmmm, I do like the way you think."

Five minutes later they pulled into Marc's driveway. Walking in, Marc said, "I'm getting a bucket of ice, two glasses, and I'll meet you upstairs."

"Don't be too long," Lisa said, smiling.

When Lisa got upstairs, she grabbed her bag and went into the bathroom to shower and change. Marc came in the room and set the bucket and glasses on the nightstand, dimmed the lights, and folded back the covers. Then he went to the guest bathroom to take a quick shower. Ten minutes later, he walked in the bedroom to find Lisa lying on the bed in a red lace see through top with matching panties.

Marc walked toward Lisa as she stood up.

"You look beautiful."

"Is that right? But, what do you think of the back?" she asked, as she turned around.

"Damn!"

The top was actually backless and held together by a small gold chain and the underwear was a thong.

"I take it you approve."

"More than approve." Then he kissed Lisa on the back. "I want to make love to you, tonight."

"Mmmm," was all Lisa could manage.

"But there is something I have to do first. Follow me."

Following him into his office, Lisa watched as went to his cabinet and pull out a manila folder.

"Come here."

"What's this, a prenup?" Lisa joked.

"No," he laughed. "But...Sit down." He pulled Lisa onto his lap when he sat in his desk chair.

Lisa opened the file and red the contents. When she finished she looked at him.

"Last night we got caught up in the moment and never got to talk about it. So, I wanted to do it tonight. You said that you trusted me and so I wanted you know everything."

Lisa looked back at the papers and noticed that each paper was dated every six months.

"Thank you for showing me this. Somehow you seem to always put my mind at ease. I am also negative. I can show my test results."

"Nic told me –"

"I know she did. I went almost every month for testing for the last six years. My doctor got so tired of me that she told me to stop coming to her office. I had to be sure, you know?"

"I understand. Now that that is out of the way we can move on to better things."

Looking around his home office, Lisa said, "You know what this room needs?"

"What?"

"A memory. Something that hits you every time you walk into this room."

"Like what?"

"I was thinking…" Lisa turned around in his lap and swung her leg over his head to face him in the chair.

"I thought you might have meant a picture or something."

"What's better than a memory of your favorite moment, you can replay over…and over… and over in your mind?" she whispered in his ear, as she grind on the hardness she felt against her inner thigh.

Lost for a minute, he finally said, "You mean right her, right now?"

Lisa nodded.

Marc didn't hesitate. "Come here, Mrs. Cavell."

"Ooo, I like the sound of that."

Their kiss started out slow and sensual, with Marc's hands in Lisa's hair.

Breaking the kiss, Marc whispered against her lips, "You are so beautiful."

Slipping his hand between them, Marc rubbed Lisa through her lace underwear.

"Ohhh," Lisa moaned.

Their kiss became more passionate. Feeling her move against his hand, he moved her panties to the side and started to rub her clit. As she moved her hips, she started to moan louder.

"Oh, Marc, yes. Don't stop. Marc, I'm cumming."

Dropping her head on his shoulder, she heard him say, "Do you need a minute?"

"No, I'm great," she chuckled.

"Good, because I want you so bad."

Kissing him deeply, Lisa freed Marc from his pajama bottoms and began to stroke him.

"Oh, Lisa."

All of a sudden, Marc lifted Lisa up and pushed inside of her.

"Oh," she gasped.

"Are you okay?"

"Yes," Lisa said, looking at him.

As they made love in Marc's chair, they held each other close and called each other's name. Moving faster and faster in the chair, they both got louder. They climaxed together at a fast pace and loudly.

After catching his breath, Marc looked up at Lisa, "You are so not what I expected."

"And what did you expect?"

"A beautiful woman, who was a little more...tame. I didn't think you would be –"

"Freaky? Oh, baby, you ain't seen nothing yet."

"What you got?"

"Well..." Lisa leaned close to his ear and whispered.

"For real?"

"For real."

"You can do that?"

"And..."

"You've done this before?"

"I've been out of practice a long time. Think you can get me back into shape."

"Oh, your shape is fine. But, I'll be happy to help in any way I can." Marc stood up, and Lisa wrapped her legs around him, as he carried her back into the bedroom.

Laying her on the bed, he said, "How about some champagne?"

"I would love some."

"Let me ask you something. Did you ever think when we first started working together that we would end up here?" he asked, as he poured the champagne.

"No."

"Never?"

"No. My imagination never got that far."

"But you did think about me. How far did it go?"

"Last night. What about you?"

"I knew you were the one. From the moment you step out of your car, ignored me completely, and walked into the building, I was in love."

"I did not ignore you."

"Yes, you did. I remember I parked right next to you on your first day. I got out of my car first and I was putting on my suit jacket when you stepped out. Needless to say, I was speechless. I watched you get out of the car; well I watched your legs. Anyway, I said good morning, you mumbled a reply and walked right past me. I was in love."

"I did not ignore you. It was my first day at work, I was nervous. And I remember it a different way. I remember sitting in my car trying to get up enough nerve to go in, when you pulled into the parking space next to me. I also remember looking over at you and thinking to myself that you had the most beautiful dark hair. You got out of your car and I watched you put on your jacket. You were the most handsome man that I had ever seen. I knew you were spoken for. I got out of my car, knowing that you would probably look right past me, but you didn't. You actually looked at me like you'd seen a ghost. So, when you finally spoke, I thought you were crazy and just wanted to get out of that garage as quickly as I could."

"Why did you think I would look right past you?"

"I was still healing. And I figured someone like you would not want to deal with all of my baggage. So, yes, I did mumble a hello and got the hell out of there. After that I only saw you in passing. But, I would always turn my head before you noticed me looking at you."

"Well, then you never caught me staring at you. We wasted three years."

"No we didn't. We spent three years getting to know one another, working together, and then becoming friends. That was not a waste. I love you. There is nothing wasteful about that."

"Same here. How do you feel?"

"Extremely happy!"

"Good. I think now is as good of a time as any to discuss some things."

"Like?" Lisa said, taking her second refill.

"Like, how do you feel about me being Catholic?"

"I think your religion is interesting and would love to learn more about it. What about you?"

"I'm fine with it. But, I don't know everything. I guess we both have something to learn."

"What are your expectations from marriage?"

"Jump right to the serious stuff, huh?"

"Yep,"

"Okay. I only know from my parents what marriage is. My mother worked and still managed to take care of me and my dad. She taught me how to appreciate the woman in my life, to always be a gentleman, and to respect her. My dad taught me to be a man. He took care of his family and never mistreated my mother. You know," Marc chuckled. "They still hold hands and kiss, and every time they hear *The Way You Look Tonight*, they dance. They're great parents. When I was growing up I never needed for a thing."

"You are very lucky. They sound like great people. They remind me of my grandparents. I remember when I was little I would see them dance together, or they would get up early in the mornings and eat breakfast together. Every morning I would hear them talking. I never heard them argue. As I got older, I knew that's what a marriage was supposed to be."

"Were these your mother's parents?"

"No, my dad's."

"Oh. You sound like you spent a lot of time with them."

"Every summer and on weekends during the school year. They were married for fifty years before he passed away."

"That is something to aim for."

"We'll make it."

"I know we will," he said, then kissed her. "I promise to be everything you need me to be. I promise to never do anything that will hurt you or let anyone hurt you."

"And I promise to love you every day of our lives. I promise to never lie to you or let anyone come between us. Lastly, I promise to do everything you need or want."

"You can keep that promise right now. Come here," he said as he sat both of their glasses on the night stand.

For the remainder of the night, they made love, only stopping long enough to say, I love you. They finally fell asleep later that night wrapped in each other's arms and in sexual bliss.

Chapter Twenty-Two

"Marc? Marc?" Lisa whispered in his ear.

"Hmm," he stirred, slowly opening his eyes.

"Good morning, sleepy head."

"Good morning."

"Breakfast is served."

"Breakfast?"

"Yep," Lisa said, setting the tray across his lap.

"Look at this. You didn't have to cook breakfast for me."

"I wanted to. As you can see, you have an omelet, sliced strawberries, French toast, orange juice, and coffee. Now eat up."

"Have you eaten?" he asked, as he cut into the omelet.

"While I cooked. I hope you don't mind me wearing your shirt."

"As sexy as you look, I don't mind at all."

Lisa smiled and watched him eat.

"Are we going to church this morning?"

"That is up to you. My mother and grandmother aren't going. So…"

"Oh, alright. Then next Sunday."

"Anything in particular you'd like to do today?"

"Since, it's going to be such a nice day, how about we go down to the park and have a picnic? Then, I figured when I got you in a good mood, I'd ask you to move in with me," Marc said, watching the stunned look on Lisa's face.

"S-Say what?" Lisa stammered.

"I want you to move in with me."

"Marc, we –we just got engaged yesterday."

"I tell you what, we'll shower, dress, and then we will pack a lunch and walk down to the park. Deal?"

"Ok," Lisa said, still in a bit of a shock.

Setting his tray to the side and getting out of bed, Lisa said, "I'll take the tray down and start the dishwasher."

"Ok. I'll make the bed."

When Lisa walked back in the room she heard the shower running.

She walked into the bathroom and knocked on the glass shower door, and said, "Hey, you need help with your back?"

Without saying a word, Marc pulled Lisa into the shower.

"Wait, your shirt," Lisa laughed.

"Can easily be removed."

Kissing Lisa and unbuttoning the shirt, he then leaned her against the shower wall."

"I thought we were gonna take a shower?"

"We are," Marc said, and picked up the soap.

"Picking the soap up doesn't make it a shower."

"Let me handle this."

Marc rubbed soap all over Lisa and then himself.

"Damn this," he said. The next thing Lisa knew he picked her up and pushed inside her. Marc thrust into her over and over, while she loudly proclaimed how much she loved him.

"Oh, Lisa," he said, as he came.

"Don't stop, I'm cumming."

Once they both caught their breaths, Marc said, "I'm sorry, I couldn't help myself. I never can when I'm around you."

As they slid to the shower floor, Lisa said, "You never have to apologize for that. You don't even have to ask."

"God, I can't wait to marry you."

"Come on."

They finished showering and then got dressed. Marc in gym shorts, a tank top, and running shoes. Lisa was dressed in white shorts, pink and white layered tank tops, and a pair of white tennis shoes.

They went downstairs and packed a basket with cold cuts, fruits, and bottles of water.

"Ready?" Marc asked.

"Yep," she said, heading out the back door ahead him.

***

James was sitting on the back pew half listening to the church announcements and half wondering why Lisa or her family didn't come to church. Then he heard something that caught his attention.

The church secretary was saying, "And Sister Beverly Dodson would like you all to send best wishes to her granddaughter, Lisa. She got engaged to Mr. Marc Cavell on yesterday."

James was fuming. He inched out of the isle and stormed out of the church, leaving the church clapping for Lisa's and Marc's engagement.

***

Lisa and Marc found a spot under a tree and laid out a blanket. Marc set the basket down and playfully tackled Lisa down on the blanket.

Laughing, Lisa said, "Security, a crazy man is on the loose."

Rolling over and pulling Lisa on top of him, Marc said, "Now, when security shows up it's you who gets arrested."

"Then let me make this worth my while," she said, then kissed him.

When they separated Lisa raised up so Marc could sit up.

Pulling Lisa to sit between his legs, he said, "Ok, now let's get some things straight. After we're married I want you home every day cooking and cleaning, and catering to me."

"Yeah, right," Lisa said, elbowing him.

"Oww, okay. Seriously, what are your thoughts on being married?"

Looking up at him, and then turning around to face him, "Well, first off you have to take care of me and keep me accustom to the life I have. I want a bigger house; I want to quit my job and more diamonds. I want to do absolutely nothing."

"Yeah, right," Marc laughed.

Laughing, Lisa said, "I just thought I'd be honest."

Pushing the hair out of her eyes and stared into them.

"You ready for the real answer?"

"Yes."

"First, you are the most beautiful man I've ever met. No one has ever made me as happy as you do."

"That's not an answer."

"Alright. I don't believe in divorce. Marriage is about teamwork and being there for one another. I believe that a man is and should be head of the house, but only if he is truly a man. A wife that knows her husband is a strong willed, smart man that will take care of her should trust his judgment. Now, don't get it twisted, a man should believe the same thing about is wife. He should trust that she is also doing what is right for the family. Now, you turn."

"Honestly, I fill the same way. A marriage is about give and take. And I don't believe in divorce, either. I believe in forever," he said, close to her lips and then kissing her.

After a moment, Lisa pulled away, "Don't even try it. Let me ask you something, how badly do you want kids?"

"I do want kids, but we already discussed this topic."

"No we didn't. We discussed the fact surrounding children."

"Look, nothing would make me happier than having a beautiful little girl who looks just like you."

"Or a handsome little boy that looks just like you."

"But we can always adopt a child and give him or her a happy home."

"Okay. Now, on to the next subject. I think we need to talk about the moving in issue."

Lisa reached into the basket and pulled out a Tupperware bowl of fruit. She took out a handful of grapes and fed one to Marc.

"I think I had this fantasy once."

"Anyway. Like I was saying, we just got engaged last night. Don't you think we're jumping ahead?"

"Nope," Marc said, as he ate another grape.

"Are you sure?"

"You know, you ask a lot of questions. At work you trust my decisions, why can't you do that now?"

Looking into those dark sexy eyes of his, Lisa said, "I do trust your decisions, but –"

"Then trust me when I tell you that I love you and want to spend every moment with you."

"You sure you won't get tired of me?"

"Never."

"I don't know, I've never lived with anyone before, have you?"

Hesitating, he said, "Yes, but it wasn't a good experience."

"What happened?" she asked, then bit into a strawberry and put the other half in Marc's mouth.

After swallowing, he said, "You never know a person until you live with them."

"Enough said. The thing is that I love my house and you love your house –"

"I want you." Looking at her for a minute, he said, "I tell you what, I know things are moving kind of fast. So, what I propose is that we continue to go between each other's homes. Wait, there's an "if". There is a vacant lot right at the end, you see it?"

"Yeah."

"Now, here's the "if", only if we buy the lot and build our new home to live in as husband and wife."

"Are you serious?"

"Yes. But you do know that means selling our current homes? We put all in or nothing."

"All in," Lisa said, kissing him.

"Let's eat."

After they ate, Lisa turned around leaned back against Marc.

Watching boats and people go by, Marc said, "Will you stay the rest of the week?"

"I don't know, I might have other plans."

Tickling her, he said, "Say you'll stay. Say it, say it."

"Okay, okay. I'll stay," Lisa laughed.

"Good. Now, how about we go out to dinner tonight?"

"No, I want to spend the rest of the day in bed."

"I like that idea better."

"We can watch movies, I'll make dinner, and we can make love. And not necessarily in that order."

"Mmm."

"Mmm."

They sat quietly and watched the world go by, until Lisa said, "I want to marry you next year."

Marc didn't say a word, he listened.

Lisa continued, "I'm not going to dwell on my past or let my past dictate my future. My mother tells me on a regular basis, that one bad man doesn't mean they're all bad."

"True."

"But, I didn't believe that. And now that I have taken that chance, I don't want to wait."

Marc continued to be quiet, so Lisa said, "I like the strong silent type, but say something. What do you want?"

"I would marry you now if you were ready. But, I am willing to wait. I don't want you to feel pressured. Do you?"

"No, not at all."

"With the proposal, the moving in, everything that has happened over the weekend, do you feel pressured?"

"No. I actually feel just the opposite. You are such a good man. If it wasn't for Carol, I don't think I would have gone out with you."

"I was hoping I had a little to do with it," he said.

"You did," Lisa said, kissing his neck.

"We've only been going out for almost three weeks."

"But we've known each other for three years."

"Yeah, but only professionally and just friends."

"Would you say you know me?"

"Better than anyone I have ever been with."

"I can say the same about you." Then turning back around to face him, she said, "Do you want to back out of this engagement, be –"

Marc put his finger against her lips, and said, "Lisa, baby, no. That's not what I'm saying at all. Proposing to you was the best thing that I have ever done."

Lisa leaned in and kissed him.

When they stopped, Marc said, "What does that mean?"

"That means September 18, 2010."

"Are you com –"

"You know, you ask too many questions."

Laughing, he yelled, "I'm getting married!"

People that were walking by or sitting near them smiled at them and watched the two kiss under the shade of a tree.

Chapter Twenty-Three

Leaving the grocery store, Lisa and Marc headed to Lisa's house so she could pack for the week.

"God, I know those flowers need watering, but I know it smells wonderful inside. Probably needs a little airing," Lisa said, as unlocked her door.

"Yeah, I think I might have gone a little overboard," Marc was saying as Lisa put in her alarm code.

"I thought that was the most roman –" Lisa stopped in her tracks when she saw her living room in disarray. "Oh, my God!"

Every rose was torn into pieces and every vase was demolished. The living room looked like a typhoon had hit.

"Wait, a minute," Marc said, walking in ahead of her.

They walked around the living room listening for any sounds in the house. When they went to check upstairs, they noticed none of the other rooms were touched, only the living room. Heading back downstairs, Lisa was calling Nic as Marc surveyed the damage. She saw him pause in front of her mirror.

When Lisa noticed he was staring at her mirror, she said, "What's wrong?"

"Nothing. Why don't we go outside and wait for the police?"

"Marc, let me go! What's wrong with the mirror?"

"Lisa, wait!"

She broke away from his grip and walked over to the mirror. Written in marker was one word...*Congratulations*. Lisa stared at the mirror for what seemed like an eternity.

Marc walked over and turned her away from the mirror and pulled her close. She didn't say anything, she stood still in his embrace.

"It's okay. Come on let's go outside for some air."

He led Lisa out of the house and they sat on the porch. The entire two minutes it took Nic to get to the house, Marc kept assuring Lisa everything was going to be okay.

"Lisa, what happened?" Nic asked, the minute she jumped out of her truck.

"It's a mess in there, Nic," Marc answered for a stunned Lisa.

Nic walked pass them into the house and couldn't believe what she was seeing. "Did you touch anything?"

"No. We just made sure the house was empty, and then we came out here," Marc said.

"What does the rest of the house look like?" Nic asked.

"Apparently like you guys left it Friday. The roses and the mirror were the only things touched from what I could tell," he told her.

"The mirror? What, on top of the fact that I'm gon' shot first and *then* ask questions when I see his ass, he got seven years bad luck too?"

"He left a message," Lisa finally said, coming into the house.

Nic went over to the mirror and then quickly looked at Lisa. "How the hell does he know?"

"I don't – oh, my God. He was at church a week ago. I'm sure he went today thinking he would run into me there. Instead he heard the announcement my grandmother gave the church secretary. He knows," she said, looking at Nic and Marc.

Everyone stared at each other. Nic's partner and a couple more cops came through the front door.

"Hey, John. Can you get these guys to see if there are any fingerprints? Whatever they can find," Nic said, to her partner.

"Yeah. How you doing Lisa?" John asked.

"I've been better. John this is my fiancé, Marc. Marc, this is John."

The two men shook hands.

"Come on, guys, let's let them work and we'll go outside," Nic said.

"Hey, Lisa, you mind if we check the messages. Your dial says you've got twenty messages," John said.

"Go ahead."

Pushing the button with a pencil, they all listened to the messages.

"This is your grandmother, Lisa. I just wanted to tell you and Marc that I wish you two the best. Call me."

"Hey Lis, sorry I didn't make the barbecue. But I was told that it was enough to make you cry. I can't wait to see that rock. I heard it was big enough generate heat from the sun. Call me."

"Stephanie," Lisa said smiling.

His voice stopped everyone in their tracks, "I hope I get an invitation to the big day. But, even if I don't, I'll be there."

Then, "I see you're not home yet. I'll wait for you."

Next message: "How could you marry someone else? What about what we had? This ain't over Lisa."

The next few messages were hang ups, but the last one was show stopper.

"I'm sure by now you've seen my handy work and gotten my message. I told you a long time ago you can't get away from me. Don't think ol' rich boy gon' be able to save you. Because if I have to go through him to get to you…I will. I'll see yo' ass dead before I see you with somebody else. See you soon, beautiful."

No one said anything. Then John said, "We're gonna need someone to make a copy of each one of these messages. Somebody get my recorder out of my car."

"Lisa you can't –"

"I know," Lisa said, cutting Marc off before he could finish his sentence. "I guess you're gonna get your wish."

"What wish?" Nic asked.

"Marc asked me to move in with him today."

Nic looked at them standing together. They looked right together. "I'll help you pack," Nic said.

They headed upstairs while Marc stayed downstairs talking to John.

When they made it to Lisa's bedroom, Nic said, "Are you okay?"

"I wanna kill him," Lisa said.

"Look, for right now calm down. Just pack what you need and then we'll try to find this asshole and then I will personally let you kick his ass."

"How can I let Marc go through something like this?" Lisa asked.

"Have you guys talked about this?"

"No. There was never a reason too."

"Well, there's a reason to, now."

"I can't let him put his self in danger because of my shit. How can I ask him to do that?"

"You can't."

"What man wants this in his life? I love him, Nic. With everything in me, I love that man. But I can't do this to him."

Marc stood outside the doorway and listened to them talk.

He heard Lisa say, "I think I better find some kind of way to let him down easy. I mean you heard James on that tape. I don't want Marc to get hurt because of my mess."

Sighing, Nic said, "How do you know Marc's gonna let you go? I mean, have you really looked at your hand. Look at it. Marc loves you. Trust me on that. I talked to him on Saturday morning. I believe that man will never let anything happen to you. And besides have you seen him? I only saw him with his shirt open and I can tell he can take care of himself. Marc's not gonna let you go without a fight, Lisa."

"She's right, I'm not," Marc said, walking into the room.

Nic looked at Lisa and then said, "I'm going downstairs to see what they've found out so far."

When Nic left the room, Marc said, "I'm not letting you go. I heard what you said and I understand how you feel. But we can get through this. I just need you to believe in me…to believe in us." Walking closer, he said, "Will you do that?"

Lisa looked at him, and then said, "You heard what he said. You didn't sign up for this."

"I signed up to love you until the day this earth ends. That's all that matters. I will protect you. I will never let anything happen to you. Don't give up on us now before we even get started."

"Are you sure about this?" Lisa whispered.

"More than anything in this world."

"Okay."

They stood in the middle of Lisa's bedroom wrapped in each other's arms.

"We're gonna get through this. I promise," he whispered, kissing the top of Lisa's head.

"So, I guess I can pack a few things until Nic and her partner are through with the house and then I'll be able to come back home."

"I don't want you to ever come back to this house. But, I also know that you're not ready to move in with me yet. So how about we cross that bridge when we get to it? When you think you're ready to come back here, then we'll talk about it.

They packed two of Lisa's suitcases and then headed downstairs. Marc went and put the luggage in Lisa's trunk and then came back in the house.

Lisa was asking Nic, "So, what happens now?"

"You go with Marc and I will call you later. Lisa you have to tell your mother."

"I know, I'll call her."

"And also expect calls from Pat and Carol."

"Don't I know it? See you later," Lisa said, as she hugged Nic.

✳✳✳

Lisa and Marc made it to his house and brought in the grocery and Lisa's luggage.

Taking her bags upstairs, while Lisa unpacked the groceries, Marc said, "I'll make some room in the closet and dresser for you."

Lisa put the groceries away and wandered outside on the balcony.

Coming up behind her and putting his hands around her waist, Marc said, "Are you alright?"

"Yeah, I'm fine."

"You can talk to me."

"I know. I'm just thinking some things through, that's all."

"Are you hungry?"

"No."

"I tell you what. Why don't you go take a long hot bath and then I will meet you upstairs with dinner. You have to eat."

"Alright. Thanks."

Marc watched Lisa head upstairs and it broke his heart that there was nothing he could do to change her mood right now. He decided to make grilled chicken for dinner. He knew Lisa had this thing for grilled chicken sandwiches with cheese. As he cooked, he could hear the jets going upstairs. Marc didn't know what he was going to do about James. His first instinct was to find him and beat the hell out of him, but he didn't know where to look. Somehow, he knew that James would pop up and then Marc would get his chance.

Twenty minutes later, Marc headed upstairs carrying a tray with everything they needed for their dinner. When he walked into the bedroom, Lisa was sitting on the bed in towel putting on lotion.

"I hope you're hungry by now," Marc said.

Looking at the tray, Lisa smiled. "I think I can do with a bite."

"Go ahead and eat while I jump in the shower."

"What about your food?"

"It'll keep."

Lisa finished getting dressed and took the tray back downstairs. Putting the chicken in the microwave to keep it warm while Marc showered, she also decided to open a bottle wine. She definitely could use a drink. After warming the chicken up, she headed back upstairs with the tray. She set the tray on the bed and waited for Marc to come out of the bathroom.

"You haven't eaten yet?" he asked, five minutes later when he came out of the bathroom.

"Waiting for you."

Marc put on a pajama pants, while Lisa was already in a pair of silk blue pajamas.

Looking at her, Marc said, "Please tell me you don't own any flannel nightgowns."

"I don't own a one."

"Thank God," Marc said, coming toward the bed.

"Eat up. I took the liberty of warming everything up."

"Thank you. Now, you eat."

"Yes, sir."

Marc picked up a remote from the nightstand and turned on the television.

"I was wondering which one it was," Lisa said.

Laughing, he said, "No wonder you're sitting here looking lost."

"I know you're a sports man. What kind of sports are you into?"

"All of them. What about you? Do you like any?"

"My favorite is boxing. I can deal with a little football and hockey."

"You like boxing?"

"Correction, I love boxing. Diehard fan."

"A woman truly after my heart," he said, as he kissed her neck.

As he flipped through channels, Lisa said, "I called my mother."

Marc stopped flipping channels and looked at her. "What did she say?"

"She was livid. She agreed that I should stay here for the week. But, there was so much cussing I didn't really get a word."

"She's worried about you, that's all."

"Yeah, I know."

Deciding to watch a movie with Angeline Jolie, they finished eating and started on the wine.

By nine, the kitchen was clean and they were in bed, in each other's arms, listening to soft music.

"What am I going to do?" Lisa finally asked.

"What are we going to do?" Marc corrected her.

"He's not going to stop, Marc. I can't let him invade your life, too."

"You are my life. So, therefore, he's already in it. We can get through this. Now, forget about him for tonight."

Taking a deep breath, Lisa looked up at Marc, "Do you own a pajama top?"

Laughing, he said, "Yes, I just never wear them."

"Good, that means my work is already half done," Lisa said, as she climbed on top of him.

"What are you doing?" Marc asked, with a huge smile on his face.

As she unbuttoned her top and let it slide off her shoulders, she said, "I'm seducing you. Is it working?"

Marc rose up and took one of Lisa breasts into his mouth.

"Mmm, good answer."

Marc switched from breast to breast as Lisa pulled him closer. She could feel him getting harder against her inner thigh.

She started to move her hips against him and heard him moan. Quickly, Marc rolled her over onto her back and came up on his knees.

"Now, who's seducing who?" Lisa laughed.

Without giving an answer, Marc slipped Lisa's pajama pants and underwear off and dropped them on the floor. Without hesitation, he kissed Lisa softly on her most sensitive spot. He kissed the inside of her thighs and then started to lick her into oblivion. She hadn't felt this good in a long time. James was the farthest thing from her mind.

"Ohh, Marc," she moaned.

It seemed to Lisa that he had found his home, because he was not coming up for air. She continued to moan and pull him closer. When she finally came, the feeling was so strong Marc had to hold her until she stopped shaking.

When she could finally speak, she said, "Oh, my God. What got into you?"

"The question is what's about to get into you?"

Marc pushed inside Lisa, and she welcomed the feeling of his body covering hers.

Their love making was slow and soft. There was no urgency like there was the night before. They had all night and they used every single minute. With whispers of I love you, to moaning sexual words in each other's ear. When they were finally spent, it was two o'clock in the morning. Lisa was lying on his chest as he stroked her back.

The rest of the night Marc lay awake. Once forgotten James was the front runner in his brain. What the hell was he going to do about this guy?

Chapter Twenty-Four

The alarm went off waking them up at five-thirty.

"Good morning, Mona Lisa," Marc said, kissing her neck.

"Good morning," Lisa said, kissing him on the lips.

Lisa got out of bed and put on the clothes that she discarded last night and headed into the bathroom.

Coming out ten minutes later, Lisa said, "What would you like for breakfast?"

"You," he said, heading into the bathroom.

"What else?" Lisa said, as she began to make up the bed.

"That's it," he called from the bathroom.

Walking into the bathroom when she finished making the bed, Lisa said, "Cereal it is." Lisa laughed, as she slapped him on the butt. "Meet you downstairs."

After finishing his morning routine, he headed downstairs.

"You're just in time," Lisa said, when he walked into the kitchen.

Marc sat down at the island and asked, "What does your day look like?"

"Just the meeting with John at ten. How about you?"

"I have a meeting with Mr. Keene."

"Good luck."

"You wanna join us?"

"Nope," Lisa said, rinsing her bowl out then putting it in the dishwater.

"Why not?"

"It's okay for you to take the lead on this one. I'm fine with doing the paperwork, research, and not dealing with him," she said leaning against the counter.

"But we're a team and I don't want to do this without you."

"You won't. I just can't deal with him. Besides, you know if I do and he says something I don't like, we'll lose the account."

"You're over exaggerating; I've seen you under pressure."

"He wants you, just go along with it. Please."

"Okay."

"Thank you," Lisa said, pulling him closer. "How about I give you a real thank you?"

"What do you have in mind?"

"Follow me."

Lisa led him into the living room and pulled chair from the table and gently pushed him in it.

"I had this planned for yesterday, but with everything…"

"Yeah, I know. But what did you plan?"

Lisa went over to the radio and turned the CD player on. Joe's voice came through the speakers. Lisa let her hair down from her ponytail as she danced slowly. She then slowly unbuttoned her top and let it slip off her shoulders. She then threw it at Marc. Lisa walked slowly toward Marc slipping her pajama bottoms off her hips. Kicking them to the side when she slipped out of them, she stood in front of Marc in nothing but her lace underwear.

Walking over to him, she gave him a lap dance. When she sat in his lap, she instantly felt how hard he was. She began to move in his lap and could hear him moan in her ear. Then she swung her left leg over his head and turned to face him and continued to move in his lap.

"Mmm," Marc said looking at her.

"Enjoying the show?" Lisa purred in his ear.

"Most definitely."

"Good, 'cause you're gonna love this." All of a sudden Lisa did a back flip out of his lap and landed in a spilt on the floor in front of him.

"Damn! You are really not what I expected."

Lisa came out of the split and her panties at the same time.

Standing up and walking toward him again, she said, "How was that?"

Marc didn't say anything, he leaned in and kissed Lisa's stomach. Pulling her closer to him, he moved up to her breast, giving each one its due attention, while Lisa ran her fingers through hair.

"Mmm, that feels good," she moaned.

Marc stood up quickly and the sudden movement made Lisa gasp. He kissed her deeply, while bringing her down to the floor. Never breaking their kiss, Marc kicked off his pajama pants. He pushed inside of her so hard that she let out a loud moan. Lisa wrapped her legs around him as he pounded into her. Lisa called his name over and over.

She then rolled him over and got on top. He grabbed her hips and came up to kiss her.

Breaking their kiss, he whispered, "Turn around."

Without hesitation, Lisa turned around. Marc then pushed into her from the back. He pushed into her over and over, harder and harder.

"Yes! Yes! Harder!" Lisa screamed.

"Oh, Lisa!" Marc said, as he exploded inside her. Then Lisa climaxed not too far behind him.

They both collapsed on the floor, breathing hard. Then they looked at each other and burst out laughing.

"Oh, my God," Lisa said, still trying to catch her breath. "Where did that come from?"

Kissing her shoulder, he said, "I didn't hurt you did I?"

"Yes, but I liked it."

"I heard," Marc said, laughing.

"Was I too loud?"

"You could never be too loud. No one has ever turned me on like you do."

"And no one will ever love you like I do, either," Lisa said, looking into his eyes.

Marc smiled as he caressed her cheek.

Looking at the clock, Lisa said, "We better start getting ready. Or do you think you can move?"

"I think I can make it. How about you?"

"I think I'll be skipping into work this morning."

They spent the next hour showering and getting dressed for work.

"You ready?" he asked.

"As I'll ever be," Lisa said, walking downstairs. "I'm driving today. Do you think you can handle it?"

"I trust you," he said, as he set the alarm.

After getting in and driving out of his circular driveway, Lisa hit the gas pedal.

"Have you ever been pulled over?"

"When I first got the car."

"But not since then?"

"I thought you said you trust me?"

"I do."

They made to work in no time flat. Lisa had to admit that it was better than maneuvering through expressway traffic.

"Good morning, Shirley," Lisa and Marc said, as they went into the parking garage.

"Good morning, Ms. Jenson...Mr. Cavell."

Lisa parked, then said, "See safe arrival."

They got out with their briefcases, and then Lisa hit locked the doors.

"Nervous?" Marc asked.

"Not one bit. You?"

"None whatsoever."

When they made it to the top floor, Marc walked Lisa to her office.

"Well, look at the happy couple," Carol said.

"Good morning, Carol," Marc said.

"Morning, Marc."

"I'll see you later, beautiful," he said and kissed Lisa.

"Okay."

Lisa walked into her office as if nothing happened; knowing Carol was going to follow.

"Don't you even try to act like everything is normal."

"What? Everything is normal."

"Lisa, you're getting married, aren't you excited?"

"Nope," she said with a straight face.

"Stop lying."

"Okay, okay. I've been waiting all weekend to see you guys again. I'm so happy I could burst."

"I can tell. You're glowing. But, there's something else, too. Oh, somebody had a good morning."

Lisa couldn't hide the smile that spread across her face.

"Unh huh, that's what I thought. Go head, girl! You got six years to make up for. Wear his ass out," Carol said.

Laughing at friend, Lisa just shook her head.

"I'm really happy for you Lisa. And Marc, too. I told you the two were made for each other."

"Yes, we are."

"Now, I don't mean to bring you down. But, Nic called me yesterday."

"I knew she would. I've never seen anything like it, Carol. All those beautiful roses Marc bought for me were ruined."

"What has Marc said about everything?"

"That's the thing; he hasn't said anything about James's threats. He's been concentrating on making sure that I know he's not going anywhere. Although, I did want to take a break. I can't bring something like this into his life."

"I take it he didn't agree."

"No. He made me promise not to give up on us before we even get started."

"Good promise."

"You think I'm doing the right thing?"

"Yes, I do. You deserve to be happy and Marc does that. He is not going to let anything ruin that."

"He asked me to move in with him. That is, before we found out about my house."

"Are you gonna do it?"

"I haven't decided yet. For right now, I'm spending the week at his house because I can't go home."

"Look, don't dwell on it. The right answer will come to you in due time. You ready?"

"Yeah. What's on the calendar for today?"

"First, you have a ten o'clock meeting with John, and at three you have meeting with Mr. Thompson."

"Good. Will you please call Nic and Pat and see if they're free for lunch? If they are, tell them to meet us at Huey's on Union. Oh, can you also call Sarah Blakely and find out why she hasn't sent over her information yet?"

"Will do. Oh, before I forget. This is for you," Carol said, handing Lisa a box.

Lisa looked at the box that was outstretched in Carol's hand.

"It's okay, it's from Nic."

With a sigh, Lisa took the box and opened it. Inside was a picture frame. When she pulled it out, it was the picture Nic took of them Friday night.

"You two look good. That dress is gorgeous."

Right then, her desk phone rung, "This is Lisa."

"Did you open your box yet?" Marc asked.

"Yeah, how did you know I got a delivery?"

"Because I also got one. And, might I add, you look beautiful."

"You look so handsome."

"I'm going to blow mine up to the size of the opposite wall in my office and hang it up."

"You better not," Lisa laughed.

"Okay, how about half the size, then?"

"No."

"Well, my first meeting has arrived. I'll see you later."

"Okay."

"I love you, Mona Lisa."

"I love you, Marc."

After hanging up, Lisa made room on the small table behind her desk where her vase of flowers still bloomed. Thirty minutes later, Lisa headed to John's office.

"Come in, Lisa," John said, after Lisa knocked.

"Good morning, John," Lisa said, walking into the office.

"Good morning."

For the next hour and a half Lisa and John discussed the Thompson account. They went over all of the pertinent information concerning Mr. Thompson's second company, and also future plans for further investments.

Then, John said, "Is there anything else you're working on?"

"A security firm checking out options. The owner's name is Sarah Blakely and Blakely Security Systems is the name of her company. She was supposed to send over her company's information, but we haven't received it yet. So, Carol is checking on that now."

"Alright. Looks like you're on top of things, as usual. Keep me posted."

"Sure thing," Lisa said, gathering her files.

"Oh, by the way, congratulations," he said, looking at her ring.

Smiling, she said, "Thank you, John."

Lisa headed back to her office, but when she got there, Carol wasn't at her desk. Lisa went into her office and got to work. Opening a file Carol left on her desk, Lisa started her day.

"Your back," Carol said, walking into the office.

"Just got back, what's up?"

"First, Nic and Pat will meet us at twelve."

"Okay."

"And second, there's a problem with the new account."

Looking at her watch, Lisa said, "Uh oh, tell me on the way."

Locking up, they headed for the elevator.

"My car or your car?" Lisa asked.

"Not funny," Carol said.

"I promise to drive the speed limit. And it's not that far."

"Alright, just remember you're carrying precious cargo."

"Anyway," Lisa laughed.

Once they were in the car, Carol said, "Okay, give me the bad news."

"Honestly, I'm a bit confused. That's why I brought this," Carol said, referring to the file in her lap.

"What's that?"

"I'll get to that. First, I placed a call to Mrs. Blakely, and get this…"

"What?"

"She said she's never approached us about conducting any business."

"What?!"

"Now, I'm thinking either she's crazy or we are."

"I don't understand, she said she's never come to us or sent anyone?"

"That's right."

"Then who the hell was that in my office?"

"That's the million dollar question. But what I needed to show you was this."

Lisa took the photo that Carol handed her. Sitting in the car in the parking garage next to the restaurant, Lisa stared at a photo.

"This is the lady who came to my office. If she's not Sara Blakely, then who the hell is she?"

Carol sighed, and then said, "Lisa, I don't know how to tell you this."

"Just say it."

"Her name is Linda Harris."

"I don't know a Linda Harris. Why would she lie about her na –" Right then it dawned on Lisa who this woman was. "Please tell me this is not who I think it is. Tell me how common the name Harris is. And tell me what I'm thinking is wrong."

"I wish I could, Lisa. But, I'm thinking the same thing."

Lisa sat behind the wheel of car, staring out the front windshield, seeing nothing.

"Look, let's go in, have lunch and you can talk to Nic and see if she can find something out about this woman," Carol said.

Still a little dazed, Lisa got out and followed Carol into the restaurant.

"There they are," Carol said, spotting them first.

Following Carol to the table, Lisa felt a tug on her arm

"Hey beautiful, want a drink?" a man at the bar asked.

"No, thanks," Lisa smiled.

"Hey, wait a minute. Give me a chance to show you what nice guy I am," the man slurred.

"Look, I said no," Lisa said, trying to snatch her arm away.

Over at the table, Carol saw what was going on and was about to head back toward Lisa. But, Pat grabbed Carol's arm and said, "Wait, this is gon' be good."

They heard Lisa say, "Look, I told you no. Now let my arm go."

"You stuck up bitches are all the same," he slurred.

Before he knew what hit him, Lisa had snatched his hand off her arm and had turned his arm up behind his back.

"Hey, bitch you trying to break my fucking arm?"

"Correction, I will break your fucking arm. Now, I've had a bad day already and it's just noon. You really don't want me to take my stress out on you, do you?"

"Excuse me, is there a problem?"

Lisa looked at the young man who appeared next to her. She figured he must have been a manager.

"No, there's no problem. My friend here just had too much to drink, that's all. Isn't that right?"

The man was in so much pain that he couldn't speak.

"Ma'am if you let him go, I'll take care of it."

"Thank you," Lisa smiled and let the man's arm go.

"Girl, you still got it," Pat said, laughing and giving Lisa a high five when she made it to the table.

"You know it," Lisa laughed.

"Okay, let's see that ring again," Pat said.

Lisa put her hand out so they could take a look at the four carat Princess cut diamond ring set in a Platinum band.

"The man did good, very good," Pat said.

"Thank you," Lisa beamed. "Let's order so I can tell you all the reason why we're here."

After the waitress took their orders, Lisa said, "Okay, ladies, I called you all here to ask you…to be my bridesmaids."

"Of course," Carol said.

"You know we will," Pat said,

"You know it," Nic added.

"Great."

"Who's going to be your maid of honor?" Nic asked.

"Well, I'm not going have one."

"Why not? It's tradition," said Carol.

"Because you all mean so much to me. You guys have been there for me through all the important things in my life. Pat, we've been best friends since we were thirteen. Nic, you saved my life. And Carol, you pushed me toward the man I'm going to marry."

"Pushed, dragged," Carol joked.

They continued to talk over lunch and made plans to start dress shopping as soon as possible.

"Before we leave, Nic, we need your help on something," Carol said.

"What?"

"Well," Lisa said, opening the folder they brought in with them. "This lady came to my office a week ago needing financial advice. So we set up a meeting to meet this week."

"But we never heard from her again," Carol added. "And today I called her. I spoke with a Mrs. Blakely, which is the client's name. But, when I talked to her, she said she's never been to see us."

"What?" Pat said.

"Then I did some research and came up with this," Carol showed them the photo.

Then Lisa said, "This is the lady who came to see. Her name isn't Mrs. Blakely."

"Then who is she?" Nic asked.

"Nic, her name is Linda Harris," Lisa said.

"Say what? Are you kidding me?" Nic asked.

"Unfortunately not. That's why we need you to find out if she really is who we think she is and what she wants," Lisa told Nic.

"I'll call you with anything I find out."

"Thanks."

"No problem. But if she is who you think she is, are we going to pay her a visit?"

"Hell, yes."

The ladies paid for lunch, passed around hugs and split up to head back to work.

On the way back to the office, Carol asked, "What do you think this Linda Harris wants?"

"To see who her husband is stalking."

"What if she thinks it's something else?"

"What else could it be?"

"How 'bout she wants to see the woman her husband is having an affair with?"

Lisa was shocked by Carol's statement she swerved into another lane. When she gathered her composure, she said, "Are you kidding me?"

"Lisa, this woman came to your office. Don't you think it's possible that she's been following him around. She has been seeing him come to your office almost every day. Lisa, she thinks you're the other woman."

Pulling into a parking space in the garage, Lisa put the car in park and turned off the ignition. She sat there and mulled over what Carol just told her.

"I can't believe this. How much worse can this get," Lisa said, more to herself than to Carol.

"Come on, we can't sit here all day."

When they got into the office, it was back to business as usual. Lisa sat down at her desk to turn on her computer, when Carol walked in.

"Good news, Mr. Thompson can't make it."

"Why, what happened?"

"Said he had to leave the country, and that he will reschedule when he comes back."

"Alright."

Lisa went back to working on some other accounts that were on her to do list.

"Lisa, Nic is on the line,"

"Damn, that was quick. You found something already?" Lisa asked when she picked up the phone.

"Lisa, it's his wife."

"How do you know for sure?"

"I have a friend in –"

"A high place," Lisa said, finishing the sentence. "I want to see her."

"I'm on my way," Nic said and hung up.

Lisa grabbed her purse and jacket and walked out to Carol's desk.

"You're going to see her?"

"Yes. So do me a favor, when Marc comes, give him my keys and tell him that I'll see him at home."

"Call me later."

"I will."

By the time Lisa made it downstairs, Nic was pulling up in front of the building.

"Hey," Lisa said, as she got in.

"Long time no see," Nic said, joking.

During the ride, they talked about everything except the elephant in the room.

"So, do you have any ideas for the wedding?"

"I had an idea for the colors."

"What?"

"I was thinking cream and maroon. What do you think?"

"That sounds pretty. But don't have us in anything ugly."

"I never pick out anything ugly, Ms. Thang."

"Good."

Twenty minutes later, they were in front of a building not too far from where Lisa worked.

"Now, we're here. What are you going to do?"

"I'm going to slap the hell out of her."

Laughing, Nic said, "Don't go in here and get arrested."

"How can I get arrested? I'm bringing the cops with me."

259

They got out of the truck and walked into the building.

"Good afternoon, how may I help you?" the receptionist asked.

"Hello. I'm here to see Mrs. Linda Harris," Lisa said.

The receptionist must have noticed the gun under Nic's jacket, because her eyes looked like they were about to pop out of her head.

"It's alright, she's a cop," Lisa told her.

"May I tell her who's here to see her?" the receptionist asked.

"Mrs. Harding," Lisa said, quickly.

"One moment please. Yes, Mrs. Harris, there is a Mrs. Harding here to see you...No, ma'am." Then she whispered into the phone, "The police...Alright." Hanging up the phone, she said to Lisa, "She'll be right out."

Within in the next minute, Sara Blakely a.k.a. Linda Harris came to the front. When she saw who was waiting for her, you could tell this was not a meeting she was expecting to have.

"Nice to see you again," Lisa smiled.

"Can you come into my office please?" Linda said.

"I'll wait out here," Nic said.

Lisa followed Linda Harris to her office.

When they made into her office, Linda said, "How –"

"Don't even think about asking me anything. I want to know why?"

"Why what?"

"Look, I am too old to be playing games. Why did you come to see me?"

"I wanted to see the bitch that's breaking up my marriage."

"Say what?"

"You heard me," Linda said, from behind her desk.

"Have you actually talked to James? Do you have any idea who I am?"

"I don't have to talk to James. And I already know you're the whore who is breaking up my home."

"First off, you call me another name and they gon' need security in here. Second, you need to talk to your husband."

"He's never home for me to talk to him! He's always with you. Every time I walk into a room he hangs up the phone. He comes home late. Don't you care that he's married? All he does is sit and stare into space. He's consumed with you!"

"That's true, but not for the reasons you think," Lisa told her. Sighing, Lisa said, "Look, I am not having an affair with James."

"I can't believe you're going to stand there and lie to my face. I have followed him to your office almost every day."

"Uninvited, I might add."

"Do you really think I'm going to believe a word you say?"

Lisa couldn't help herself, she started to laugh.

Linda Harris saw red, "What the fuck are you laughing at? You wreck my home and you think it's funny? If we weren't at my job –"

"Girl, please. You need to calm down. We need to talk."

For the next fifteen minutes, Lisa told Linda everything. In short form, of course. When she finished, she sat and looked at Linda.

"I don't believe you," Linda Harris said.

Lisa wasn't shocked by this.

"Would you please tell your secretary to ask the other woman to come in?"

Sighing, Linda pushed a button on her phone, "Please tell the other young woman to come in, Carla."

A minute later, Nic walked into the office.

"Hello, I'm Detective Nicole Harding," Nic said.

"You brought the police here. What are you having me arrested?"

"No, nothing like that," Lisa said.

"Mrs. Harris, this is a copy of a restraining order that I issued to your husband last week. As of Sunday, he has broken into Lisa's home and vandalized it. Has Lisa also explained how she and James know each other?"

Linda was still reading the restraining order.

"Mrs. Harris, did you hear me?" Nic asked.

"What's the meaning of this? Why would you get a restraining order against a man you're having an affair with?"

"Exactly," Lisa said, chuckling.

"You really think this shit is funny?"

"Look, Mrs. Harris," Lisa began. "I am not having an affair with James. He is the one who won't leave me alone. I have told him, my fiancé has told him, and even the police, but he still will not leave me alone. Now, I don't know what kind of problems you and James are having and frankly I don't give a damn. What I do care about is the fact that he won't leave me alone and you coming to my office."

Cutting in, Nic said, "Mrs. Harris, I'm sure Lisa has told you that her and James use to date. Did she also tell you that he almost killed her and in fact killed her unborn child?"

"I don't believe you," Linda said, looking at both of them.

Without hesitation, Nic took out six Polaroid photos and tossed them on the desk in front of Linda. Lisa was shocked, but quickly recovered at the sight of the photos of her that were taken while she was in the hospital. She could hardly recognize herself. Linda on the other hand couldn't believe her eyes. She looked between Lisa and the photos several times before she finalized they were the same person.

"Get out!" Linda said.

Nic picked up the photos and said, "Please let him know that the police are looking for him. Have a nice day."

Walking out to the parking lot, Lisa said, "Have a nice day? I can't believe you said that."

"She called us liars. I couldn't help it."

"You know she's going confront him."

"I hope we find him first," Nic said, starting her truck.

On their way back downtown, Lisa called Carol to tell her she was right.

"Don't worry about coming back here. I've already locked everything down. Marc came by and got your keys. He wanted a million and one answers, but I told him you would explain everything," Carol said.

"Thanks Carol. I'll see you in the morning." Lisa hung up the phone and sighed.

"Marc already gone?" Nic asked.

"Yep. You can take me to his house."

"Will do."

Twenty minutes later they pulled in Marc's driveway.

"I guess he hasn't made in yet," Lisa said.

"Are you going to tell him?"

"Yeah. I mean I have to, don't I?"

"Yes, you do."

"Well, let me get in this house and prepare myself. Thanks for today," Lisa said, as she hugged Nic.

"No, problem, sweetie."

"Can I have these?" Lisa said, picking up the Polaroid's.

"What are you going to do with them?"

"Burn them."

"Be my guess."

"See you later."

"Bye."

Lisa went in the house and put in the alarm code. She noticed he had six messages, but didn't check them. No one would call his house for her. Making sure she set the alarm back, Lisa headed upstairs. Walking into the bedroom she put her briefcase and purse on one of the chairs by the balcony sliding door and went into the bathroom.

Turning on the water, she poured her powdered milk in the warm water and began to undress. Lisa slide into the warm water and leaned her head back on the tub. The house was completely silent so she could think with a clear head. She reached over and picked up the photos and stared at them. She had never seen the photos, so they were a little earth shattering. She couldn't believe what she looked like then. A lot had happened today and it seemed as if things were not stopping anytime soon.

Lisa was so caught up in the pictures she hadn't heard Marc come in downstairs. In fact, she didn't hear him until he was standing in the bathroom doorway.

"What happened to you today?"

Lisa jumped a mile when she heard voice.

"Baby, I'm sorry. I thought you heard the alarm beep."

"My mind was somewhere else."

"What are you looking at?"

At first Lisa hesitated, then she handed him the pictures. She watched the expression on his face change as if he could feel the pain that caused the bruises. Then Lisa saw the realization that came into his eyes when realized it was her.

"Oh, my God. Where did you get these from?" he asked as he sat down on the edge of the tub.

"Nic had them. She needed to prove a point today."

"To who?"

Lisa closed her eyes because she didn't want him to see the tears that were welling up in eyes.

"Oh, Mona Lisa. You can tell me," he said.

"I – I –" Lisa stammered. Then she broke down crying. She didn't know why. She just knew she couldn't hold it back any longer.

"Oh, baby. What's wrong?"

"I'm sorry, I'm getting your suit wet."

Marc then did something Lisa never expected. He took off his shoes and got in the tub with his clothes on. Despite the tears Lisa burst out laughing.

"Now, it doesn't matter."

"I guess not."

Pulling Lisa close to him, he said, "What happened?"

Leaning her head on his shoulder, she said, "You remember the new client I told you about?"

"Yeah, the uh security firm, right?"

"That's the one. Anyway, I hadn't heard from the client, so I told Carol to call and find out what happened. Come to find out, the Sara Blakely that Carol spoke to never came to see us."

"So –"

"Before you even ask, Carol did some research and found out that the woman who claimed to be Sara Blakely is actually Linda Harris."

"And who is she?"

"Marc, she's James's wife."

"What?!"

"Yeah, that's why Nic and I went to see her today. She actually thought that I was having an affair with him."

"So how did she take it when you told her the truth?" Marc asked turning on the hot water.

"You know you're ruining your suit."

"I'll buy another one. Keep talking."

Lisa sat up and turned toward him and began undress him. She dropped each wet garment onto the floor as she took them off him.

"Finish your story."

"She didn't believe anything I said. Then when I called Nic into the office she still didn't believe us. Nic even showed her the photos. She stared at them and then told us to get out. Marc, she even said that she had been following him to my job almost every day.

When Lisa finished undressing him, Marc reached over and turned on the jets.

"I got to thinking, maybe if I stay right here in this tub nothing else bad could happen to me."

"Well, I don't know about that," he said, chuckling. Then becoming serious again, he asked, "Lisa, what were you going to do with the pictures?"

"I didn't mean to look at them. I couldn't help myself."

"What are you going to do with them?"

"I'm going to burn them."

"Good answer. And don't worry, we'll figure something out. Just let me do the worrying for you tonight. Now, come on and get out of this tub so you can eat."

"I'm not hungry."

"That's okay, you can watch me eat," he said, wrapping a towel around himself. He held a towel up for Lisa to walk into when she climbed out of the tub. Wrapping the towel around her and hugging her, he whispered, "Everything is going to be fine. I won't let him hurt you ever again. Do you believe me?"

"Yes," Lisa said, looking him straight in the eyes.

As she changed, Marc cleaned up the bathroom and found a bag to put his suit in.

"Maybe the dry cleaners can save it." Lisa said, as she pulled a tank top over her head.

"Doesn't matter."

After Marc changed they both headed downstairs.

"I brought Chinese home," he said.

"I guess I can do with a little something."

As they were about to walk into the kitchen, the doorbell rang.

"I'll get it," Marc said, turning back toward the door.

"Marky!!"

Before he knew what was happening, he was being tackled and kissed.

"Oh, Marky, aren't you a sight for sore eyes? I flew straight through so I could see you. I am so happy see to see you," she said, and then kissed him again.

"Gabriella, what are you doing here?" Lisa heard Marc say.

"I'm here to see you, silly. I had to get away with from my parents. I needed a fix," Gabriella purred.

Marc noticed movement in the corner of his, and turned to see Lisa standing in the kitchen doorway with box of Chinese food and chopsticks watching the scene. Evidently, Gabriella saw Lisa too, because she all of a sudden got quiet.

"Hello," Gabriella said, looking at Lisa like she must be in the wrong house.

"Hello," Lisa said, still standing in the kitchen doorway eating.

"I repeat, Gabriella, what are you doing here?"

"I was hoping to have our famous date weekend. You remember going to daddy's cabin and —"

Lisa couldn't help it, she started choking and had go in the kitchen and get some water.

"Uh, Gabriella, I'd like you to meet someone," Marc said, loudly. "Gabriella, this is Lisa Jenson, my fiancée."

Gabriella's neck snapped toward Lisa, when Marc's information finally sunk in.

"Fiancé?" Gabriella said.

Lisa almost felt sorry for her. Almost. Lisa just continued to watch the show while she ate. She could tell that Marc wished he was anywhere else but here.

"Lisa, this is Gabriella Hues."

"Hi," Gabriella said, with obvious attitude.

Lisa put down the container and walked over to her. She stood eye to eye with Gabriella or at least tried too. Gabriella was a couple feet taller than Lisa, at least with Lisa being barefoot.

"How do you do?" Lisa smiled, with her most fake smile.

"I guess congratulations are in order."

"Thank you," Marc said.

"I guess that means you're off the bachelor's list," Gabriella said.

"I'm happy to say that I am," he said, smiling at Lisa.

"How long have you two been engage?"

"We got engaged over the weekend," Lisa smiled, as she looked down at her ring.

She heard Gabriella gasp at the sight of the ring.

"Huh, just missed the mark. Should've shown up Friday," Gabriella said, watching Lisa's reaction.

"What did you say?" Lisa said, walking closer. Then Lisa caught herself and smiled, "Sorry, to have beaten you to the four carat punch." Lisa then looked at Marc and said, "I'll take my food upstairs so you can talk to your friend."

"No, wait," Marc said.

"It's okay, talk to your *old* friend. It was nice meeting you, Gabriella." Lisa kissed Marc, grabbed her food, and headed upstairs.

Marc turned back to Gabriella and said, "It was nice of you –"

"So, that's it? You're going to marry her?"

"What else is there?" Marc said.

"What about us?"

"Us? I haven't seen you in a year. You moved out and left me, remember?"

"Yes, but I'm back. So tell your little friend she can leave," Gabriella said, trying to walk pass Marc into the living room.

"Gabriella, you can't just walk in here. And Lisa is going to be my wife.

"You finally got the one woman no one could measure up to."

"What are you talking about?"

"You don't think I remember who she is? You've pined over that woman for the last three years and now you've finally got her. I had to listen to you time after time about how great she is, how great she is with this or that. You never loved me, it's always been her."

"I'm sorry Gabriella, you're right. I love her. I always have."

"But, I love you."

"Gabby, you don't love me. I've found the woman that I'm going to marry and love for the rest of my life. You were right when you told me to find the right one. And I have. It was nice seeing you again, Gabriella. Take care of yourself," Marc said, as he opened the front door.

"You'll miss me," she said, and turned walked out the door.

Marc closed the door and leaned against it. He knew when he went upstairs he had a lot of explaining to do. Ready to face the music, Marc headed upstairs.

***

Lisa was upstairs in the bedroom trying to keep herself busy enough so she wouldn't go to the top of the stairs and listen. She knew she didn't have anything to worry about. But she was curious. She could hear their voices, but not the exact words. Pacing back and forth in the bedroom, she was about to head back downstairs when she heard the front door close. Trying to calm herself, Lisa got on the bed and leaned back against the headboard and tried to concentrate on her sweet and sour chicken.

Marc walked into the bedroom and found Lisa sitting on the bed eating and watching TV.

"Sweet and sour chicken good?" he asked, testing the waters.

"Yeah, and don't worry, I left you some," Lisa laughed.

"Thanks. I'll be right back."

Before he walked out, he looked back at Lisa and saw that she was still eating and watching TV. He headed downstairs, put everything they needed on the tray and went back upstairs.

"So, what are we watching?" he asked, as got into bed.

"We are watching The Mummy part three. It's not called that, but that's what it is generally."

"Good enough for me."

They talked about the movie. Some parts of the movie even made them shout at the TV. By the end of the movie Lisa still hadn't brought up Gabriella and this confused Marc.

Lisa noticed Marc staring at her and said, "What's wrong?"

"Just looking at you."

Lisa smiled and went back to looking at television. Once again she caught him staring at her. "Marc, what's wrong – oh, I get it. You're waiting on me to bring up Gabriella. I tell you what, you talk, and I listen. Then it's over. Deal?"

"Yes. First off, I thought you would be pissed about her showing up like that. I've been waiting for you to cuss me out, yell at me, hit me, anything."

Lisa laughed and said, "What good would that have done? Besides, I would never do those things. That's not how we solve our problems."

Marc continued, "I know, but –"

"Most women would. Yeah, I know," Lisa said, finishing his thoughts.

"Yes, but you're not most women."

"Damn right, and I'm not one for beating around the bush, either."

"Point taken. I met Gabriella about four years ago. We dated on and off for the first year and a half. After the second year mark, we decided to try a more serious relationship and she moved in with me. And no that is not a habit of mine."

"What?"

"Asking the women I date to move in with me."

"Good to know."

"During what was supposed to be a serious relationship, neither one of us put forth a real effort. She took more shopping trips to other countries than the law allowed. She was the ultimate party girl."

"And what was your flaw?"

"Me? Well, I committed the ultimate wrong."

"You cheated on her?"

"I was in love with another woman."

"Oh."

Lisa stared into Marc's deep brown eyes and smiled.

"So, we stopped kidding ourselves and she moved out."

"But you kept sleeping together."

"Yes. But it's been over year since the last time. And I'm so sorry for any disrespect this may have caused. Are we okay?"

"I wasn't mad or angry with you, Marc. With everything that is going on in my life that I have brought into this relationship, I have no right to get upset. Like you said, we all have baggage."

After they ate, Marc took the tray downstairs and cleaned up the kitchen. When he came back into the room he was holding a legal pad and pen.

"What's that for?" Lisa asked.

"If we're getting married, I think we should start planning a wedding. And these brochures are for contractors."

"Okay."

Taking the notepad and pen, Lisa started to write while Marc flipped channels and finally stopped on a station with a basketball game.

"Alright, first what are you favorite colors?" she asked.

"Basic. Black and white."

"I can work with that."

"What are yours?" he asked.

"Maroon and brown. But I think I can work with the black, white, and maroon."

"What's next?"

"Your groomsmen."

"My best man is my best friend from New York, Tim. Then Steve and of course my dad."

"Full names please. Timothy Caldwell, Steven –"

"Roberts, I know. And your dad?"

"Vincent Cavell. And my mother's name is Isabella Cavell."

"Isabella. That is a beautiful name."

"Speaking of parents, have you told your father yet?"

"No," Lisa said, without hesitation.

"Why?"

"Because I haven't talked to him in months."

"Lisa, you haven't talked to your father in months?"

"Yeah," Lisa said, showing no emotion.

Marc reached over and picked up the cordless and handed it to Lisa.

"I don't want to."

"Why not?"

"Because, he won't care."

"You don't know that."

"Look, my dad and I have an acquaintanceship. Not a father and daughter relationship."

"At least call and tell him you're getting married. If you haven't guessed, you're going to need someone to walk you down the aisle."

"And I do. Anthony."

"That's a good idea, but he's still your dad. Call him."

Sighing, Lisa took the phone and dialed his home number. She dialed his home number because she knew it was a good chance he wouldn't be there. She was wrong.

"Hello," a deep voice answered.

"Hi, dad."

"Lisa?"

"Yeah, it's me," she said, looking at Marc.

"How are you, baby?"

"Fine, you?"

"I'm doing pretty good. How is your mother?"

"She's fine. Have you talked to Anthony?"

"Last week. How was his trip?"

"He said he enjoyed it."

"How's work?"

"Work is fine. Um, dad I have some good news."

"I could use some good news."

"I'm getting married."

Lisa didn't hear anything but silence on the phone.

"Did you hear me?"

"Married?"

"Yes, married."

"How did you meet him?"

"We work together. He's good man and I love him."

"So when is all this going to happen?"

"We're getting married next year."

"Well, you make sure to send me an invitation."

"Of course."

"Look, I have to go. I have a dinner meeting in twenty minutes."

"Alright, bye."

"Bye, sweetheart."

Click.

Lisa handed the phone back to Marc and just looked at him.

"I could figure out most of it."

"He said to send him an invitation."

"No congratulations? He didn't ask anything about me or want to meet me?"

"No to all of the above."

"I'm sorry."

"Marc, it's okay. He has never been that involved and I'm good with that."

"Well, I'm not," Marc said, picking up the phone.

"What are you doing?" Lisa asked, while she tried to grab the phone.

"I'm calling him back."

"Marc, no. Just let it go. For me."

"I want you to be happy on your wedding day."

"I will, baby. As long as you're at the altar waiting for me."

"And I will."

"Good," she said, taking the phone away from him.

"Now let's move on to places. Do you have any ideas?" he said.

"Not a clue. But I figured since we're from different religions, we should have it in a common area."

"What about your family?"

"They don't care about that. Besides, it doesn't matter where we get married as long as we get married."

"Really?"

"It does matter, but that was nice of me to say," Lisa laughed.

"Cute. Anyway, how about the ballroom in a nice hotel?" Marc asked.

"That could work. But, I have a secret."

"What?"

"I've always wanted to have a beautiful wedding at the Botanic Gardens."

"I thought you never thought about stuff like this?"

"Just a little," Lisa blushed. "Especially, when I was helping Pat plan her wedding."

"I tell you what, Saturday you and I will go look at the Botanic Gardens."

"What about your parents? They're supposed to be here this weekend. Friday morning to be exact. And I doubt if I can go home by then, but I can go to my mother's house."

"Why, there's enough room here."

"Marc, I can't stay here with your parents here. What will they think?"

"That two people who love each other can't bear to be without each other," he said, staring into Lisa's eyes.

"You can't sweet talk me with those big brown eyes."

"Damn. Well, then I'll just have to beg."

Marc leaned over and started kissing Lisa on the neck.

"This is your idea of begging?"

"You could call it negotiations," he whispered.

When he went down the cleavage of the tank top she was wearing, she said, "I see your point. But you know we can't do this with your parents here."

"The hell we can't. I can be quiet if you can."

"I'll try."

"Good enough for me," Marc said, as he pulled Lisa beneath him.

As they kissed, Marc realized he was hearing bells.

"That's never happened before," he said looking down at Lisa.

"It's not mine," Lisa said.

"Hold that position. I'll be right back." He got out of bed to search for his cell phone. "Marc Cavell…Yes, sir, Mr. Keene. How are you?"

Lisa rolled her eyes at the mention of Mr. Keene's name.

"Um, no sir. I'm sorry I want be able to join you. I have a lot of work to do," Marc said, smiling at Lisa. "Oh, she is…Good-bye."

"What did he want?"

"To have drinks," Marc said, as he turned his phone off and plugged it up. "And he also told me he hopes she's worth the work."

"I figured that's what he said,"

"Now, where were we?" Marc asked, as climbed back into bed.

Laughing, Lisa said, "I was about to go sleep. I don't know about you."

"Go ahead. I'm sure I'll be able to find some way to amuse myself," he said, and then crawled under the covers.

Lisa then felt him kiss her stomach.

"You know I can't sleep if you do that."

Popping his head up from under the covers, he said, "Yes, you can. Just close your eyes."

Marc went back to kissing her stomach and moving down to her inner thighs.

"Mmm," Lisa moaned.

Making his way back up, Marc felt Lisa's hands in his hair. Pushing Lisa's shirt over her head and kissing her deeply they both knew sleep was not in the near future.

Chapter Twenty-Five

The next few days were pretty much a blur for both Lisa and Marc. Friday, Marc took off so he could pick his parents up from the airport.

"Are you nervous about meeting his parents?" Carol asked, sitting in Lisa's office.

"A little."

"When will the parents meet?"

"Tonight, actually. We figured it'll be better to get it over with. And tomorrow Marc and I are going to look at the Botanic Gardens for a possible place for the wedding."

"That'll be beautiful, Lisa."

"And on Sunday, we ladies will go dress shopping. That way Marc can spend some alone time with his parents."

"Just let me know what time."

"I will."

"Have you guys made any more plans about the wedding?"

"We've come up with the black, maroon, and cream. I've worked out a way to use all the colors. My dress, of course, is white. And I think you guys will wear maroon with black silk scarves around the waist or draped around your necks, hanging to the back. And I'll wear maroon scarf wrapped around my waist. The groomsmen will have maroon cumber bums and ties. Like I said, I have plans but nothing definite."

"Those are some great ideas. Do you have a wedding planner?"

"Yeah, y'all."

Carol burst out laughing. They were soon interrupted by the phone ringing.

"Lisa Jenson...Hey, baby...That's great...I can cook...But –...Okay, if you so...Me and mom will meet you all there...Bye."

"What happened?"

"He wants us all to go out to dinner. He says his mother wants to get to know me."

"She can't get to know you while you're moving around."

"That was the point."

"Nervous now?"

"Petrified is more like it."

"Don't worry, they'll love you. And then you and Marc can live happily ever after."

"From your mouth to God's ears."

Carol and Lisa wrapped up the day and by five o'clock they were leaving.

"Mama!" Lisa called out when she walked into the house.

"I'm upstairs," her mother said.

Lisa went upstairs to her mother's bedroom, "Hey."

"Hey. How do I look?" Janice asked, as she twirled around. She was wearing a white blouse with black slacks. She was also wearing a pair of pearl earrings and matching pearl necklace. Lisa always thought her mother could wear anything.

"You look good. I really like the pearls."

"Thank you."

"I'll be ready in half an hour," Lisa said, heading to her old bedroom.

"Where are we going for dinner?" her mother said.

"The Macaroni Grill."

By six-fifteen, Lisa was ready to go. She was dressed in a black dress with a pencil knee length skirt and black heels. She decided to wear here hair down.

"How do I look?"

"You look great. Where'd you find the jewelry?"

"Where I always get my costume jewelry."

"Gordman's. I forgot."

"Are you ready?"

"Yep."

On the way to the restaurant, Janice was saying, "Are you happy, Lisa?"

"Extremely, mama."

"You must be. You didn't even pause. Have you thought about everything that goes along with marriage? I mean, it's not just you anymore. There's someone else in the picture."

"I know. Marc has being understanding with that. He is really a good man and I love him. And before you say I told you so, there's no need, because I already know. And I also want to thank you mama for not letting me give up."

"I am so happy for you, baby. Marc is truly a good man and any blind man can see how he loves you."

"Thank you, mommy."

Thirty minutes later Lisa pulled into the restaurant parking lot and found an empty space near the door.

As Lisa and Janice was walking toward the doors, they heard a young man say, "Excuse me, ladies, would you like to have dinner with us?"

'Us' were two handsome men.

"I'm sorry, we already have dinner plans," Lisa said.

When Lisa and her mother walked in the restaurant, she spotted Marc with his parents at a table. Lisa also noticed how beautiful his mother was and how Marc looked so much like his father.

"Are you ladies sure you won't have dinner with us?"

Lisa smiled when Marc spotted them at the door and got up to greet them.

"No, thank you," Janice said, as they walked away.

Marc, meeting them half way said, "Hello, Mrs. Jen –, Janice."

Smiling and receiving the kiss Marc planted on her cheek, Janice said, "Hello, Marc."

"Hello, Mona Lisa," he said and kissed Lisa.

"Hello, to you, too."

Leading them over to the table, he said, "Mom…Dad, this is Lisa Jenson and her mother Janice Jenson. Lisa…Janice, these are my parents Isabella and Vincent Cavell."

Hellos were said around the table and Marc and his father helped Lisa and her mother with their chairs.

"So, Lisa, tell us about yourself. I mean, Marc has told just about everything. At first we thought you were a figment of his imagination," Marc's mother said.

Smiling, Lisa said, "There's really nothing extra about me. I just want you to know that I believe in and trust in every decision your son has made since we started working together. I hope to make as good a partner in life as in our work relationship. I'm also a little strong willed. But I get that from her," Lisa said, tilting her head toward her mother.

"Well, at times he needs it. The Cavell men feel they should have their way all the time, so I'm glad Marc found someone that won't let him have his way all the time."

"I don't mean to cut in," Janice said. "But, Marc, you have to be the same with Lisa. Because she can be just as hard headed."

Laughing, Marc said, "Yes, ma'am."

During dinner they all laughed and talked. The parents laughed about mistakes Lisa and Marc made in their younger years, while Marc and Lisa sat and laughed embarrassingly, at the stories. By the time dinner and dessert had been eaten everyone had become friends and well on their way to becoming family.

Walking out the restaurant, Marc said, "Did everyone enjoy themselves?"

"Yes." Everyone said in unison.

"Good. Mom…Dad, you can take my car home, I'm gonna ride with Lisa to take her mother home."

"Marc, you don't have to do that," Lisa said.

"See, what I mean," Janice whispered to Isabella.

"Yes, I do. But I have remedy for that. May I?"

"Be my guest."

Standing in front of Lisa, Isabella took her hand and said, "It is obvious that your mother has raised you to be a strong woman, but let me ask you something. Do you love my son?"

"Yes, ma'am, I do."

"Would you protect him from any harm or pain?"

"Yes, ma'am."

Isabella than took Marc by the hand and joined his hand with Lisa's and said, "Then sweetheart, let him do the same for you."

"Yes, ma'am," Lisa said.

Hugs were then exchanged between the parents, and Janice and Isabella exchanged phone numbers. Marc's parents got in his car and pulled away as Marc opened the door for Lisa and then her mother.

Getting in the backseat, he said, "I hope you ladies enjoyed yourselves."

"We really did. Do you have enough room back there, Marc?" Janice said.

"Yes, ma'am, if Lisa lets the top back."

"You don't have to tell me twice," Lisa said, hitting the button. "Oh, mom don't forget we are meeting Pat, Nic, and Carol to pick out dresses on Sunday."

"I won't, what time?"

"I was thinking about right after church."

"Fine with me."

Thirty minutes later, Lisa was pulling into her mother's driveway.

Walking into the house and cutting on lights, Janice said, "Well, kids I thank you for dinner and Marc you have lovely parents."

"Thank you, Janice."

"Alright, I am going up to bed, lock up when you leave."

"Okay, mama. Good night."

"Good night."

"So, did you enjoy dinner?" Marc asked, pulling Lisa closer to him.

"Yes, I did. Your parents are great."

"Thank you. And they really loved you."

"I hope so."

"You ready to go home?"

"Yeah. You drive," Lisa said, after she locked the door.

Marc helped her into the car and then got in himself.

Instead of taking the expressway, he took the scenic route home.

"What time do you want to get out tomorrow?" Marc asked.

"How about ten, we can check a couple of places out. What are your parents doing this weekend?"

"Whenever they're here, they go sightseeing."

Driving through Downtown, the traffic was bumper to bumper. People walking around and loud music was coming from the clubs and cars.

"Hey," this kid yells at Marc, while they were stopped at a light.

Marc and Lisa looked over. "Yeah," Marc said.

"Man, that's a bad ass car. Let's trade."

"Nah, that's okay."

"Fuck that car! His bitch his fine as hell!" another guy in the car said.

Lisa turned around a looked at him, but before she could say anything, Marc pulled off.

"Dumb ass," Lisa said.

"Don't worry about him. I have plans of my own."

"And what are those plans?"

Without answering, Marc turned onto Riverside Dr. Then he said, "Wanna park?"

"As long as you promise not to behave."

"Oh, I promise."

Parking in the parking lot along the river, Marc turned the car off but left the radio on.

"So how is this for an end to a great evening?" he asked.

"I think it's a wonderful ending. I haven't done this in a long time."

"Me neither. How did your work day go?"

"Pretty good. We pretty much got everything covered."

Turning toward Lisa, he said, "So are you ready for your birthday?"

"Yeah, but it's still three weeks away."

"Never too early to plan."

"I usually have dinner with Pat and Nic and as of my second year with the firm, Carol."

"Am I invited this year?"

"Of course," Lisa said, then leaned over and kissed him. She then pulled away quickly. "Did you feel that?"

"I was about to," Marc said.

"No, I felt water. I think you better let the top up."

"How about down?" he said, reaching for the straps on her dress.

Laughing, Lisa said, "Let the top up."

Letting the top up and then turning back to Lisa, he said, "Now, back to you."

As they kissed, the rain began to come down hard.

"Marc?"

"Yes," he answered, between kisses.

"Shouldn't we go home?"

"First, I love that you think of my place as home, and second, I want to sexually harass you first and then sneak you in the house like I was sixteen again."

"I'm willing to play along if you are."

The rain fell harder outside as the windows began to fog up.

Twenty minutes later, Lisa broke the kiss and said, "We need to leave before we get arrested for what I have in mind."

Without a word, Marc started the car and backed out of the parking space. They made it home in a minute flat.

"We have to be quiet. I don't want to wake my parents."

Giggling, Lisa walked into the house, "Do you want something to drink?"

"No, I want you upstairs and naked."

"Yes, sir."

Making it upstairs without making a sound, they were all over each other the minute they were in the bedroom.

"I can't believe we're gonna do this with your parents in the next room," Lisa whispered.

"You don't have to whisper, the walls aren't that thin."

A second later they were completely naked and Lisa was headed toward the balcony.

"Are you coming?"

"Yeah, but you first."

As the rain fell on them, Marc picked Lisa up and she wrapped her legs around him as he thrust inside her. Moaning softly, and holding on tight to each other, they made love in the rain. After Lisa climaxed twice, Marc carried her back in the room, but he left the balcony door open.

Laying her on the bed, he continued to kiss her. Turning Marc over, Lisa straddled him and guided him inside of her. He held her hips and guided her to his own pace.

"Marc, I'm coming," Lisa said, trying not to be loud.

Suddenly, he rolled over and continuously rammed into her until she couldn't take it anymore.

"Turn over," Marc whispered between kisses.

Doing as she was told, Lisa turned over. Marc slammed into her from the back so hard, that she had to bury her face in the pillow in order not to scream. Marc's pace speeded up until he came inside of Lisa. Neither of them moved for the next couple of minutes.

Then Marc rolled onto his back and kissed Lisa's shoulder as he pulled her close to him.

"Have I told you how much I love you?" he asked, when he caught his breath.

"I love you too," Lisa said, between breaths.

Covering up and laying in each other's arms they talked until they finally fell asleep to the sound of the raining falling outside.

✳✳✳

Knock, knock. "Marc are you and Lisa awake?" Isabella said through the bedroom door.

"Yeah, mom we're awake."

Kissing Lisa on the forehead, he said, "Wake up, Mona Lisa."

"Breakfast is on the table when you two are ready."

"We'll be down in few minutes, Mom."

"Alright."

"Wake up, sweetheart," Marc whispered in Lisa's ear.

"I'm awake," Lisa said, opening her eyes.

"Good morning."

"Good morning."

"How did you sleep?"

"I slept great. How about you?"

"Same here. Hungry?"

"More than anything else."

Getting out of bed and going into the bathroom, Lisa slipped her robe on.

"I thought I hid that," Marc said, referring to her robe.

"You did, but I found it."

After washing her face and brushing her teeth, Lisa put on her workout clothes. While Marc was in the bathroom, Lisa made the bed with new linen and picked up their clothes that they shed the night before.

"I'll meet you downstairs," Lisa called out as she left the room.

Walking into the kitchen, she said, "Good morning."

"Good morning. Oh, please don't tell me you're a health nut like my son," Isabella said.

"Afraid so, but the way I eat, I'd better be."

"Music to my ears. Come and sit down and I'll fix you a plate."

"How are you this morning, Lisa?" Mr. Cavell asked.

"I'm fine, Mr. Cavell. How about yourself?"

"I'm fine, honey. But will you grant an old man a request?"

"Mr. Cavell, you are far from being old, but yes."

Laughing, he said, "Well, thank you. But I don't want to hear any of that 'Mr. Cavell' stuff. You can either call me Vincent or dad. I've always wanted a daughter."

"Alright, Vincent."

"Here you are dear," Isabella said as she placed a plate full of food in front of Lisa.

As Lisa cut into the blueberry pancakes, she said, "So what are your plans today?"

"Well, we'll be doing some sightseeing down here. And Marc said that there is a casino not too far from here."

"They're quite a few."

"Really?"

"Yes, ma'am."

"Lisa."

"Sorry, Isabella."

"Good morning," Marc said, walking into the kitchen.

"Good morning," everyone said in return.

As Marc leaned in to kiss his mother on the cheek, Isabella said, "You are just in time, here's your plate."

"Thank you. What are you guys going to do today?"

"We were telling Lisa that we were going to do some sightseeing and going to one of the casinos," Vincent said.

"You two have a full day, I see," Marc said.

"Yep, and we should be getting on our way," Isabella said to her husband.

"Alright. We'll see you kids later."

"Bye," Lisa and Marc said.

Marc and Lisa talked about their plans for the day while they finished eating breakfast. Fifteen minutes later, they were done cleaning the kitchen and heading upstairs to get a workout in.

By ten-thirty they were dressed and out the door.

"Today is definitely a top down day," Lisa said as they walked out to her car.

"Shotgun!" Marc said.

"I guess that means I'll be driving today."

Hitting the button on to unlock her car doors, Lisa got in and started the car. Letting the top down, she said, "Where to first?"

"Let's start with The Peabody first."

"Peabody it is."

Lisa drove out of his driveway and headed into the middle of downtown. Even though weekend traffic was heavy, they made it to the hotel within a couple of minutes.

Getting out when the valet opened her car door, Lisa handed him her keys and took the ticket he handed her.

"Any baggage, ma'am?" the valet asked.

"No."

Walking into the hotel and over to the desk, Marc said, "Excuse me, we're looking for Mrs. Lena Collins."

"Are you Mr. Cavell?"

"Yes."

"Mrs. Collins is running a little behind and asks that you please give her a few more minutes."

"Of course."

"But you are welcomed to look around."

"Thank you."

Marc and Lisa decided to go upstairs and look at the ballroom. As they looked around the room, Marc asked, "Can you see yourself walking down the aisle to me here?"

"I can picture that anywhere," Lisa said, as she hugged him and then kissed him.

Then they heard, "I can see we can't wait for the wedding," Lena Collins said, walking into the ballroom.

Laughing, Lisa said, "Sorry about that."

"No problem at all. You must be the bride, Lisa. And the groom, Marcello. Did I pronounce that right?"

"Yes, but you can call me Marc."

"Alright, Marc. Now, let me show you where you're going to have your wedding."

For the next hour, Lena gave them the complete spiel about the hotel and the ballroom. The price was Lisa's main concern, even though Marc said it shouldn't be. And soon they were walking out of the hotel.

Giving the valet the ticket, Lisa said, "What do you think?"

"I liked it, but this is about you. What do you think?"

"I haven't decided yet, but I do think you should drive."

"Where to next?" Marc asked, pulling out of the parking garage.

"The Botanic Gardens."

Taking the scenic route, gave them plenty of time to discuss some more ideas for the wedding. They had already decided to incorporate both of their religions into the ceremony. Moving down the list Lisa had brought with her, they were coming up with some great ideas for the wedding.

Looking around as they walked into the Botanic Gardens, Lisa could definitely see having their wedding here among the tulips.

"Good morning, I'm Alex Johnson," a man greeted them as they entered the information center.

"Good morning," Lisa and Marc said.

"What can I do for you this morning?"

"Well, my fiancée and I are looking venues to have our wedding," Marc said.

"Congratulations! Let's get you two a packet and take a look around," he said, leading them to the front desk.

His entire speech lasted about twenty minutes. He was straight to the point, answered all their questions, and let them look around for themselves. When they finally left, Lisa was impressed.

"So what do you think?" she asked Marc, as they pulled out of the parking lot.

"The price is just slightly under The Peabody. So, price is not an issue. We wouldn't have to worry about flowers for the wedding," he laughed.

"True," Lisa laughed.

"What's your opinion?"

"I think it's beautiful and I already have some ideas."

"Hungry?"

"Yes."

They stopped at restaurant and were seated on the patio and given menus. The waiter took their drink orders and gave them the specials for the day.

As they waited for their lunch, they continued to talk about the venues in comparison.

"What do you really think?" Lisa asked.

"I think I'll marry you anywhere."

"So will I. But we need to find a place that we both can agree upon."

"What do you think about having our wedding outside?"

"I never thought about it, but I kind of like the idea. Where do you have in mind?"

"I know this guy who happens to owe me a huge favor and who happens to own a huge house. He just might let us use it if I beg hard enough."

"Call him. I want to see it."

"Alright," Marc said as he pulled his cell phone out and went through his contact list. After a minute he said, "Yes, is Mr. Herbert in...Tell him Marc Cavell is calling..."

While Marc was on the phone, Lisa was busy eating her sandwich and writing down some more ideas for their wedding.

After pressing the end button on his cell phone, Marc said, "Let's take a ride."

"What about your food?"

"I'll eat later, come on," Marc said, as he laid some money on the table and pulled Lisa's chair out for her.

"Where are we going?" Lisa asked from the passenger side, when Marc got on the expressway.

"Cordova."

"So, how do you know this Mr. Herbert?"

"Lesley Herbert was a client from my beginnings at the firm."

"What type of company does he own?"

"Actually, he has multiple companies. Herbert Industries covers the gamut of steel, oil, and even pharmaceuticals. And that's just the tip of the iceberg."

The rest of the ride consisted of making decisions on a band or DJ. They both preferred a DJ. Other small decisions were made also. Like a suitable number of people to invite.

"Let's say one hundred and fifty," Marc said.

"One hundred and fifty? You don't think that's too many people?"

"No. We both have big families."

"We gonna need a great caterer, but cheap."

Laughing, Marc said, "Is there such a thing?"

"We'll find out," Lisa said.

After a half hour drive, Marc turned and drove through a large iron gate. Lisa couldn't help thinking the house looked like a castle. The house was exquisite. It was built with stone instead of brick and an elaborate lawn that was the size of two football fields. The lawn was very well manicured.

"This is beautiful," Lisa said, as Marc helped her out of the car.

The front door opened as they walked up the steps.

"Marc," the man called as he met them at the door. Lesley Herbert was nothing like Lisa had imagined him. Lesley Herbert was a very handsome man. He was dark skinned, with a low hair-cut and as far as Lisa could tell, in great shape.

"Les, how you doing, man?" Marc said, as they shook hands.

Looking at Lisa, Lesley said, "Who is this beautiful sister?"

"This is my fiancée Lisa Jenson. Lisa, this is Lesley Herbert."

"How do you do, Mr. Herbert?" Lisa said, shaking his hand.

"No, the name is Lesley. My father is Mr. Herbert. Come on in and get the lay of the land."

Lisa walked in and instantly fell in love with the high ceilings and extravagant chandeliers.

"Now, Marc tells me that you have agreed to marry him. Do you feel that you're in any danger? Wink if you don't want to say it front of him."

Laughing, Lisa said, "Right now I feel safe. But, if the need arises, I'll let you know."

"Alright, alright, that's enough," Marc said. "We have business to take care of."

"We'll talk later," Lesley whispered loudly to Lisa behind his hand. "Okay, the first to see is the east wing. The pool is on this end, so I don't know if it will provide a lot of space."

Lesley opened the doors and let them walk out first.

"This is breathtaking, Lesley. You have a beautiful home," Lisa said.

"Thanks. Now, let's see what's behind door number two," Lesley said, as they walked toward the west wing. "As you can see there is a big dining area, if you choose to have the reception inside. What about this scenery?"

As Lisa looked around she realized that she didn't like this end so much. It was too closed in for her taste.

"I see this is not what you had in mind. Good thing I saved the best for last. Follow me."

He then led Lisa and Marc through a door that lead to the kitchen off the dining area. The kitchen was huge. Going out the back door, they ended up on the patio of the backyard.

"How does this suit you?" Lesley asked.

Lisa was instantly mesmerized. "This is perfect!"

Marc came up behind her and whispered in her ear, "Do you approve?"

"I approve tenfold."

"Now, would you do me the honor of having your wedding here?" Lesley asked.

"Yes and thank you so much," Lisa said.

"No need to thank me. Besides I owe this man a lot."

"If you don't mind, I want to take some pictures."

"Not at all."

When Lisa was out of earshot, Marc said, "Thanks, Les. Man, you have made her day, which will make my life."

As the men talked, Lisa took pictures of the grounds and the back of the house with a camera she had brought along.

"Marc, we're cool. Besides any woman who has you talking about marriage deserves to have the very best. How did you guys meet, anyway?"

"We work together."

"She works with you?"

"Yeah, she's been there for about five years."

"Hate I missed her."

"I'm glad you did. But, honestly, I almost missed her myself. When I first tried to meet her, she wouldn't give me the time of day. So you know I had to find out more about her. But once again, she walked right passed me.

Then she was promoted and I got my chance to find out some things about her. And, well, I fell in love," Marc said, as he stared at Lisa and smiled.

"I can see that and I can see why. She is a truly beautiful woman."

"Yes, she is."

As Marc watched her, he thought to himself how happy he was that he hadn't missed her.

"So, when is the date?" Lesley asked, as they all walked into the house.

"September eighteenth of next year," Marc said.

"Then you two have a lot of work to do. I tell you what, I'm gonna be in and out of town, but I will let the staff know to let you guys have free run of the place for planning."

"Thank you so much," Lisa said.

"No problem at all. Can you two stay for dinner?"

"I wish we could, but my parents are in town."

"Rain check, then?" Lesley asked.

"You got it," Marc said.

"And thank you for seeing us such short notice," Lisa said, as she shook his hand.

"You're welcome. I'll see you two soon."

As they got in the car, Lisa said, "It is so nice of him to let us use his house."

"Now, we can scratch that off the list."

"So –" Marc was then interrupted by the ringing of his cell phone. "Marc Cavell...Oh, hi Mom, where are you guys...Really...No, we'll be able to fend for ourselves...Have fun...Bye." Hanging up, he then said to Lisa, "My parents have decided to have dinner at one of the casinos."

"That's nice."

"She asked if we wanted to join them, but I said we could fend for ourselves. That's okay isn't?"

"You're the one driving. I go where you go."

"I like the sound of that," he said, kissing Lisa's hand. "So, what do you want to do?"

"No idea."

"I haven't done any music shopping in a while. Why don't we head to Wolfchase Mall?"

"Okay."

Marc headed east on the expressway.

Thirty minutes later, they were parking in front of the Wolfchase Galleria. Going from store to store, they looked around to see if anything peeked their interest. Finally walking into the music store, Marc went over to the jazz section and Lisa went to the R&B section. After a few minutes, Lisa joined Marc in the jazz section with a stake of CDs in her hand.

"You got enough time to listen to all those?" Marc joked.

"I work better while listening to music," Lisa laughed. "What did you get?"

"Wynton Marsalis, some Coltrane, and I had to replace my Al Jarreau CD. What did you get?"

"Joe, the new Sade, Trey Songz, Maxwell, Robin Thicke, and Aerosmith –"

"Aerosmith?"

"Yes, I said Aerosmith. What?"

"I never thought you would like Aerosmith."

"That's what you get for thinking," Lisa laughed.

"What else?"

"Stevie Wonder and Mary j. Blidge."

"Is that all?"

"All I can tote," Lisa laughed.

Taking the CDs from her they headed to the cash register.

Leaving the store, they continued to window shop, when Lisa stopped and said, "That is beautiful." She was looking at a beautiful fur coat. It was a black, full length coat.

"Why don't you try it on?"

"Are you crazy, we're planning a wedding?"

"I didn't know they charged to try something on."

"Anyway, moving on," Lisa said, about to walk away.

"Unh-unh, come on," he said, pulling her into the store.

"Nooo," Lisa said, laughing.

"Excuse me, can you help us?" Marc asked a salesperson.

"Sure, what can I do for you?"

"My fiancée would like to try on the coat you have on display in the window."

"A lady with great taste. Come on, honey," the clerk said, as she led Lisa to the back of the store.

While Lisa was in the back, Marc was up front checking out the men's selection.

"My, it looks as if it was made for you," the sales lady told Lisa.

"You're just saying that. But, you're right." Lisa couldn't help but smile at her reflection. She had never thought about actually buying a fur coat, but she was now. She had nice coats, but not a fur coat.

Watching from up front, Marc couldn't help but stare. She looked amazing. But he was bias; he thought she looked amazing in anything. He couldn't help but think how lucky he was to have her in his life.

"Excuse me," Marc said to another salesperson.

"Yes, how can I help you?"

"Well..." Marc then explained to the salesman what he wanted to do. "Can you do that?"

"Yes, sir."

"Here is when and where, and here is my card."

"Hey, what are you doing?" Lisa asked, joining him at the counter.

"I just bought this coat, but they don't have in my size. So they have to order it for me."

"Oh, that is nice."

"How did the coat fit?"

"Like a glove."

"Good, now where to?"

"Home, I am tired."

"Home it is."

Walking out to the car, Lisa's phone rang. When she looked at the screen, she saw it was Nic. "Hey, girl. What's up?"

"Hey, where are you?"

"Me and Marc are just leaving Wolfchase, why?"

"Lisa, I need you to meet me at St. Francis."

"St. Francis, why? Is mama and Anthony hurt?"

Marc stopped to look at her at the sound of fear in Lisa's voice.

"They're fine. Everyone is fine."

"You wouldn't be telling me to come to St. Francis if everybody was fine. What's going on?"

"It's Linda Harris."

Chapter Twenty-Six

"What?" Lisa said.

"Yeah, they just brought her in. She's okay, just a little shaken up. But she asked me to call you. She wants to see you."

"Why?"

"That she wouldn't tell me."

"I'm on my way." Hanging up the phone, she looked at Marc, "I need to go to St. Francis Hospital."

"Why, what happened?"

"He beat her up," Lisa said, staring off into space.

"Wait a minute, Lisa look at me. Who beat up whom?"

"James. He beat his wife up. She had Nic call me. She wants to see me." Looking up at him, she said, "I want to go see her."

"Are you sure?"

"Yeah."

"Okay."

Marc opened her door and closed it when she got in and went around and got in. Looking over at her, he said, "Are you sure?"

"Yeah, I'm sure."

Marc started the car and pulled out of the parking lot. Taking the expressway, they made it to the hospital in twenty minutes flat. Holding on tightly to Marc's hand, they met Nic in the emergency waiting room.

"Hey, girl. Hey, Marc," Nic said, when they walked in.

"Hey, how is she?" Lisa asked Nic as she hugged her.

"Like I said on the phone, she's a little shaken up. Her bruises look worse than they really are, but other than that the doctor said she would be fine."

"Can I see her?"

"First, are you sure? You don't have to do this," Nic said.

"I'm sure."

"Follow me."

Nic lead them through the security doors and flashed her badge at the nurse's station. Stopping in front of the First door they came to, Nic said, "Remember what I told you, it's not as bad as it looks."

"Okay."

"Do you want one of us to go in with you?" Marc asked.

"No, I'll be fine," Lisa said, squeezing his hand before she let go.

Knocking softly on the door, Lisa pushed it opened. She tried not to appear shocked when she saw Linda Harris, but she couldn't help it.

"It's not that bad, I'm okay," Linda said.

"Déjà vu. I used to say the same thing. How did this happen?" Lisa asked.

"I finally confronted him about you and he didn't like what I said."

"What did you tell him?"

"The fact of him going to see you and following you. Oh hell, I told him everything. Next thing I know we were fighting. When he left, I called the police and your friend showed up. I thought she was a detective?"

"She is."

"Anyway, she brought me here herself. She said to make sure I was alright. I think she didn't feel safe with leaving me at home alone in case he came back."

"You're probably right. Are you really alright?"

"By the doctor's standards, yes. But I'm gonna take some time away. I'm going to my sister's for a while; she lives in Connecticut."

"Good for you."

"Is your fiancé with you?"

"Yes, he's out in the hall with Nic."

"Can I meet him?"

"Sure." Lisa opened the door and told Marc to come in.

Marc walked in and said, "How are you feeling, Mrs. Harris?"

"Better than I look, Mr. –"

"Cavell, Marc Cavell."

"So, you are the most hated man in Memphis? It's nice to meet you."

"It's nice to meet you, too."

"Lisa, I asked your friend to have you come because I needed to tell you that James knows about your engagement. I thought I was telling him something new, but he already knew. He never told me how he found out, but he does know. He said that there isn't going to be a wedding. I really don't know how he found out."

"Church," Lisa said.

"What?" Linda said.

"My grandmother had our engagement put in the church announcements."

"Meaning that he's been going to your church, too," Linda said.

"Yes," Lisa said, looking at her.

"More news to me. Well, when is the wedding?"

"September eighteenth of next year," Lisa said.

"Congratulations," Linda smiled, sadly. "But a piece of advice. Move up the date. He is not going to let you get married. No matter how hard this is for me to say, he is not over you. And as the old say goes, if he can't have you...no one can."

The three of them were silent in the room for what seemed like a lifetime.

Linda was the first one to break the silence, "Both of you, please be careful. I have never seen him like this. I don't know what he might do."

"Sadly, I have seen him like this. Take care of yourself, Linda," Lisa said, and gave her a hug.

Walking out of the room, Lisa saw Nic talking to three young men. When they saw Lisa come out of the room, Lisa could hardly believe her eyes.

"Lisa?"

"Joseph? Oh, my God!"

All three men went to Lisa and exchanged hugs with her.

Then Lisa said, "Marc this is Joseph, Michael, and Shaun. James's sons." They shook hands with Marc.

"Look at you boys...men now. You are all so handsome."

"Thank you," they said in unison.

"How is she?" Joseph asked.

"She's fine. The doctor said she could go home today. You don't have to worry."

"What happened?"

"I think its best that she explains that, Shaun," Lisa said.

"Where is dad?" Michael said.

"I have men out looking for your father now," Nic chimed in.

"Does this have to do with you?" Joseph asked.

"What? Why would you ask that?" Lisa said.

"I talked to him about a couple of weeks ago. He said that he had run into you and that you guys had been seeing each other. He said that he and Linda are getting a divorce and that..."

"And that what?" Lisa and Nic asked at the same time.

"That y'all were getting married."

Lisa was too stunned to even speak.

"That's not true," Marc said. "We are getting married."

The boys looked at Lisa with the same expression on their faces that she knew mirrored her own.

"Can we go in?" Joseph asked.

"Sure. Look here is my card, please call. I would love to have you guys at my wedding."

"Okay."

They each gave Lisa a hug as they went into Linda's room.

"Wow, they have grown so much. The last time I saw them I think Joseph was twelve, Shaun was ten, and I think Michael was about six. Now, they're grown men."

"Are you okay, Lisa?" Nic asked.

"Yeah, I'm fine. Thanks for calling me."

"No problem. Look, we are looking for him, but he could be anywhere. So, be mindful of your surroundings. Both of you."

"Will do," Marc said.

"Call me later," Lisa said, as she hugged Nic.

"Okay."

They left the hospital and headed home.

"Are you alright?" Marc asked.

"Yeah, I'm fine."

They made it home and unpacked the bags from the car. Walking into the house, Lisa headed upstairs with the bags while Marc checked his messages. Coming upstairs a few minutes later, Marc walked in the bedroom and said, "My parents haven't come back yet."

"They must be having a ball."

Marc sat on the bed next to Lisa, "Are you sure you're alright?"

"I am. I've never saw it from this end before. I had gotten kind of use to being the one people looked at. I guess I am just tired."

"Why don't you take a nap? I'll wake you later for dinner."

"What are you gonna do?"

"I'm gonna do a little work. Unless you want me to stay."

"I don't want to keep you from your work."

"You come first."

"I like the sound of that. But I'll be okay. Go get some work done."

"Alright." Kissing Lisa, Marc went to his office.

While Lisa was lying down, he was in his office trying to get some work done. Unfortunately, he couldn't concentrate for thinking about what Linda had said. Unlocking his bottom desk drawer and taking out a Colt .38 that he thought he would never need, he made sure it was loaded. Putting it back in the drawer and locking it, Marc sat back in his chair and stared out the window at nothing in particular.

After a few minutes, he got up and went back into the bedroom. Quietly he climbed into bed and pulled Lisa close to him.

"What took you so long?" Lisa whispered.

"I thought you were asleep."

"I was waiting for you."

After a couple of more sentences, they both fell asleep.

✳✳✳

Waking up around six-thirty, Marc said, "Baby, are you hungry?"

"Yeah, I could do with a little something."

"How about a big something?"

"Mmmm, even better."

"What do you feel like eating?"

"I'm open, surprise me. Do you want any help?"

"Nope, you lay down."

"That I can't do, I have a wedding to plan."

Marc headed downstairs to start dinner, while Lisa went to his office to do some research on the computer.

Starting with caterers, Lisa came up with three catering companies that were of some interest to her. Then she moved on to florists and decorations, and most importantly a photographer. Wanting to print some things off, she looked at Marc's printer to make sure there was paper in the tray. There wasn't any. Lisa was about to call his name, but he walked into the room before she could.

"Just the man I wanted to see."

"I hope so. What do you need?"

"Paper for the printer."

"Open the cabinet door underneath."

Doing as he instructed, she pulled a stack of paper out and put it in the paper tray.

"Can I use one of these big binders?"

"Take whatever you need. There are other supplies down here too," Marc said, coming behind the desk. "Let's see, dividers, pens, legal pads, staples, and anything else you can think of. Go crazy!"

"I do love a prepared man," Lisa said and then leaned in and kissed him.

"I shall return. I'm going to check on dinner," Marc said, after another kiss.

Lisa turned back to the desk and began to set up the binder. She used the dividers for dividing each department. On the cover of the binder she wrote Cavell and Jenson Wedding. Inside the binder every aspect of a wedding had its own section. Pressing the number four speed dial on her cell, Lisa put her Bluetooth in her ear and waited for Pat to answer.

On the third ring: "Hello?"

"Hey, girl, what are you doing?" Lisa said.

"Hey. Nothing lady, just sitting here reading."

"You, reading?"

"Yes and it's not work related."

"What?!"

"Girl, your little cousin is a godsend. She is efficient and a hard worker. I love that girl."

"I'm glad it's working out. It's about time you got a break."

"I told her if she continues to work for me and finishes college, I can get her a leg up after she graduates. You know she's taking up accounting?"

"Yep."

"That girl is so much like you at that age its pitiful."

"I'll take that as a compliment. Now, the reason I'm calling is to put you to work."

"What do you need?"

"Your expertise on wedding planning."

"Okay, hold on. Let me go to my office."

"While you do that, where is Lewis?"

"He's watching a movie in the den, that's why I left, I didn't want to disturb him."

"Well, aren't you a good wife."

"Yes, I am."

"Let me ask you something. Is it –"

"Before you even ask, yes it is hard. I'm not trying to scare you, but you have to consider someone else from now one. And that will be hard for you because you've been by yourself since you moved out of mama's house. So you're gonna have to learn how to submit."

"I know that, he's working with me on that. But that's not my problem."

"Then what?"

"All this crap that has happened lately with James."

"I know, and Nic called me earlier, too. Let me tell you this, if Marc hasn't bounced yet he's in it for the long haul. We all come with some baggage, Lis. Besides you prayed about this relationship, right?"

"When I first realized I was having feelings for Marc, I prayed for an answer. It has been a long time since I've been interested in someone and I didn't trust my judgment."

"And after plenty of praying, how were you answered?"

"Marc didn't judge me for all my baggage. He said he loved me and that's all that mattered to him. And I believe him."

"That's all that matters."

"Now that that is out of the way. Help your sister with her wedding."

"Okay, okay. Where you want to start?"

"Well, I typed in "wedding" in the search engine and came up with about thirty billion links."

"Calm down. It's not as bad as it looks. What you need to know is that the two major wedding web sites are tietheknot.com and weddingchannel.com. Everything else leads to one of those sites."

"But, which one is better?"

"I used both. So you go on tietheknot.com and I'll go on weddingchannel.com."

"Okay," Lisa said, typing.

For the next hour Lisa and Pat checked out both web sites, changing screens when the other found something interesting on the other web site. Thirty minutes later, Marc brought Lisa's plate and a glass of wine.

"I could have come down," Lisa told him.

"No, stay. I'll be right back," he said, heading back out of the room.

"Okay, Pat. I'm back."

"The most important thing to do is print off to do list. That way you can keep up with everything."

"Just printed one out."

"Before I forget, how did the search for a place go today?"

"Oh, girl, it went great! Marc has a friend, who owns a beautiful home. I took some pictures and I am sending them to you now."

"What's the friend's name?"

"Lesley Herbert."

"Lesley Herbert? *The* Lesley Herbert?"

"Yeah, you know him?"

"Not really, just in passing at a couple of business dinners. That man is Bill Gates rich."

"Yeah, I could tell that by the house. Have you gotten the pictures?"

"Opening them right now. Oh, Lisa! It's beautiful."

"I know, right?"

"Lisa, this is where you're getting married," Pat said, sounding excited.

"I know!"

"I cannot believe you're getting married."

"Me neither."

"Look, honey, I have to fix dinner. So I will see you tomorrow."

"Yes. We are meeting at two at Here Comes the Bride."

"I'll be there."

"Alright, bye."

"Bye. And tell Marc I said hello."

"Same to Lewis."

Taking out her earpiece, Lisa said to Marc, "Pat says hello."

"How is she?" Marc asked, from the couch.

Lisa took her plate and glass of wine over and sat next to him. "She's fine. She is helping me plan."

"I plan on helping, too."

"I know, sweetie," Lisa said, leaning in to kiss him.

"Monday, I'm going to call some contractors and see if we can get some meetings."

"Sounds good to me."

After they finished eating, Marc took their plates downstairs to clean up the kitchen and Lisa got back to work. He came back upstairs with the bottle of wine they were drinking.

"Refill?" he asked.

"Sure," she said, holding her glass up.

"So, what do you have so far?" he asked looking at the to-do list.

"Starting with that for right now. And now I am looking at dresses and bridesmaid dresses. I'm gonna print off a couple of examples for the girls to see. And then print off some examples of wedding dresses."

"What do you have in mind?"

"I have an idea of what I want, but I don't think I have ever seen any dresses made like it."

"Then have it made."

"Who would – " And then it dawned on Lisa. "I'll be right back." A minute later, Lisa came back with a card.

"Who's that?"

"My dressmaker. I met this lady who owns the store where I bought the dress that I wore to the Keene party."

"Mmmm," Marc said, smiling wickedly.

"Anyway," Lisa said, dialing the number on the card.

Lisa knew the store would be closed; it was almost nine. But to her surprise, the phone was answered on the third ring.

"Liz's Closet."

"Hello, is Elizabeth Crawford in?"

"This is she."

"Mrs. Crawford this is Lisa Jenson. I came into your store about a month ago and I bought three of your dresses. You gave me your card and told me you made dresses and gowns. Well, I'm getting married and I wanted to talk to you about making my wedding dressing."

"Congratulations."

"Thank you."

"Well, when would you like to come in?"

"I was hoping tomorrow at two, if it's not too soon."

"That'll be fine. How many are coming with you?"

"Four."

"Okay, Ms. Jenson. I'll see you tomorrow."

"Thank you, Mrs. Crawford. Good-bye."

"Good-bye, dear."

After hanging up, Lisa said, "That's done, now I can send each of the girls a text about where to meet."

After sending out the text, Lisa said, "Now, it's your turn, Mr. Cavell."

"What do I need to do?"

"First, we need to talk about changing our wedding date."

Marc was both shocked and relieved that Lisa was even open to want to talk about it.

Lisa continued, "I know you remember what Linda Harris said. And I also know that you've been thinking about it, because I have too. So, what do you feel is best for us?"

"I have been thinking about what she said. But I didn't want to pressure you, that's why I didn't say anything. If we could set up a wedding in a month, I'd be happy. Sooo, how about March seventeenth?"

"Your birthday?" Lisa asked.

"Yep."

"But, what about the house? What if it's not finished by then?"

"That's the only part I haven't figured out yet."

Lisa's cell went off indicating she had text messages. All three ladies responded back with okays.

"So, will you call Les tomorrow and let him know about the date change?"

"Yeah."

"Second, how will we explain to our parents that we moved the date?"

"Tell them you're pregnant."

Both of them started to laugh at that one. Then they heard Marc's alarm beep, letting them know that his parents made it home. A minute later they came upstairs.

"Marcello?" Marc's mother called out.

"We're in my office, Ma," Marc called out.

"Hey, kids. How was your day?"

"Eventful," Marc said. "What did you guys do?"

"Well, we went on Beale St. and bought souvenirs, and then we went to three different casinos. It was so much fun," Isabella said, excitedly.

"And your dear old dad won eight hundred dollars, playing a slot machine," Vincent boasted.

"Way to go, Dad!"

"Congratulations, Vincent!"

"Thank you, thank you."

"Where did you go?" Lisa asked.

"Harrah's Casino, Horseshoe, and Sheraton Casino," Vincent said.

"So, what are you two up to?" Isabella asked.

"Wedding planning," Marc said.

"Oh, we're just in time,"

"Actually, you are Mom. Lisa and I need to talk to you guys."

"About?" his father asked.

"We have decided to move the wedding up."

"Really?" Isabella asked.

"Lisa is pregnant," Marc blurted out.

"No, I'm not. Marc is just joking," Lisa said, quickly.

"Why, then?" Isabella asked.

Lisa took the lead on this one, and said, "Because we love each other and we don't want to wait."

"Will you do it even if we don't approve?" Marc's mother asked.

Shocked by the question, but only for a moment, they both answered 'yes' in unison.

"Good. Look you two, no one can tell you what's best for you anymore. You two have been taking very good care of yourselves and each other. We, as parents, have raised you right and we stand behind you one hundred percent."

"Thank you, Mom and Dad," Marc said.

"Thank you," Lisa said.

"You're welcome. Now, me and your father are going to bed and let you get back to planning."

"Goodnight," they said, as they headed out of the room.

"What's next?" Marc asked, smiling.

Chapter Twenty-Seven

The next morning consisted of Lisa getting up and getting ready for church. By ten she headed downstairs.

"Good morning, all."

"Good morning, dear," Isabella said.

"Morning," Vincent said.

"Do you want some breakfast?" Isabella asked, as she stood scrambling eggs at the stove.

"Oh, no thank you. I just wanted to wish you two a safe trip home, before I left for church."

"Thank you, sweetheart," Isabella said, hugging Lisa.

Then Lisa went over and hugged Vincent.

"Now, you remember to call me if Marc starts to act up," he said.

"Yes, sir," Lisa said, laughing.

"I heard that," Marc said, walking through the back door.

"Good," his father said.

"Good morning," Lisa said, receiving the kiss he gave her.

"You look beautiful this morning."

"Thank you. Did you have a nice run?"

"Yeah. I tried to get back before you left."

"I was just saying good-bye to your parents."

"I'll walk you to your car."

"Alright. Again, have safe trip."

"We will," Isabella and Vincent said in unison as they sat at the kitchen table.

Walking to front door, Marc said, "What time will you be back here?"

"About four."

"Okay. I'll meet you back here when my parent's flight leaves."

"What time is your parent's flight?"

"Four."

"Okay, then dinner will be ready by five."

"I'll be here."

They kissed and then he watched her pull away. Going back into the house, Marc walked into the kitchen to eat breakfast with his parents.

"What do you two want to do today?"

"We have seen just about everything we wanted to see," Isabella said.

"Okay, but since you guys haven't been out here in a while, let's do some shopping.'

"Alright," his parents said.

"Can I just say that I love you guys and I want to thank for being there for me for every important milestone of my life. So with that said, I want the truth. What do you two think of Lisa?"

His father spoke first, "Son, you have always made your own decisions, some of them bad and some of them good. But no matter what the consequences you stood and took them like a man. And I am proud of every decision you have made in your life, including this one. I think she will be a great wife to you as long as you are a great husband to her."

"Thanks, Dad," Marc said, kissing his father's cheek. "Mom, you're awfully quiet. What do you think?"

"Marc, I'm from the old world and growing up we never saw couples mix. I remember every girl you brought home through the years and they were somehow wrong. But as you got older, you began to make better choices. And now I am happy to finally tell you that you have found your wife. We love Lisa, son. And she's perfect for you. Now, don't take too long with giving me grandchildren."

Kissing his mother's forehead, Marc said, "Thanks, Ma. We want."

An hour later, Marc and his parents packed his trunk with their bags and set out to do some shopping and some more sightseeing before their flight.

✳✳✳

Church was over by one-fifteen and Lisa and her mother split up from her grandmother and brother and headed for the mall. Getting there, Lisa saw that Carol had already made it.

"Hey, lady," Lisa said, as she hugged Carol.

"There's the bride," Carol said returning the hug.

"Hello, Mrs. Jenson."

"Hey, Carol and I keep telling you to call me Janice," she said as they hugged.

"Hello, ladies," Pat said, walking into the store and hugging everyone.

Five minutes later, Nic arrived, "Hello, hello, hello."

"Okay guys, I wanted to talk to you before we go in."

"What's going on, Lis?" Pat asked.

"Well, Marc and I have made a decision about the wedding."

"What?" her mother asked.

"We decided to move the wedding date up."

"How far up?" all the ladies asked. Then they looked at each other and burst into laughter.

Laughing, Lisa said, "March seventeenth."

All the ladies looked at Janice as if waiting for her reaction.

"Why are you changing the date?" her mother asked.

"Because we love each other and don't want to wait."

"Will you do it no matter what I say?"

Without hesitation, Lisa said, "Yes."

"Well, we better get in here and get these fittings started."

When they entered the store, they were greeted by the owner, Elizabeth.

"Good afternoon, ladies. How may I help you?"

"Hi, I'm Lisa Jenson. I called you on yesterday about my wedding."

"I remember you now. The maroon strapless, blue chiffon, and the black halter, right?"

"Yep, that was me."

"And you're getting married, that's great. Well, let's get started, ladies. So, when is the big day?"

"March seventeenth."

"Okay, so we have to get busy."

For the next few hours, they talked about colors, designs, materials, and measurements.

"So, how much are we looking at?"

"All together we are looking at twenty-five hundred dollars. Each dress is one hundred and eighty, the mother of the bride's dress is one seventy-five, and your dress is fifteen hundred. This price includes everything. Does that sound fair?" Elizabeth asked.

"That sounds more than fair and thank you so much."

"You're welcome."

After getting her receipt for the deposit, they traded information for future fittings. Going out to the parking lot, hugs were passed around before everyone split up.

Lisa and her mother went grocery shopping, before she dropped her mother off at home.

Making it back to Marc's place by four-thirty, she unpacked the grocery bags and brought them in the house. While she unpacked the bags and put up the grocery, her cell phone rang. Looking at the caller I.D., she didn't recognize the number so she let it go to voicemail. A couple of minutes later, her cell rang again. Seeing Marc's name on the screen, she answered, "Hey you."

"Hey, I know I'm late, but my parent's flight was delayed. So, I just left the airport."

"Don't worry, I'm also running late. How far away are you?"

"Twenty minutes."

"Alright."

After hanging up, Lisa went upstairs to change out of her suit and take a quick shower. Twenty minutes later she was back downstairs and starting dinner.

About five minutes later she heard the alarm beep and Marc saying, "Honey, I'm home."

"I'm in the kitchen."

"It smells good in here. What are we having?"

"We are having meat loaf, green peas and rolls. I had my mother do the meat loaf at her house. So dinner will be ready in ten minutes."

"Good. I'm going up to take a quick shower."

While Marc was in the shower, Lisa set the table, opened the doors to the balcony, lit candles and turned off the lights. With the sun going down, she thought it would generate a nice mood. After going through his CDs, she settled on R. Kelly. His new CD would also create the right mood.

Looking up to see Marc coming downstairs, Lisa said, "You are just in time."

"Good. Because I am starving."

He pulled Lisa's chair out for her and then sat down himself.

"How did the dress shopping go?"

"Dress shopping went great. Elizabeth is going to do all the bridesmaids dresses, my mother's dress, and my dress for twenty-five hundred. What do you think?"

"I think that's a good deal. Are we paying for everyone's dress?"

"No, they are all paying for their dresses. I am paying for me and my mother's dress. Do you think your mother would want her dress made too?"

"Wouldn't hurt to ask, I'll call her tomorrow."

"Let me do it."

"Okay."

"So, how do they really feel about me?" Lisa asked.

"Who?"

"Stop playing, you know I mean your parents."

"My parents love you. My mother is already talking about grandkids." Realizing what he just said, Marc said, "Baby, I'm sorry. I –"

"It's okay. We'll just have to sit them down and explain everything to them. So, did you enjoy dinner?"

After dinner they talked as they cleaned up the kitchen and put the leftovers away.

"Do you want to watch a movie?" Marc asked.

"No, I want to sit here and watch the sun set and listen to some soft music."

"I like that idea better," Marc smiled.

Cuddling on the couch as they listened to music and watch the sun go down. They didn't say a word. They were completely relaxed at just being with each other. Without any words. When they finally decided to go upstairs to bed, Lisa could hear her voicemail alert go off on her phone, but she ignored it. There was nothing important enough to disturb tonight.

Chapter Twenty-Eight

The next couple of weeks went by quickly. Between meetings at work, meetings with contractors, decorators, coordinators, and photographers, Lisa wasn't even aware that her birthday was this weekend.

Carol was the one to remind her, "So, what are you and Marc doing for your birthday?"

"My what?" Lisa asked, sitting in front of her computer typing.

"Your birthday," Carol said, slowly.

"Why would I be thinking about that? My birthday isn't until the fif –" Lisa trailed off and looked quickly at her calendar. "My God, my birthday is this weekend. I've been so wrapped up with everything, I completely forgot."

"Well, I can understand that, you guys have a lot on your plates right now. So, how about all us girls go out Friday after work? That way you and Marc can spend the rest of the evening together."

"Okay, I'll see what his plans are and let you know."

"Alright. Well, dear, I am going to head home. Do you need me to wait for you or has Marc come back from his meeting?"

"No and no. You don't have to wait for me, I'm going to be here at least another hour and I'm going to meet him at home."

"How does it feel to be staying with him?"

"Not as weird as I thought it would be. I just couldn't go back to that house. I loved my home and James tainted it. But, I must admit that I am happy."

"Have you found a buyer yet for your house?"

"Yeah and at a very good amount. It's more than I had anticipated."

"Well, I am happy that you are happy. I'm just glad that you're safe now."

"I am happy. Now, get out of here and don't forget to tell Charles hey."

"Okay, and you sure you're gonna be alright?"

"I'll be fine. I'll see you in the morning."

"Bye."

After Carol left, Lisa got back to work. When she looked at the clock again she couldn't believe that an hour had passed so quickly. Packing up and leaving for the day, she locked up and headed for the elevator. As she got on the elevator and pushed the button for the garage, someone stuck their hand between the doors before they closed. Before Lisa knew it James was in the elevator with her.

"Hey, baby," he said.

Lisa was so shocked she couldn't speak.

"Miss me?"

"Wha – What are you doing here?" Lisa stammered.

"To see you, baby," James said cornering her in the elevator.

Staring at the numbers as the elevator went down, Lisa was trying to figure out a way to get out.

"Oh, don't worry about that," he said stopping the elevator. "Now, we can't be disturbed."

Taking deep breaths, Lisa calmed herself and said, "Please, just say what you have to say and let me go."

"Let you go? Oh, no baby. That's one thing I will never do. How can you ruin my life and then marry someone else?"

"What? James, we have been over for six years. Hell, you got married," Lisa said, getting upset.

"I loved you more than life itself. I told you I was sorry."

"Damn this. Look, you say what the fuck you got to say and then leave me the hell alone. I'm not afraid of you anymore. You can't hurt me. What you wanna do, beat me up, rape me, and scare me into coming back to you? You've done all those things to me already and as you can see they didn't work. And speaking of things that didn't work, your little breaking and entering didn't do the trick either. The police are looking for you and when they find you I hope they lock your ass up. I'll make sure of it."

"Lock me up? How do you know it was me? It could have been your so-called fiancé. He looks a little shifty to me. You might want to be careful of him."

"Get the fuck out of my way," Lisa said, shoving James to the side and trying to press the elevator button.

Next thing Lisa knew she was being shoved up against the back of the elevator. James raised his hand as if he was going to slap her, but this time Lisa didn't flinch.

"Please, do it. Give me a reason," Lisa said, standing up to him. She refused to let him see fear in her ever again.

"You better be lucky I'm in a good mood. But I'ma tell you this, you turned my wife against me. So that means you owe me, and I do plan on collecting. You and what's his name can plan all you want, but that wedding will never happen. I'll see you dead before I see you marry someone else. Besides, you can't have a wedding without a bride."

He then hit the start button and the elevator began to move again. James then cornered Lisa again and pressed himself against her, "You feel that? It used to be a time you couldn't get enough of me. Don't worry you'll get the real thing real soon."

He then forced Lisa to kiss him and then walked off the elevator when the doors opened to the garage.

Steadying herself and trying to keep from breaking down, Lisa walked quickly to her car, while looking over her shoulder. When she got in the car and started it, she broke down.

Tap, tap, tap.

"Ahhhhhh," Lisa screamed.

"Lisa, it's me baby. Unlock the door."

Looking into Marc's eyes, she unlocked the door and he opened it.

"Baby, what are you still doing here? I went home…Lisa what's wrong? Look at me. What happened?"

"He…he…he…he was here Marc," Lisa stuttered. "He caught me while I was getting on the elevator. I – I thought I would be safe, how could I be so st – stupid?" Lisa sounded as if she would start hyperventilating.

"Shhh, it's okay," Marc whispered in her ear. "Come on, come on." Marc helped her out of her car and locked it up for the night.

"I can't leave my car here."

"It'll be okay, besides you aren't in any shape to drive," he said, as he stood there holding her tight until he felt she had calmed down.

After getting her into the car and pulling out of the garage, Marc didn't want to push the issue, so he just let her talk when she was calm enough. Getting her in the house, Marc took her upstairs and ran her bath for her, just like she liked it. He undressed her and helped her into the tub. He stayed with her and even helped her with her back. Even though she complained about being babied, she let him help.

"Can you give me a few minutes?" Lisa asked. Her voice barely above a whisper.

"Are you sure?"

"Yes."

"I'll be right downstairs if you need me. I bought some chicken salad and some honey wheat bread. Just like you like it."

"I'll be down in a minute."

"Okay."

Marc kissed her and walked out of the bathroom. It broke his heart and scared him to death to see her like this. On his way downstairs, he was already on the phone.

"Hey, Nic. I need you to come to my house...He showed up at our job. Nic, you gotta find him or so help me God I will...I don't know what he did but I have never seen her like this...Okay, okay."

Pressing the end button on his phone, Marc went into the kitchen and started to make sandwiches. He had never been this mad in his life. *What if he...Oh, God, what if he raped her?* he thought to himself. After gathering everything they needed, he headed out of the kitchen. To his surprise, Lisa was sitting on the couch wrapped in a blanket.

"I hope you don't mind. I brought a blanket down with me."

"This is your home. How are you feeling?"

"Better."

Ding dong.

Lisa jumped at the sound of the doorbell. It broke Marc's heart to see her this way. Opening the door, Marc let Nic in.

"Hey, where is she?"

"In the living room."

Walking into the living room, Nic went over to the couch and hugged Lisa.

"How are you?" Nic asked.

"I'm fine, just a little on edge. What are you – Oh," Lisa said looking at Marc.

"He was supposed to call me, Lis. James violated the restraining order. I already have people out looking for him, but I have to ask you some questions."

"No he did not rape me or hit me. He pushed me a couple of times, but mostly he just made threats."

Marc couldn't help but sigh a breath of relief.

"Tell me what happened from the beginning."

Lisa went over what happened from beginning to end. Every now and then she snuck a look at Marc. When she finished, she felt exhausted.

"I think that's it. Do you need to go to the hospital?" Nic asked.

"No. I'm fine. Really, I am."

"Do you still have your gun?"

"Yes," Lisa said. This bit of news she could tell shocked Marc. "I was going to tell you."

"Marc, do you carry a weapon?" Nic asked.

"Yeah."

"Are you licensed?"

"Yeah."

"Good. For right now I would advise both of you to be very careful and if need be to start carrying, then do. I am telling you this as a friend, not a cop. Are you sure you're alright?" Nic asked Lisa.

"I'm fine."

"Good. Now, moving on. Damn, this is a nice house! Lisa, why didn't you get one of these houses?"

"Anyway."

"Hell, if you had I'd spend more time over there."

"Yeah, right. You were damn near over my house every day."

"This is really a nice house, Marc."

"Thank you, but this is Lisa's home too."

"Then, lady of the house, show me around."

"Come on, nosy."

As Lisa showed Nic around the house, Nic was talking to Pat and Carol on the phone.

"Y'all should see this house. Lisa found herself a rich man."

"I did not," Lisa laughed.

"Add their checks together; they could buy us all houses."

Lisa could here Pat and Carol laughing over the phone.

After the tour, they came back downstairs to find Marc watching a game.

"Alright, guys I'm gonna go. But don't worry, I'm gonna find this asshole and then kill him," Nic said, as she hugged Lisa.

After Lisa locked up, she went and cuddled up on the couch with Marc. Kissing her on top of the head, he said, "Are you alright?"

"I'm fine, but I don't want to talk about me. Are you okay?"

"I'm okay."

"You're lying."

"So are you," he said, looking down at her. Then he pulled Lisa onto his lap and held on as tight as he thought she could possibly take it.

Taking a deep breath, he said, "I don't know what I would have done if something happened to you. The fact that I wasn't there to protect you is killing me. I –"

"It's okay, I'm okay. I should've left when Carol did. I should have known better. But I'm alright, we're alright."

Kissing him on the forehead, Lisa balled up in his lap. She had never felt this safe in her life. They stayed like that until the game was over, and then went upstairs to bed. Even though neither of them could sleep, they both stared out at the water and talked about the wedding.

"So, what other traditions can we add to the wedding? I want this wedding to represent us both," Lisa said.

"And it will."

"How about we speak our vows in Italian?"

"What about your side of the family? We want both sides to enjoy the wedding."

"I know. But it would be so romantic."

"Do you know any Italian?"

"No, but I have always wanted to learn."

"Okay, repeat after me. Ti amo, lo sposerete?"

"Mmmm, you sound so sexy. What did you say?"

"I said 'I love you, will you marry me?'"

"Ti amo, too."

"Fast learner."

"More, more."

"Okay. Lei e` la donna piu` sessista che mai ho incontrato."

"Translation."

"You are the most sexist woman I've ever met."

"I like the sound of that in any language," Lisa laughed.

"Okay, one more. Lei mi everything mai ha volute in una donna. L`ho amata prima che l`ho saputa anche. And that means: You are everything I've ever wanted in a woman. I loved you before I even knew you."

Lisa looked up at him smiled, then kissed him. For the rest of the night, Marc whispered Italian in her ear.

***

The next day they had a meeting with Paul about the Keene account.

At the end of the meeting, Paul said, "So, you two, how are the wedding plans coming along?"

"Great," Lisa and Marc said.

"All I want to know is, will John and I be receiving an invitation?"

"Of course," Marc said.

After leaving the conference room, Marc said, "Are you still clear today to leave early, to go see the plans for the house?"

"Yeah, one, right?"

"Yep."

Splitting up at his office, Lisa went to her office and was surprised to find Pat waiting there flipping through a wedding magazine.

"Hey, girl. What are you doing here?"

"Hey lady," Pat said, putting the magazine down. "It's about time you showed up. Carol said you were in a meeting, but damn!"

"You should talk, Mrs. Workaholic. Now, what are you doing here?"

"I needed to talk to you."

"About?"

"Me and Lewis just left the doctor, and –"

"You're not sick are you? Or Lewis?" Lisa asked, as she sat next to Pat on the couch.

"No, no, nothing like that. Lisa...I'm pregnant."

"What?! Oh, my God!" Lisa screamed as she hugged Pat. "I'm so happy for you guys."

"Thank you. Now, the second reason I'm here is to invite you and Marc to a dinner we're having tonight."

"Tonight? You're supposed to be resting, how are you going to cook?"

"I'm not. Mom and Phaedra are cooking as we speak. So be at my house at seven."

"Okay. I can't believe this...you're pregnant."

Just then Carol walked in, "What did you just say?"

Pat smiled and said, "She said that she couldn't believe that I'm pregnant."

Carol made a high pitched sound as she came over and hugged Pat.

"Oh, and you and Charles are invited to dinner tonight at my house."

"We will be there. What time?"

"Seven o'clock."

"Okay."

"Have you called Nic?" Lisa asked Pat.

"Yeah, I wanted her to meet me here, but she was out and wasn't answering her phone. But I left here a message. Trust me I will be hearing from her," Pat laughed. "The other night I talked to her she was out with Michael. What's up with those two?"

"They are becoming very close, aren't they? Well, we will corner her about that later," Lisa said.

"So, what do you wanna have?" Carol asked.

"Actually, Lewis wants a girl and so do I, but I have to say a part of me wants a boy."

"No, you have to have a girl, so you can name her Lisa."

"Girl, please," Pat laughed.

"Knock, knock. Room for one more?" Marc said, standing in the door.

"Always, but guess what?" Lisa said.

"What?"

"I'm pregnant," Pat said.

"Congratulations, Patricia. To you and Lewis."

"Patricia? Marc, family calls me Pat. You're our brother-in-law now."
"That's right," Carol said.
Then Pat and Carol hugged Marc. Lisa couldn't help but smile.
"Wait don't move." Lisa got her camera and said, "Say, mommy."
"Mommy!"
After taking the picture, Pat said, "Look, I need to run a couple errands. I will see you guys tonight."
"Bye," everyone said in unison.
"Are you ready?" Marc asked Lisa.
"Um, yeah. Carol, I left everything written down if need be. I talked to Mr. Roberts, he's supposed to call me later, but that will be on my cell. And I think that's it," Lisa said, closing her briefcase and putting on her jacket.
"Okay and we will see you guys tonight."
"Bye." Lisa said.
Walking toward the elevator, Marc asked, "What's tonight?"
"Pat is having a dinner at their house, are you free?"
"I'm sorry I have plans."
"What plans?"
"I was actually planning on making love to my beautiful fiancée tonight."
"Oh, well we can see Pat and her family anytime."
Laughing, Marc said, "What time is dinner?"
"Seven."
"I guess I can change my plans, but I'm sure she won't be happy about this."
"I know she won't."
"Hey, you two, do I have to write you up for sexual harassment?" John said, laughing.
"I keep telling her this is not the place for that. I think you should write Ms. Jenson up for breaking the rules, you know, to teach her a lesson," Marc said.
Laughing, Lisa said, "Funny, I'm gonna remember that later."
Getting on the elevator, they heard, "Wait for me."
When John held the door it was Melody who walked on.
"Thank you, Mr. Peterson."

"You're welcome, Melody. What floor?"

"Oh, the garage, like everyone else. Hello Mr. Cavell...Ms. Jenson."

"Hi, Melody," Lisa said.

"Melody," Marc nodded.

While Marc and John talked, Lisa and Melody waited in silence. Pushing her hair behind her ear, Lisa heard Melody take sharp breath.

"Ms. Jenson, your ring is beautiful. Where did you get it? And it's on the ring finger. You're getting married?"

"Yes, I am," Lisa smiled.

"Congratulations! Who's the lucky man?" Melody asked, smiling.

"I am the very lucky man," Marc said.

Talk about shocked into silence. Lisa almost felt sorry for her...almost. Melody finally said, "Well, congratulations to you both."

Lisa could practically see steam coming out of her ears. Everyone went in their own direction when the elevator doors opened.

As she got in the car, Lisa's cell phone rang. "Lisa Jenson...Yes, Mr. Roberts...Well, if you want me to look at them immediately, you can email them to me...And I'll call you first thing in the morning...Goodbye."

"Everything alright?"

"Yeah, just getting some figures. Mr. Roberts is either hiding something or I'm losing my touch."

"That could never happen," Marc said, giving her hand a squeeze. "So, what do you wanna do for your birthday?"

"I don't know, but the girls want to take me out for drinks after work. But I wanted to know what your plans were first."

"Honestly, that'll be great. While you celebrate with your friends, I can catch a game with Steve. Then we can go out for dinner."

"That'll work."

Walking into the contractor's office, Marc said, "Marc Cavell for Peter Williams."

"One moment please," the receptionist said.

As they sat down, Marc asked Lisa, "Will you keep an opened mind about this one?"

"Of course, why would you ask me that?"

"Because the other three contractors have decided to go into other professions because of you."

"I am not that bad."

"Okay."

"Mr. Cavell, Mr. Williams will see you now."

"Thank you."

They walked into Mr. Williams' spacious office.

Mr. Williams stood up and came from behind his desk to greet them, "Mr. Cavell, please come in. Nice to finally meet you."

"You too, Mr. Williams. And this is my fiancée Lisa Jenson."

"Nice to meet you," Lisa said.

"The pleasure is mine," Mr. Williams said, obviously flirting with Lisa.

"How nice," Lisa said, pulling her hand from his grasp."

"How about we get started?" Marc said.

"Yes, lets. Now, Mr. Cavell, per our first meeting I made some sketches of your ideas."

Showing them the sketches, Marc and Lisa looked over them.

"These are amazing," Lisa said.

"Thank you," Mr. Williams said, leaning into Lisa.

Smiling, Lisa maneuvered on the other side of Marc, pretending that she was trying to get a better look at the blueprint.

"Your husband explained what you were looking for in great detail."

"It's perfect," Lisa said, looking at Marc.

"As you can see, there will be four bedrooms, three baths, den, and a huge kitchen."

"So, how much are we talking?" Marc asked.

"We're talking the house with specific amenities for each of the rooms and the landscape, so it's close to the three hundreds."

Looking at Lisa, Marc said, "Can we swing that?"

"If we were able to do this, how soon can you start and how long will it take?"

"Well, my team and I can start breaking ground as soon as next week. And I think we could finish this job in less than six months. Permitting everything going as planned. Our last job, which we finished last week, was building new homes in Southaven."

"Yes, we saw those. They are very good. So, what do you think?" Lisa asked Marc.

"I think we both agree he's good. So alright," Marc said.

After they both wrote checks for their half of the deposit, they shook hands on the deal and left.

"I think I will have to watch this guy," Marc said in the elevator.

"You have nothing to worry about."

"I know that," he said, and kissed Lisa.

Making it home by two, they were still talking about the plans for the house.

Going into the kitchen, Lisa said, "Can you believe we're gonna have our own home together?"

"We already do."

"You bought this house. I didn't have anything to do with that."

"You made it a happier place."

Lisa walked over to Marc and kissed him.

"And if you want to help, I could always use some help with the mortgage."

"I'll write you a check."

"I bet you would. Are you hungry?"

"Yes, but not for food."

"Mmmm, well let me give you what you're craving."

"Come on," Lisa said, about to walk out of the kitchen.

Marc grabbed her by the waist, "Unh-unh, where you going? You got the stairs and the balcony, and now I want you right here right now," he said, as he kissed her on the neck softly.

Taking each other's clothes off as they slid to the floor, Lisa said, "I hope none of your neighbors, have a telescope."

"You didn't think about that when we were on the balcony. Now, get naked."

Chapter Twenty-Nine

After making love in the kitchen, they went upstairs to shower and rest before Pat's party.

Lying in bed, Lisa said, "I can't believe Pat is pregnant. She and Lewis have been trying to have a baby since they first got married."

"How long have they been married?"

"About four and a half years. They were going to Jamaica to get away and try to get pregnant. So, I guess they'll go to celebrate instead."

"That reminds me, we haven't talked about where we're going for a honeymoon. Do you have any ideas?"

"Not really. I thought about somewhere tropical, but I also thought about...never mind."

"No, tell me. I want to know."

"Ever since I was young I've always wanted to go to Italy," Lisa said, turning towards him.

"Really?"

"But this is your honeymoon, too. Where do you want to go?"

"Actually, I was thinking Paris. How much vacation time do you have saved up?"

"A lot."

"How about we do both? We could take two weeks. A week in Paris and a week in Italy."

"Can we do that, I mean we're building a house?"

"Honesty time, I make roughly two hundred and eighty thousand after taxes, you?"

"A little more. I have Anthony. So, about two hundred and ninety thousand."

"Good, then you pay for the trip."

"I don't think so," Lisa laughed.

"Hey, you can't blame me for trying. Tomorrow, we'll look up travel agencies and then we'll see what we can find on our own."

"Okay."

Looking at the clock, Lisa said, "Let's take a nap, we have a couple hours to kill."

Marc rolled over and set his cell to ring at 6:00, and then pulled Lisa close to him.

***

By six forty-five, Lisa and Marc were dressed out the door.

"Let's take your car," Lisa said.

"Only if you drive," Marc said, tossing her the keys.

Pulling out of the garage, they took the expressway out east to Pat and Lewis' house. Lisa turned into the cul-de-sac and couldn't believe all the cars that were there. Finding a spot directly across from the house, they got out and headed toward the house.

Ringing the doorbell, Lisa said, "I hope they heard us."

Just then, Pat's mother answered the door, "Lisa!"

"Hey, Mama! How are you?!" Lisa said, hugging her.

"I'm doing great, I'm about to be a grandmother," she said, closing the door. "Now, who is this beautiful man?"

"This is Marc. Marc, this is my second mama, Mary Furrow."

"Well, you are the lucky man who has finally caught our Lisa. Nice to meet you."

"It's nice to meet you, Mrs. Furrow."

"Ooooh, he's gentleman. It is nice to meet you, too. But you can call me Mary or mama."

"It's nice to meet you, Mary."

"Come on, everyone has been waiting on you, Marc."

"Me, why me?"

"You see, when Lisa was younger, she said she would never get married. So the family can't wait to meet you."

Laughing, Marc said, "Okay."

Walking into the living room, Mary said, "Look who finally showed up."

Hugs and introductions went around the room. Next they moved to the kitchen.

"It's about time," Pat said, as soon as she saw them.

"You knew we were coming, Mommy," Lisa said, as she hugged Pat.

"Okay, everybody, this is Lisa's fiancé, Marc. Marc, this is everybody."

"Hello, ladies. Um, am I the only man here?"

"No," Pat said, laughing. "They're out on the patio smoking those god awful cigars. You can go right out that door."

"I'll be back," he said, kissing Lisa and then walking out to the patio.

As soon as he closed the door, just about every woman in the room said, "DAAAAAAMN!!!"

"Girl, what runway did you get him off of?" Pat's sister, Pamela asked.

"He is fine as hell," one of Pat's cousins added.

"I told y'all. Show them your ring, Lis," Pat said.

Lisa held her hand out for everyone to see.

"Girl, that is beautiful," Mary said.

"So, where are you guys getting married?" a young woman asked.

Lisa knew her face, but couldn't think of her name.

"We're getting married at his friend's house."

"Is it a big house?"

"Yeah."

"You make me sick," Pat blurted out. "I'll tell them. His friend is Lesley Herbert. Before you even ask who he is, he is in business and is Bill Gates rich."

Laughing at her friend, Lisa said, "Why is all this music playing and no one is dancing? Come on, ladies."

Lisa opened the door to the patio, and said, "Hello, gentlemen."

Walking over to Pat's father, Larry, they hugged and she said, "Hey, dad. How are you?"

"Great, how's my third best daughter?"

"I'm fine."

"Now, there is a crazy rumor going around that you're getting married. Please tell me it isn't true."

"Yes, it's true."

"My heart is broken to lose another daughter, but congratulations, sweetie."

"Thanks, Dad. Where is the father to be?"

"There he is," Larry said, pointing at another group of men.

Walking over to them, she said, "There's the new daddy! I am so happy for you two."

"Thank you, Le Le. I was just telling Marc that you two will be having a few soon."

"You moving a little fast, ain't you?" Lisa said, laughing.

Then raising her voice, Lisa said, "Gentlemen, there is a room full of women waiting to dance with husbands, boyfriends, one-night stands, and baby daddies, so come on in."

When Lisa walked into the living room everyone was dancing. She saw Nic on the floor dancing with Marc and just shook her head. Finding her mother on one of the couches, Lisa sat next to her.

"Enjoying yourself, Mama?"

"I was until Nic stole my dance partner," Janice said, laughing.

"Excuse me ladies. Lisa, do you want to dance?" Michael asked.

"No."

"It's just one dance, come on."

Looking at her mother for help, her mother said, "Stop being mean and dance with the man."

Sighing loudly, Lisa said, "Okay."

Lisa went out on the floor with him, even though she didn't entirely want to. Just as they were getting into the song, it was changed over to Gerald Levert's Awesome.

"Thanks for the short dance," Lisa said.

"Wait. One more? Besides they're keeping your fiancé busy. I want to talk to you."

Hesitantly, Lisa took his hand. She said, "Talk."

"You know, I really do care deeply about Nicole."

"She's a great woman."

"Yes, she is. That's why I wanted to talk to you. I know you don't like me. But, I'm not that bad of a guy."

"Look, Nic is a grown woman, who knows what she's getting into. Now, I might not be that fond of you, but I trust Nic's judgment. And if she says you're a good guy I believe her."

"Well, is there anything I can do to change your mind?" he asked pulling Lisa closer to him.

"And how would you do that?"

Leaning in to whisper in her ear and moving his hand down to the lower part of her back, Michael said, "Given the right chance, I think we can go through a long list of possibilities. What do you think?"

"I think you're still an ass," Lisa said, walking away from him.

Then she felt someone grab her arm, "Come with me," Pat said, pulling her into the bathroom. "I saw that," she said, when she closed the door.

"You saw what?" Lisa asked, looking in the mirror.

"Don't play stupid with me, I saw Michael coming on to you."

"That's not what he was –"

"Tut-tut, stop it. What did he say?"

Sighing, Lisa said, "He said that he cared deeply for her and he knew I didn't like him."

"And?"

"And, was there anything he could do to change my mind?"

Just then there was a knock on the door and Carol and Nic walked in.

"What are you two doing and why is Carol dragging me in here?" Nic asked.

"How are you and Michael?" Pat asked Nic.

"We're fine, why?"

"How do you feel about him?" Lisa asked.

"I like him. A lot," Nic said, smiling.

"That's what we wanted to know," Lisa said.

"But –"

"We were making sure you were happy," Lisa said, cutting Pat off.

"I am."

"Good. Oh, and mama said she's gon get you about stealing her dance partner."

"I gave him back," Nic said, smiling and then walked out of the bathroom.

"What's going on here?" Carol asked.

"Michael made a pass at Lisa," Pat said.

"He what?"

But that didn't come from Carol. It came from Nic, who had walked back into the bathroom.

"What did he say to you?" Nic asked.

"He just asked was there anything he could do to change my mind about him. That's not really a pass," Lisa said.

"How did he say it?"

"He whispered it in my ear."

"Did you feel like he was making a pass at you? You know you think to clearly to jump to conclusions."

After taking pause, Lisa said, "Yes, I do think he was making a pass at me."

"What are you going to do?" Pat asked Nic.

"I'm going to shoot him."

Before anyone could stop her, she was already out the door. They followed her out of the bathroom and watched Nic as she talked to Michael. Then Michael looked right at Lisa, and headed in her direction.

"What lies did you tell her? You –"

"Is there a problem? Because if there is, you talk to me. Not her," Marc said, standing in front of Lisa.

"Michael, you need to leave," Pat said.

Looking at Lisa, Michael said, "Bitch."

Lisa grabbed Marc and said, "Marc, no. You can't hit him, he's a cop. But, I can."

Before anyone could stop her; Lisa had punched Michael in the face.

"Lisa!" Carol yelled.

Pat and Carol pulled her into the bathroom, while Lewis, Marc, and Nic took Michael outside. Five minutes later, Nic came into the bathroom.

"Is he gone?" Pat asked.

"Is he pressing charges?" Carol asked.

"He is not about to tell someone a woman gave him a black eye. How's your hand, Ali?"

"I'm good. How are you?"

"I'm fine."

"Are you mad at me?"

"No, but you could have told me. We have been friends too long."

"I know. And Pat, I'm sorry for spoiling your party."

"Girl, please. Does it sound like you spoiled anything?"

They all started laughing and left out of the bathroom.

"Your hand okay," Marc asked.

"Yeah. I'm sorry for doing that, but I couldn't let you hit him. He would have arrested you for sure. I didn't hurt your manhood did I?"

"No, actually, Lewis welcomed me to the club?"

"What club?"

"Something called Wives Who Can Whip Ass. He said it was a club I had to belong to since we're getting married."

"Very funny."

"Let's dance slugger."

"Um, Pat, is Lewis' brother Brandon married?" Nic asked.

"Nope, he's single."

"Gay?"

"Nope."

"Wanted?"

"Nope."

"See you later," Nic said, before walking over to a smiling Brandon.

Laughing, Pat and Carol found their husbands and joined everyone else that was dancing.

By eleven o'clock everyone was telling Lewis and Pat congratulations and leaving. After making sure Nic was gonna be alright, Marc opened the door and helped Lisa get in the car.

When he got in the car, Lisa said, "Had fun?"

"I did and I even got a client out of it."

"Who and how did you do it?"

"Xavier Hill. We were all talking about the market and I guess he liked what he heard."

"Xavier is a good guy. He started his own software company."

"Yeah. We have a meeting tomorrow morning."

"That's great."

"How long did you two date?"

"Huh?"

"Huh. You heard me."

"About two years. How did you find out?"

"When he found out that I was your fiancé, he started talking about how lucky I was. And he had this kind of far off look in his eyes."

"It only lasted a couple of years."

"Why didn't it work out?"

"You know how it goes, boy meets girl, girl loses boy to another woman. And then boy marries other woman. But, we managed to remain friends."

"Is he still married?"

"No."

Making it back home, they went into the house and locked up for the night.

"Are you cold?"

"Just a little chilly."

"How about I set up a small fire in the bedroom? We'll open the balcony door so we can get the full effect."

"Sounds like a plan."

Walking into the bedroom, Marc started the fire and Lisa sat on the bed to take her shoes off and put them in the closet.

When Marc finished with the fire, he said, "Come here."

"What?" Lisa said, smiling as she came out of the closet and walked over to him.

Without saying a word he unbuttoned her blouse and slipped it off her shoulders and kissed her. Following suit, she unbuttoned his shirt.

"Wait a minute," Marc whispered against her lips. Then he pulled all the cover off the bed and laid them down on the floor in front of the fire.

Helping Lisa down on the floor, he said, "I think every time I look at you, I love you more."

"Can you believe that in five months we're going to be married?"

Marc pulled the chopsticks out and let her hair fall around her face.

"Yes, I can. And the months are not going by quick enough for me."

Marc reached over for the remote to the radio and turned it on, and Robin Thicke's voice came through the speakers. As they kissed, Robin Thicke sang about sex therapy. For the rest of the night, Marc repeatedly told Lisa that it was all about her tonight. He brought her to climax so many times that she had lost count. They were so close to one another that they were almost one. Lisa thought to herself that her nights of romance were starting to outnumber her nights of loneliness.

That next morning was a busy one for Lisa. She had three meetings before noon and a surprise visit.

"Lisa, there is a Xavier Hill to see you," Carol said over the intercom.

"Send him in." Smiling, Lisa got up from her desk to greet him as he walked in. "Hey, Xavier. How are you?"

"I'm great. How are you?" he asked, as they hugged.

"I'm doing fine. What brings you here today?" Lisa asked, as she sat on the couch and gestured for him to sit.

"Well, I just had a meeting with your – with Marc. And I decided to stop by before I left."

"How did the meeting go?" Lisa asked, acting as if she didn't hear him hesitate on the word fiancé.

"It went great. I really look forward to working with him."

"Glad to hear it."

"So, he tells me the wedding is in five months. Nervous?"

"A little, but I'm mainly happy. Marc is a wonderful man."

"He has to be to get you to talk about getting married."

"I'm not just talking about it, I'm doing it."

"You know I always thought me and you would get married."

"How in the world did you think that and you've already been married?"

"Trust me that is something I have always regretted. Letting you go. You're a very special lady, Lisa."

"Thank you, X."

Laughing, he said, "I haven't heard that in a long time, Le Le."

They were quiet for a minute, then he said, "I know I shouldn't say this, but I'll kick myself if I don't. I hate I missed my chance in marrying you. You were the first woman to be my friend and lover. Hell, you were my first. I'll always regret not getting you back when I had the chance. Unless I still have a chance?"

Lisa looked into the eyes of this man that she loved so deeply when she was young, and said, "No, you don't."

"Can I ask you something?" Xavier said.

"Sure."

"Are you happy?"

"Extremely. I'm better than happy, I'm loved."

"Good, you deserve it. Now, I'm going to leave before I make an even bigger fool of myself."

"Don't say that. You and I will always be friends. That is a promise we made to each other before you got married, remember? Nothing has changed. You showed me there was another side to love other than sex. Honestly, for a long time a part of me waited for you to come back. But then Marc came into my life and now I can't picture my life without him. Besides after you got married I knew I had to let you go."

"After my divorce I wanted to tell you how I felt. I guess I missed my chance. I thought you would slam the door in my face."

"I would never do that to my friend."

"Now that I have gotten that off my chest, I better go."

As they stood up, Xavier Hill, Lisa's first love, hugged her tight and kissed her on the cheek. Before he walked out, he said, "Would you have let me in?"

"Yes, I would have."

"Be happy, Le Le, you deserve it. See you at your wedding." And then he was gone.

Standing there in her office, Lisa felt a little sad. She stood at the window and looked down on the traffic and out at the water. And then she smiled. She could not remember being this happy in a long time and she knew why. Picking up her phone, she dialed Marc's office extension.

Chapter Thirty

"Happy Birthday," Marc whispered to Lisa early Friday morning.

"Thank you, baby."

"So, how does it feel to be twenty-nine?"

"Wonderful. In fact, this is the happiest birthday I have ever had."

"It hasn't even started yet."

Getting out of bed to begin their day, Marc asked, "What time do you think you'll make it home?"

"We won't be out long. So probably around seven."

"Okay, I'll meet you here. Where do you want to have dinner?"

"I don't know. Why don't you surprise me."

"How about I reserve a table at Wendy's?"

"That's a good one," Lisa laughed.

After eating and working out, they got ready for work. While Lisa was in the shower, Marc opened the glass door and stepped in.

"Hey, wait your turn," she laughed.

"I just thought you needed some help washing your back."

"Yeah right."

"Okay, how about I give you your first gift."

"And what would that be?"

He said nothing, only kissed her softly on the lips. "I plan on us being a little late to work today."

"Oh, you do?"

"Mmm-hmm," he said, kissing her neck.

"Mmmm," Lisa moaned.

Smiling, Marc said, "I see you agree with the plan."

He then moved down to kiss and suck each breast. He could feel her hands in his hair. Going even lower, he kissed her stomach softly and then he lifted one of her legs and placed it on his shoulder. Then he kissed her on her inner thigh as he rubbed her clit softly. He could hear her moaning become louder as he started to suck on her clit.

Lisa's hands were in his hair as she moved her hips to the rhythm of his tongue. As she climaxed, she called out his name loud enough for the whole entire city to hear.

Standing in front of her and letting her catch her breath, he said, "Did you like your first gift?"

"Yes, I did."

"Good," he said, and then kissed her deeply.

This time he picked Lisa up and as she wrapped her legs around his waist, Marc pushed into her. Pressing her against the shower wall, he continued to go deeper and deeper.

"Oh, Marc. Yes, yes."

He thrust into Lisa harder with every stroke, until they both came together. Breathing hard they slid to the shower floor of the shower.

Letting the water fall on them, Marc laid his head against the wall and said, "Happy birthday, Mona Lisa."

"It is now," she said, and kissed him.

After showering and getting dressed they left for work, making it there by nine forty-five.

"Good morning, Carol," Lisa said, walking into the outer office.

"Happy Birthday!" Carol said, while handing Lisa an envelope.

Opening it, Lisa read the cover, "Today you've finally become a woman, tomorrow…" Lisa opened the card and on the inside it said "an old woman."

Lisa started laughing and hugged Carol, "Thank you, and not funny."

"Charles and I thought it was hilarious. Now, your second card." Carol handed her a pink envelope. Opening and reading this one, there was a castle on the cover and under it, it read: "Far, far away…" When Lisa opened the card, she read the handwritten inscription: *A beautiful princess named Lisa was born. Like many princesses she had her choice of princes. But no man was ever able to slay the dragon that guarded the heart of the beautiful princess. Year after year a prince would come only to be turned away. Finally, Prince Marc arrived and though the dragon had grown stronger over the years, Prince Marc continued to fight. But, soon with patience and persistence, the prince finally killed the dragon. Winning the princess' heart, Prince Marc climbed the tower and kissed Princess Lisa, thus gaining her trust and most importantly her heart. And they lived happily ever after.*

Lisa I love you with all of my soul. Happy Birthday, baby. Now walk into your land of dreams.

Lisa looked at Carol, but she couldn't speak for the lump in her throat.

"Come on," Carol said, opening Lisa's office door.

When Lisa walked in, there were red roses everywhere. There wasn't an empty space in the room, except her desk.

"How does he do this?" Lisa whispered.

"Well, I called them yesterday and they delivered this morning. How did I do?"

"You always seem to outdo yourself."

"I wanted to replace the ones you lost."

"Marc, this is beautiful!" Lisa said, as she walked over and kissed him.

"Mmmm, I'm gonna start giving you flowers every day."

"Stop it, we're at work," Lisa said, trying to move away from him.

"Lock your door," Marc whispered, as he kissed her neck.

"We can't."

"Oh, yes we can. Do you remember a promise you made me?"

"Ooooo, you gon' bring that up? You know you wrong for that," Lisa said, laughing.

"Okay, I got something better. I dare you."

"Oh, so you want dare me?"

"Yep. What you got?"

Smiling, Lisa said, "Lock the door."

She never saw Marc move so fast.

"Um, Carol hold my calls."

"Will do."

Marc came over behind her desk and leaned her against the window and kissed her. Reaching up, he cracked open the window to the right of them.

Turning her chair around, Lisa pushed Marc down in the chair.

"What would you like me to do?" she asked him.

"Mount up."

Straddling his lap, Lisa kissed him deeply. Marc pushed her skirt up around her hips, while Lisa unbuckled his belt and undid his pants. Marc entered her with one thrust.

"Oh, Lisa," he moaned into her ear.

"Don't stop, Marc," she whispered.

Getting out of the chair still holding Lisa, he said, "I've always wanted to do this."

Then he pushed all of her things off the desk and laid her on it. His tempo speeded up as Lisa tried not yell out loud.

"Marc, I'm cumming."

Those words just made him speed up and thrusts harder.

After his climax, Marc laid his head on her stomach and said, "You are killing me."

"I think that's the other way around," she said, breathing hard.

They both used Lisa's bathroom to clean up, then they cleaned up her office. Sitting on her couch, Marc held her in his arms.

"Now, let's see you conduct a meeting."

They both burst out laughing.

Sighing, Lisa said, "This is the best birthday I have ever had."

"I'm glad, but it's not over yet. We still have tonight."

"What have you done now?"

"It's a surprise."

"You can't keep doing this, I haven't given you anything."

"Yes, you have. You. You've given me your hand in marriage and that's enough until the day I die."

They kissed each other and then decided to get the work day started, at least what was left of it.

After Marc left, Carol walked in the office, "Ready to start birthday girl?"

"Um, yeah. What's first?"

"Well, Mr. Roberts is here for his meeting."

"How long has he been here?"

"A couple of minutes. You need more time to, uh...gather your thoughts?"

Lisa burst out laughing, "Please tell me you didn't hear us."

"No. Just the crash of desk items," Carol said, straightening certain items on her desk.

"I cannot believe I just did this. Okay, okay, get a grip," Lisa said, as she was trying to stop herself from smiling.

"You ready?"

"Give me five minutes."

Carol went back out to her desk. After five minutes she showed Mr. Roberts in.

"Hello, Mr. Roberts. How are you?" Lisa said, standing in front of her desk.

"Good, how are you?" Mr. Roberts said, shaking Lisa's hand.

"Do you have everything we will need?"

"Yes, I decided to bring it over myself. I don't trust the delivery guys."

"Well, I can understand that. But this is the only thing I needed from you, I hate that you had to come all this way for one file."

"Well, actually Ms. Jenson, I was hoping to talk your assistant into a lunch date."

"Really?" Lisa said, smiling.

"Yeah. So, you'll call me if there's any problem."

"Of course, Mr. Roberts."

Lisa couldn't help but laugh, when Mr. Roberts closed her door. For the rest of the day, Lisa tried to concentrate on the account she was working on. But, she kept picturing her and Marc on the desk and in the chair.

Answering her phone after the first ring, "This is Lisa."

"Thinking about me?" Marc said, softly.

"Yes, no matter how hard I try not to."

"How was your meeting?"

"Difficult."

"I'm sorry, is there anything I can do?"

"No, you've done enough."

"I'm nowhere near finished, Mona Lisa."

"What does that mean?"

"Be ready by eight."

"Okay."

"I'll see you then."

At five, Carol walked into Lisa's office and said, "Let's go birthday girl."

"I am ready. Where are we going?"

"We are taking you to Chili's, let's go."

Lisa rode with Carol to the restaurant where they were supposed to meet Nic and Pat. Getting there first, Carol and Lisa got a table and ordered drinks.

"Happy birthday!" Nic and Pat said when they made it to the table. They each gave Lisa a birthday card that Lisa found hilarious.

"These are so going in my collection."

"How many rounds have we missed?" Pat asked.

"This is the first," Lisa said, lifting her glass.

Pat ordered Ginger ale and Nic ordered a Margarita.

"So, what did Marc get you?" Pat said.

Caught off guard, Carol choked on her Bahama Mama, "I'm sorry, that went down the wrong way."

"Well," Lisa said, after nudging Carol and sipping her Strawberry Martini. "He wrote me a fairytale and filled my office with red roses."

"He wrote you a fairytale?" Pat asked, as she wiped away a tear.

Nic, Lisa, and Carol looked at her like she had lost her mind.

"Hormones?" Nic asked.

"Yep. It's gotten so bad, I cry at Halloween commercials."

"It'll be over soon. Are you getting morning sickness?" Carol asked.

"Morning, afternoon, and night."

"Keep drinking Ginger ale and eating crackers."

After listening to Pat's wonders and woes of being pregnant, they talked about the wedding plans, and other crazy birthday's they all had spent together. After paying for their drinks, hugs were passed around and everyone split up to go home.

Carol pulled into Marc's driveway a couple of minutes later and said, "This is nice."

"Come on, I can give you the tour."

Walking into the house, Lisa put in the alarm code and walked into the living room.

"Follow me," Lisa said.

"Wow, look at that view," Carol said, looking out the balcony door.

"I know right," Lisa said, as she turned on the lights.

They both were shocked to see a big white box with a red bow on the coffee table. An envelope was tucked in the bow. Lisa opened the envelope and read the note inside.

"What does it say?" Carol asked.

Smiling, Lisa read, *"If you're reading this, then I haven't made it home yet. So, until I do, I hope this will keep you warm."*

Lisa then lifted the top. "Oh, my God," Lisa and Carol said at the time.

Lisa took the fur coat out of the box, when Carol said, "Lisa, it's beautiful."

Lisa was speechless, as she wiped tears away and stared at the coat.

"What's wrong?"

"Nothing. It's just that a month or so ago, Marc and I were shopping and I saw this coat in the window. I wanted it so bad. But there was no way I was going to pay five thousand dollars for a coat, while we're paying for the house and the wedding. I can't believe he did this."

"Try it on!"

Lisa stood and slipped into the coat, and said, "How do I look?"

"You look wonderful. Like it was made for you. Well, I am gonna get out of here so you can really start your birthday celebration."

"Okay. And thank you again for the birthday drinks."

"You're welcome, sweetie."

They hugged and then Lisa watched Carol get in her car and drive away.

Locking the door and setting the alarm, Lisa put the box away and went upstairs to see how she looked in the coat. Looking at her reflection, Lisa smiled. Then she got an idea. First, she called The Pier and ordered dinner. She was able to talk the matri d' into having the food delivered. For an extra amount, of course. Looking at her watch, she figured she had enough time to set everything up.

After her shower, Lisa curled her hair and then put on her makeup. Hearing the doorbell and telephone ring at the time, she headed downstairs to answer them both. Lisa picked up the cordless phone when she got downstairs.

"Hello?"

"Hello, gorgeous," Marc said.

"Hey, where are you?" Lisa said, as she opened the door and let the delivery guy in.

"Unfortunately, I'm caught in traffic on the expressway."

"How long will you be?" Lisa asked, as she paid the delivery man.

"The way this traffic is, February is looking pretty good. But don't worry; we're still going to celebrate your birthday. By the way, did you like your gift?"

"Marc, I love it and I love you. I can't believe you did this."

"Did you try it on?"

"Yes, and it fits perfectly."

"I'm glad you like it. Okay, now we're moving. Give me about fifteen minutes."

"Will do. Bye."

"Bye."

Putting the phone on its base in the kitchen, she made sure the table was set perfectly and then she ran upstairs to change. Lisa changed into a pair of four inch heeled shoes that buckled around the ankle, with a black thong and a diamond incrusted chain belt. She sprayed on her favorite perfume, Donna Karen, and then put on her new coat.

Lisa went back downstairs and turned on the radio. Soft music came through the speakers. She made sure the fire in the fireplace was going strong. She heard Marc's car pull into the driveway. She then stood next to the dinner table.

When Marc walked in, he dropped his gym bag by the door and said, "Mona Lisa, are you upstairs?"

"No, I'm right here," Lisa said, as she stood there, with her coat wide open. "So, how does the coat look?"

After finding his voice, Marc said, "You're wearing a coat? Oh, my God. You look...I can't even find the words. Sexy even seems like an understatement."

"Thank you," Lisa said, walking toward him.

"Your perfume is intoxicating."

"Thank you, again. Should I model for you?"

"I'm glad I showered at the gym. I don't want to miss a thing."

"I figured as much."

Marc sat on the couch as Lisa stood in front of the fireplace.

"As you can see, the coat closes perfectly to keep me warm. And opens to reveal what's on the inside. Do you like?"

Marc nodded.

Lisa heard the intro to Alicia Keys' song, *Like You'll Never See Me Again.* "Dance with me."

Marc got up and pulled her close. They danced to the song in front of the fireplace.

"I thought we were celebrating your birthday."

"We are. Unless you had your own plans."

"I had something planned, but –"

"Do I have enough time to change?"

"Yes, but you've done all this. I can cancel mine."

"No. I tell you what, tomorrow will be your pamper day."

"You sure?"

"Yes."

"Okay, but uh…can you keep this on?"

"Oh, yeah."

Marc put out the fire, while Lisa put the food away. They headed upstairs to change for dinner. Lisa put on a black backless dress that snapped around the neck. The dress had a split that came up to the thigh and her back was out down to an inch above her butt. She was still wearing the shoes and the thong and the belt could be seen across the lower part of her waist.

"How do I look?" Lisa asked when Marc walked out of the bathroom.

Biting his bottom lip, Marc groaned with lust. "I still can't find the words."

"Well, you look good enough to eat," Lisa said.

"I like the sound of that."

Marc helped Lisa with her coat and then put on his coat.

"Which car are we taking?" Lisa asked.

"Neither," Marc said, as he opened the front door.

"Then how –"

Just then a limo pulled into the drive.

"Is there anything you haven't thought of?"

"I hope not."

After locking up, they got in the limo and were on their way.

"So, where are we going?"

"To the top of the world," Marc smiled.

"A clue. Come on, tell me."

"You'll see. And speaking of seeing, the image of you standing there in just this coat and a thong is something I will never forget. Ever."

"Good."

Soft jazz played as Marc poured them both a glass of champagne. About thirty minutes later they heard, "Sir, we're here."

Lisa looked out the window at the Clark Tower and looked at Marc. "Top of the world. I get it."

Marc helped Lisa out of the limo and asked the driver if he would be alright?

"I'll be fine, sir. I will be here when you're ready."

Taking Lisa by the hand, they walked into the lobby of the building to the elevator. Waiting for the elevator with another couple, Lisa thought at first sight that it might be a grandfather with his granddaughter. But after seeing how the young girl was all over the man, Lisa knew that couldn't possibly be true.

Getting on the elevator, the much younger woman said, "Excuse me, but are you a model?"

"No, I'm not," Lisa said.

"Yes, she is known as the most beautiful woman in the world," Marc smiled.

"I knew I've seen you before. You're a model! Did you hear that, honey?" The young woman said to her companion.

"Yes, dear. It's very nice to meet you," the older gentleman said.

Finally making it to the thirty-third floor, they got off the elevator with young girl still gushing over Lisa.

"Reservation for two under Cavell," Marc told the host.

"Yes, Mr. Cavell. This way."

Marc and Lisa followed a waiter to their table that had a great view of the city. Marc helped Lisa with her coat and then pulled her chair out. Marc could swear he heard every man in the room grunt with lust when they saw the back of Lisa's dress.

He didn't even think he could make it through dinner without attacking her.

A second later, a waiter came to the table and said, "Would you like to see the wine list?"

"No. I want you to bring us the best bottle of champagne you have," Marc said.

"Yes, sir."

"So, Mona Lisa, is your fan club still watching you?"

"No. And you know you wrong for telling her that. Getting her excited for nothing."

"I don't think it's for nothing. You *are* the most beautiful woman in the world."

"You are crazy."

"Only about you," he said, and leaned in to kiss her.

"Your champagne, sir," the waiter said.

"Ah, thank you."

"Would you like to order now?"

"Are you ready? You want to start with an appetizer?" Marc asked Lisa.

"Um, yeah."

"We will start with the Shrimp Beignets. How does that sound to you?"

"Perfect," Lisa said.

"Very good. I shall return with your appetizer."

After the waiter left, Marc said, "You look incredible. I don't think I will be able to contain myself."

Smiling, Lisa said, "Who said you had to?"

"I do like the way you think."

Lisa leaned in a kissed him. "I want to thank you for today. The roses were beautiful."

"Like I said, I wanted to replace the ones you lost."

"You didn't have to do that. I still remember how beautiful they were. How beautiful you are," Lisa said, as she kissed his hand.

"Sir, your appetizer," the waiter said.

"Thank you," Marc said.

"I shall return when you are ready to order."

Marc poured himself and Lisa a glass of champagne.

"A toast. To the most beautiful, most sweet, kind hearted woman I've ever met. I love you so much, Lisa Jen – You know what, we are only five months away from the wedding, so I am going to say, I love you so much, Lisa Cavell. Happy birthday, baby." Marc leaned in and kissed Lisa.

"Marc, you have done more for me than you realize. Because of you, my heart is happy and I know what love really is."

Clanking their glasses together they took a sip and continued to talk through a glorious dinner of Tilapia for Lisa and a Pork Shank for Marc. For dessert they shared a Semifreddo. And two bottles of champagne. After paying for dinner, Marc and Lisa left the restaurant feeling wonderfully, mildly, drunk. The driver got out of the car the minute he saw them and opened the door.

"Take the scenic route home, please good sir," Marc told the driver.

"Yes, sir," the driver laughed.

As they settled in the backseat, Marc said, "Did you enjoy dinner?"

"Yes, I did. But you know, I think I'm drunk."

"Well, this is a good time to take advantage of you, isn't it?"

"Have you ever made love in the back of a limo?"

"No, but it is on my to-do list."

"When we get home, scratch it off your list."

As they both kissed, they helped each other out their coats. Marc then unsnapped the top of Lisa's dress and let it fall to her waist. He then began massaging her breast as if they were a lump of clay. Soon their sweet kisses turned into something more primal and passionate.

Breaking the kiss, he moved down to suck the nipple of each breast that throbbed with passion. Moving one hand up her thigh along the split, he heard her whisper his name as he rubbed her through her panties.

"Ohhh, Marc," Lisa moaned.

Moving her panties to the side, he instantly started to stroke her clit. Then he whispered, "I want you cum for me, baby. Can you do that?"

"Yes," Lisa moaned.

He made small circles slowly around her clit and with each passing moment the movement speeded up.

More quickly than she intended to, Lisa grabbed his wrist and said, "I'm cumming, Marc. Ooooohhhh, Marc."

"Don't stop now; I want you to keep going."

After he was satisfied with the three orgasms he gave her, he whispered, "How do you feel?"

"Horny," Lisa said, and then kissed him. Straddling his lap, she continued to kiss him and undue his pants. "Your turn."

She then dropped to her knees on the limousine floor and took as much of Marc in her mouth as she could.

"Oh, shit," he moaned.

Lisa quickened her rhythm, when she felt his hand in her hair.

"Damn." She heard Marc say.

She felt the vein in his penis harden in her mouth, but still continued to take him even deeper into her mouth.

"Oh, shit. Lisa baby, I'm about to cum."

"No, not yet." Lisa slowed her rhythm. She kept him close to orgasm, but never let him conquer it.

Not being able to take it anymore, Marc pulled Lisa up onto his lap. He pulled her dress over her head and threw it to the side. Pulling her down on to his shaft, they both moaned loudly at the same time.

"Did I hurt you?" Marc said, as he pushed her hair out of her eyes and then kissing her deeply.

"Yes, but I liked it."

In the back of the limo, Marc made love to Lisa with all the force in his body. As they climaxed together, they could feel the car slow down and come to a stop. Marc straightened his clothes, while Lisa put her coat on and picked her dress up of the limousine floor.

When the driver opened the door, Marc got out and then helped Lisa out of the car.

"Thank you," Marc told the driver and then handed him a hundred dollar tip.

"Thank you, sir. You two have a good night."

"We will," Lisa said.

The minute they were in the house, Lisa dropped her coat to the floor. "So, where were we?"

Marc walked up to her and kissed her. Breaking the kiss, he said, "We were right here."

As they kissed again, Lisa helped Marc undress before they both fell on the couch.

"Turn over," Marc said, against her lips.

Lisa happily obeyed and turned over. He thrust inside of Lisa with so much passion and force, that after a short time they climaxed together. They collapsed on the couch breathing hard and unable to move.

After catching his breath, Marc said, "It is now eleven o'clock. You have one hour left of your birthday. How was it?"

Sitting up, and moving in close to Marc, Lisa said, "This has been the best birthday I have ever had. And it's all because of you. You have made my birthday an event from beginning to end. And I thank you for that. Thank you so much."

"You're welcome, Mona Lisa. But as I said, you still have one hour left. And there is one more surprise."

"No, there is nothing else I could possibly want for my birthday."

"I think there is." Marc put his pants back on and headed into the kitchen. Lisa heard him in there milling around in the kitchen as she buttoned up his dress shirt that she practically tore off him a few minutes ago.

"Surprise!" Marc came out of the kitchen with a small cake, a carton of ice cream, bowls and spoons.

"I can't believe you! You know I forgot all about a cake."

"I didn't. Wait a minute, one more thing."

He then lit the one candle he put in the middle of the cake.

"Happy birthday, sweetheart. Make a wish."

Lisa looked into Marc's eyes and blew out the candle.

"What did you wish for?"

"I can't tell you that. But I can tell you that it has already come true." Lisa then leaned over and kissed him.

"Cut your cake," Marc said. "To end your birthday right, what would you like to watch?"

"An old movie. How about *In This Our Lives?*"

"Betty Davis."

For the next couple of hours they sat and watched the movie, ate cake and ice cream. In Lisa's mind, a perfect ending to a perfect day.

Chapter Thirty-One

As the months went by, wedding plans became final; the house had begun to form. By mid-December, it was actually looking like it would be ready by the time they were married. Marc and Lisa continued to work together and plan their lives together. They spent Thanksgiving with Lisa's family and even cooked their first Thanksgiving dinner at home. Christmas and New Year's was spent in New York with Marc's family. He took her to Rockefeller Center for ice skating and to see the Christmas trees. Christmas day was spent getting to know Marc's aunts, uncles, cousins, nieces and nephews, and childhood friends. However, New Year's Eve was spent in a Hilton Suite, in a Jacuzzi.

After the New Year, everything was back to normal. Work was in overdrive; Lisa had three new clients and all of them demanding all of her time. Marc was being kept busy with the Keane account, and the house.

Considering there had been no sign of James in months. Lisa thought that he might have gotten the picture and gave up.

The final fitting for the ladies bridesmaid dresses left them all satisfied. And that was a feat within itself, Lisa thought. They all agreed to wear the black scarves draped around the neck and hanging to back. The bridesmaid's dresses were made to look like party dresses. They were maroon, little above the knee in length, with pencil thin skirts.

The groomsmen and Marc would be wearing black tuxes with maroon cummerbunds and bow ties to match the maroon scarf that would be wrapped around the waist of Lisa's wedding dress. Lisa's wedding dress was a long, strapless gown with black beading across the bodice and the trim of the gown. Her vale was made of Italian lace.

As all the ladies tried on their dresses with all accessories, Lisa said, "You all look so beautiful."

"Pat, what's the matter?" Carol asked, as they all stood in the mirror.

"I'm as big as a house."

"Girl, what mirror are you looking in?" Nic said.

"You're not even showing yet," said Lisa.

"The hell I don't. Look at me. Y'all will be walking down the aisle, while I'm waddling down the aisle."

"Girl, please. You're having a baby. You're gonna be the most beautiful thing walking down that aisle. Well, except for me," Lisa laughed.

"Thank you, for saying that," Pat said, hugging Lisa.

"Are you ready Lisa?" Elizabeth asked.

"Yeah. How are my mother and Isabella coming along?"

"They'll be done by the time you come out."

Marc's parents came down early so they could help with the wedding. The ladies were laughing and talking when they heard a cell phone ringing.

"That's not my ring," Pat said.

"Mine either," said Nic.

"Oh, it's Lisa's phone," Carol said. "Awww, she has their picture come up when he calls. Hey, Marc. This is Carol...Yeah, everything is going good...she's back there trying on her dress. You want to talk to her...Okay...Yeah. Wait, matter of fact here she is. Hold on. Mrs. Cavell, Marc is on the phone."

"Oh, thank you. Hello...I'm fine. The dress is beautiful. You future wife really out done herself with everyone's dress. Janice and I are gonna look like queens...Yeah, we're all waiting on Lisa to come out now. How's it going on your end...Great...Oh, my God..."

Everyone turned toward Lisa as she walked out of the dressing room.

"Lisa, you look beautiful," Nic said.

"Marc, you should see her. She is breathtaking...Lisa, Marc wants you."

"Oh, okay. Where is my earpiece?"

Getting it out of her purse, Carol handed it to her.

"Hello...hey you...Yeah, everyone looks gorgeous. Did everyone's tux fit...Good...Okay, I'll see you when we get home...Bye."

"Alright, you ready?" Elizabeth asked Lisa.

Taking a deep breath, Lisa said, "Yes."

Helping Lisa with her train, they walked over to the mirror.

"Oh, my God," Lisa gasped.

"What do you think?" Elizabeth asked.

"It's amazing, Elizabeth! I can't believe it. It's exactly what I described." Looking at everyone else, Lisa asked, "What do y'all think?"

Lisa's mother walked up to her and said, "Baby, you look so beautiful."

"Mama, you're crying. I've never seen you cry."

"Well, my daughter has never gotten married before," Janice said, as she hugged her daughter.

Then Elizabeth said, "Now your vale."

After they put on her vale, Lisa looked at herself in the three way mirror and couldn't believe she was in a wedding dress. She never really expected her life to be this good, but she was happy and that's all that mattered.

"You ready to say goodbye to Lisa Jenson?" Pat asked her, as she stood next to her.

"I don't know. Did you?"

"Nope. I didn't know until I saw Lewis waiting for me at the altar."

Smiling at her friend, Lisa said, "Thanks. Love ya."

"Love ya."

After they all changed, they paid for their dresses, and left the store.

Out in the parking lot, Lisa said, "Now, does everyone have directions to the house?"

"Yeeeesssss," they all said.

"Okay, so be there at seven for the rehearsal."

They all said goodbye and split up. Lisa took her mother home and also to leave her dress there.

"Okay, mama, I'll be back at six to pick you up."

"I'll be ready."

"Lisa, I'm gonna stay with your mother. Unless you need me?" Isabella said.

"No, I'm alright. Go ahead and have fun without me," Lisa said, pouting.

"Get out of here, you big baby," Janice said.

"That's okay. I'll be lonely, but I'll be okay."

"Bye," Janice and Isabella said.

"Bye."

Lisa got in her car and was backing out of the driveway, when her cell phone rang.

"Lisa Jenson."

"No, Lisa Cavell," Marc said.

"Hello, Mr. Cavell."

"Where are you?"

"On the expressway headed home."

"Dad, Anthony, and I will meet you guys there."

"Oh, it's just me. Your mother dumped me to stay with my mother until the rehearsal dinner."

"Oh, baby. I'm sorry you lost your friend. But you still have me."

"I know."

They went over everything about the fittings, until Lisa said, "I'm home, how far are you?"

"Right behind you."

"Oh, bye."

"Bye."

"There's my soon to be daughter," Vincent said.

"Hey, Dad," Lisa said, hugging him. "Hey, Anthony. Did you enjoy yourself today?"

"Yeah. I finally have a guy to talk too."

"About what?"

"Men stuff, Lisa. Nothing you would know about."

"Marc, have you been corrupting my brother?"

"Of course not," Marc said, smiling wickedly.

Walking into the house, Anthony said, "Man, I love coming to your house. It's way better than Lisa's house."

"This is Lisa's house," Marc said, laughing.

"Thank you," Lisa laughed.

Lisa was about to walk in the kitchen, when she felt dizzy and had to hold on to the wall.

"Lisa, you okay?" Anthony asked, jumping up to catch her if she fell.

"Yeah, I'm fine. Just got a little dazed, that's all. I'm okay. I'm probably just tired."

"Well, come one. I'll take you upstairs so you can lie down," Marc said.

"No, I'm –"

"Going upstairs to lie down. It's only twelve. You have plenty of time to rest."

"But, I need to wrap everyone's gift."

"Already taken care of. Carol took the gifts out of your trunk while you guys were trying on your dresses."

"But she doesn't know who gets what."

"I gave her a copy of the list you made. Now, lay down."

"Finally giving in, Lisa laid down on the bed.

Marc laid next to her and pushed her hair out of her eyes. "Better?"

"Yeah. I guess I am tired. Go back downstairs. I promise to rest."

"You sure?"

"Yes."

"Sleep well, Mona Lisa." Marc kissed her on the forehead and left the room.

"Is she okay?" Anthony asked when Marc came back downstairs.

"She's fine as long as she rests. Between working and planning the wedding, she hasn't been sleeping like she should."

"Well, let her rest. But don't let her drive tonight," Vincent said.

"Don't worry. I won't."

"You men hungry, or is it just me?"

"Starving," Marc and Anthony said at the same time.

For the rest of the afternoon, the men sat around, ate, and watched sports. Marc went upstairs to check on Lisa, but she wasn't lying down. He went over to the bathroom door, about to call out Lisa's name when he heard her throwing up.

Knocking on the door, he said, "Baby, are you alright?"

He heard her flush the commode, and then turn on the water.

"Lisa baby, open the door."

After a minute, Lisa opened the door. "I'm alright. Just having stomach trouble."

"Do you want me to get you something?"

"Do we still have that Ginger ale?"

"Yeah. Be right back." Marc was back in less than a minute. "Here you go."

Taking the glass, she said, "Thank you. I don't know what's wrong with me. Maybe I'm catching a cold."

"Well, Monday you're going to the doctor."

"I'll be fine."

"And I'll be fine when a doctor tells me you're fine. So, Monday we're going to the doctor."

"You can't go because you have that meeting with Keene."

"I can cancel."

"No you can't. But, I do promise to go to the doctor, because I can't be sick and still plan a wedding." Looking at the clock, Lisa said, "And I think I'd better freshen up so we can get out of here."

An hour later everyone had made it to Lisa's mother's house. Janice and Anthony were in her truck, Lisa and Marc in Lisa's car, and Vincent and Isabella in Marc's car. The entire caravan headed out to Mr. Herbert's house. On the way to Cordova, Lisa's phone rang.

"Probably someone needs directions." Looking at her caller I.D., she said, "Oh, it's my mother. Hey, Mama. What's wrong...It was nothing. I just felt a little dizzy, but I'm fine...Anthony talk too much...I'm fine...I am...Monday...Yes, ma'am. And tell Anthony I'ma kick his butt...Okay, bye."

Lisa looked at Marc and saw that he was trying to keep from laughing.

"You can laugh now."

And that's just what he did...hard.

"I'm sorry, baby. I can't help it. Are you in a lot of trouble?" Marc said.

"It's not funny," Lisa said, laughing herself.

Thirty minutes later they made it to the house with Pat and Lewis, Nic and Brandon, and Carol and Charles. Steve and Marc's best friend from New York, Tim. As everyone got out of their cars, Marc and Lisa walked up the stairs to the front door. The maid opened the door just as Lisa and Marc walked up.

"Hello, is Mr. Herbert here?" Lisa asked.

"Here I am. Come in, come in," Les Herbert said.

As everyone came in, introductions were made. But, Lisa noticed when she introduced Les to her mother, how long they held hands during their initial meeting.

"Well, I see where Lisa gets her beauty. It's a pleasure to meet you, Mrs. Jenson."

"Please, call me Janice. And it's nice meeting you, too."

Everyone gave their coats to the ladies at the door.

"This house is tight!" Anthony said.

"Thank you, son. That's good right?" Les asked.

"Yes, sir," Anthony asked.

"So, everyone please follow me," Les said, as he lead them to the backyard.

With everyone standing close enough to hear her, Lisa said, "Okay, let me have you attention please. I am so happy you all could make it tonight. Marc and I just want to thank you guys for given us time out of your busy schedules. Everyone here is here because we love you and wanted you to be involved in this blessed event. Now, as far as introductions are concerned, y'all know each other, we family. But we do have a couple of new faces. Mr. Timothy Caldwell, Marc's best friend and best man. Stephen Roberts, our good friend, co-worker, and groomsman. Last, but not least, Adrian Stewart. She is the wedding coordinator that Pat so graciously talked into helping us. Baby, is there anything you want to say?"

"Um, nope. Kidding," Marc said. "Really, thank you for coming and standing behind me and Lisa. Just seeing how happy she is, is enough for me."

He then kissed Lisa on the cheek.

Lisa then said, "Pastor, if you would bless us with a prayer."

"I need all heads bowed," the Pastor began.

After the prayer, Adrian got to work.

"Alright people, I'm gonna need the Pastor and the parents."

Adrian nodded to Anthony and he pushed play on the radio. 'The Lady, Her Lover, and Lord' by T.D. Jakes came through the speakers. Adrian instructed Anthony to stop the song when the parents had made it to their seats.

"But don't instantly turn the music off, let it fade out by turning it down," Adrian told Anthony.

Next Adrian lined up the groomsmen and the bridesmaids and told Anthony to play the next song. The groomsmen and bridesmaid would walk down the aisle to 'Spend My Life with You' by Eric Benet and Tamia. Again when they made it to their spot, Anthony faded the song out.

When it was Marc and Lisa's turn to come down the aisle, they each chose not to use their music. They wanted that to be a surprise to one another.

After everyone was in place, the minister went through the ceremony. When Lisa and Marc were presented husband and wife, Adrian had them all descend the steps following Marc and Lisa.

"Now, everyone has their partner and place. We're not going to practice this to death, so just remember your timing when marching down the aisle," Adrian said.

"Okay. Everyone ready to eat?" Les asked.

Everyone went into the house, where a beautifully set table was in the dining room. Everyone feasted on samples of the dinner for the wedding.

"Alright guys, Marc and I decided to have you all help us choose what we're having for the wedding. So, eat up and then tell us what you like," Lisa said.

As everyone ate and talked, Lisa couldn't stand the smell of the food.

"Baby, are you okay?" Marc asked.

"Yeah, sweetie. I'm just still having a little stomach trouble."

"I asked the maid to bring you a pitcher of Ginger ale."

"Thank you."

"Lisa, I have a few questions if you don't mind?" Adrian said, as she pulled a chair up next to Lisa.

"Sure."

"First, how many hostesses do you have?"

"Three. Stephanie Brooks, Brooke Ford, and Erica Simmons."

"Okay. And what's the little boy's name that will be ringing the bell?"

"Jayden Aniello."

"Alright. I think that is everything."

"Okay. Um, excuse me for a minute," Lisa said, getting up and rushing to the bathroom. Coming back to the table a few minutes later, she said, "What did I miss?"

"Nothing, really. Except that Les has been chatting up your mother and Anthony since we started eating," Marc whispered.

Looking at them, Lisa couldn't help but smile. Anthony even seemed to be enjoying himself. Lisa then asked Marc, "How old is Les?"

"He's forty-eight, why?"

"Just checking. I don't want my mother robbing the cradle."

Laughing, Marc said, "I wouldn't worry about it."

"Why?"

"Because it's hard to get you Jenson women's attention."

"True. But it's worth it when you do get it."

"You got that right," he said, leaning over and kissing her. "Three weeks. Just three weeks and you will officially be Mrs. Lisa Cavell. You ready?"

"Yes, I am. Are you?"

"I've been ready since the day I saw you in the parking garage."

"Hey, hey, you two, cut it out. You're in public," Nic said.

"We were just talking," Marc said, laughing.

"About what?" Carol asked.

"Your gifts," said Lisa.

"Uh oh, we get gifts too?" Pat said, laughing.

"Yes, you do. But first I want to thank Carol for going outside of her bridesmaid duties and wrapping your gifts."

Everyone thanked Carol, while Marc and Lisa unpacked the gifts.

"Okay, bridesmaids first. You guys mean so much to me. You're not just my friends, you're my sisters."

As they opened their gifts, Pat said, "Oh, my God!"

"Yeah, what she said. Are these real?" Nic said in shock.

Laughing, Lisa said, "I knew you would ask that, and yes, they are."

Each bridesmaid received a pair of diamond encrusted hoop earrings. As they all hugged and thanked Lisa, Marc handed out the groomsmen gifts.

"I don't have a speech, so just open them."

Laughing, Steve and Tim opened their gifts.

"Oh, man! I was about to buy one of these. I can keep my money in my pocket now," Tim said.

"Thanks, man!" Steve said.

The groomsman gifts were Movado watches for gifts.

"Okay, now the parents," Lisa said, as her and Marc picked up two boxes each. Lisa went first.

"Marc and I decided to buy gifts for the other's parents. So, Isabella…Vincent, I chose these gifts for you to show how much I thank you for welcoming me into your family. I hope you like them."

"And, Dad, I had them engrave yours," said Marc.

Vincent and Isabella opened their gifts and seemed to be stunned by what they saw. Isabella had started to cry silently, when her husband looked into her box and said, "You did this?"

"Yes," Lisa said, as she pulled a chair closer to Isabella. "Marc told me a couple of years ago about when he was younger you house was robbed. And that among the things that were taken was your engagement ring and that it was a family heirloom. So, Marc described what it looked like and I had the jeweler make an exact duplicate. I know it can't replace the original, but I hope it brings you some happiness."

"It's beautiful. Thank you. But, if this going to be a family heirloom, I should give this to you."

"I tell you what, hold onto it for me."

"I'll do you one better. I'll give it to my grandchild."

"Deal," Lisa said, as they hugged.

Isabella then turned to her husband, "What did you get?"

"A watch. A very nice one, might I add."

"It's a Rolex, Dad. Turn it over," Marc told him.

"What does it say?" Isabella said, trying to see the back.

"Per ogni tic di questo orologio, è per ogni minuto che ci sei stato per me." Vincent stood up and Marc hugged.

"What does that mean?" Pat asked.

"It says, 'For every tic of this watch, is for every minute you've been there for me'. Thank you son…and daughter," Vincent said, with a strained voice.

Marc then walked over and kneeled by Janice's chair.

"I hope I chose the right gift for you. I kind of went out on my own and did this. When Lisa and I first started dating, I noticed how her face lights up when she talks about you. She once told me that you were the strongest woman she knew and if she could be anything like you, she knew she could succeed at anything. I wanted to give you something that would show you how much I thank you for trusting me with one of your most precious jewels. So I decided to give you one back. It's no way as priceless as the gift you've given me. But I hope you like it."

Janice opened the box and gasped. "My Lord."

"What is it, Ma?" Anthony asked, as he and Lisa looked over her shoulder.

355

"Marc," Lisa whispered, when she saw the diamond necklace. "Marc, thank you so much. This is beautiful! And I also want to tell you that I am very happy my daughter opened her heart to you."

"Thank you," Marc said, as he and Janice hugged.

"Anthony, open your box," Lisa told her brother.

Anthony opened his box and found a diamond face Movado watch.

"Awww, man! Look, Ma. Look what they got me. This is tight!"

"Read the back," Lisa told him.

"I Love You, Big Brother," Anthony read.

"Since you always think you're older than me anyway," Lisa laughed.

Without saying a word, Anthony hugged Lisa tight, and then he hugged Marc.

"Thank y'all. I can't wait until my boys see this," Anthony finally said.

"You're welcome," Lisa and Marc said.

"And we haven't forgotten you, Adrian. Thank you for helping us."

"You're welcome."

"Pat told me that you were Victoria Secret crazy. Since I am also a nut –
"

"Amen," all three bridesmaids said.

Laughing with everyone, Lisa said, "Anyway, I got every scent they had. You have the lotion, body spray, and shower gel."

"Thank you, girl," Adrian said, as she hugged Lisa.

"So with that all done, I hope you all like your gifts. Because those will be last ones you see from us for a while."

"Hey, have you guys decided where to go on your honeymoon?" Pat asked.

"We are spending a week in Paris and then a week in Rome," Lisa said.

"If it wasn't for our wonderful guardian angel, Carol, we would have had to settle for Paris," Marc said.

"Settle?!" Nic said. "Well, if you feel Paris is settling, then you stay here and I'll go."

For the rest of the dinner, they talked about the wedding, agreed on what food to serve and the best friends of the bride and groom tried to outdo each other with the most embarrassing stories about them. By ten o'clock, everyone was getting ready to leave.

Walking out with her mother, Lisa said, "So, do me and Anthony have a new daddy?"

Laughing, Janice said, "No, but I do have a date for tomorrow."

"Do you want me to chaperon?"

"No, thank you. But, I do want to know –"

"Never been married, no children, owns quite a few companies, hardworking, an all-around good guy," Lisa said.

"I just wanted to know what to wear? However, I do appreciate the biography," Janice said, laughing.

Hugging her mother and brother goodbye, Lisa then went over to where the girls were waiting.

"So, really, did everyone like their gifts?"

"Girl, yes!" Nic said.

"Um, we have been watching you all night, and well...are you pregnant?" Carol said.

"NO!"

"Don't get all huffy. You are a grown woman and about to get married. It's okay," Nic said.

"Nic, you know I can't have children. You all know that."

"Honey, I don't care what a doctor says. God is in the blessing business. And if he says this is the time, then it's time. When are you going to the doctor?" Pat said.

"Monday."

"Okay. Afterwards I want you in my office," Pat said.

"Alright, but I'm telling you guys it's probably just exhaustion or stress."

"We'll see," Carol said.

After hugging everyone, they got in their cars and headed home.

Chapter Thirty-Two

"Good morning, Lisa."

"Good morning, Dr. Sydnor."

"It's been a while. How have you been?"

"I've been doing great. I'm getting married in two weeks and work is well."

"Congratulations! Okay, tell me everything. Who is the guy?"

"His name is Marc Cavell," Lisa said, showing his picture.

"Very handsome."

"Yes, he is."

"How did you two meet?"

"We work together."

"Oh. At Morgan & Peterson, right?"

"Yes."

"Well, congratulations. So, now that we are caught up, what are you here for? I see in your chart that they have already taken blood. Blood pressure is good, cholesterol is great. You are in good shape. What's this about dizziness and throwing up?"

"It's been going on for a couple of weeks and I just figured its exhaustion. But my family made me come in and get a check-up."

"From what you have told me it could very well be exhaustion. With your job being very demanding and on top of that planning a wedding, these things along could cause stress. When was your last cycle?"

"I'm late. I usually have it at the beginning of the month."

"Okay, have you thought of the fact that you might pregnant?"

"No! You told me that I couldn't have children after what happened."

"No, I told you it would be difficult. Not that you couldn't."

"That couldn't be it, it's exhaustion."

"How would you feel if you were?"

"I don't know. I mean, I came to terms with not being able to a long time ago."

"How would your fiancé feel?"

"He wants children. I don't know how soon he wants children."

"In case it is exhaustion, I want you to rest. If you have a coordinator, use her. Don't try and take everything on yourself. Okay?"

"Alright."

"I'll have all your results in a couple of days."

"Okay."

After leaving the doctor's office, Lisa headed to Pat's office. Since her doctor was in the same area, Lisa made it there in less than ten minutes. Getting off the elevator on the fifteenth floor, she walked into Pat's outer office.

"Look at you looking all professional and working hard," Lisa said, as she watched Stephanie at her desk.

"Hey, Lisa!" Stephanie said, as she got up from behind her desk and hugged Lisa. "Wait, I'm at work. Hello, Ms. Jenson. How are you today?"

"I'm fine, Ms. Brooks," Lisa said as she laughed. "So, how is school?"

"School is good. I got an A on my paper for my Economics class."

"Great! Congratulations."

"Thank you. Now watch me work. Excuse me, Mrs. Cole," Stephanie said, as she pressed a button on her desk phone.

"Yes, Stephanie?"

"Ms. Jenson is here to see you."

"I'm sorry, but I don't know a Ms. Jenson."

Lisa laughed and said, "How about a Mrs. Cavell?"

"Yes. Please send her in, Stephanie."

"Oh, Stephanie, did Adrian call you?" Lisa asked.

"Yeah, she told me everything. And sorry I couldn't make it."

"Don't be. School comes first."

"And Mrs. Cole told me about the house and the gifts. That –"

"Gifts. I'm glad you said something. Here is yours, Brooke's, and Erica's gifts. I hope you guys like them. And don't forget to wear them for the wedding."

"Thank you, Lis."

"Open it when you have time."

Buzz

"Yes, Mrs. Cole?"

"Is that crazy woman still lurking around out there?" Pat asked.

"Yes, I am. See you later, Stephanie."

"So, what did the doctor say?"

"Hello to you too," Lisa said, walking into Pat's office.

"Hey. What did your doctor say?"

"Nothing. Just told me to rest more and that she'll have my results of the blood test in a couple days."

"In a couple of days? We can't wait that long."

"You don't have to wait. I told you, its exhaustion. Enough about me. How are you feeling these days?"

"Fat, but happy. Lewis is going all out for the nursery."

"That's great. And you're not fat, you're gloriously pregnant."

"I know. Anyway, how is work?"

"Work is going well. I have a couple of meetings tomorrow. But they're fairly easy to please."

"Have you talked to your husband?"

"No. After I leave here I'm stopping by the office. Have you talked to Nic?"

"Yeah. She called a few minutes before you got here."

"Well, I am not going to keep you from your work. Tell Lewis I said hey. And stay off your feet," Lisa told Pat as they hugged.

"You do the same."

After saying goodbye to Stephanie, Lisa headed to her job to pick up some files and to see Marc. Pulling into the parking garage and parking, Lisa decided to head to her office first.

"Hey, Carol," Lisa said, walking up to her desk.

"Hey, lady. What are you doing here?"

"I came here to pick up a couple of files for my meetings tomorrow."

"Well, I'm glad you stopped by because we have some changes."

"What?"

"Mr. Richards had to change his appointment to ten and Mr. Stabler sent some information to your email that you need to look at."

"Is that all?"

"Actually, no. You got a letter today," Carol said, handing her an envelope.

"From who?" Lisa asked, taking the envelope.

Seeing the name, Lisa sighed.

"Thanks Carol."

Lisa walked into her office and sat on her couch. Opening the letter that Linda Harris sent her, Lisa noticed her heart rate speed up.

Dear Lisa,

I know this is a surprise, but I wanted to let you know that I'm doing well. I've been

going to counseling. I guess I'm trying to find out where I lost myself. I know it's been pretty quiet on your end. James has been here trying to get me to come back. But I really don't see that happening. I mean he is not the man I thought I married. He seems to be so full of hate and I didn't see that at the beginning of our relationship. I'm sending this letter in hopes that it finds you safe and happy. I talked to the boys and they said that you were getting married on the seventeenth. I'm happy to hear that. I told them to take lots of pictures for me. They also promised not to tell their father. It's odd how they know him. I wish you all the happiness in the world. Be happy, Lisa.

Linda

Lisa laid her head back, sent a prayer up to the heavens above for Linda. Gathering her things and printing a few emails, Lisa left her office.

"Okay, Carol I'm gonna go see Marc before I head home."

"Alright. Hey, what did your doctor say?"

"That I need rest."

"That's not what Pat told me."

"Y'all think y'all slick, don't it?" Lisa laughed.

"A little," Carol giggled.

"I'm not pregnant."

"We'll see."

"Bye, Carol."

"Unh-huh."

Making it to Marc's office, Lisa said, "Hello, Barbara. Is Marc in?"

"Hi, Ms. Jenson. Yes he is, but Melody is in there right now."

"Really?"

"If you can wait –"

"No, I can't," Lisa said, and walked into Marc's office.

Walking into Marc's office, Lisa found Marc sitting behind his desk and Melody leaning over him with her blouse unbuttoned.

"Shit," Marc said when he saw Lisa standing in the door. "Lisa, baby it's not what you think."

"Careful Marc, you're beginning to sound like the average man."

"I'll just leave you two to talk," Melody said, almost running for the door.

She didn't make it. Lisa slammed and locked the door.

"Please Melody, stay."

"Mr. Cavell, should I hold your calls?" Barbara said over the phone intercom.

"Tell her yes," Lisa said.

"Um, yeah Barbara."

"So, who's first?" Lisa asked.

"Lisa, it's not what you think. I was telling Melody that she was out of line. I have told her that over and over. Lisa, baby, look at me," Marc said standing in front of Lisa. "After everything we have been through I have never considered being with another woman. Remember what I told you Saturday? It's been you since the day I saw you. Only you."

Marc couldn't tell if Lisa believed him or not. She had on her poker face and it was killing him not being able to read her.

"Yeah right," Melody said, chuckling.

"Your turn," Lisa said looking pass Marc to Melody.

"Me? I'm not about to explain myself to you."

Lisa walked passed Marc toward Melody and without meaning to Melody took a step back.

"Has Marc ever made a pass at you? Smiled seductively? Rubbed up against? Given you any idea that he was interested in you?"

"No. But that's because you are always around."

"Is that right?"

"Yes, that is right. Just because he acts perfect around you don't mean a damn thing. Don't believe that he is going to be a good boy when you two get married."

Lisa slapped her.

"Lisa –"

Lisa put her hand up to stop Marc from talking.

"Now, it's my turn. I have watched you time and time again make passes at Marc. And I have watched time and time again how he has ignored them. It must really hurt that he has looked over you only to marry someone else. But let me help you to understand something. I am nowhere near as nice as I seem to be. Don't take my smiles and dismissive attitude as weakness. I am so not what you think I am. Trust me. I advise that whatever business you have with Mr. Cavell, you leave it with Barbara. You are dismissed." Lisa walked over, unlocked and opened the door.

Not wanting to leave like some five year old that has been reprimanded by her teacher, she didn't have a choice. Melody walked to the door faster than she wanted and left.

"Baby, wait. Don't leave like this. Talk to me."

Lisa gathered her things and left the office without saying a word.

"Damn!" Marc said. He quickly picked up his phone and made a call.

When Lisa got back to her car, she dialed Nic's phone and took deep breaths.

"Harvey."

"We need to talk."

"Where?"

"Where are you?"

"The precinct."

"I'm on my way."

Fifteen minutes later, Lisa was walking through the door of the police station.

"How you doing? I'm here to see Detective Harvey."

"You're Lisa, right? She said you were coming. But she didn't say you were beautiful."

"I guess she didn't mention that I was engaged either."

"Go on back."

"Thank you."

Walking through the double doors, Lisa walked to Nic's desk.

"Hey, girl," Nic said, when she saw Lisa.

"Hey."

Looking at Lisa, Nic said, "Follow me."

Lisa followed Nic into a small room and sat the table.

"This looks just like the ones on TV."

"Everybody says that. Now, what happened?"

Lisa told Nic about the letter from Linda and what happened in Marc's office.

"Do you believe him?"

"Yeah."

"Did you tell him?"

"No."

"Let him sweat, huh?"

"No. It's just that I was so mad. I couldn't even look at him. But on my drive over I calmed down."

"So, you do believe him?"

"Yeah. Do you think I shouldn't? I mean, why would he put so much work into me if he could have had her so easily?"

"Oh, no you don't. I'm not even answering that. Only you know how you feel. No matter what you decide, you know we got your back. But to be honest, talk to him when you get home. But to the best part, you slapped her?"

Lisa couldn't do anything but laughed.

"You slapped her?" Nic laughed.

"I didn't even think about it. I had been trying to remain a lady this entire time, but this I couldn't let slide. And besides she can't tell what I did without explaining what she did. But I think I got my point across."

Laughing, Nic said, "I bet you did. I also bet you scared the hell out of Marc."

"Stop. I'm supposed to be mad."

"Okay, okay. But I still would have paid good money to see the expressions on their face when you closed and locked the door."

"You know you wrong Nic," Lisa laughed. "But let me get out of here. I feel like I'm on Law & Order."

"So, exhaustion, huh?"

"Yes. Who called you?"

"Pat, Carol, and I had a conference call," Nic said, laughing.

"Now y'all talking about me?"

"You know we don't believe you, right?"

"It is just exhaustion."

"Yeah, right!"

"I better go before this turns into an interrogation."

"Well, go home and get some rest."

After leaving the station, Lisa stopped off and picked up a bottle of her favorite wine and headed home. Making it home, she set the alarm, got a glass out of the kitchen and headed upstairs. Putting her things away, Lisa ran her bath and lit candles. Slipping into the tub and resting her head on the back of the tub, she listened to Maxwell and drank a glass of wine.

There was so much going through her mind; the possibility that she might be pregnant, Linda's letter, James, and seeing Marc and Melody in his office. That last one was driving her crazy. She tried not to let her mind run off on crazy tangents. Marc loved her and she loved him. Most importantly she trusted him.

"You know, that song reminds me of you?" Marc said, from the bathroom doorway where he was leaning against the door jam.

So caught up in her thoughts, Lisa didn't even hear the alarm beep.

"It's a beautiful song." Lisa said, without looking at him.

"Lisa –"

"Don't. Just don't Marc. You don't have to explain."

"Why not? You're not leaving me are you?"

"Marc, I was never gonna leave. It's just that I was so mad. I didn't want to say anything that I might regret."

Sighing, he kneeled next to the tub and kissed Lisa's neck, "I thought I'd lost you."

"Well, as long as you remember that feeling. I never have to worry about you cheating."

"I'd never want to hurt you. The look on your face when you walked in my office almost killed me. I love you so much, Lisa."

Looking in his eyes, she smiled. God help her she believed him. "I love you, too. Now, tell me what I walked in on."

"As usual, she was coming onto me. I was sitting behind my desk and she came around the desk, undid her top, and then you walked in. That's it. I swear."

"Where you attracted to her?"

"No. I have never been attracted to her. So, are we okay?"

"Yes."

"Come on," he said as helped her out of the tub and wrapped a towel around her.

Lisa cleaned up the bathroom, while Marc took her wine and glass to the kitchen.

Coming back upstairs, he said, "Come here."

Marc pulled her onto the bed next to him. Holding on tight to Lisa, he whispered, "Twelve days left."

"Yep."

"I couldn't work at all after you left."

"I'm sorry."

"You have nothing to be sorry about. I shouldn't have been in that predicament. I'm the one who's sorry, baby."

Lisa turned toward Marc and kissed him, "Let's forget about it."

"Done."

Marc untied the towel as she untied his tie and unbuttoned his shirt.

"Do you think we do this to much?" he asked.

"There is no such thing."

Their kisses soon became more passionate as Marc kicked his pants off. Thrusting into Lisa, she called his name softly. This time there was no dying need to have each other, just soft kisses, and tender touches.

A couple of hours later, wrapped in each other's arms, Marc said, "I've never heard this song before."

Aerosmith was now playing.

Feeling him play with her hair, she said, "I heard it on a movie."

"What movie?"

"Armageddon. I thought it was a beautiful song."

"What's it called?"

"I don't wanna miss a thing."

Marc reached over to the table by the bed and put the song on repeat.

"I take it you like it, too."

"Yeah."

"When are Isabella and Vincent coming home?"

"I don't know. I talked to my father after you left and he said they were going out to dinner and a movie."

"That's nice. Wait, you talked to your dad after I left?"

"I told you I thought I'd lost you. So, I called my dad to talk to him."

"And what did he say?"

"He told me to pray and get my ass home as soon as possible. His exact words."

They laid there quietly holding one another, listening to the music. By six o'clock, they had their own dinner and a movie. They ordered a large pizza and watched movies until they went to bed.

The next few days seemed to run into each other as if one day was never ending.

But on Friday, "Lisa, your doctor is on the line," Carol said over the intercom.

"Thanks. Lisa Jenson."

"Hey, Lisa. Sorry about taking so long getting back to you, but we got backed up in the lab."

"That's okay. I figured I was fine. I am fine, right?"

"Actually you're better than that. You're pregnant."

Lisa was speechless.

"Lisa, are you there?"

"Um, yeah. Yeah, I'm here. Are you sure?"

"Positive," Dr. Sydnor said laughing.

"I've already set you up for an appointment on Tuesday at eleven o'clock. The doctor's name is Dr. Avery. Can you make it? I know your wedding is that Saturday, so I tried to make it before the big event."

"Yeah, yeah I can make it. Thank you, doctor."

"Congratulations, Lisa."

"Thank you. Goodbye."

The rest of Lisa's day was spent in a fog. She couldn't believe she was pregnant. After work Lisa drove to the house completely stunned. At least she was going to have the house to herself. Marc was playing ball and his parents were having dinner with her mom and Les.

When she made it home, Lisa walked to the front door still in disbelief about what Dr. Sydnor told her. Then out of nowhere, Lisa was shoved into the house. As she fought back, she was slapped across the face. Falling to the floor, Lisa looked up and saw James standing over her.

"I told you I would be back."

Lisa's first instinct was to fight, but she couldn't risk it. She wouldn't risk him hurting her baby. Marc's baby.

"This is a nice house. It took me a little while to find where you moved to, but I did."

"What do you want? What are you doing here? I thought you were in Connecticut." Lisa asked, as she pulled herself up onto the couch.

"Connecticut? How did – Oh, Linda. Yeah, I was up there. But as you can see, I'm back."

"Unfortunately."

"So, where is ol' boy?"

"My husband will be home soon."

"Don't call him that!" James shouted.

Lisa didn't even flinch at the sudden rage in his voice.

"What do you want?"

"I want you."

"No."

"No?"

"I will never come back to you. Now get out before I call the police."

"Then if you want comeback to me, you will have to suffer for your choices."

Lisa couldn't help herself, she started to laugh.

"What's so fucking funny?!"

"You are. You want me to suffer? What the hell you think I been doing?" she asked, turning serious.

"You haven't suffered like I have."

"I cannot believe you. You think I didn't suffer? I'm the one who spent two weeks in a coma. I was the one with six broken ribs, my eyes swollen shut. And worst of all, I'm the one who lost a child. I was depressed for a year, a year over that and your sorry ass! So, don't tell me about suffering! Now get the fuck out of my house!"

"I know I hurt you. But I love you and I will do anything to make it up to you."

Lisa reached for the phone by the couch, but James yanked the cordless phone from her and slammed it against the wall.

"You are not going to get away that easy, Lisa. You –"

Before he could finish the phone rang.

"It's Marc."

"Let it ring."

The phone stopped ringing before the answering machine could pick up. A moment later Lisa's cell phone rang.

"Damn it, answer it! But you better not –"

"Try anything? Yeah, right," Lisa said, finishing his sentence.

Reaching into her purse, Lisa felt her gun that Nic told her to carry.

Pulling out her phone and pushing the green button, she said, "Hello...Hey...Yeah, I'm fine...No, I'm on my home now...I plan on it... No, go ahead and play ball, Marcello...You don't have to come home, I'll be fine...No, Marcello...I love you, too. Bye."

"You don't love him! You love me!! Say it!!"

Lisa didn't say a word.

"SAY IT!!"

Again, Lisa didn't speak.

"Do you want me to hurt you?"

"Too late."

"I told you I was sorry for everything I did to you. When are you gon' let that go?"

"I should ask you the same thing. And what about now? Are you sorry for this too?"

This time it was James who didn't have answer.

"That's what I thought. I can't believe I'm going through this again with you. I mean, what are you going to do hold me hostage?"

"No, I've decided on one better. If you don't wanna be with me –"

"No, I don't."

"If we can't be together in this life, then I guess we'll have to meet on the other side," he said, as he pulled out a gun.

That statement hit Lisa like a ton of bricks.

"That's right, sweetheart. What's that old saying...If I can't have you, no one can?"

***

"Marc, are you sure?" Nic asked, as she and couple of cops ran out of the precinct.

"Nic, I spoke to her. We decided that we should have a safety word after he showed up at work. He's in the house, Nic!"

"Where are you now?"

"On my way home."

"Do not go in that house. Do you hear me?"

"But he –"

"Don't go in that house. I will meet you there."

Nic closed her phone and dropped into her partners lap.

"Nic, we're not gonna be any help to Lisa if we're wrapped around a pole. Slow down," her partner said.

"He's gonna kill her, John."

Nic got to Marc's house in record time. She found Marc a couple houses away waiting for her.

"Have they left house?" Nic asked, when she walked up.

"No."

Nic dialed the house number while Marc told her partner everything. Unfortunately, the answering machine picked.

"Lisa, pick up…pick up. Marc said you were on your way home and that you should be there by now. I don't wanna have to come over there. I –"

"Hey, I'm here," Lisa answered.

"I know he's there."

"Yeah, girl."

"What is he doing?"

"Nothing, right now."

"Does he want you to leave?"

"No."

"I got a few people here who are going to get you out. Marc's here too."

"I know. I'm just tired. But, I have to go."

Then the line went dead.

"She's okay. Is there another way into the house?"

"The back door on the patio that leads into the kitchen."

"Key. Is she carrying her gun?"

"Yeah, ever since you told her to."
After three more cars of police pulled up, Nic told them to follow her.

Chapter Thirty-Three

"So tell me something," James said.

"What?"

"Do you really love him?"

"Yes. And, why do you keep asking me that? I told you I love him. God, why are we even talking about this?"

"We are talking about this because I want you to tell me the truth."

"I am telling you the truth," Lisa said, calmly.

"You love me, not him. Do you know what I had to go through to get you back?"

"You will never get me back," Lisa said, but James kept talking as if he didn't hear her.

"You never even checked your surroundings," he scoffed. "I'd been following you for months before I came to your office."

Now, Lisa was afraid.

"You've been watching for how long?"

"I have always known where you lived and worked."

"The letter," Lisa said, thinking about the letter he sent her.

"Then I married that bitch. I thought she could make me forgot about you. She tried, anyway. She did everything I asked, but I couldn't forget you. I love you, Lisa. I love you."

"Then if you love me like you say you do, let me go. You don't have to do this. You wanna make up for the things you've done to me? Then let me go."

Lisa had never seen someone change. But it was as if James had completely changed right in front of her. He didn't even look like his self anymore.

"Let's go upstairs." He grabbed Lisa and pulled her off the couch. But before it was out of reach she grabbed her purse.

"Why are we going upstairs?"

"I have a gift for you."

"And what's that?"

"I want to make love to you one last time. And we're going to do it in the same bed you sleep in with him. Then I'm gonna leave you there for him to find."

Lisa's mind completely shut down. She couldn't think of anything to stop this from happening. Being pushed into the room all she could see were the flashes of Marc and her in this room. And now all that would be tainted by this one moment.

"What do you usually wear for ol' boy?" James asked, as he went through the dresser draws.

Lisa didn't answer him.

"Bingo! Put this on."

He threw the red see through top and panties that Lisa wore her first weekend with Marc.

When Lisa didn't move, he said, "I said put it on!"

"James you can't do this. What about your boys? They wouldn't want you to do this."

"Don't talk about my sons."

"Think about how this would make them feel. You can –"

"Shut up! You don't know anything about how they feel. Look, I'm done talking. Change clothes."

"They love you, James. They –"

"If they really loved me, they would have told me about the wedding next week."

Lisa felt like she had been kicked in the gut.

"Oh, you thought I didn't know. Well, I figured instead of a wedding there'd be a funeral."

Lisa just stared at James as tears rolled down her checks.

"Are you getting it now?" he asked.

"Yeah, it's either me or you," Lisa said, softly. Lisa got up from the bed and walked toward James. "James, do you love me?"

"I always have and always will," he said, looking at her with that same look that used to make her weak in the knees. Now it just made her sick.

"Then, let me go. You have to let me go. Please."

James suddenly grabbed Lisa by the throat.

"All you care about is yourself! What about me?! What about how I feel?!"

"Let me go!" Lisa said, as tried to push him away.

James then hit her with the butt of the gun across the face and pushed her to the bed. Lisa felt like her face exploded. She tried to keep from passing out and keep him from pulling her clothes off, but both were a losing battle. He laid his gun on the nightstand out of her reach and started to rip her blouse open, as she screamed and tried to fight him off. He then reach up her skirt and ripped her stockings and panties off.

"James, no!!!" she screamed.

"SHUT THE FUCK UP!!!" he screamed in her face. He then started to unbutton his jeans.

"Oh, God no," Lisa moaned.

When he shifted his weight off of one of her legs, Lisa kneed him and punched him in the face. As screamed from the pain, Lisa wiggled free and reached into her purse.

✳✳✳

After Marc unlocked the door, Nic and her partner went in first followed by three more cops. After looking around downstairs, they were about to head upstairs when they heard James yell and two gunshots.

"Shit," Nic said, as her and her partner went up the stairs quietly.

The other policemen spread out to check every room on the second floor, while Nic and her partner stood on either side of the master bedroom. Nic opened the slowly and her and partner peered in. At first sight, Nic could see James lying on top of Lisa on the bed. Neither was moving.

Nic rushed into the room. "Oh, my God! Lisa! Keep Marc out of here," Nic told the other policemen. "Oh, God, please don't do this to us. Not now," Nic prayed.

She checked James's pulse and it was shallow, she pulled him off of Lisa to check her for a pulse, but Lisa opened eyes and called her names.

"Oh, thank you, Jesus. Thank you," Nic said, as she pulled Lisa off the bed. "Are you hit?"

"No, he – I –. Is he dead?!" Lisa said, hysterically. "Don't let him die."

"An ambulance is on the way. Let me get you out of here."

On the way out of the room, Lisa took one last look at James. She could have sworn he was smiling.

"Come on. Marc is waiting downstairs," Nic told Lisa.

"Nic, I need to go to the hospital."

"He –"

"No. I need to see if my baby is okay."

Nic stopped and looked at Lisa, "Your baby?"

"Yes. But don't tell Marc. I want to make sure everything is alright first."

"Okay."

Nic helped Lisa downstairs to where Marc was waiting.

"Lisa," Marc said, as he ran up the stairs to meet her. "Oh, baby. Are you alright? Did he –"

"I'm okay," she said, crying, as she held on to him as tight as she could.

"Oh God, thank you," Marc said, kissing her all over her face.

Nic went back upstairs to talk to John.

"So, is he gonna live?"

"They don't know yet, its touch and go. He was hit center mass. Over a few centimeters he would be dead."

"That doesn't make me happy."

As the paramedics wheeled James out, Nic thought she saw him smiling. Following the gurney downstairs, Nic watched as Marc shielded Lisa from seeing James.

"No, wait. Nic is he gonna be okay?" Lisa asked, breaking away from Marc.

"I don't know, but don't worry about that. Your ambulance is here. We're gonna meet you at the hospital."

Marc and Lisa went out and got into the second ambulance.

***

"Alright, Lisa, everything looks fine. You won't need stitches, there's not a lot of swelling. And as far as I can tell the baby is fine."

"Thank you, doctor. Oh doctor, can you tell me how far a long I am?"

"From my estimations, a month. Give or take a week."

"Really?"

"Yep."

"Have you told your fiancé, yet?"

"No, I wanted to make sure the baby was fine first."

"Alright. Do you want me to send him in?"

"Please."

"I'll see you later."

A second later, Marc was standing next to her bed.

"Hey, you. How are you feeling?" he asked, as he caressed her cheek.

"Better now. How about you?"

"Blessed and happy that you are safe."

"Is my mom here, yet?"

"Not yet, but Nic called her and she called me. I told her what happened and she should be here soon. Are you sure you're fine?"

"Yes. But..."

"I know," Marc said, climbing into bed with her.

They lay their quietly on the bed until Lisa's mother and grandmother came in.

"Lisa, are you alright?" Janice said, as she burst into the room.

"I'm fine, mama," Lisa said, as they hugged.

"Hey, baby," Lisa's grandmother, Beverly said as she hugged Lisa.

"Hey, Grandmama. Where's Anthony?"

"He's out in the hallway," Janice said.

"Why?"

"He's a little upset right now. He'll be in when he's ready."

"I'll go talk to him," Marc said.

He kissed Lisa on the forehead and walked out.

"How's he doing?" Janice asked about Marc.

"I don't know yet. We haven't had a chance to talk to yet."

"Tell me what happened so I can go upstairs and pull this asshole's plug. Sorry, Mama. Tell me what happened, Lisa?"

Lisa took a deep breath and told her mother and grandmother everything that happened. When she finished she knew that it was only God's will that kept her mother from walking out of the room and finding James's hospital room.

"I am so happy you're okay, baby," her grandmother said.

Lisa watched her mother stand by the bed with her eyes closed. Lisa could tell she was still fighting with her anger.

So, she felt now was the best time to tell them.

"There's something I need to tell you two."

"We're listening," Beverly said.

"I talked to my doctor this morning before leaving work. And she gave me the results of my blood tests."

"And what were they?" Janice asked.

"Well, according to Dr. Sydnor, one of you will be a grandmother and another a great-grandmother."

Janice and Beverly looked at one another, then at Lisa.

"Are you saying that…that you're pregnant?" Janice asked.

"Yes."

"Oh, my God! My baby is having a baby! Is everything alright? Are you and the baby okay?" Janice asked.

"We're both fine. But keep it quiet. I haven't told Marc yet. I wanted to make sure the baby was fine before I said anything."

"Oh, baby we're so happy."

"Knock, knock," Nic said.

"Hey," Lisa said.

Nic came in with Pat and Carol right behind her.

"Hey, sweetie," Pat said, as they hugged.

"Hey, honey," Carol said.

"You guys don't have to look so gloomy. I'm fine. Really, I am."

"Are you sure?" Carol asked.

"I am. Did you tell them, Nic?"

"Nope. I still can't believe it."

"What?" Pat said.

"I'm pregnant."

"No! Are you serious?" Pat asked.

"Yes."

"I'm going to be an aunt!" Carol said, laughing.

"Yes, all three of you are."

"Our babies are going to grow up together."

"Pat don't cry. This is good news," Lisa said.

"I know. I cry at everything now. My hormones are crazy. You'll know what I mean soon."

Everyone talked a few minutes more until the nurse came in and said that there were too many visitors in the room.

"Nic, can I talk to you for a minute?" Lisa said.

"Yeah."

Everyone said that they would be back later to see Lisa before they filed out of the room.

Once they were alone, Lisa said, "How is he?"

Nic sat in a chair next to the bed, "From my understanding, he is still in surgery, but they don't know if he'll make it."

"Are his sons here?"

"Yeah, they're upstairs."

"What happens now?"

"Nothing. It was self-defense, even if the worst happens. Look, I have to go take care of some paperwork and let you rest. I'll be back later."

"Thank you for saving me again," Lisa said, crying softly.

"Hey, stop that. No need in thanking me. You're my sister and I love you."

"I love you, too."

"I'll be back later. Get some rest."

Lisa watched Nic walk out of the room.

She was lying there looking out the window when she heard, "Lisa?"

Lisa looked at Anthony as he was standing in the doorway.

"Heeeyyy. It's about time. I thought you left with mama and grandmamma."

"No, Marc took them home so I could see you. How are you feeling?"

"Good."

Anthony pretty much did all he could do no to look at Lisa.

"Anthony?"

"Hmm?"

"Look at me. I'm not as bad as the first time."

Anthony finally looked at Lisa and smiled.

"See?"

"Yeah."

"So are you ready for next week?"

"Yeah. I'm even bringing a date."

"Who?"

"Kesha."

"Really? How did that happen?"

"Don't get all excited, we're only friends."

"Okay."

"So, mom said you wanted to tell me something."

"Sit down," Lisa said, patting the bed. "I wanted to know if you were ready to be an uncle."

"You pregnant? Awww, man. Lisa that's great!"

"And don't tell Marc. I want to tell him."

"Okay. But I hope it's a boy."

Laughing, Lisa slapped his arm.

***

After returning to the hospital from dropping off Janice and Beverly at home, Marc went to the nurse's desk.

"Excuse me, can you help me?"

"Of course, what can I do for you?" the nurse asked.

"I was told that a family member was brought here and I am trying to find out what room he is in."

"What's his name?"

"James Harris."

The nurse typed the name into the system and then said, "Yes, he just got out of surgery about twenty minutes ago. He is in room three-sixteen."

"Thank you."

Marc headed up to the third floor. Following the arrows he found room three-sixteen and without hesitation he walked into the room. Standing by the door, he just watched the machine push air into James's body. Walking closer to the bed he saw that James was waking up.

"How you doing?" Marc asked James. "You know who I am?"

James was unable to talk with the tube down his throat, but Marc could tell that he recognized him.

"I just came to see how you were feeling," Marc smiled.

James just continued to lay there and stare at him.

"Do you remember what I told you would happen if you ever came near her again? Hmm?"

Marc just watched James lay there. Then the weirdest thing happened, James smiled.

"You must have thought I was joking."

At that moment Marc put his foot on James's breathing tube. Almost instantly James started straining to breath. Marc stood there and watched James fight to breath.

"I know you will never leave her alone. So I have a little solution of my own."

Before closing his eyes, Marc's smile was the last thing James saw.

✳✳✳

"Knock, knock."

Lisa and Anthony looked toward door. Lisa was shocked to Linda standing there. Then she walked in and let Joseph, Shaun, and Michael come in.

"The roles have been switched," Linda said, as she walked over to the bed.

"It would seem so."

"How are you?"

"Fine."

Lisa looked at the boys, but she really didn't know what to say. So, instead she said, "Linda, this is my brother, Anthony."

"Hello, Anthony," Linda said.

"How you doing?" Anthony said, as they shook hands.

"This is ridiculous. The boys wanted to come see how you were. They were afraid that you wouldn't want to see them," Linda said.

"I don't know what to say to you guys. But, I am truly sorry for what happened. I tried to lead this down another road. To talk to him, but he wouldn't listen. I really did –"

"We understand, Lisa. We wanted to tell you how sorry we are. We didn't think he would go that far," Joseph said.

"I know you didn't. I just don't want you to hate me. I tried to keep it from going this far."

"We all did," Michael said.

"Look, we just came in to see how you were and now we are going to let you rest."

"I will still see you all next week, right?"

They all agreed and then said their goodbyes.

A few minutes later, Marc came into the room and said, "I found a couple of stragglers lurking the hallway claiming they know you."

Then his parents walked into the room.

"We'll only stay a minute," Isabella said.

"Hey," Lisa said, smiling.

"How are you doing?" Vincent asked.

"I'm fine. I'm sorry about all of this."

"Don't be. Marc told us what happened. Vincent and I went to the chapel and prayed for you. We even prayed for that young man's soul. We aren't staying, just wanted to make sure you were okay. We will see you tomorrow," Isabella said, as she and Vincent kissed Lisa on the cheek.

"Goodnight," Lisa said.

"We'll see you tomorrow, too," Isabella told Marc and then kissed him on the cheek.

"Okay. I'll call you," Marc said, hugging his parents.

After his parents left, Lisa and Marc stared at each other from across the room.

But, Lisa was the first to speak, "Did you tell them everything?"

"Yeah," Marc said, after taking a deep breath.

"Marc, I –"

"Lisa, me first. Nic told me what you said about James. Lisa, I can't do this."

"You can't do what, Marc?" Lisa asked. It felt like she couldn't breathe. Whatever was coming next, she did not want to hear.

"I promised you I would keep you safe. And I feel like I let you down."

"That's not true. I have never felt safer than when I am with you. I know if it is within your power you would let nothing or no one hurt me. I know that."

"If it's within my power. You never have to worry about him again."

Lisa watched Marc over by the window, then she said, "Come here. Please."

Marc walked over to the bed and lay next to Lisa.

"Somewhere in this relationship I forgot to protect you. You were always there for me, but I never tried to understand your part in this."

"That's not true. I didn't mean that you don't care about me or my feelings. I just want you to be safe. I'm sorry I got upset."

"Don't be, you're allowed."

"Now that I've vented, your turn."

Lisa took a deep breath and told Marc what happened. They cried together, Marc because he was thankful for Lisa's safety and Lisa because everything finally hit her.

After a while, Marc said, "Are you up for next week?"

"Nothing could keep me from going down that aisle."

Marc leaned in and kissed her softly on the lips.

There was a knock at the door, and then Nic walked in. "Hey, stop that. Is any place safe from you two?"

Laughing, Marc and Lisa said, "No."

"What are you doing back here so soon?" asked Lisa.

"I needed to talk to you."

Marc was about to move, but Nic told him to stay where he was.

"Lisa, there were some problems. He died, Lisa."

Looking at Marc, Lisa asked, "When?"

"About a half hour ago," Nic said.

"I'm safe now," Lisa said, still looking at Marc.

"What will happen now?" Marc said.

"Nothing. Like I told Lisa earlier, it was self-defense. Lisa, are you gonna be okay?"

"Yeah. How are Linda and the boys?"

"They're in shock."

"Oh, God," Lisa said, and broke down crying.

"I'm gonna leave. I'll see you tomorrow." Nic hugged them both and left.

"I love you, Mona Lisa."

"You saved me."

For the rest of the night, Marc held Lisa while she cried.

The next morning Marc went home to change and get Lisa a change of clothes.

"Lisa?"

"Yes."

"Hi. I'm Dr. Leonard Avery."

"Oh, I thought I wasn't supposed to see you until Tuesday."

"Well, Dr. Sydnor called me and told me what happened. I wanted to see you as soon as possible."

For the next hour, Dr. Avery examined, questioned, and poked Lisa.

"Okay Lisa, from my examination you and the baby are healthy."

"How far along am I?"

"A month. So, I'm going to start you on prenatal vitamins. And do me a favor, slow down on the exercise."

"Will do."

The doctor gave her a prescription and gave her his card with another appointment. After Marc brought her clothes, she changed, signed her discharge papers and left the hospital.

"Where to?" Marc asked.

"Home."

"Are you sure?"

"We have to go back at some point. I will not let this put my life on hold. Let's go home."

They made it home and Lisa walked into the house first. When she walked into the living room she started taking deep breaths.

"Are you alright?"

Lisa nodded yes. She then walked slowly up the steps. When she made it to the bedroom, she stood outside the closed door. She took a few more deep breaths and then opened the door. Lisa couldn't believe what she saw.

"Everyone chipped in," Marc said, standing behind her.

The bedroom had fresh paint, new carpet, and a new bed. Lisa had to admit the room was beautiful.

"Thank you," Lisa said, and turned to hug him.

"I know this won't erase everything, but I hope this will help. But maybe I shouldn't have brought you back here so soon. We can go to the Peabody. We don't have to sleep in our honeymoon suite."

"No, I can do this. Besides I won't be sleeping much this week anyway."

"So, you still plan on marrying me?"

"Absolutely."

They stood in the middle room holding onto each other tightly.

Chapter Thirty-Four

The funeral was on Wednesday. Lisa sent flowers. Marc didn't understand why, but she explained that it was something she needed to do.

The week of the wedding was complete havoc. They packed for their honeymoon, which they would be leaving for on Sunday morning. Their wedding night would be spent in a suite at the Peabody. On Friday, last minute errands were being ran. Making sure all bills were paid and the flowers, the food and the cake would be delivered on time.

Answering her phone, Lisa said, "Lisa Jenson...Hey, mama...no I'll be there in another hour...No, I've only talked to her on the phone, but she said she would be there around six...I'm leaving my car at your house...Yes, I have...Okay, bye. God, you would think she's getting married tomorrow."

"Her little girl is getting married tomorrow, she's making sure there aren't any problems," Marc said, from the passenger seat.

They were on their way to pick up Marc's pastor at the airport.

Pulling up to the pick-up line, Marc said, "There he is." Getting out greeting him, Marc said, "Father Martin! How are you?"

"Marcello, it's good to see you."

"The car is over here. How was your trip?"

"It was good. Hello, Lisa. How are you doing?" Father Martin, said as he shook Lisa's hand.

"Hello, Father Martin. I'm great, I'm getting married tomorrow."

They all got in the car and left the airport to take Father Martin to his hotel.

"So, are you two ready for the big day?"

"Yes," Lisa and Marc said.

They continued to talk on the way to the Holiday Inn hotel.

After getting Father Martin settled in his room, Lisa and Marc headed home.

"Wait, turn here."

"Why?"

"Because I want to talk to you."

Lisa turned into the parking lot on the river.

"Come on," he said, getting out of the car.

Getting out of the car and following him, Lisa hit her door lock button. Taking hold of her hand they walked over to the tree where they had their picnic.

"Okay, what do you want to talk about?"

"I wanted to spend some alone time with Lisa Jenson. No wedding talk, no honeymoon travel talk, just Marc and Lisa."

"Okay, me first. I can't wait to be your wife."

"I said no wedding talk."

"I'm not talking about our wedding. I'm talking about our marriage. I'm talking about waking up to you, coming home to you or with you, going to bed with you. Having good and bad times with you. Everything that involves a marriage," Lisa said, as she stared into his eyes.

"I cannot believe I was lucky enough for you to choose me to love. I want to thank you for loving me. After everything that has happened before me you still took a chance and opened your heart to me. And with everything that has happened these past months you have never closed your heart to me. Thank you for that. And for that alone I will love you for the rest of my life on earth and in heaven."

They stood in the park, under the tree and kissed.

A few minutes later they made it home, they walked into the house hearing Isabella talking and then a male voice that was not Vincent's. As they walked into the living room, Isabella was sitting on the couch talking to man Marc had never seen.

"Hey, Mom. Where is –" But before Marc could finish his sentence, his dad walked out of the kitchen holding a tray of coffee.

"Hey, Son. You and Lisa are back just in time. We have company," Vincent said, more to Lisa than to Marc.

"I can see that we do. Hello, I'm Marc and this is my fiancée, Lisa."

"Marc," Lisa said, squeezing his hand.

Turning to look at her he didn't understand the look on her face. "Are you okay?" Marc asked.

"No," Lisa said, staring at the man on the couch.

"Hello, Lisa," the man said, as he stood.

"What are you doing here?" Lisa asked.

"I came to see you, obviously."

"Why?"

"Wait, did I miss something?" Marc asked.

Since Lisa didn't answer him, Isabella said, "Marc, this is Mr. William Jenson, Lisa's father."

Marc stared at him for a minute and then looked at Lisa.

"Mama told you where I was."

"Yeah. I called her after I read about what happened."

"What newspaper delivers week late information?" Marc asked.

"Marc, don't," Isabella said.

"No, it's okay, Mrs. Cavell. I deserve that," William said.

"You damn right! You didn't even come to see her in the hospital? Everybody else was there."

"Fermarlo, Marcello! Just stop it!" Isabella said.

Marc looked at Lisa, who hadn't said anything since her initial questions.

"Lisa," Marc whispered.

Lisa took a deep breath and gave Marc's hand a squeeze. "Can William and I have some privacy please?"

Isabella and Vincent headed for the stairs.

"Marc, come and help me pack," Isabella called, without turning around.

Lisa smiled and nodded for him to go upstairs.

"I'll be upstairs if you need me," he said, then kissed her on the forehead and went upstairs.

"He really loves you," William said, once they were alone.

"How would you know?"

"I can tell. He stood up to your father to protect you. He's a good man."

"Again, how would you know?"

"Lisa, I just wanted to make sure you were okay."

"Are you serious? That question would have been better in a hospital room over a week ago...when I needed you. But as usual you weren't there."

"I know that I'm a little late."

"A little?" Lisa scoffed.

"Look, I don't want to have the same conversation with you that I just had with your mother."

"We won't. I could never say those words."

"Are you really alright?"

"No, William, I am not. I was attacked in my home, almost raped and killed. No, William, I am not alright. Mama said that she called your office and your house. You never returned her calls. So how worried were you really?"

He was about to walk over to Lisa, but she put her hand up to fend him off. Wiping away tears, Lisa took a deep breath and stood up a little straighter.

"I...I wish I knew what to say to help you." William said.

"You don't have to say anything. I've been waiting on you to change since I was old enough to know better. And I'm tired of waiting. Consider yourself daughter-free. Anthony can make his own decision. But me, I'm done. I have spent so much of my life, trying to get you to love me. But nothing worked. Then I spent another part trying to get men just like you to love me. I'm done, William. Done. I have a good man up there, who loves me so much. And family and friends who have loved me all of my life that I overlooked, because I was always waiting for you. Tomorrow I'm getting married in front of those same people. You can consider yourself off the guest list."

"I'm sorry I haven't been the best father to you or Anthony. I tried to be there for you –"

"I've heard this before and I don't want to hear it again." Lisa walked over to the patio door, and then said, "Goodbye, William."

After a couple of minutes of silence, Lisa watched her father's reflection walk out. She closed her eyes and willed herself no to cry. A few minutes later, she felt a hand on her shoulder and turned around and hugged Vincent.

After a moment, he said, "You know all parents don't get it right the first time. For some of us it takes a while."

"You didn't need a while."

"Yes, I did. It took me a long time to realize that a child needs both parents. It's never too late to straighten things out. When he realizes that, he'll be back. But, until then, I'm here."

"Thank you," Lisa whispered, through her tears.

Vincent saw Marc come downstairs and let Lisa go into his arms. She and Marc stood there a long time without saying a word.

"Okay, you two that's enough of that. We have to go," Isabella said, coming downstairs with her suitcase and dress.

Vincent and Marc helped Lisa and Isabella with their bags.

"Anthony should be here later. Don't corrupt him to much tonight," Lisa said, laughing.

"He called while your dad was here and said he'd be here in an hour," Marc said.

"Oh, okay."

Marc opened Lisa's door for her, and said, "I'll miss you."

"Me, too."

"Okay, okay. We have to do," Isabella said, getting into the car.

Marc and Lisa kissed one last time before she started the car.

Kissing her again, Marc said, "I'll see you at the altar."

"I'll be there," Lisa said, and kissed him.

"The ladies have to go son," said Vincent.

Pulling out of the driveway, Lisa said to Isabella, "I miss him already."

"It'll wear off," Isabella laughed. "I'm kidding. If you both are good to one another, and I know you will, it'll be good for the rest of your lives."

"Like you and Vincent?"

"Just like me and Vincent."

"Thank you, Mom."

"You're welcome, Daughter."

Walking into her mom's house, Lisa said, "Hello, hello, hello. The bride is here."

"Hey," Pat said, walking out of the kitchen.

Hugging her, Lisa said, "How long you been here?"

"About thirty minutes. Lewis dropped me off. I don't know what they're doing at your house, but he couldn't wait to get rid of me. How you doing, Isabella?"

"I'm fine. How are you?"

"Ready to pop. Come on, everybody is in the kitchen."

When Lisa got in the kitchen, she said, "Hey, Mama...Hey, Grandmamma. Y'all cooking for an army?"

"Just a small one," Janice said. "Hey, Isabella."

"Hey, Janice. How you doing today, Beverly?"

"I'm great! My grandbaby is getting married tomorrow," Beverly said, happily.

"So, where do I start?" Isabella said.

"First, you can give me your things. Lisa and I will take them upstairs," Pat said.

"Thank you, sweetheart. You sure it's not too heavy for you?"

"No, I'll be okay."

After Pat and Lisa left the kitchen, Janice said, "How did it go?"

"Not good at all. I had to take Marc upstairs with me and Vincent. He was on the verge of attacking the man. But they didn't talk long, and after he left Vincent went downstairs to talk to her. I don't know what was said, but she seems to feel better."

"I hope so," said Janice.

"Look honey, she'll be okay. You raised a very strong daughter. She will be fine. Now, where is a free apron?"

"Right here," Beverly said. "My shift is over."

"Where are you going," Janice asked.

"I am going to talk to my granddaughter."

✳✳✳

"How do you feel?" Pat asked when they made up to Lisa's old bedroom.

"A lot stronger than I thought I would."

"Well, in that case...Are you ready? I mean really, really ready."

"More than that. Marc is an amazing man. I love him so much."

"Good answer."

Knock knock knock

"Come in," Lisa said.

"Room for one more?" Beverly said, walking into the room.

"You can have my spot. This baby is greedy," Pat said, heading out the door.

"You sure it's the baby?" Lisa laughed.

"Yes."

"Hey, bring Nic and Carol up when they get here."

"Will do," Pat said, before closing the door.

"I wanted to tell you how proud I am of you," Beverly said, when the door closed.

"Grandma, I'm just getting married."

"It's more than that. It's because you're you. You have always made me proud. And now you're making me a great-grandmother. I love you, baby girl."

"I love you too, Grandma."

As they hugged there was a knock on the door.

"I guess our time is up," Beverly said. "Come on in."

Isabella walked into room. "I'm not interrupting am I?"

"No, honey. I'm going downstairs to make sure that child of mine hasn't burned down the kitchen.

After the door closed, Isabella said, "Your mother said that you had something to tell me."

"I've wanted to tell you something for a week now, but we were never alone."

"Okay, what?"

Lisa took a deep breath, and said, "Isabella, I'm pregnant."

"Oh, Lisa! I can't believe it! Why didn't you two tell me?"

"Marc doesn't know yet."

"Why not?"

"Because the day I found out was the day I was attacked. I wanted to make sure the baby was going to be okay before I told him."

"I can't believe this. How far along are you?"

"A month."

"I truly cannot believe this!" Isabella said, with tears in her eyes.

"Don't cry Isabella. You're gonna make me cry."

"I have to call Vincent."

"Tell him to not tell Marc. I want to tell him for a wedding/birthday gift."

"Oh, I will. I am so happy for you two. And now I must go downstairs to whip your mother for not telling me." Isabella left the room beaming from ear to ear.

Lisa sat in her room and looked around at all the old pictures on her wall and dresser. Pictures of her and Pat through their teen years, college years, even up to now. She smiled.

"We're here," Nic said, as they walked into the room.

"Hey," Lisa said, as everyone hugged.

"Are you ready for your bachelorette/slumber party?" Carol asked.

"We brought gifts for you, we have movies, and plenty of Liquor…for me and Carol," Nic said.

"Yeah, yeah. Don't rub it in!" Pat laughed.

Carol and Nic hung their dresses in the closet along with Pat's.

"Here you go, Lisa," Carol said.

Carol handed Lisa a maroon cloth covered box with a black bow.

"Thank you. I decided to tell Marc that he's going to be a father through his wedding gift."

Lisa unwrapped the box and took the top off. Inside was a silver baby rattle.

"Lisa, it's beautiful," Nic said. "But, what is the inscription?"

"It says Qui è a belle ragazze poco," Lisa read.

"What?" all three ladies said.

"And when did you learn to speak…what was that?" Carol said.

"Italian. And Marc taught me."

"I bet he did," Nic said.

"Anyway," Lisa said, with a smirk on her face. "It means, here's to beautiful little girls."

"Awwww, that is so sweet," Pat said. "I know you. What does the inscription really mean?"

"Well, when Marc first proposed, I gave him every excuse in the book to not get married. But when he kept dismissing them, I finally told him I couldn't have children. Again, he dismissed it. He told me that nothing would make him happier than to have a beautiful little girl that looks just like me. So, I had the jeweler put it on here."

"You ladies come on out of there. It's time for dinner," Beverly said.

"You don't have to tell me twice. I haven't touched a thing today in anticipation of this dinner," Nic said.

"Me, too," Carol said.

"I'll be down in minute. Let me wrap this up," Lisa said.

As she finished up the box, there was another knock on the door.

"Why do y'all knock? I already know you in the house," Lisa joked. But her smile froze and her eyes grew ten times their size when she saw who walked in.

"Hey, baby."

"Robert?"

"Who else?"

"AHH! I can't believe you! You said you couldn't make it."

"You know better than that."

Lisa couldn't believe it. This was one of her favorite people in the whole world. Robert and Lisa had been friends longer than her and Pat.

"You know I couldn't miss my best friend's wedding," Robert said, as they hugged tightly.

"When did you get in?"

"A couple of hours ago."

"I can't believe you're here," Lisa said, hugging him tightly again.

"Not for long. There is a bachelor's party going on with my name on it."

"Do you know how to get there?"

"Yeah. I got directions from the groom. So, you gon' get married on me, huh?"

"Yes, I am. He's wonderful, Robert."

"Got to be to get your attention. Look, baby girl, I got to go. But I will see you tomorrow before the wedding. I want to see Lisa Jenson before she leaves."

"You better. Oh, God. Robert I am so happy you came," Lisa said, as she walked him downstairs.

Robert went in the kitchen to say goodbye to everybody and then Lisa walked him out to his car.

Leaning against his car, Robert said, "I know what happened. Nic called me. Are really okay?"

"I am."

"I tried to get here as fast as I could."

"I know you did. I'm just happy you're here now."

"This is Robert you're talking to. Are truly okay?"

"I am. It was hard at first, but I'm better now."

"Good. Now, it's time to party. See, you tomorrow, baby girl."

"Bye."

Lisa watched her best friend back out of the driveway. After he drove out of sight Lisa went back in the house to join the others at the table.

Once she was seated, her mother said, "Happy now?"

"Ecstatic!" Lisa beamed.

"Alright, before we eat I'd like to say a prayer," Beverly said.

The ladies held hands and bowed their heads.

"Lord, we first want to give honor to you for bringing this family together again. We are also thankful for you bringing us through another ordeal. We ask that you keep your protective arms around us, Lord. We thank you for our health, our minds and our souls. I want to send out a special prayer that tomorrow goes off without a problem. That nothing will keep the bride or the groom from meeting one another at the altar. In Jesus' name, Amen."

"Amen!!!" Everyone said.

"Let's eat," Janice said.

The ladies passed bowls, plates, and cups around the table. They talked and laughed about old times and filled Isabella in on what Lisa was like when she was younger. During dinner, Lisa stopped to look at each of the women at the table. Each woman contributed to her life a great deal. She couldn't help but feel loved at this table.

✳✳✳

"Alright man, you ready?" Tim asked.

"Depends on what you got planned," Marc laughed.

"Come on, it's me."

"I know! And don't forget Anthony is here."

"Man, please! How old are you, eighteen?"

"In another month," Anthony said.

"Close enough and happy birthday! Gentleman, it is my pleasure to bring to you Passion, Ecstasy, and Obsession!"

Tim pushed play on the remote and Lil Jon and the Ying Yang twins boomed through the speakers. The ladies walked into the living room from the downstairs bathroom.

"So, where is the groom?" one the ladies asked.

"Here he is right here."

Steve put a chair in the middle of the room and Tim practically threw Marc in the chair.

"Damn, you fine."

"Thank you," Marc said, smiling.

"You ready for this?"

The ladies gave Marc and the other fourteen men in the room the best show they ever had. Anthony had the best time of his life. The ladies performed for three hours and the guys enjoyed every minute of it. After the ladies left, the guys went on Beale St. and participated in getting Marc drunker than he had ever been. This was a night he wouldn't soon forget...or remember.

***

Back at the Jenson house the ladies were still laughing and talking. Lisa started opening the gifts they had brought for her. She received lingerie (edible and regular), perfume and lotions. There was Victoria Secret paper, boxes, and bags everywhere.

By eleven, Isabella, Janice and Beverly had went to bed, but Lisa, Pat, Nic, and Carol stayed up to do a little girl talk. Nic and Carol drank enough for all four of them, while Lisa and Pat stuck to juice and water. The ladies finally fell asleep around three, and again, full in both senses of the word.

Chapter Thirty-Five

"Wake up, sleeping beauty," Janice said, sitting next to Lisa on the couch where she was sleeping.

"Mmmm, I'm awake. What time is it?"

"It's nine. Come on, it's time for you and baby to eat."

"Okay. Where is everybody?" Lisa said, as she yawned.

"Waiting for you."

Lisa went into the downstairs bathroom to wash her face and brush her teeth. Walking into the kitchen, Lisa received applause and cheers.

"What is all this for?"

"It's your wedding day!" Carol said.

Everyone sat around the dining room table and held hands as Lisa's mother said grace.

After grace, Janice said, "Everybody eat up. I don't want anybody fainting from starvation today."

"If we eat all of this we won't be able to fit in our dresses," Nic said.

The ladies ate breakfast and talked about what might have happened at last night bachelor's party.

By mid-morning, everyone was dressed and ready to head out. Lisa was in her mother's bedroom when she heard her phone beep. Putting in her voicemail password, Lisa pushed one, and the first message was from Marc.

"I got your message this morning, and I had to tell you that I love you and I'll see you at the altar. Bye, Mona Lisa."

"Marc?" Janice asked.

"Yeah. Is everyone ready?"

"Yep. We're waiting on you. Are you ready?"

Lisa looked at her mother and smiled, "Yeah, Mama. I'm ready."

"Well, then, let's go get married."

Carrying her dress and Janice carrying her accessories bag, they went downstairs.

Nic, Pat, Carol, and Isabella rode in Nic's truck. While Janice, Lisa, and Beverly rode in Janice's truck.

As the caravan of cars pulled away from the house, Lisa said, "So, you and Lesley have become very close, huh?"

"I don't know how I feel yet. For right now, we're good friends."

"Uh oh."

"What?"

"That's how Marc and I started."

"Not funny. Anyway, change of subject. How far a long are you; you never told me?"

"I'm a month."

"You mean I'm going to be a grandmother in eight months?"

"Yes, you are."

"Well, I better get ready," Janice said, laughing. "So, that means you knew during the rehearsal dinner?"

"No. I didn't find out until that Friday."

"Friday? When –"

"Yep. But the doctor said everything was fine."

"I can't believe my baby is having a baby. Did you tell William?"

"No. It's not like he would care."

"Lisa, he has a right to know. I'm not telling you what to do, I'm just asking you to think about it."

"I will," Lisa said, dialing her phone. "Yes, my name is Lisa Jenson and I'm calling to confirm the delivery of the flowers for my wedding today...Yes...Thank you. Now, to call the caterer. Hello, yes my name is Lisa Jenson and I'm calling to confirm the delivery for the Cavell and Jenson wedding...Yes, and the cake...Alright, thank you. Well, everything is being delivered as we speak," Lisa said, as she put her phone away.

"That's good."

Pulling into the drive at Lesley house, Lisa said, "Oh, I forgot to do one more thing." Taking her cell phone out again, she dialed another number. "Hey, Danny. This is Lisa...Yeah, we're here...Okay, bye. Danny says he's about five minutes away."

As they all walked into the house, Les greeted them, "The beautiful ladies have arrived."

"Hello, Les," Janice said.

"Hello, Janice. Aren't you looking radiant this morning?"

"Thank you."

"And the beautiful bride and gorgeous bridesmaids."

"I like this man," Nic said.

"Let's get you to your rooms. We don't want your groom seeing you before the wedding. He's been lurking around here trying to find you all morning. Follow me, ladies. Now, the groom and groomsmen are in the west wing, so there is no way you will run into each other."

"Thank you, Lesley," Lisa said.

"You're welcome, sweetheart. Janice, can I talk to you for a minute?"

"Sure."

Once they were out in the hallway, Les said, "I missed you last night. Did you miss me?"

"Of course, I did," Janice said, kissing him.

"Have you thought about what asked you?"

"Yes. But, I already answered you."

"I'm not accepting that answer and I'm going to keep asking you. Eventually you'll make me the happiest man on Earth and agree to marry me."

"We've only known each a month. I just need a little more time."

"Okay. But, I will keep asking until you say yes."

"I hope so," Janice said. She kissed him and told him she would see him in a little while.

"What was that about?" Lisa asked when her mother walked back into the room.

"None of your business."

"I –"

Knock knock knock

Nic answered the door. "Lis, there is a very handsome man at the door that says he's here to do your hair."

"Nic, let the man in," Lisa laughed. "You made it!" Lisa said, as she got up to hug Danny.

"Yeah, but I passed it the first time. This is house is nice! So, how many heads do I have?"

"Mine, my mother's, the groom's mother, but let me see if there are any more."

"You do that and I will start with your mother. Come on mother of the bride. I will be done with you quick with this short mane of yours. How do you usually curl it?"

"Actually, my beautician usually curls it away from my face."

"Okay, we will start with that."

Lisa walked into the other and said, "Ladies, Danny is here for hair. Who wants the hook-up?"

"How many heads does he have?" Pat asked.

"Three."

"I'm fine," Carol said, taking hot rollers out of her hair.

"Me, too," Nic said, with rollers still in her hair.

"Well, in that case count me in," Pat said, following Lisa out into the adjoining room.

"Okay, Danny. Just one more."

Knock knock knock

Pat opened the door to let Isabella and Vincent in.

Vincent walked over and hugged Lisa and said, "Bella told me. I am so happy! Not only do I get a daughter today, but I also get a grandchild."

"Marc didn't here you, did he?"

"No. He and the other guys are downstairs. I have to go round them up, it's almost show time."

Kissing Lisa on the cheek, he left.

By one, the ladies were dressed, with makeup and hair in place. Janice and Isabella looked amazing in their dresses. Janice was in a maroon dress with marching coat, and Isabella was in a cream colored dress with matching coat. The photographer and video engineer came upstairs to take pictures of the bridesmaids, hostesses, and the mothers.

After giving Lisa a beautiful upsweep, Danny said, "What do you think?"

"I love it, thank you."

"Alright, now that I am done, I am going to join my wife downstairs. Goodbye, Lisa Jenson," Danny said, and walked out of the room.

The video engineer came over and asked Lisa if she would like to say something to her future husband.

"Okay. Marc, sweetie it is now one-forty-five and as you can see I'm not dressed yet. But, I just wanted to tell you I love you and I can't wait to marry you. See you soon."

"Great, now I'm going back downstairs to get some more footage."

The photographer waited outside until Lisa was dressed. After she was in her wedding gown and veil, he took shots of all the ladies together. Then Lisa, Janice, and Isabella together. And a few of Lisa and Janice together. Everyone thought the shots he took of Lisa standing on the balcony with the sun shining at her back was beautiful.

"Done. I have to go reload for the ceremony," he said, and left the room.

"Alright, ladies it's two-fifty. Let's go," Adrian said.

Each bridesmaid and Isabella hugged Lisa as they left.

Janice was the only one to stay.

"You look beautiful, baby," Janice said, hugging Lisa without creasing her wedding gown.

"Thank you, mommy."

"I have one more surprise for you. See you out there, baby."

"Okay, but what –"

Janice went to open the door and let Robert in.

"Oh, my God. I have never seen you look so beautiful," Robert said, staring at her in amazement.

"I beg your pardon," Lisa smiled.

"You know what I mean," he laughed. "I just had to see you, before the wedding. You look absolutely beautiful."

"Thank you."

"Alright, you ready for this? I won't be the only man in your life anymore."

"I know. But, you will always be the one man who never left my side in anything. I feel like my life would not have been complete if you hadn't been in it. Thank you for being my friend."

"You are most definitely welcome, Lisa Jenson. And most of all thank you for being my friend, partner in crime and all that. Now, let's go get you married."

Lisa kissed Robert on the cheek and took his arm as he led her out of the room.

Anthony was standing outside the door waiting for them.

"Y'all ready to do this?" Lisa asked.

"You know it," Anthony smiled. "Lisa you look great!"

"Thanks, little brother." Lisa took Anthony's arm and held onto Robert's arm. "Two of the greatest men in my life," she smiled at each one of them. "Now, let's go get the third," Robert said.

***

Walking out the side door, Lisa could hear the music playing. She had to stop before going behind the curtain so Marc wouldn't see her.

"Lisa, me and Robert have a gift for you," Anthony said.

"I can't take another gift. I'm wearing make-up."

"Anthony asked me to walk with you two down the aisle. Is that okay?" Robert said.

Lisa looked at her brother, kissed him on the cheek, and then said, "Father knows best."

They all stood behind the curtain and watched the ceremony.

First to go down the aisle were the mothers. Janice and Isabella walked down the aisle to 'The Lady, Her Lover, and Lord' by T.D. Jakes. Once they were in place, the music smoothly changed to 'Spending My Life With You' by Eric Benet and Tamia.

"They look so good," Lisa said, as all her friends walked down the aisle.

Then she heard the intro to Marc's song. They each picked a song that they wanted to dedicate to each other. And Lisa picked 'I Do' by Boyz II Men. She held her breath until Marc came into view. Once she saw him she could breathe again.

"He looks beautiful," Lisa whispered to herself. She watched as he made it to spot by the stairs. Lisa, Anthony, and Robert walked behind the curtain to wait until it was Lisa's turn to walk out.

"Alright, Jayden. Are you ready?" Adrian asked.

"Yes," Jayden said, shyly.

"You know what to say?"

"The bride is coming."

"That's right. But, I want you to say it really loud, okay?"

"Okay."

"Here's bell. Get going little man."

And Jayden ran like the wind, as he rang his bell and yelled at the top of his lungs "THE BRIDE IS COMING! THE BRIDE IS COMING!"

He shouted that until they had to catch him and stand him up by Marc.

"Alright, Lisa this is your moment. You look gorgeous!"

"Thank you."

"Whenever you ready."

Lisa heard the music begin. She couldn't place what the song was but she stepped from by the curtain with her two escorts. Everyone stood up when they saw her step out. Then Lisa heard a voice she thought she would never think to hear at her wedding. When she heard him sing the first word she knew exactly who it was before she saw him.

Brian McKnight began to sing one of Lisa's favorite songs. When she felt Anthony and Robert tug her arms, she remembered that she should be walking. Brian McKnight was singing at her wedding, she couldn't believe it. She looked up at Marc and he winked. Lisa walked down the aisle to 'Still in Love' by Brian McKnight. And it was song by Brian McKnight.

Anthony and Robert led Lisa down the aisle toward Marc slowly as Brian McKnight serenaded her.

When they made it to the step, Anthony and Robert handed Lisa over to Marc.

"Is that who I think it is?" Lisa mumbled to Marc, once he was in ear shot.

"Yes, it is."

Lisa and Marc walked up the steps to their pastors and to their new lives.

"We are gathered her…" Pastor Williamson began.

Fifteen minutes later, Father Martin, "I now pronounce you husband and wife. You may kiss your bride."

Marc lifted Lisa's veil and as they kissed, Pastor Williamson said, "I give you Mr. and Mrs. Marcello Cavell."

Applause and cheers went up, just as white doves took flight. Marc and Lisa descended the steps as family and friends clapped and cheered.

After taking pictures with the entire wedding party, Lisa and Marc took pictures together. Showing their rings, kissing, and feeding each other cake. Lisa also took pictures with the groomsman, and Marc took pictures with the bridesmaids.

Once everyone was seated, the toasts began.

"I just want to tell my son how much his mother and I love him," Vincent began. "No matter what choices you made we have been behind you. You have always made us proud. And today you have made us even prouder. You have given me a beautiful daughter. Congratulations, you two. We love you."

"To Marc and Lisa," everyone said.

Then it was Janice's turn. "Lisa, baby you have always been the light of my life. You have been a gift from God. I love you so much. And I want to tell you that you have me made proud every day of your life. And today is no different. You married a man that loves you and will love you for the rest of his life. Love each other and be good to each other. I love you both."

After all the toast, the reception carried on with champagne flowing and Brian McKnight singing. He sang 'Never Felt This Way' for Lisa and Marc's first dance.

"As they danced, Lisa said, "I can't believe we're finally married. I love you, Marcello Vincent Cavell, with all of my heart."

"And I love you, Mrs. Lisa Denise Cavell."

"And how did you get Brian McKnight to sing at our wedding?"

"I told you Tim works in the music industry."

"Yeah, but you didn't tell me what he did."

"He produces the music."

"Are you kidding me?"

"No."

"Well, thank you, Tim. And thank *you* for marrying me today."

"No, thank you. I worked hard to get you, woman."

Laughing, Lisa said, "And now that you have me, what are you going to do with me?"

"Oh, I got plans. You hear that?"

"Yeah."

Everyone started to tap their glasses for Marc and Lisa to kiss. And they obliged willingly. After singing a few songs, Brian McKnight talked with Lisa and Marc and wished them well in their marriage.

"Please stay. Have something eat. We have more than enough."

"Thank you. I will."

"Enjoy yourself."

After the dance was over, they went back to the table to eat.

For the next hour, everyone drank champagne and ate a wonderful meal. As the cake was being served, Stephanie brought two bags to their table.

"Okay, it's gift time. Who's first?" Marc asked.

"You," Lisa said.

"Alright, your gift was hard one to find, but it kind of fell in my lap a couple of days ago. I hope you love it."

"I will."

Lisa opened the cream colored box to find a medium sized velvet box inside. Taking out the box and opening it, Lisa gasped.

"It's done?" she asked.

"Yes. And it will be ready to move into the day we get back from our honeymoon. I have a few friends and family that will move everything for us and when we get back you can start decorating. I love you, Mona Lisa."

"Oh, my God! Oh, I love you," Lisa said, as she kissed him. "Now me." Lisa took a deep breath, and said, "I didn't think I would be this nervous, but here goes. Marc, I promise to make you just as happy as you've made me. I hope this gift is the first step."

Marc hadn't noticed that everyone at the head table was watching them. He untied the bow and lifted the top. At first he looked confused, but then he read the inscription.

"Qui è a belle ragazze poco." Marc looked up at Lisa. "Are you...Are you...Does this mean what I think it means?" he stammered.

"Yes," Lisa laughed.

Marc picked Lisa up out of her chair and hugged her. He kissed her all over her face as the wedding party started to clap.

"You're positive?"

"Very positive."

"How far along are you?"

"A month."

"Does anyone else know?"

"Just the people up here."

"Well, let me make the announcement." Marc ran upstairs to the veranda where the DJ was and said, "May I have your attention. I have the best announcement in the world. Today is a great day for me, it's my wedding day, my birthday, and now my beautiful wife has given me another gift...Fatherhood. I'm going to be a father!"

The applause was loud and long.

"I love you, Lisa."

Marc jogged down the stairs, where Lisa had ran to meet him in the middle of the dance floor and kissed him.

For the rest of the night, everyone ate, drank, and danced. By nightfall, it was time for Marc and Lisa to leave. As they walked out the front door, everyone threw rose petals at them.

"Marc, I feel that you and your beautiful wife should leave in style. So, here is my gift to you two," Les said, as he opened the door to the white Rolls Royce.

"Thank you, for everything," Lisa said, kissing him on the cheek.

"Yeah, thanks man," Marc said, shaking his hand and giving him a hug.

After they got in the car, Lisa said, "Are you ready?"

"I told you. I've been ready since the first day I saw you," Marc said, as the car pulled away.

The End

Epilogue

One Year Later...

During the honeymoon, Lisa and Marc made love, did some sightseeing, made love, ate, and made love. After their honeymoon, they arrived to their new, furnished home. As the months passed, Lisa got bigger. Pat had a beautiful baby boy, which she named Michael Jayden Cole. Nic and Brandon were still dating and even talking about moving in with each other. Carol and Charles were still in love. Anthony graduated high school and is currently attending TSU and majoring in engineering.

The second week in November, Lisa gave birth to a beautiful six pounds, eight ounce baby girl. They named her Elise Marie Cavell. Lisa and Marc truly had a good life. Lisa was even planning another wedding...her mother's. Lesley Herbert proposed to Janice Jenson on his forty-ninth birthday, which Janice happily accepted.

Between family and work, Lisa's plate was pretty full, but she loved every minute it. The baby was growing and becoming more gorgeous every day. Marc and Lisa made a promise that work ended the minute they walked across the threshold of their home.

Lisa thought of all this as she watched Marc pace up and down the nursery floor trying to get Elise to go to sleep. She was already a daddy's girl. Lisa never would have expected her life to end up like this, but she was happy. And that's all that matter.

"What are you thinking about?" Marc asked, smiling.

"Just happy about where I ended up," Lisa smiled, as she walked into the nursery.

Dear Survivors,

As the writer of this novel and as a victim of domestic violence myself, I dedicate this book to you. As women, we have a fountain of strength that keeps us going for our family, our friends, and most importantly ourselves. Every day we find a reason to carry on. You must realize that you don't have to lie in the bed you made. You can always get up!

Don't believe that there isn't anything better out there for you. If you are in an abusive relationship, be it physical or verbal; please do not believe that this is the way things should be or that things will eventually get better. Because they won't. There is life after him. Believe me, I know it is.

Just remember that God didn't bring you this far for you to give up. You have the strength to change your situation. To change your life. I know at times it feels hopeless, but never give up. Go to your family or friends, you don't have to go through this alone. I went through two years of abuse without telling anyone. Afraid of what my family might do or even say. I kept things bottled up and it took a toll on me both mentally and physically. Remember that you can overcome anything; you can come out of anything. Be strong, pray often, because it truly does changes things.

Sincerely,
Author Laura T. Johnson
Survivor

Made in the USA
Charleston, SC
04 September 2015